HIS EYES CARESSED
HER TREMBLING BODY

Gazing hungrily at Samantha's towel-clad form, Chris observed huskily, "That's quite a costume you've got on...."

Samantha could feel the color rising to her cheeks. Her heart yearned toward him, and she longed for the exciting warmth of his embrace. But once again the disturbing thought of his relationship to Felicity curbed her soaring emotions.

"Chris," she hedged, "the clinic— "

"I know," he interrupted teasingly. "You've got to get back to the clinic. You might be needed there."

Dark eyes shining, he leaned toward her. As he reached out to trace the delicate line of her cheekbone, Samantha flinched involuntarily, and his features suddenly hardened.

"Just remember you're needed here, too," he said quietly. Then he turned away, leaving her aching for him in every fiber of her being....

AND NOW…

SUPERROMANCES

Worldwide Library is proud to present a sensational new series of modern love stories — SUPERROMANCES

Written by masters of the genre, these longer, sensuous and dramatic novels are truly in keeping with today's changing life-styles. Full of intriguing conflicts, the heartaches and delights of true love, SUPERROMANCES are absorbing stories — satisfying and sophisticated reading that lovers of romance fiction have long been waiting for.

SUPERROMANCES
Contemporary love stories for the woman of today!

JOY HOWARD
STORMY
PARADISE

A SUPERROMANCE FROM
WORLDWIDE

TORONTO · NEW YORK · LOS ANGELES · LONDON

Published April 1983

First printing February 1983

ISBN 0-373-70060-1

Printed in Canada

CHAPTER ONE

"THERE IT IS, MISS. Off the left wing."

Samantha's heart leaped as the pilot tipped the plane unexpectedly to give her an unobstructed view of Good Providence Island. Nor was the leap entirely the result of the abrupt turn.

"It's so tiny," she murmured, staring out the small high window of the old DC-3, fascinated by the blur of green and brown now coming into view far to her left.

The pilot laughed. "Yeah, just nine miles long," he observed as he wrenched the yoke of the plane to return it to the horizontal. "Thirteen miles from the next island in the chain, and that's just another coral key. Nothing on it to speak of."

Samantha nodded as the pilot's voice droned on, reciting the problems of communication with Good Providence, the cost of flying there, the difficulties a storm could create. She tried to pay attention, knowing that all of this should interest her! It was her future home he was discussing. But though she knew she would later wish she'd listened, her mind was too full to attend to such details as how many gallons of fuel this one flight consumed.

Good Providence Island—her home at least for one year, the length of her contract. As she watched the tiny dot expand and take shape before her wide green eyes, she clenched her hands in fear and anticipation. What would her new life be like? She had trained and planned and hoped for it so long, through years of college and medical school and then all the postgraduate training and a long series of special courses: family practice, childhood diseases, obstetrics and finally tropical medicine. At the time it had seemed like a lot of training, but now?

Now she was thousands of miles from home, closer to Japan, New Guinea or the Philippines than even the west coast of the United States. It took twelve hours to fly to Hawaii via Guam, nearly six more to Los Angeles. And those flights came after you got from tiny Good Providence to the island of Halekai—a jouncing hour or two by the Inter-Island Airlines, an impressive-sounding operation that had turned out to be this single DC-3 operating on whatever schedule and pattern its pilot chose.

The closer the plane drew to the island, the more fervently Samantha willed it to slow its inexorable flight. She found herself wishing she had taken an additional year of residency, one more fellowship in. . .in *something*, anything to delay the moment's approaching so quickly, so inevitably—the moment when she would be the only physician on an island inhabited by hundreds of men and women and children. All of those people would depend on her for their well-being, perhaps their very survival. The knowledge that before this day there had simply been no doctor on the island failed to comfort her. So much rested on her shoulders, and at the moment those shoulders felt very frail.

Samantha wriggled her cramped body awkwardly, seeking a comfortable position on the hard leather seat. As she stared out the small window, struggling fruitlessly to listen to the pilot's words, she could see the island slowly taking shape. The vague purple-and-green haze grew into solid bands of color, white at the base, then lines of greens and purples and browns mounting to the highest point she could see. Even from the air the rugged outline of the mountain ridges was apparent. High purple and brown peaks, craggy cliffs stretching fingers down to the water's edge in one or two places and the typical rounded dome of a volcanic mountain just to the left of center.

Closer still, and specks of deep green became visible against those seemingly barren cliffs. As Samantha's gaze moved slowly down from the rounded peak of the volcano, she could see patches of scrubby trees clinging to the slopes. Still lower, a swath of rich lush green cut across the base of the slopes, reaching nearly to the sea. Then finally came the thin band of white that would be the sand at water's edge.

"Hang on now!"

The pilot's warning came a moment too late, just after the lurch of the plane told of their sudden descent. Samantha clenched the bottom of her seat as she had through most of the flight and glanced anxiously behind her at the boxes stacked crazily in the expanded luggage compartment, on the seats and in the narrow aisle of the old airplane.

"Serviceable," had been the pilot's answer to her unspoken question when she'd looked askance at the tin tail dragger awaiting her on the runway at Halekai, the nearest large island in the five-hundred-mile-long chain to which Good Providence belonged.

"I'll get us there," he had promised when she continued to hesitate before the rickety set of stairs. "Come on; we're late already."

Samantha had known the departure was already late because of her, though she couldn't be blamed for delays in her flight from Hawaii—a flight by way of Wake Island, Guam and an atoll whose name she hadn't caught. Still, she was determined not to cause more trouble or to seem afraid, and so she had scrambled up the uneven stairs only to stop with shock when she saw the plane's interior. A few seats remained, way up front. Otherwise the cabin was bare. Or, more accurately, it would have been bare had it not been for the baggage strewn casually around the floor.

"You can pick your way to the front, can't you?"

The pilot's voice had revealed his impatience while Samantha stood dazed at the cabin's entrance. As quickly as she could she had worked her way through, over and around the scattered boxes of supplies, the open bags of groceries, the canvas sack leaking mail onto the floor, the unwrapped scythe leaning crazily against a new rocking chair gaily adorned with a bright red ribbon but otherwise un-wrapped, unlabeled, unidentified.

Casual as was this beginning, the flight had seemed only more so. The pilot stopped at two or three islands in the chain, landing on gravel runways and dirt strips with equal aplomb and, it seemed to Samantha, necessarily equal damage to his cargo. But when she had looked curiously at the rocking chair partway through the flight, she'd seen that it stood undamaged in the same place and at the same angle as on takeoff. Shrugging, she'd decided that the pilot must know more than it seemed.

Still, the cavalier arrival at a little airport where no one awaited them and a second where pigs and children played heedlessly on the runway had done nothing to calm her nerves, already frazzled from fifteen hours in the air. Usually their landing would be greeted almost immediately by men in Jeeps or women on foot, coming to collect their packages; but once the pilot excused himself and hopped on a waiting bicycle to deliver a bundle in person. Then Samantha had huddled in what small shade she could find under the wing of the plane, waiting anxiously for his return.

Now, as they approached Good Providence, she wondered what kind of a reception to expect. Surely there would be a welcoming party for the new doctor, the island's first and only physician. Or perhaps she would be expected to carry her bags on a bicycle or load them on a wheelbarrow and push them—but where should she even take them?

Samantha shook her head nervously. *Someday this*

will all seem funny, she told herself, gritting her teeth to fight against her rising panic.

The plane had dropped several hundred feet, banking sharply as it did. Tilted as it was, it blocked Samantha's view of the island, but she knew from the changing color of the water that they were very near. The endless purples of the deepest ocean had shaded first into a vibrant midnight blue, and then all at once they became the light blue green of the lagoon. Dark splotches in raggedy patterns testified to coral growth on the ocean floor within the lagoon. There the sun seemed to glisten through the shallow water clear down to the white sand.

With a sudden rush the land came up. A swath of glittering white beach and then a blur of low green bushes intruded into Samantha's hazy view. And then, with a final bump of the low tail, the plane ground to a halt. She was on Good Providence.

"George? Over here." The pilot looked around for only a moment before beginning to unload Samantha's luggage. Catching sight of a young man leaning lazily against an open Jeep, he called on him to help. "You're taking her to the Big House, aren't you?"

When that failed to arouse the man, the pilot straightened up. Placing his hands on his hips, he growled, "Come on, George. She's your responsibility now."

His head nodding roughly at his single passenger left no doubt in Samantha's mind that she was the person being discussed. *What a welcome,* she thought with a shiver, pausing uneasily in the process of collecting her hand luggage. But at last the indolent young man wandered nearer to the plane.

"Yeah," he muttered indifferently, "I guess she's mine now."

With no more greeting than that, he took the hand luggage from Samantha and returned to the Jeep. The pilot shrugged and shook his head. "I'll help you," he said after a quick look at her flushed face.

He worked efficiently, if a bit roughly, and in a few minutes her suitcase and medical bags were loaded onto the Jeep. At this, George, who had climbed into the driver's seat, glanced at Samantha. "That it?" he asked with minimal interest.

She nodded. "I shipped the rest weeks ago," she explained.

"Did you now?" he said with an insolent grin. "Can't say I've heard that anything's arrived yet."

Samantha's heart sank. Limited in what she could carry on the flights, she had shipped most of her clothing, her books and several boxes of medical supplies well in advance. If they hadn't arrived, starting the clinic would be even harder than she'd anticipated.

As he placed the last bag precariously on top of the pile on the Jeep's rear seat, the pilot interrupted her thoughts, "Aw, don't worry. George doesn't know everything." He smiled awkwardly at her in an attempt at reassurance.

A tight-lipped nod was the best Samantha could manage in return, and she was grateful when George started the Jeep's engine.

"Bye, Miss...uh, Dr. Hall," the pilot shouted over the roar of the Jeep.

Samantha waved forlornly, feeling as though the only link with her previous life, the only safety line, was snapping before her eyes. *Don't exaggerate,* she warned herself as she jerked her attention from the past to the present.

Her uneasiness only intensified as George thrust the car forward, squealing around the corner of the airport and onto what she later learned was one of the island's two paved roads. But at his snorting laugh as he mockingly repeated the pilot's word "doctor," something inside her snapped.

"Slow down," she demanded abruptly. "You can drive like this when you're alone if you wish, but there's medical equipment in those bags. And if you do insist on driving like this, you might just need that equipment someday!"

Shocked, the young man glared at her for a moment as though thinking of a suitable response. But he did slow down; and in the silence that followed, Samantha had a chance to look around her.

George guided the Jeep along a narrow road between scrubby trees and low bushes. An occasional tall coconut palm reached gracefully toward the brilliant sky. The sun glinted off the road, creating dancing waves of light and heat.

Beyond the low brush Samantha could see up into the hills. Now the green band she had observed from the plane resolved itself into lush fields planted thickly with sugarcane. Here and there among the cane she caught sight of a flash of a light-colored shirt or the glint of a bronzed arm raised in work or in greeting, and once, high above the fields, she caught a fleeting glimpse of a thin silvery ribbon that could only be a waterfall.

Even over the pungent odor of gasoline from the Jeep she could sense the light tang of ginger and citrus, and from everywhere she was assaulted by the luxurious heady perfume of tropical flowers. Her gaze returned to the bushes that lined the road: looking more closely this time, she could see dots of red and yellow and bright orange, the half-hidden flowers whose multiple scents so richly perfumed the air.

At last, signs of habitation appeared—first a stray house or two and then small groups of buildings. Samantha stared curiously at the houses as the Jeep slowed to make way for the children, dogs and goats that threatened its progress. The houses were unlike anything she had ever seen or expected to see on a tropical island in the Pacific. Except for the palm trees and exotic flowers in the yards, the houses could have been transplanted exactly as they were to an old seafaring town in New England. One- and two-story Cape Cod-style houses built of clapboard were painted white or pale shades of blue, beige or green. Each had shutters in contrasting hues, open to let in what air still stirred on this muggy day. Unconsciously Samantha's eyes roamed to the roofs of the houses, seeking the railing of a widow's walk looking out to sea. But the builders had stopped short of that, it seemed, in their recreation of a New England coastal village.

How odd, Samantha thought as she gazed around her. Suddenly her eyes were caught by a new sight, a glimmer of white partway up the slope of the mountain, above the small village. She squinted as she concentrated on the shimmer of light, struggling to identify what she saw. Finally she gave up, turning to George in her curiosity.

"What's that?" she asked the silent driver. "That patch of white up on the hill?"

He glanced quickly in the direction she pointed. "Oh, that's the Big House." Catching her puzzled look, he added grudgingly, "Where Mr. Girard lives."

"Oh." Samantha grew quiet. Christopher Girard was her employer, and though she had never met him—her interview in the States had been conducted by his representatives—she had heard a great deal about him. She knew that he ran the sugarcane plantation that was the island's sole industry—in fact, its sole reason for being inhabited. She'd gathered that the plantation had belonged to the Girard family for years, even generations, and that Christopher Girard ran not only the plantation but practically the entire island.

Her curiosity mounted now, and she struggled to see the house perched on the slope. But they were too far away, and the sun was too bright for her to gaze into the hills for more than a moment at a time.

Oh, well, she consoled herself. The pilot had said they'd be going there, so she'd see it soon enough.

Suddenly realizing this meant she was about to

meet her employer, Samantha groaned inwardly. There had been no place for her to wash at the runway that constituted the whole of the island's airport. With the one hand she could spare from supporting her baggage in the rocking Jeep, she struggled to smooth her curly hair. But it was hopeless. She had traveled in the lightweight shirtdress for more than half a day now, and the most wrinkle-resistant material had its limits. She could not wipe the smudges off her face, let alone freshen her makeup. In spite of the heat, Samantha shivered in nervous anticipation. What a way to meet her employer!

Her anxiety continued to mount as the white dot on the hill grew larger. Ahead she could see a fork in the road, the right-hand branch staying close to the shore and the left heading up into the hills, obviously going to the Big House. She bit her lip fearfully as they neared the fork, hanging onto the metal door for strength as well as for support against George's inevitably rough turn.

But to her shock he did not take the left-hand fork. Instead he continued along the coast road, giving the other path not even a glance.

"Where are we going?" Samantha demanded to know.

He looked at her strangely. "Where did you think we were going?" he asked.

"To the Big House," she snapped back, tired of his insolence.

"Nah." He shook his head. "I'm taking you to Widow Tarai's."

"But...Mr. Girard is expecting me," she began quickly, then added more tentatively, "isn't he?"

George shrugged. "He's not on the island."

That burst of conversation apparently exhausted George's capacity, for he lapsed into a silence too marked to be interrupted. Samantha huddled into her seat, unsure what to think. Though she was grateful not to have to report to her employer with a smudged face and wrinkled dress, it had never occurred to her that Christopher Girard might be away from the island. True, she had never met him, but at least they had corresponded. In all the thousands of miles she had traveled, she had thought of him as the one person she knew on the island, and now he was not here to greet her.

Fortunately Samantha had little time to brood before George pulled up in front of a neat two-story house, slamming on the brakes as he forced the car to a screeching halt.

"Well, here we are," he announced, leaning back lazily against the seat.

He seemed in no more rush to help her unload her luggage than he had been to load it. Sighing, Samantha climbed down from the Jeep and began to take out her bundles. Suddenly the horn blared as George leaned against it. Her nerves already on edge, she leaped back at the sound, but a quick glance at the impertinent youth showed her how much pleasure he would get if she made a fuss. So, saying nothing, she continued to lift her bags out of the back seat.

"Here, let me help you."

The voice was cheering, and Samantha turned gratefully to meet a chubby red-cheeked woman who could only be "Widow Tarai." That guess was confirmed as the white-haired woman clasped Samantha's hand warmly in both of her own and quickly introduced herself.

Her good-natured scolding accomplished what Samantha's exasperated looks had not, and George scrambled out of the Jeep to carry the heavy cases into the house. As she trailed up the path behind Mrs. Tarai, Samantha had time for only a brief glimpse at her surroundings, but what she saw went far toward making her feel more comfortable.

Like most of the houses she had noticed en route, this one was well cared for. Glistening under a new coat of paint, it showed its age only in its style and in an occasional charming unevenness of its wallboards, not in its condition. Tropical flowers grew profusely on bushes set at intervals in the yard, and roses climbed on vines up to the front porch. Although the grass was sparse and dried to a faint greenish brown, it was neatly trimmed. The walk was formed of sand brushed smooth and neat, and huge conch shells offered their peach and pink lips to the sun in front of the porch. Without being studied or artificial, the effect was enchanting.

All the time they carted the bags into the house and up the stairs, Mrs. Tarai talked. If she felt short of breath as they marched up and down the steep staircase, she didn't reveal it in her voice, which went on and on, soothing even in its busyness.

"You'll just stay here a few days," she said as she heaped the last of Samantha's bundles onto the high white bed. "I hope it will be all right?"

Her eyes betrayed anxiety as she glanced at Samantha, standing dazed in the middle of the small room to which she had been led.

Samantha recovered hastily. "The room? Oh, it's fine," she responded without looking around. Then, as Mrs. Tarai fussed with the curtains at the window, she realized that her response had been inadequate. She glanced about the room, then allowed herself to slow down and look more closely.

Although small and simply furnished, the room was neat and absolutely immaculate. Snowy curtains hung at the two windows, set at angles from each other to allow ventilation. There was a small chest and a wardrobe, a low bench on which her biggest suitcase now rested, and a high narrow bed covered with crisp, inviting sheets.

"It really is lovely," she added, smiling warmly at Mrs. Tarai.

The older woman sighed with relief. "I'm so glad, my dear," she breathed quickly. "You see, I didn't know you'd be staying here until just yesterday, and then...." She spread her hands as if to show how helpless she had felt.

"You did a wonderful job," Samantha insisted. Awkwardly, afraid she might offend the kind old woman, she went on, probing as delicately as she could. "You didn't know till yesterday?" she prompted.

Reassured that she'd succeeded in preparing the room to her guest's demands, Mrs. Tarai returned more volubly, "Yes. Well, I thought you'd be at your own house, you know."

Samantha nodded warily. That was what she had thought, too.

"Mr. Girard rushed to get it all done, but, well, one thing after another. . .you know, my dear. And then he had to leave the island, and when he's not here, oh, it all just goes to pot, it does. So it's not quite ready—your house, or, I guess, the clinic." Mrs. Tarai looked at her quickly. "But you'll be all right here, and it's only for a little while," she reiterated.

"Is it far from here—where I'll live? And the clinic?" Samantha asked.

"No, not at all," Mrs. Tarai answered hastily. "Just a few steps. Felicity—that's my daughter—can show you later if you'd like. She's not here right now. But maybe you ought to rest a little first anyway, and then have something to eat?"

Samantha nodded. Now that she no longer had to run to catch another plane, the exhaustion of her long days of travel began to set in. Grateful for the suggestion, she quietly thanked Mrs. Tarai, then, barely pausing to wash her face, returned to her room. For a few minutes she rummaged in her luggage; but at last, too tired even to remember what she'd been looking for, she stripped off her well-worn dress and stretched out on top of the covers, pushing aside one or two bundles that rested on the bed. The last images to drift through her mind were pictures of a mountainside dotted with the green of trees and sugarcane, with one white house. Then she slept, too tired even to dream.

WHEN SAMANTHA AWOKE, the sun was low in the sky and her curtains were tinted with a delicate blush of reflected light. Stretching luxuriously, she rose from the bed and walked to the window. From this view she could see only the village, not the ocean, but even the tropical sun reflecting reddish gold off the sides of the mountains was a scene of beauty she had never before known.

Rested and excited now, she dressed hastily and trotted down the stairs. The smells rising from the kitchen suggested that Mrs. Tarai was as good a cook as she was a housekeeper, and Samantha's stomach reminded her forcefully that she hadn't eaten since the flight from Guam to Halekai, hours before.

"Well, do you know what day it is?" Mrs. Tarai's voice greeted her with a teasing lilt.

"I'm not sure," Samantha laughed. "Ever since they told us that we'd lost Thursday crossing the International Date Line, I've been hopelessly confused!"

Mrs. Tarai smiled at her as she motioned for her to take a seat. "Felicity will be down in a minute, so we can all eat together," she explained.

For a few minutes they chatted comfortably about the trivia that can begin a relationship: Samantha's long journey, Mrs. Tarai's housekeeping, the good smells of dinner. Suddenly, placing a finger to her lips, the widow cocked her head toward the stairs.

"No, she's still in her room," she said. She moved hastily to sit close to Samantha. "I just wanted to tell you how glad I am that Mr. Girard arranged this job for Felicity—and I hope it'll work out," she whispered.

Samantha looked at her, confused by her words as well as by the abrupt confidence.

"Don't you know?" Mrs. Tarai gazed at her in disbelief. "I thought you would have heard, or at least George would have told you."

"Told me what?" Samantha asked, withholding comment on the silent insolence her driver had displayed earlier that day.

"Felicity will be working with you, assisting you, at the clinic," Mrs. Tarai explained. "Mr. Girard had the idea, and I think it's grand." She glanced at Samantha awkwardly and continued quickly, "I mean, his deciding to bring a doctor to the island was the most wonderful thing he could have done. But what he's trying to do for Felicity is important, too."

She paused for breath, then rushed on. "Felicity's been sort of restless since she finished up at the high school—you know how young people can get," she added, as if Samantha were her own age instead of just a few years senior to the young woman she was describing. Barely waiting for Samantha's acknowledging nod, she continued, "And Mr. Girard thought this might do the trick for her. He brought her some first-aid books to read, and he got her a uniform and...." She paused, cocking her head again, then rose swiftly, placing a warning finger to her lips.

"Wasn't it a beautiful sunset?" she asked loudly as she busied herself ostentatiously over the large pot of fragrant chowder that bubbled on the stove.

Samantha looked up as Felicity entered the room and found it took an effort to keep from gasping. Before her stood one of the most sensuously beautiful women she had ever seen. As Mrs. Tarai quickly performed the introductions, Samantha struggled not to stare from daughter to mother and back again, as if wondering how the pleasant-looking but ordinary Widow Tarai had produced such a marvel. Finally she gave up the struggle and gazed in frank admiration at the striking beauty of the young woman, at eighteen barely more than a girl, but fully mature with her rounded form.

An extremely attractive woman herself, Samantha felt no jealousy to preclude her appreciating another's beauty. While she was slender and petite, with delicately chiseled classic features and short curly hair of the lightest auburn hue, Felicity was built on a larger scale, with black hair curving negligently around her face and across her shoulders. Its disarray and the brightly flowered sun dress she wore offered a sharp counterpoint to the beautiful regularity of her features. Her warm tawny skin suggested what Samantha had guessed from the Widow Tarai's name: if the widow was a New England grandmother in appearance, her husband must have been a native islander. Felicity's eyes, unlike Samantha's sparkling green ones, were as black as her flowing mane and fringed with thick lashes. But those eyes were dark and sullen, and the expression on her face marred the perfection of her beauty.

At last Samantha found her voice again. "I hear you'll be working with me," she said encouragingly.

The young woman scarcely responded. The merest nod of her beautiful head seemed to take all the energy she had.

Samantha tried again. "Have you studied much first aid?" she asked.

Felicity shook her head languorously. At this Mrs. Tarai interrupted, walking over to the table and brandishing her dripping ladle menacingly. "Felicity, why don't you answer Dr. Hall's questions," she said in exasperation.

The young woman shrugged her elegantly expressive shoulders. "I've read a little," she admitted.

Samantha groaned inwardly. Although she continued to try to make conversation with Felicity during the few minutes that remained before Mrs. Tarai mercifully served their dinner, it was a nearly hopeless effort. If this was what the widow meant by saying that Felicity was a little restless, she was being kind. Felicity was more than a little restless: she was sullen and childish and difficult, in spite of her striking beauty.

Samantha knew she would have to try to work with her. For whatever reason, Christopher Girard thought it would be a good idea, and he was her employer. But there were limits to what she might hope to accomplish—and to what she was willing to tolerate.

Dinner consisted of a steaming chowder, chock-full of fresh fish and seafood and served with great slices of a sweet homemade bread. Pineapple and bananas followed, with coffee to finish the meal. But as good as the food was, hearty and spicy and warming to Samantha's tired heart and body, the conversation was equally bad. Every subject Mrs. Tarai introduced, Felicity scoffed at. Eventually the two other women talked together, tacitly agreeing to ignore the young beauty who sat with them as though she was not quite sure she belonged there.

At last the awkward meal was over, and Samantha hastened to cut off Mrs. Tarai's attempt to convince her daughter to take "Dr. Hall" to see the clinic.

"It's late, and I'm tired," she explained, cautious not to let Felicity think she had won in some strained battle for power. "Why don't we go tomorrow morning instead," she suggested.

"Felicity?" her mother prompted the young woman, who still lounged gracefully at the table.

"I guess," she answered reluctantly.

"Do you start work tomorrow, Felicity?" Samantha asked, determined to understand this difficult young woman's role.

Felicity shrugged. "If you want me to," she answered at last. "Chris—I mean Mr. Girard—" she amended at a shocked look from her mother, "said I should start whenever you need me."

"Yes." Samantha spoke firmly. "We can go to the clinic first thing in the morning, then, and you can help me set up the supplies I've brought."

Mentioning her supplies reminded her of the missing trunk. A hasty inquiry produced no satisfactory answer; Mrs. Tarai had not heard of any other luggage arriving on the island. "But Felicity can check in town tomorrow," she added with a frown at her daughter.

"Okay," Samantha sighed. There was obviously nothing to be done tonight even if she wasn't so weary she could barely see the stairs to climb them.

With a formal good-night to Felicity and a warmer one for the widow, Samantha retired to her room. Looking with dismay at the open boxes and half-unpacked cases sitting helter-skelter about the room where she'd left them earlier, she seated herself heavily on the bed.

Listlessly she bent down to retrieve the shirtdress she had tossed on the floor in her earlier exhaustion. Her eyes roved about the room, and she compared the numbers of her cases with the small chest and single wardrobe before her. It would be impossible to fit her belongings into this minute room. But then, she would only be staying here a few days, so it scarcely paid to try.

She leaned back against the bed, so tired she was near to despair. An extreme lassitude pervaded her body, making her limbs feel heavy and weak. Her head rolled forward in her exhaustion, and she could feel the tears welling up in her eyes. What an awful beginning. She moaned beneath her breath as she sniffed, helpless against the tears that insisted on rolling down her face.

Greeted by a sullen lazy man who carried none of her bags and then seemed all too eager to get her killed on the road. Shown to a room in someone else's house instead of the private home she'd been promised. The clinic wasn't ready, her luggage had disappeared, her employer wasn't even on the island.

Her employer. She sat up, riveted by the thought of Christopher Girard. "Chris," Felicity had called him. Against her usual good nature, a suspicion began to form in Samantha's mind. Felicity wasn't only restless and bored; she was very, very beautiful. Perhaps more than kindness to an elderly widow lay behind Christopher Girard's helping Felicity get a job. . . .

Samantha shuddered. If that was the case, she could be stuck with an unwilling, probably incompetent helper for a long time. She rolled over onto her stomach in her frustration.

Mrs. Tarai obviously thought that Christopher Girard was some kind of a god. Getting a doctor for the island, finding her daughter a job, taking care of everything. What had she said—that when Girard was off the island, nothing went right? Words to that effect, anyway. Well, nothing had gone right today.

Mrs. Tarai's "god" seemed incapable of preparing a house on time, when he'd had months of notice. He couldn't prevent luggage from being lost. He sent a scruffy youth to meet her plane and saddled her with an obnoxious untrained assistant.

To be fair, Samantha forced herself to remember that she hadn't expected any assistant at all, and it was hardly Christopher Girard's fault if her trunks were lost. And as she realized this, she began to think of her employer in a new light.

This man, this one human being, had the most astonishing power over the lives of hundreds of people. Without him, none of the people on the island would have jobs or plane service or medical care. Without him, they would be left to eke out a subsistence living through farming or fishing. What kind of a world was it that depended so on one individual? And what kind of a man could he be? An autocrat? A dictator who reveled in his power? A playboy who found jobs for his women as so-called medical assistants—or a decent man who tried to help out the only child of an elderly widow?

For the first time Samantha realized how much she, too, would depend on Christopher Girard. That her life would be intimately affected by him was already apparent: her housing, her job, her assistant—all were selected and controlled by him. In spite of her professional training, her fellowships and scholastic prizes and her preparation for this job, she felt terribly unprepared. And she was frightened. It had never before occurred to her with such graphic power that she was thousands of miles from anyone she knew, isolated on a tropical island and uncomfortably dependent on the pleasure or whims of one man—a man she hadn't even met.

As she drifted off to sleep a few minutes later, Samantha's mind whirled with images of George leaning defiantly against the Jeep, Felicity sullenly rejecting her efforts at friendly conversation, the missing luggage sinking heavily to the bottom of the Pacific Ocean. All the sweet scents of tropical flowers wafting in her open window on the gentle night breeze could not dispel the powerful ugliness of what she had seen and what she feared. Over and through all of the pictures there hovered a great unknown, the vaguely imagined form of Christopher Girard. Images floated through her mind: Girard guiding a troop of docile farmers like scouts on a hike, Girard motioning furiously with the whir of a heavy whip, Girard floating above them all to be transformed into some vast bird of prey that lighted on the topmost frond of a coconut palm, there to sit and pelt the helpless islanders with the hard nuts from the tree while Samantha ran around frantically trying to tend the wounds he inflicted. With this final image, distraught and exhausted as she was, Samantha at last sank into an uneasy slumber.

CHAPTER TWO

"OH, LORD...look at this place!"

It was early the next morning, before the sun rose high and hot in the tropical sky. Samantha stood at the open door of the small house to which Felicity had reluctantly led her and stared in dismay at the scene that confronted her. From where she stood she could see into the two main rooms on the first floor, the two rooms that were to comprise the clinic. Far from being "not quite ready" for use as a medical facility, they looked as though they had barely weathered a typhoon and might never be made ready for any use at all.

Boxes were upended, their contents spilling forth into the floor. Loose papers were strewn around as though they had been flung by an angry giant. Chairs stood on tables or on each other and some of the tables themselves lay on their sides like wounded animals. Drawers gaped, supplies and papers dripping out of them to the ground. And everywhere, on the floor and the furniture, in the opened cupboards and in the lamps scattered about the rooms, there was dirt. Not just dust and an occasional cobweb, but great handfuls of dirt, piles of sand, ground-in mud.

It looked as though someone had upended a wheel-barrowful of dirt and then decided that one barrow-ful was not enough.

As Samantha stood in dismay, her hands clasped to her open mouth, she heard further evidence of the horrors that awaited her. The scurrying sounds of mice scampering to hide now that light streamed in from the open door did nothing to ease her disgust and frustration.

But even as she let her eyes take in all the ugliness of the frightful scene before her, she could feel that frustration began to shift to something else—anger. And as that anger deepened and intensified, it began to take a useful shape.

No longer was she dizzy with the lingering effects of her long journey or dazed by the changing time zones and the remains of jet lag. No longer did she want to return to the sanctuary of her small room at Widow Tarai's and snuggle into her narrow bed for one last catnap. This mess had to be cleaned up, and she was both strong enough and angry enough to do it.

Abruptly she turned to face Felicity, who had remained outside at a safe distance. "Come on," she commanded. "We're going to get to work."

Looking cautiously past her, Felicity motioned at the disgusting scene with a languid wave of her expressive hand. "To work? In there?"

"That's right," Samantha responded grimly, closing the door behind her.

"But. . . it's so dirty!" Felicity stared at Samantha.

"And we're going to clean it," Samantha announced.

Without waiting for the girl's response, Samantha strode down the street, retracing her steps to Widow Tarai's. Felicity, seeing no choice and perhaps aroused by the surprising reaction of the young physician, followed her tamely enough until they neared her mother's house. Then she spoke, though her tone remained cautious.

"Do you really mean we're to clean those rooms by ourselves?" she asked.

Samantha stopped walking and turned to face the young woman. Placing her hands firmly on her hips, she looked Felicity sternly in the eye. "Do you have another suggestion?"

Felicity's eyes dropped first, and slowly shaking her head, she allowed Samantha to lead her into the widow's home.

It took Samantha only a few minutes to rummage in her suitcase for an old pair of shorts and a halter top. Slipping out of the cool skirt and blouse she had donned when she thought her day would be spent arranging a few supplies in cabinets and starting to teach Felicity a filing system, she quickly dressed in an outfit more suitable for the heavy cleaning she would be doing.

Mrs. Tarai, horrified by Samantha's terse description of the clinic, offered to help. But Samantha refused even to consider the offer.

"I've got Felicity's help," she reassured the old woman with more confidence than she felt. "But

I will need some things to clean with," she added.

Half an hour later, she and Felicity returned to the other building, laden with buckets, rags and brooms, jars of soap and disinfectants and cans of bug spray. For their walk down the street Samantha had tossed a light cotton shirt over her halter, feeling uncomfortable about appearing in the village in such skimpy attire. But Felicity obviously experienced no similar constraint. If she looked on curiously as Samantha paused to slip into the overblouse, Samantha found it hard not to look askance at Felicity walking along in her skintight short-shorts accompanied only by the bra of a bikini.

Shrugging, Samantha reminded herself that she now lived in the tropics, where customs were different. Still, she noticed that the women who greeted them on the street seemed to frown at Felicity's costume.

These thoughts and all other disappeared in the next hour as the two women plunged into the work before them. At least Samantha plunged in; Felicity's involvement was more nearly a tiptoeing around the edges of the job. When Samantha watched her, Felicity worked, or at least kept herself busy. But when Samantha's head disappeared inside a cupboard, her assistant's energy seemed also to disappear.

Samantha couldn't help being aware of the girl's lackadaisical approach, but she was unsure just what to say. It seemed best simply to make Felicity aware that she knew she was slacking off and to try to motivate her by her own example and obviously watchful eye.

For a while the watchful eye worked, however little effect the example had. Together the two women scraped dirt out of the highest cupboards, struggled to set furniture upright, carted armloads of papers and debris out the door. Within a very few hours the sun had gained its full morning strength, and as the heat intensified the work became increasingly unpleasant. Still Samantha pushed them on. She could begin to see the progress they had made, and she was reluctant to ease up.

Just before noon she decided it would be reasonable to take a break for lunch and suggested this to the younger woman. Felicity turned to look at Samantha, her answer quick and tight.

"I'll quit for lunch all right," she announced harshly. "I'll just plain quit!"

Samantha pursed her lips and exhaled slowly, forcing her temper to stay within bounds. "I know you're hot, Felicity. So am I. Let's have those sandwiches and drinks your mother packed, and we'll both feel refreshed."

But Felicity shook her head stubbornly. "I'm going to feel a lot more refreshed than that," she announced, thrusting her broom noisily aside. "I'm going swimming!"

Samantha tried one last time to save the situation. "Do you mean you'd like a quick swim before lunch? That's fine," she offered.

"No." Felicity glowered at her, rejecting the compromise. "I've had it."

Angry now, Samantha strove to keep her temper. "You're supposed to be working for me," she reminded the young woman who stood before her, beautiful even in her sulky fury.

"Sure, as your medical assistant," the girl rejoined. "Not as a scullery maid."

Samantha refrained from stating the obvious: that she, too, was performing the disagreeable work of washing floors and gathering dead bugs from drawers. Instead, she simply glanced warningly at the girl. Felicity caught the veiled message that her job might be at stake, but her reaction was not at all what Samantha expected.

Laughing indolently as she walked toward the door, Felicity tossed her mane of wild black hair over her shoulders. With a knowing smile she announced, "I'm not worried. Chris wouldn't let me lose this job so easily!"

There was nothing Samantha could say or do as she watched Felicity strut off down the narrow road. Furious at her attitude and more than a little worried about what this would mean for their working together in the future—as well as for her own relationship with Christopher Girard—Samantha was too upset to eat. Hastily she swallowed some of the fruit juice Mrs. Tarai had packed with the sandwiches and then returned to her task.

Her fury gave her renewed strength, and she attacked the work with angry energy. By midafternoon she had nearly completed one room. The furniture was restored to its normal position, the drawers were cleaned and shut, the floor had been swept and washed, the cupboards had been brushed out and washed with disinfectant. All that remained now was to douse them liberally with bug spray and let them air dry.

Wishing for at least the third time that she'd thought to borrow a stepladder from Mrs. Tarai, she clambered up on top of the shelf that covered the lower cabinets. By standing on tiptoe she could just reach the topmost shelf of the highest cabinet, but her position was precarious and she had to cling to a lower shelf with one hand as she stretched to full length.

She had sprayed one cabinet and moved cautiously over to the next when an unexpected sound interrupted her. Frightened, she turned quickly, nearly losing her grasp on the shelf.

"Here, careful now," a deep resonant voice said in warning, and a pair of warm strong arms encircled her thighs.

"What . . . ? Let go of me!" Samantha stammered as she looked down at the tall rugged stranger who clasped her so intimately.

"And have you fall?" His tone was quizzical, teasing but somehow reserved.

"I won't fall," she insisted, hanging onto what shreds of dignity remained in her control. But there were very few shreds left her, considering her near-total disarray, the dust on her abbreviated costume and the flush that spread upward from the point on her thighs where the stranger's arms lingered. Now that she stood secure again, his grasp seemed more nearly a caress than a means of support, and again she tried to extricate herself.

"Hey, what are you trying to do?" The strange man laughed as she wriggled to free herself from his grasp.

"Get down," she answered breathlessly, helpless to fight the strength of his encircling arms.

"That's easy," he grinned. But he made no move to release her.

"Will you please let me go?" she asked, her voice at some fine border between the command she longed to give and the plea she feared would be ignored.

"Let me help you down," he countered. Then, keeping his eyes on her face so that she found she must return his steady gaze, he eased her forward on the ledge. Still holding her in the tight circle of his strong arms, he slipped her feet off the cupboard and glided her slowly down toward the floor, keeping her close against him all the time. As her soft tired body slid along his lean hard one, guided and controlled by the power of his wiry arms, Samantha could feel rising in her sensations she had rarely experienced before, and never in a situation like this, never while she half lay in the arms of a total stranger.

At last the lean strong man set her on her feet. But though she could stand alone, he did not yet release her. His hands, which rested on her shoulders, were gentle in spite of their large size in comparison to her petite limbs. And still his gaze compelled her to stare into his eyes. Gasping for breath, Samantha felt suffused by a warmth that had nothing to do with the heat of the tropical afternoon or her own day of hard labor. Whether the stranger was affected, too, was hard to tell, but at last she forced herself to break away from this odd silent embrace.

"Who are you?" she asked as she backed off to stand behind a table at some distance from the dark man.

"I could ask you the same question," he responded.

"But you...just walked into my house," she gasped.

"Ah, well, actually it's my house," he said with an odd grin.

For a moment Samantha looked confused, then suddenly she understood. She flushed at having been caught in such a state of grubby disarray and then blushed all the more furiously as she remembered his actions—and her reactions. Holding on to the table in a sudden wave of dizziness, she spoke as calmly as she could.

"You must be Christopher Girard."

"And you must be Samantha Hall." He walked toward her with his hand outstretched.

Instinctively she sought to back away, then realized he meant only to shake her hand. Embarrassed to extend her dust-covered hand to his, she wiped it quickly on her shorts.

"That's not going to help, you know," he announced as he clasped her hand in a hearty greeting. "Anyway, you already attacked me with a layer of dust," he continued, smiling slyly as he added, "or did you forget?"

"Who attacked whom?" she retorted angrily.

"Yes, well, we won't worry about details, will we? We both enjoyed it, after all."

"I'm not enjoying any part of this encounter," Samantha answered quickly.

"Really?" He raised his eyebrows quizzically. "My sensors must be failing," he added, shaking his head in a mockery of disbelief. "Usually I know very well when a woman is enjoying herself."

Having no answer but another blush, Samantha stood quietly, steeling herself against his next quip—or move. But to her relief Christopher Girard walked away from her, glancing about the room before returning his gaze to her.

"What have you been doing?" he asked at last.

"What does it look like?" she responded, remembering her earlier anger at the condition of the clinic he was supposed to have made ready for her arrival. "Cleaning."

He glanced at her strangely. "Cleaning?" he repeated.

"Yes," she lashed out at him in anger and frustration at all his unkept promises. "Did you think I could see patients in. . .in a pigsty?"

A line furrowed his brows, revealing his confusion. Suddenly he surveyed the room again, taking in the buckets of soapy water, the bags of wrapped garbage, the empty bottles of disinfectant. With a loud angry exclamation he strode over to the entryway, staring into the second room, still looking as it had when Samantha first saw it hours before. Returning to the front room, he stared for a moment at Samantha, alarming her by the expression of barely controlled fury that cut across his face. Abruptly, without a word, he disappeared into the back part of the house, and a moment later she heard his footsteps charging across the rooms on the second story.

Realizing she had been too shocked and upset by the condition of the clinic to consider what the rest of the house might look like, Samantha sank to the floor in despair. It might take weeks to make the house habitable and to get the clinic ready, and she just wasn't sure she could face that, with no help from Felicity and considering the disturbing, teasing arrogance of her employer.

At last she heard his footsteps descending the stairs, taking them two at a time from the sound. Instinctively she glanced up when he entered the room, steeling herself for the worst. But there was a small grim smile on his face as he gazed down at her.

"They left the second floor alone," he said enigmatically.

"They?" she prompted, puzzled by his words.

Christopher Girard paused, then reached out a hand to help her up. When she hesitated, he sighed in exasperation, "I'm not going to bite."

His voice revealed his tension, and Samantha, loath to be the recipient of the fury she sensed building in him, slipped her hands into his, allowing him to pull her up to stand beside him. She stood expectantly, waiting for him to explain his strange comment. After a final angry appraisal of the room she had spent the entire day cleaning, he grasped her hand in his and led her to the door.

"We'll talk somewhere else," he announced.

Samantha motioned meaningfully at her attire, acutely conscious of the brevity of her shorts and the smudges of dust on the bare skin revealed by her skimpy halter.

"All right," he sighed. "It's just that the sight of this room makes me so damned angry."

His voice trailed off as he glanced around for a place to sit. Finally he pulled two chairs over near the open window where they would be touched by the gentle breeze. Motioning Samantha into one, he seated himself on the other. Samantha looked around hastily, hoping she could find her cotton overblouse and slip it on to cover herself, but it was nowhere to be seen, and she didn't want to provoke either anger or a more disturbing reaction in the man who sat impatiently expecting her to join him.

As she waited for him to speak, Samantha had her first chance to take a good look at her employer. Girard was dark and rugged, lean and powerfully built, with wiry arms whose embrace she remembered all too well. Even seated he appeared tall, and she guessed correctly that he stood several inches more than six feet. Like Felicity, he had black hair and eyes, with the same kind of thick lashes. Like her, too, he emitted a powerful sensuality, but in him it had the ability to disturb Samantha. There the similarities ended. Not only was he tall and attractive, but he also carried not one unnecessary ounce on his hard masculine body, as was made obvious by his thin cotton shirt open nearly to the waist and tucked inside a distressingly tight pair of jeans. Now that his earlier impassioned anger had dissipated, his eyes sparkled with energy and life; before them, Samantha's green eyes dropped.

"Do I pass inspection?" In spite of the teasing words, his voice had a depth and resonance that vibrated in Samantha to the tips of her toes.

Blushing, she looked up to deny what he had seen, then knew it was useless.

"Don't be embarrassed," he laughed. "My inspection was every bit as thorough."

Furious with herself for letting him see her studying him, furious with him for reminding her of her deshabille and her unwitting acceptance of his earlier embrace, she spat out at him, "Can you explain all of this?" She motioned angrily around the room. "Why wasn't the clinic ready for me?"

He shook his head. "It should have been. There were just one or two things left to do when I last saw it. And believe me, it didn't look like this three days ago."

"Well, then, can you explain how it got this way?"

Sighing, he answered, "I wish I could." For a moment it seemed he was considering saying something else, but finally he concluded with a shrug, "Someone got in and messed it up, I suppose."

She looked up, startled. "Why would anybody do that?" she asked. Suddenly a terrible thought occurred to her, and hesitantly she put it into words.

"Don't the people want me here? Don't they want a doctor?"

Quickly he leaned forward, clasping her small hands in his large ones. "It's not that. They want you here all right."

For a silent moment his restless eyes revealed the internal debate he underwent, but once more they grew hard and expressionless as he answered blandly, "It must have been vandals, perhaps from another island."

With this, though she felt he was not telling her the whole story, Samantha had to be satisfied. Briefly they discussed some other topics, and again she became aware of the extent of his power on the island. Did she need a refrigerator to store drugs? He would get it. Were her accommodations at Widow Tarai's acceptable? If not, he would change them. Had she considered what furniture she might like in the house? She had only to tell him and he would arrange to add to what he had already put in place.

As they talked, Samantha felt herself beginning to respond to this fascinating man in a new way. Although the few letters they'd exchanged while she was considering the job had given her a vague sense of his life on the island, and his business representatives had told her more, she had not altogether recognized the extent of his authority. Now, as he talked calmly about what she might need and mentioned with no special pride one or another thing he could do for her, her vague recognition began to take a new, distinct shape. He seemed acutely aware of his

power and his responsibility, balancing the undoubt-
ed pleasure of the first against the demands of the
second in a way that helped her to understand why
Mrs. Tarai regarded him as she did. No god, certainly, but a man with considerable control over the lives
of others.

As he spoke of the various people she could expect
to see among her first and most faithful patients, she
let her mind drift a little. Listening enough to catch
those details that might be useful to her later, she
released a part of her mind to observe Christopher
Girard. There was no question that he was a striking-
ly handsome man, looking strong and lithe like a
Greek statue. She watched in fascination as he
stretched one bare arm along the windowsill, noting
how his leanness let her see the tendons moving when
he tensed and relaxed his fist. Remembering the sensation of those arms wrapped around her thighs and
gliding up her body, she felt a little thrill run through
her. She wanted to shake herself like a puppy in the
rain, shedding not the unwanted water off the dog's
back but the unwanted sensations that permeated her
being. Forcing herself to pay attention to his words,
she turned her eyes away from Christopher Girard. It
was a tiny movement, but he caught it nonetheless.

"Where's your mind off to now?" he teased with a
trace of exasperation.

Embarrassed, she took refuge in a reasonable excuse. "Just tired."

"Jet lag, I suppose," he offered sympathetically.

She nodded, glad for the neutral explanation.

"And then all of this, today," she added, waving around the room with a heavy arm.

His lips pursed in anger. "You won't be doing it tomorrow," he assured her. "I'll send a crew over to do the work, and you're to take the day off."

Gratefully Samantha smiled, stifling a yawn as she did. Not thinking to ask where he would find the laborers or how he could afford to spare them from their regular jobs, she simply accepted his ability to solve this particular problem. It would be good to rely on someone else right now, especially after this exhausting day.

Suddenly he looked at her strangely and asked, as though he had just thought of it, where Felicity was. "Did you send her out for something?" he suggested.

Without thinking, Samantha laughed. "Are you kidding?" she asked incredulously. "She took off hours ago."

To her shock, Girard stood up so fast he knocked over the chair on which he had been seated. Grabbing it hastily with one hand before it could clatter to the ground, he stared at Samantha.

"I am not kidding," he announced sternly. "What do you mean, she took off?"

Frightened at the look in his eyes, Samantha suddenly remembered all her earlier suspicions about this man and the assistant he had saddled her with. Tense with aroused anxiety, she forgot to meet his stern gaze as she answered simply, "Felicity left here just before lunch."

"And you don't know where she went?" His glinting eyes, as hard as rocks, revealed his fury.

Angry herself now, Samantha fought back the desire to ask whether she was Felicity's supervisor or her baby-sitter. Instead she spoke calmly. "I think she may have gone swimming."

"Swimming," he repeated slowly.

Suddenly her temper got the better of her. It wasn't enough that she had to clean the filthy room alone when her supposed assistant disappeared, but now she was being held responsible for a flighty girl whose own mother couldn't control her. Rising to face Girard, she spoke harshly.

"Yes, swimming or dancing, or maybe she's just loafing with that lazy George you sent to meet me yesterday. She decided she's just too good for this work and she left. And that's all I know!"

The storm passed, Samantha realized her legs were shaking, and she hastily seated herself again, determined not to attract Girard's attention to her nervous reaction.

But he seemed unaware of her. Slowly he walked toward the door. Hooking his thumbs into the loops of his belt just behind the curve of his waist, he stared out into the street, quiet now in the late-afternoon heat. At last he turned back to her, speaking in a stony voice.

"I see." For a moment he said nothing else; then, looking at Samantha with a tense wistfulness, he added, "Look, I know she's young and flighty, but her heart's in the right place." He paused, then added with conviction, "It'll be better when she's working in the clinic. When she was younger she was always taking care of injured animals, and she's got a special way with sick children. I think she can help you—a lot."

Samantha bit her lip to control her expression of dismay. After her outburst and what she had said, he still wanted her to work with Felicity Tarai. He claimed he could "see," but he couldn't; he was blinded to the real flaws of the girl. Bitterly she thought of the likeliest reason for his being so blind, and that thought did not improve her temper.

Lectures about shared responsibility and the need for Felicity to obey her if she was to help with patients sprang to her mind and died there as she sat fuming. There was nothing more she could say right now. Like it or not, she would have to accept Felicity's presence, if hardly her help.

Sighing, Samantha rose again, planning now to close up the clinic and return to her lodgings at Mrs. Tarai's. But Girard forestalled her, placing a hand gently on her shoulder to prevent her leaving. Although his touch was light, her skin burned from the contact, and she was grateful when he released her once she had seated herself again.

"What did you mean when you said I'd sent 'lazy George' to meet you yesterday?" he asked, an inquisitive look in his dark eyes.

She shrugged. "You seem to run everything else here, so I assumed you'd sent him," she explained, sarcasm slipping into her words and her tone.

He ignored the tone and picked up only the fact. "George isn't the most energetic man on the island, I'll admit, but he's not lazy," he protested.

Hurt that he seemed to be doubting her words, Samantha glowered at him. "Oh? Maybe you think that I *should* carry all my luggage after traveling sixty-five hundred miles and spending fifteen hours in three planes?" she snapped, adding, "*If* you can call that last puddle jumper an airplane."

"It's a good plane," he insisted quickly, before responding to her real objection. "No, I don't think you should have carried your baggage," he agreed, and then added jokingly, "I think there are better roles for women than lugging suitcases."

At her grunt of impatience he moved close to her, placing one finger under her chin and tilting her head so that he could look into her frosty green eyes. "Look, Samantha," he began firmly, "I don't know why George behaved as he did. It's not his usual way, and I'll find out." Speaking more to himself than to her, and glancing angrily around the room, he went on softly, "There's a lot I have to find out about."

Warmed by his first use of her given name, feeling somehow protected by his words and the gentle touch of his fingers on the tender skin of her face, Samantha began to relax. But his next words cut through her growing peace and reminded her of her anger.

"Meanwhile, you'll be a good girl and trust me?" he asked in a tone she could only classify as patronizing.

Squirming under his observation, she grimaced. "I'll do my work," she said at last. "That's what I'm here for."

He gazed at her, surprised by her angry response; but finally he spoke, apparently accepting that he would get no other answer. "Just so you don't give up," he shrugged.

"I'm no quitter," she answered hastily, unwilling to speak of how much this job meant to her both as a professional and a personal challenge.

If he was surprised by her vehemence, Girard didn't reveal it in words or actions. He simply said, "Good," then stood in silence, as if curious to observe her next move.

Samantha sat quietly in her chair, afraid even to speak again lest she lose the tenuous hold she had over her flooding emotions. Finally Girard started to walk toward the door, as though he was leaving. But as he reached the doorstep he paused and turned around to face her.

"I heard you were missing some bags," he said.

"Yes." She twisted around in the chair to look at him. "Another part of my grand welcome," she quipped, trying to convert her confusion and anger into a casual joke but slipping awkwardly into an unpleasant sarcasm.

He looked at her strangely, then said calmly, "They'll be here tomorrow...unless you need them tonight?"

Startled, Samantha rose from the chair and rushed toward the door. "No, tomorrow will be fine," she agreed hastily. Then she probed anxiously, "Where did you find them? Are they all right?"

He nodded his answer to the last question and responded to the first. "They'd been misplaced, it seems. I found them when I was going through some supplies at the depot on Halekai yesterday, and I flew them over in my Beechcraft today." He paused, looking at her knowingly before concluding, "I figured you wouldn't want to wait another week or so for the supply boat."

Sheepishly she nodded her appreciation for his understanding. But it was difficult to say more than the most perfunctory thanks as he stood there, arrogantly certain of his constant success.

"Well, then, I'll see you tomorrow," he announced. But still he remained, looking down at her from his full height.

"Yes, I suppose so," she answered, finding herself oddly incapable of meeting his gaze.

"Samantha?" He whispered her name this time, his voice suddenly husky.

Surprised, she looked up at him just in time to meet his face bending toward hers. Giving her not a minute to object or react in any way, he brushed his lips lightly against hers.

"Welcome to Good Providence," he said softly as he straightened up again.

Before she could say or do anything in response, he had disappeared out the door, and in a moment the street was as empty as if he had never been there.

This was a strange man, she thought as she stood

in the doorway of what would soon be her home. He found trunks no one else even knew to be missing, he ran the lives of hundreds of people, and yet something about what had happened to the clinic seemed to be beyond his understanding or control. Clearly he had been baffled by the ransacking of the two rooms. Yet if she was no quitter, it was apparent that he wasn't, either. He obviously intended to learn what was behind the mystifying events of the past few days and then to use his power to resolve the problems.

Gazing out the door to where she had last seen him walking down the street, Samantha lifted her hand to her face, stroking her fingers lightly across the lips he had touched with his own.

Gentle and fleeting as his kiss had been, it left her fully aware of another power he had over her, the intense male power she had sensed from the first moment of contact between them. It was a strange welcome she had been given, Samantha thought as she prepared to leave the house for the night, a disturbingly wonderful welcome to her new life. She had taken this job because she sought adventure as well as a way to make herself useful, she mused as she walked slowly back to Mrs. Tarai's. It began to seem that she might find more adventure than she'd anticipated—and adventure of a new kind, too.

CHAPTER THREE

THE NEXT MORNING dawned with the sparkling clarity Samantha would soon learn to expect on this Pacific island. By afternoon it might grow hazy as the intense heat rose from roads and reflected off the buildings. But except when it rained, morning invariably arrived with the sun glittering on the water and the air so clear and fresh she could often glimpse the next island, a tiny coral key more than a dozen miles distant.

Once Samantha saw that the team of men and women Chris had sent over to put the clinic in order could work as well without her as with her, she adopted his suggestion of taking a day off. She would move into the house and set up the clinic on the following day, with help promised by the same team of workers now attacking the mess with such diligence and energy. How much assistance Felicity would provide was another matter, but Samantha had noticed some difference in her attitude at breakfast this morning. She seemed more alert, helping her mother clear the table and offering to show Samantha a secluded cove for swimming if she wished.

"That sounds nice, but I think I'd like to explore

the village first." Samantha smiled, adding quickly, before the young woman could revert to her previous coolness, "Could we go after lunch?" Within minutes they had made their plans.

As Samantha wandered through the village a little later, she found herself avidly considering what might have caused the change in Felicity. She conceded that it was possible her initial impression of the girl had been incorrect: maybe Felicity had been in a bad mood. But that seemed unlikely, given Mrs. Tarai's comment. She wondered what role Christopher Girard's return had played, finally deciding that if she couldn't know the cause she could at least be grateful for the effect and try to encourage the newer, more helpful kind of behavior.

By this point in her ruminations, Samantha had reached the center of the small village. The shops had been open since seven, their doors wide to catch the breeze off the ocean. Over the entrances to the food stores hung strips of brightly colored plastic, which Samantha soon learned let in the air and the customers but helped keep out the flies. Once she had explored the butcher's shop and the small grocer's, she knew why keeping out the bugs mattered so much: meat lay unwrapped on refrigerated counters and poultry hung from hooks on the ceiling; cheeses, fruit and vegetables likewise had no protection from the myriad large insects of the tropical island. Yet though the shops were dark and spare, they were spotless, and there was adequate refrigeration.

In both the butcher's and the grocer's and in the

other stores she visited, Samantha introduced herself—unnecessarily, as it turned out. Everyone knew of her arrival. The DC-3 stopped at Good Providence only if it had a passenger to discharge or pick up, and that did not happen very often. Shopkeepers and shoppers alike recognized the petite redhead as the long-awaited Dr. Hall and greeted her warmly.

Any lingering doubt Samantha had about the islanders' wanting her was dispelled as one person after another, in the stores and on the street, came up to her and shook her hand in welcome. Some of the hands that reached out for hers were almost as pale as her own; others were a deep warm brown. But most ranged somewhere in between, from lightest gold to richest copper, for the mixed blood of the majority of the islanders attested to the long peaceful intermingling of two races, two cultures.

The butcher called his wife out from their rooms behind the shop, and she walked proudly with Samantha to the little general store. There the wife tended the counter, but she called to her husband, and he left his late breakfast to greet the newcomer and offer her credit. At the garage Samantha found a special welcome, for the mechanic held out to her the keys to a small blue Datsun wagon, the car she had been promised by her contract. The license plate read DOC-1, and from the steering wheel hung a small bunch of red and yellow flowers, filling the interior with the heady fragrance of the tropics.

By the time she drove back to Widow Tarai's for lunch, Samantha felt she could fly to the top of the

Mountain of the Sun, the island's high volcanic peak, without the help of an airplane. Never in her life had she been made to feel so important, so special. Although she had expected to be needed on the island, she had not dreamed of anything like this, and the warm greetings and genuine goodwill of the islanders wiped out all of the discomfort of her first day and a half in Good Providence.

Even Felicity responded to her pleasure, showing enthusiasm for the new car and suggesting they take advantage of it to drive to one of the more distant beaches for their swim. After a quick lunch, the two women changed into bikinis and packed up towels and books for a lazy afternoon. That was all Felicity brought, but not so Samantha. Under a wide-brimmed straw hat purchased that morning in town and covered by a full-length, long-sleeved muumuu, Samantha walked to the car carrying a huge bottle of suntan oil.

Acknowledging Felicity's smothered giggle with a teasing frown, she jokingly complained as she climbed into the car, "I'll fry in this ridiculous sun of yours, and I don't want to be burned to a crisp!"

Though worry about burning her fair skin in the tropical sun was the primary reason for her full-length gown, Samantha also felt strange about riding through the village in an uncovered bikini. She knew she looked attractive in the flowered suit, but she felt uncomfortable about exposing herself to the stares of the villagers.

Felicity clearly had no such inhibitions. Her suit

was even more revealing than Samantha's, the shiny black material an effective complement to her dark coloring. As they drove through the village and along the narrow paved road, Felicity leaned far out the open window, waving and shouting to the acquaintances they passed. On an island the size of Good Providence, everyone was an acquaintance, and since most of the life of the island took place outdoors, that led to a lot of boisterous waving.

The cove Felicity guided them to lay near the very end of the paved road. Considering the curving narrowness of the road, Samantha was grateful not to have to face driving on a dirt path this first day of adjusting to a new car, but she knew that would soon come. The primary reason for having a car was so that she could visit patients who could not come to the clinic, and that included families living up in the hills. She could walk to her rounds in the village.

The afternoon passed lazily. Samantha swam twice, gasping each time as she dipped her sun-heated body into the tingly water. But the ocean was warm and she stayed in a long time when she swam. Through the clear water she could see patches of coral, and she vowed to buy a mask and snorkel at her first opportunity. In between dips she dozed lazily in the shade of a big palm, slipping out cautiously, and well coated with suntan oil, for short periods in the sun. She knew her fair skin could burn very easily and she didn't want to be her own first patient.

From time to time she tried to engage Felicity in conversation, but the girl seemed reluctant to do more than answer her simple questions. She did probe a little into Felicity's education, especially those areas that might help her decide what kinds of duties to entrust to her, and here she got more cooperation. Still, so much would depend on Felicity's attitude, and Samantha was not ready to rely on that, in spite of Christopher Girard's recommendation.

Warm and lazy, Samantha was reluctant to suggest leaving the charming cove. But by four o'clock she knew she'd had all the sun she should on her first day. Felicity seemed willing to accept that, and the two women packed up the car with a great show of shaking sand off towels and feet so as to keep the dirt out of the brand-new vehicle.

"Not that it much matters," Felicity said knowingly. "It won't look like this for long."

Samantha nodded. She had seen how mud and rust covered the few cars they had encountered while driving and could well imagine what constant exposure to dirt roads and salty air would do to the little station wagon.

As the two women walked in the door shortly before five, Mrs. Tarai's excited voice greeted them.

"Oh, Dr. Hall, this is for you." The round-cheeked woman held out a small folded note, sealed and addressed to Samantha.

Curious, she stood in the hallway to read the note. It was an invitation to dine at the Big House that evening at seven.

"May I use your phone?" she asked Mrs. Tarai,

knowing that theirs was one of the few telephones on the island.

"There's no need," the widow explained breathlessly. "Mr. Girard said you should only call if you couldn't make it. You are going, aren't you?"

Her eyes rounded with excitement. Obviously invitations from the Big House were not to be taken lightly.

"Did Mr. Girard deliver this in person?" Samantha asked.

Mrs. Tarai nodded. "Yes. Well, he wrote it once I told him you were out for the afternoon."

She paused expectantly, and Samantha realized she hadn't answered her hostess's question. She smiled briefly, amused at the elderly woman's agitation.

"Yes, of course I'll go," she said, then added politely, "Unless you were counting on me for dinner?"

Mrs. Tarai shook her head quickly and shooed her upstairs to get ready. "You'll need to leave nearly half an hour for the drive," she warned. "It won't be formal, but Mr. Girard likes his guests to dress up."

Samantha nodded, her excitement mingling with nervousness as she climbed the stairs. It was apparent that Christopher Girard got what he wanted.

While she bathed and scrubbed the sand out of her hair, she considered what to wear. She had unpacked only one small suitcase so far, deciding to leave the rest until after her move the next day. But that suitcase held only casual clothes, nothing suitable for the evening.

Back in her room, her short hair wrapped in a towel,
she opened the larger of the two suitcases she'd traveled with. Near the top lay a dress of soft shimmering
green, a green like the ocean near to shore—or like her
own eyes, she thought as she stretched the dress out on
the bed to check for wrinkles. Mercifully there were
none, and she returned to the suitcase, rummaging
until she found a pair of dainty silver sandals and
some sheer stockings to go with them. An additional
search turned up a half slip, but she couldn't find a
strapless bra, and with that dress any straps would
show. A quick look at her watch convinced her that
she didn't have time to rummage further, and so she
would have to dress without a bra.

The bodice of her gown was made of several layers
of material and covered her nakedness, but the low-
cut back and narrow halter tying behind her neck left
all of her back and most of her shoulders bare. Below
the waist the dress flared out lightly in thin layers of
diaphanous material falling just below her knees. A
narrow silver bracelet on her forearm complemented
her silver slippers. With her crop of curly auburn hair
and the slight flush of her sun-tinged cheeks, she
looked healthy and natural and altogether beautiful.
A touch of green eye shadow and a light pink lipstick
completed her makeup, heightening the striking effect of her green eyes sparkling with excitement. For
although Samantha was nervous about seeing Christopher Girard again after their strange encounter the
preceding afternoon, she was also flooded with a
sense of anticipation.

The drive into the hills above the village went smoothly, thanks to the map that had accompanied the note, and soon she had reached the side road leading to the main entrance of the Big House. As she parked her car next to the Jeep and the sporty Jaguar convertible standing before the house, she realized the name of the building was apt. Not only was the house large, it was imposing.

She barely had time to take in the expanse of smooth white stucco walls before the massive front door was opened by a butler. She walked quickly up the stairs, determined not to be caught in another embarrassing inspection, though presumably it was more acceptable to inspect a man's house than the man himself.

When she announced who she was, the butler acknowledged her with a formal bow accompanied by a distinctly informal and hearty welcome. Taking her light crocheted shawl from her, he ushered her through the tiled hallway to a drawing room opening off to her left.

"Mr. Girard is expecting you," he murmured as he stood aside to let her pass.

There were no doors along the hallway, she observed in her quick walk after the stately butler. The large rooms opening on either side were set off only by arches cutting high and wide into the stucco walls. The effect enhanced the sense of airy spaciousness apparent from her first sight of the house. She barely had time to notice this and the intricate tiled patterns on the floors along which she stepped before Christopher Girard reached out a hand to greet her.

"I'm glad you could come tonight, Samantha," he said, smiling in welcome.

She felt her heart beat faster as she looked into his dark eyes, now twinkling with apparent pleasure. Her own response was less certain but equally warm. The moment passed swiftly as he turned to introduce her to the other guests.

"This is Ed Bates, our schoolteacher, and Father Ilima, who is here from Halekai and staying with Ed. Gentlemen, Dr. Samantha Hall."

In a few minutes they had passed through the formalities of greetings and insisting on the use of first names, except, of course, for Father Ilima. Over a cool tropical drink of rum, pineapple juice and soda, they exchanged brief introductions. Samantha learned that Ed Bates, a descendant of one of the original settlers, had been born on Good Providence. After attending high school on Halekai, he had gone to the United States for further education. While in high school he had met Father Ilima, a native Micronesian who had also studied in the United States, at a seminary in California. In spite of the disparity in their ages—at thirty, Ed was at least twenty-five years younger than the priest—they had become and remained close friends.

Ed now served as the primary teacher for almost eighty schoolchildren in the first through the eighth grades. Two recent graduates from the high school assisted him, keeping order and helping students with their work while he lectured to one group or listened to recitations of another. When Samantha heard this, she gasped in shock.

"Why, that's impossible!"

The three men laughed, but it was Father Ilima who answered her. In perfect English with just a soft lilt to remind her this was his second language, he explained that until a year ago Ed had worked entirely alone.

"And you should have seen the schoolhouse," Ed broke in. "Leaky roofs, desks a century old—now, *that* was impossible!"

Confused, Samantha looked from one man to the next. Although she sensed that Chris could explain most simply, his face was expressionless and his eyes hooded. So she asked the others to continue.

"It's really quite simple, my dear," the priest said calmly. "Chris worked a miracle."

"Come now, Father," Chris's scolding voice laughed, but Samantha detected a hint of embarrassment, too.

"All right," Father Ilima conceded. "It's not perfect yet, so there's been no miracle." Then, shaking his finger at the tall dark man who sought refuge in refilling his glass, he added, "Still, it's the closest thing to one I've ever seen. And I should know!"

The laughter that greeted this solemn announcement broke off only when the butler announced that dinner was ready. Their move into the dining room interrupted the discussion, and Samantha had to wait for the answer to her question. During the bustle of seating and the tasting of wine there was no way for her to reintroduce the topic.

As the thin-stemmed glasses were filled with a delicate pale wine, Chris motioned for silence at the table and rose to offer a toast. Quickly the two other men rose, turning to face Samantha.

He began solemnly, addressing Samantha with a small bow and a flourish. "Our new physician. From her résumé and her glowing references, I knew she would grace our island with the wisdom and compassion of the best of her profession." He paused for a moment, motioning to the two men that he hadn't finished. Then, with a mischievous twinkle in his eyes and a wink intended only for Samantha, he concluded, "I didn't know she would also grace our table with her beauty."

Blushing, Samantha accepted the simpler and far less personal toasts of the other two men, then gratefully welcomed the intrusion of the servant who brought in the first course. That provided a needed interruption and the conversation shifted away from Samantha, to her relief. For a few minutes they all concentrated on the delicate fish soufflé served hot and fluffy in individual casseroles, but once the first moments of appreciative eating had passed, conversation began again. As soon as there was a lull, Samantha returned to the question of the school. This time Father Ilima answered her seriously, though she noticed that Chris once again concentrated on his food as though he was embarrassed.

"The school here had never been very good, not as

long as I'd known it," the priest began after he'd finished his soufflé. "But in the last twenty years or so it had been allowed to go to ruin. The building was never painted, no one ordered new textbooks, and for a few years the only teacher was a girl who had graduated from the high school and worked without pay."

Samantha's shock appeared in her wide green eyes. "How could that be?" she asked when Father Ilima paused to swallow some wine.

The priest glanced quickly at Chris and then, as if receiving a signal of some sort, continued softly, "Things like that happen, Samantha." Picking up his story with energy now, he went on, "Then about two years ago Ed returned to the island from the U.S. He didn't get much of a welcome officially, but he had some good unofficial friends."

The priest's surreptitious glance at Chris was unmistakable this time, and suddenly Samantha knew that it was the rugged-looking man sitting so impassively at the head of the formal table who had made the difference for the schoolchildren of Good Providence. She cocked her head slightly in his direction, looking quizzically at Father Ilima as she did so, and was rewarded with a subtle nod.

"So that's when the change began," the priest continued, knowing she had understood his hidden message. "Now Ed's got a fine building, new texts and two assistants. And next fall, as soon as he can hire two more assistants from the high school, the current ones will be shipped off to Guam to get their teaching degrees. Then we'll really see a difference."

Samantha smiled with pleasure as she heard the glow in the priest's voice and saw it in Ed's eyes. She couldn't help glancing at the head of the table, but she knew better than to comment on Chris's role in all this. Instead she turned to Ed.

"That's wonderful, but you've still got your work cut out for you," she observed.

He nodded. "We could probably hire a teacher from one of the other islands or from the States, but we'd rather develop our own talent here," he explained.

At this Chris joined the conversation for the first time. "It's not just that, Samantha," he interposed. "It's hard for the children on Good Providence. They're not Micronesians, Guamanians, Japanese or Spanish, and most of the pupils they meet on Halekai come from one of those groups. For that matter, so do most of our neighbors in the island chain, though it's true that on Guam there are many more people of American descent. But usually either they're military and stick to themselves, or they've come from Hawaii, and often they're Polynesian, very much more at home here than our islanders, virtually all of whom are descended from the original settlers. Here the children exist in a kind of miniature New England, transported thousands of miles and more than a hundred years away. Yet they really live like their neighbors, and they are governed in the same way."

"They're brought up speaking English," Ed interrupted, "but they'll need to learn the local dialect before they're full grown—and Japanese, too, if they enter business or stay on Halekai.''

"And too many of them do stay on Halekai, or go to Guam or Saipan,'' interjected Father Ilima.

"Is that a problem?" Samantha asked with interest.

"A terrible one," Ed confirmed. "On Halekai especially, because they see the resorts and the fancy restaurants catering to the tourists who arrive on their grand cruise ships—"

"And it seems to them the money flows as freely as the wine," Father Ilima finished for him.

Chris picked up the refrain. "And what do they have if they return to Good Providence? Work in the sugarcane or at the docks or in one of the shops. It's not very exciting in comparison."

"Can't they just loaf on the beaches?" Samantha's question was spoken in jest, but the answer she received was deadly serious.

"No." Chris shook his head firmly. "From the days of the first settlers it has been a law on the island that either you work for the plantation or in some other way contribute directly to the life of the island—or you leave!"

Samantha looked up in surprise. Hesitantly she asked, "Doesn't that create problems?"

"Not nearly as many problems as would arise if the law didn't exist," Chris explained. "There are provisions for dependents—children, the elderly, widows of former workers and the like. And we try to encourage people to stay, even to develop their own work—a new shop or service, for example."

Father Ilima picked up the story. "It may seem harsh, Samantha, but bear in mind that when Matthias Girard first landed here, none of the neighboring islands wanted so much as to look at his settlers. Then later, when the sugarcane plantation did so well and the island began to prosper, it was in danger of being overwhelmed by immigrants. So the laws were set up to ensure both that the first settlers worked— no work, no home—and that the island wouldn't be flooded by more people than it could handle."

"Why were the other islanders opposed to the original settlers?" Samantha asked.

Chris laughed. "You haven't heard the story, I take it?"

She shook her head. "No, but I'm interested."

He nodded. "It's an interesting tale." Pausing to offer more wine to accompany the delicious coq au vin they had all been enjoying, he continued, "Matthias Girard was my grandfather's grandfather. He was a merchant seaman, born in Rhode Island but shipping out of all the wonderful old New England seaports—New Bedford, Nantucket, Gloucester—as well as Providence and Newport. On one of his voyages he saw this area, and it seemed paradise to him after the cold austerity of the world he had come from. He wanted to settle here but knew he needed a business to keep himself afloat. Coconuts and pineapples and a little fishing might be adequate for the natives, and it was an attractive life, but it wasn't the life of a staunch old New Englander."

Father Ilima interrupted, "Don't oversimplify,

Chris. There were industries around here, though this island was uninhabited.'' Turning to Samantha he explained, ''Sugarcane, coffee and coconuts—those were the staple crops on these islands, and some had been on the trade routes since the seventeenth century. But Matthias Girard was an independent man who just had to do it all himself.''

Chris nodded. ''He was also a broody man—kept a diary with all his hopes and thoughts in it, and you can just about trace the development of his idea in its pages. When he returned home he had his plan all worked out. He took his earnings from that voyage and all his wife's savings, too, and paid for the release of some two dozen prisoners from the jails in and around Providence. Those were to be the first settlers.''

Chris paused to grin at Samantha's wide-eyed stare. ''Now do you see why the locals were reluctant to mingle with Matthias's people?''

She nodded quickly. ''I'm surprised he had the courage to mingle with them,'' she said, adding in curiosity, ''Did his wife come along, too?''

''You bet she did,'' Chris answered. ''As near as I can tell, she hated the cold winters as much as he did, and she shared his love of adventure. At last she got her chance to go to sea, too.''

Samantha looked at Ed, realizing he was the descendant of an ex-convict. As if Chris understood her thought, he spoke hastily.

''You should understand that Matthias was no fool. He chose only selected criminals: they had to have certain skills, and there were no murderers, rapists or embezzlers among them. A good burglar might show initiative; a farmer imprisoned for debt was still a farmer and could help on the plantation he planned to develop; a sailor who had jumped ship added to the experience of his crew.''

Samantha smiled in understanding. "He was a smart man," she exclaimed.

"The first practical prison reformer I've ever heard of," Father Ilima chimed in.

"And resourceful," his handsome descendant continued. "For the voyage, he turned farmers into sailors and housewives into nurses and cooks."

"There were other women, then?" Samantha looked up in surprise.

Chris teased mischievously, "How do you suppose there got to be so many islanders today?" Then he returned with merciful speed to his tale. "Once here, he set some of the people to planting cane and others to clearing land for houses. Fortunately it was a lot easier than settling America had been, for the temperatures were balmy and the people could live off the land if they had to. In fact, that's why he named the island as he did—it was a good provider and he considered it a gift of divine providence, as well as the settlers' new version of Providence, Rhode Island."

Samantha nodded. It was the right name for this bounteous land and the unhappy settlers' new home.

Chris was still talking. "As quickly as he could, Matthias supervised the planting of crops, set up grazing areas for the pigs and cows he'd brought along, convinced one or two people from Halekai to teach them how to fish the native way. He used his contacts from years as a merchant seaman to establish markets for the cane and to work out trade agreements for those things they couldn't build themselves or find on the island. It wasn't easy, but he built up the settlement, and in time the new islanders came to thank him.''

"Weren't they glad to be released from jail?" Samantha felt uncomfortable discussing the convicts with one of their descendants present. But realizing that a great majority of the islanders grew out of that small original stock, she had to assume there could be few feelings of awkwardness left.

"Sure," Chris agreed. "He didn't take anyone who was unwilling to go. But still, they were wrenched from a world they knew to a very different life, and however beautiful the island is, those first years can't have been easy.''

For a moment Samantha sat quietly, trying to imagine what those early years would have been like. No one would have starved, but there must have been hardships and fears and a great deal of loneliness. As she sat mulling this over, suddenly the serious expression on her face turned into a wide smile.

"What's so funny?" Chris asked.

Samantha laughingly told them, "Can you imagine the picture it must have made in a New England harbor when Matthias Girard loaded his ship? Cows and pigs and ducks and men and women...two of each kind, like Noah's Ark?''

The laughter in which they all joined interrupted the talk about history. Soon they moved into the living room for their coffee, Samantha feeling more comfortable with Chris than she had dared to hope.

In the next forty-five minutes the conversation revolved around more immediate concerns, ranging from the state of this year's crop to how much local Micronesian history should be covered in what grade. Shortly before ten Ed rose with a sigh and motioned to Father Ilima.

''Tomorrow's a working day for me,'' he explained to Samantha as he and the priest prepared to depart.

''I must leave, too,'' she said, standing with compunction. ''I want to set up the clinic tomorrow so that I can open it the day after.''

But as she motioned to the butler to bring her shawl to her, Samantha felt Chris's warm hand descend on her bare shoulder, a touch so light she scarcely noticed its possessive undertone.

''Would you like to see Matthias's diary?'' he asked swiftly. ''And you haven't toured the house, either.''

Torn between her feeling that it would be most proper to leave with the others and her desire to see the rest of this obviously magnificent house as well as the historical diary, Samantha hesitated. But Father Ilima's reaction convinced her.

''You ought to take up his offer, Samantha,'' the

friendly priest told her, smiling encouragingly. "It's hard to get him to show that relic."

"All right," Samantha agreed.

With Chris she escorted the others to Ed's car. It came as no surprise to see that he drove the practical Jeep and Chris the extravagant Jaguar.

Once the others had left she felt a little shiver of nerves run down her bare spine, but Chris continued to perform as the charming host he had been all evening. Leading her across the tiled hallway to a small den and unlocking a large drawer in the heavy carved desk, he drew forth a pile of papers and a series of old leather-bound journals. For nearly an hour they pored over the books together, Chris pointing out passages of special interest and Samantha alternately smiling at his ancestor's penchant for detail and frowning sympathetically as she read of the hardships of his life as a merchant seaman and later as the founder of Good Providence. When she came across an account of how they boarded the ship, counting cows and ducks and geese as well as barrels of grains and boxes of supplies, she pointed it out to Chris, and they shared a chuckle over his ancestor's Ark.

"Shall we take that tour now?" Chris asked a few minutes later when he'd replaced the journals in their special drawer.

"I'd like that," Samantha admitted. As fascinating as she found the history of the island and of Chris's ancestor, she was even more intrigued by the present—and the present owner of the Big House.

"It's obvious that Matthias didn't build this in

those early days," she said thoughtfully. "When was it built?"

"Not long afterward," was Chris's surprising response. "Matthias's son started it, and his grandson completed most of the work, though every generation has added some touch, usually in an attempt to modernize it."

They walked back into the main hallway together, Chris pointing out that the red, yellow and blue tiles laid in intricate patterns in all the rooms on the first floor were original. "Upstairs there's more wood," he explained, "but I prefer the tiles." With a wry smile he added, "Doesn't it all seem incongruous?"

She looked at him in perplexity, then suggested in a slow voice, "You mean this luxury, compared to the start?"

"Yes, that, too, of course," he acknowledged swiftly. "But the tiles are Spanish. They don't come from around here, and no self-respecting nineteenth-century New Englander would have put them in."

"That's true," Samantha murmured. She glanced at him.

Slipping his hand under her elbow to guide her through a high archway into a tiled court, he motioned expressively about the space before them. "This, too," he said, pointing out the fountain in the center and the low stone benches around the edge. "There are two additional courtyards like this, all with flowers and benches and at least one fountain."

"It's lovely," Samantha breathed. "But it also looks as though it belonged in Spain." Pausing thoughtfully, she suddenly remembered something he'd said earlier. "Aren't there Spaniards in this area?" she asked.

He smiled. "Yes, bright eyes. But it happens these came with the family."

She looked up at him expectantly, blushing with pleasure at the affectionate appellation he had used.

"Apparently Matthias talked so much about his voyages as a seaman that his son, Nathaniel, caught the travel bug. As a young man he shipped out on one of the vessels that came here to pick up the sugar, and he traveled to Mexico and Central America, the Philippines, Hawaii, Guam, just about everywhere ships went in those days. He brought back many good ideas that he later put to work on the plantation, and he brought back boxes full of this tile."

As they walked through the rooms on the main floor, Chris showed Samantha other evidence of his ancestors' travels. Pictures and wall hangings from Europe and the Far East, camel saddles from the Near East used as benches along the edges of the corridors, draperies of silk from the Orient. Altogether they created a house that was unique without being overpowering. Love and interest had gone into its design and good taste had always prevailed. Controlling everything had been the consistent desire to suit the house to its surroundings. Palm trees offered their graceful shade to the open courtyards, there were no unnecessary doors or curtains, and the whole effect was airy, cool and spacious.

Chris made no move to escort Samantha around

the upper level, and she would not ask to see it. But she told him honestly how lovely she found the house, and he seemed pleased.

Guiding her out to a terrace overhung with swaying palms, he pointed to the lights of the village far below.

"Sometimes you can see a ship from here," he said softly, "a ship going by so far away its lights seem like distant stars."

"There are stars tonight," she murmured in response. "I'll have to relearn the constellations, too; they all look so different from this angle."

They stood quietly, close together, gazing out beyond the village to the sea and stars, glimmering faintly. At last Chris broke the silence.

"Homesick?"

She shook her head. "There wasn't much home to leave," she admitted quietly.

In answer to his quizzical look, she traced quickly for him that history that he could not have learned by reading her dossier. "My mother died when I was very young, and my father while I was still in college. I've got some cousins around, but that's about it, and since I went away from home for college and medical school, well, I don't have many friends left there, either."

Chris nodded. "You outgrew them?" he suggested.

She shook her head. "We simply grew apart."

There was silence between them as each became lost in individual thoughts, though how similar these topics were Chris could have guessed more easily than Samantha. After a moment he spoke again, his voice soft and surprisingly gentle.

"Was your father a doctor?"

At this she smiled. "Yes—it's a classic story. The father is a doctor, he assumes his son will take over his practice, and then he finds himself saddled with a girl instead." She spoke with the love grown of understanding as she added, "Even my name was strictly second-best: he wanted to name his son Samuel."

Chris slipped his arm around her shoulders, though he continued to gaze out to sea. "I can't imagine any man, even your father, feeling as though he'd been saddled with you."

Relishing the warmth of his casual embrace and his apparent sympathy, Samantha murmured her response. "Oh, he got used to my being around."

Hugging her more tightly inside the shelter of his arm, Chris answered huskily, "I know how easily I could grow accustomed to your being around."

Though a lump rose in her throat, making it difficult to swallow, Samantha said nothing. Wordlessly Chris turned her around until she faced him, sliding his arm tenderly along her naked back as she moved slowly in his embrace.

"Samantha," he breathed, her name half a question on his lips. His eyes, too, seemed to ask a question, but he was too impatient to wait for her answer.

Slowly he brought his other arm up to her bare shoulder, squeezing it gently before he slipped his hand over her shoulder blade and down her back. Not until he had caressed her skin clear to her waist did he halt the inexorable descent of his warm strong fingers. Then, with the gentleness of strength held tensely in control, he pulled her toward him.

The path of his hand on her back had left a line of liquid fire that spread inward to the very core of her. Samantha's breath came unevenly as she responded to his delicate knowing touch. She longed to close her eyes and hide from him, even as she could feel herself arching toward his masculine strength. But he held her eyes with his steady gaze, willing her to look into the depths of his dark eyes.

When there was just enough space between them for the smallest wisp of a tropical breeze to move, he bent his head toward hers, only then closing his darkly expressive eyes and silently inviting her to do the same. With a sudden sharp inhalation of breath, as if he could wait no longer, he claimed her lips with his own.

The kiss began gently, almost tenderly, and Samantha felt her fears dissipating into the night. But his lips were insistent, searching and pressing hers open. As her lips parted under the sensuous insistence of his mouth, she could feel herself responding to him in heart and body. Never had she been kissed like this before, and never had she felt herself experiencing so profound and frightening a response. She sighed with pleasure and with the ache of anticipation.

But suddenly his exploring tongue began to shoot

darts of fire against her lips. Abruptly she forced herself to draw back. She wasn't ready for this, not yet, not so soon.

As if he understood, Chris let her pull away. But his lingering hands massaging her spine in fine circular motion told her that he, too, had been aroused by the depth and warmth of that single kiss. He would let her go, those hands said silently, but it was with the greatest reluctance.

As she held him back, her small hands lost against the expanse of his dinner jacket, she looked long and deep into his eyes. They smoldered with a dusky fire she understood all too intimately. But even before her ragged breathing could return to normal, she forced herself to break away from that enchanting gaze. On unsteady legs she walked toward the front of the house where her car waited, her transport to the world of sanity and cool reason.

As if unable to move, Chris didn't offer to accompany her to the car but stood leaning against the railing on the terrace, watching her as she walked slowly away. Neither spoke, not even to say a word of farewell, which would only have marred the spell in which each appeared to be equally enmeshed.

CHAPTER FOUR

MRS. TARAI wiped her hands distractedly on her bathrobe rather than on the towel dangling over her shoulder as she greeted Samantha at the door.

"Well, my dear?" she asked expectantly.

Samantha felt little surprise at the elderly woman's excited interest in her evening. She had expected it, though she hadn't thought Mrs. Tarai would wait up for her.

As if recognizing the slight awkwardness, the widow spoke hastily. "I've just made myself some warm cocoa. Would you join me?"

About to refuse, suddenly Samantha changed her mind. She knew she couldn't sleep in her current state, with every nerve aflame. A cup of cocoa and a chat with the motherly widow might soothe her agitated heart and help her tense body to relax.

As the two women sat by the kitchen table, the conversation naturally turned to the events of the evening. Choosing carefully, Samantha described what she considered appropriate. But as the talk continued, Mrs. Tarai offered comments and asked questions that surprised and confused her young listener. She seemed to know more about the house and its occupants—past and present—than an ordinary islander, even an inquisitive old woman, might be expected to know. But the story she eventually told was too intriguing to permit Samantha to do anything more than register her puzzled observation.

Once Samantha revealed that she knew about the island's history, both its founding and its more recent problems, Mrs. Tarai's tongue grew loose. At first she simply added some details about the distant past, but soon she was talking about the years she had known, and that meant the years under Daniel Girard and his son, Chris.

"Daniel married young," she began. "Why, by the time he was Mr. Chris's age he had a six-year-old boy, but he was also a widower."

Samantha looked across the table at the woman, flushed in her excitement as she spoke of those days so many years past. Thrilling with a delicious anticipation, Samantha gave herself up to the story as the widow spoke about Chris and his father.

"He loved his bride dearly, really doted on her, and when she died giving birth to Mr. Chris, he just gave up."

At Samantha's murmur of sympathy, Mrs. Tarai looked at her sharply. "It's the boy who deserves your sighs, not the father," she announced acerbically. "Oh, yes," she went on after a glance at Samantha's raised eyebrows. "The man lost his wife, but the boy lost both his mother and his father."

After the briefest pause, the widow exhaled a long

breath, as though she remembered all too painfully the days she described.

"Chris wasn't beaten or left out to starve; he wasn't even really neglected, I suppose. There was always plenty of money for whatever he wanted, but there wasn't any love, at least not from Daniel Girard. He was reared by servants and shipped off the island the first chance his father had. He spent two years on Halekai, supposedly because there was a good tutor on the island. In those days he was at least allowed home every weekend. But when he was seven, Chris was sent off to boarding school in the States. Imagine it! America! Not the islands, not even Saipan or Guam, but almost seven thousand miles away from home. And he stayed there, too, coming back only for a few months each summer, right on through college."

Samantha shuddered at her vivid picture of a terrified little boy going through the trip she had just found so nearly overwhelming. Her sympathetic reaction encouraged Mrs. Tarai to continue her story.

"Well, eventually he finished college, and there were no more excuses to keep him away. So about ten years ago he returned, supposedly to work on the plantation. That's when the trouble really began."

"Trouble?"

Mrs. Tarai shrugged. "Mr. Chris and his father didn't get along. Oh, not just because they'd been separated so long. They were so different. Daniel Girard had never cared much about the island or its people, though I suppose he thought he did his duty by them, just as he had done with his son.''

The widow gave a tight-lipped nod of satisfaction at Samantha's sharp intake of breath.

"Exactly," she said sarcastically. "But it got much worse after his wife died." Her voice softened as she continued, "Then Mr. Chris returned, and he saw the results of his father's neglect. He tried. Oh, how he tried! But the more he interfered, the angrier his father got."

The widow stirred the dregs in her cup absentmindedly, as if considering how to say what she obviously felt she must. At last she went on, her voice low and distant, as if it were traveling the great distance from that time a decade ago. "They fought something awful. Finally his father took the whole business—everything from running the plantation to overseeing road repairs and calling for emergency medical help—and gave it over to a manager, Pete Thompson."

Her voice quavered as she said that name, almost as if it hurt just to utter the syllables.

"And Chris?" Samantha prompted. He didn't seem to her to be the type who gave up.

Mrs. Tarai's face softened. "Oh, he was clever. He knew that if he opposed his father openly he'd get nowhere. Probably be cut off without funds, too, and the islanders needed money desperately for so many things. So he pretended to give in and returned to the States, claiming he had washed his hands of the whole mess. But he hadn't, not him!"

A warm smile wrinkled the skin on her apple-dumpling cheeks as she continued, "As he'd expected, his father was glad to give him a generous allowance as long as he stayed away. Well, he used some of that money for himself—went back to the university, studied agriculture and business and marketing and electronics and. . . oh, all sorts of things he thought might be useful when the day came for him to take over. And he traveled, working at other plantations around the world, too, just to learn the newest techniques and to see how other places solved their problems."

She paused, obviously admiring his diligence and foresight, then she shook her head in wonder. "But most of his money came right back to the island. He had his spies here, and they did what they could. Fixed a leaky roof, bought a pair of shoes, arranged a 'donation' of schoolbooks, found a 'scholarship' for a child to attend high school."

"Was Father Ilima one of those spies?" Samantha asked gently.

The widow smiled soberly. "He might have been. We don't talk about it."

Samantha could understand that Chris was reluctant to be treated as a hero, and she respected his modesty. But there was something else in Mrs. Tarai's expression, some veiled hint of worry her honest face couldn't hide.

"But those days are over," Samantha probed gently. "Chris is in charge now."

Mrs. Tarai looked away from Samantha, her cheeks glowing faintly. When she spoke at last, her words were neutral, and Samantha realized she was avoiding the question.

"Chris took over when his father died, about a year ago," was all she said.

"And the manager? What was his name—Pete...?"

Before answering, the widow rose and carried her cup to the little sink. Her back was turned to Samantha as she spoke, her voice again apparently neutral. "Pete Thompson. Oh, he's working on Halekai now."

Although she burned with additional questions, Samantha sensed she would get no more answers that night. Carrying her own cup to be rinsed, she soon bade the elderly woman a sleepy good-night. Tired as she was, her head whirled with thoughts and feelings excited by the evening, and it was a long time before she could even turn out the light. But at last sleep claimed her until the dawn broke many restful hours later.

EVEN WITH THE HELP of the team of workers Chris sent over, augmented by the surprisingly cooperative Felicity, it took nearly eight hours to unpack the trunks and set up the clinic. Chris stopped by once to offer a friendly greeting and see how the work progressed; but at the sight of the efficient team amid the mess of boxes, equipment and clothing strewn everywhere, he threw up his hands in a mockery of despair.

"I give up," he laughed. "This is beyond me."

Samantha joined in his laugh as she accepted the bottle of wine he held out for a housewarming gift, but inside herself she knew there was little that could truly be beyond Christopher Girard.

By four o'clock the last bottle of antibiotic was stored away, the last piece of equipment stood in place and the last file cabinet was ready to accept a record of a patient's ailment. In her living quarters, too, most of the work was done. The house had been well stocked with china and linen and even a supply of foods, both canned and fresh. Samantha had taken advantage of the presence of the strong-backed young plantation workers to rearrange some of the furniture, and two of the women helped her empty her suitcases into the dresser and wardrobe. She had moved into her new house and was ready to open the clinic in the morning.

"I deserve a holiday. After all, it's my last totally free afternoon," she announced to herself. She stood at the open door of the clinic, giving a self-satisfied look around the sparkling well-equipped rooms. "Yes," she reiterated as she walked up the stairs to her bedroom, "I'm going swimming."

Before rummaging through her dresser for a bikini, Samantha took another survey of her bedroom. Like the rest of the living quarters, it was furnished with superb good taste. When she'd seen the rooms earlier that day, she'd recognized Chris's hand in their decoration. Surely the Oriental tapestry hanging in the den had come from the Big House, as had the intricately carved oak desk and squashy leather sofa that were its major furnishings.

As practical as was the den, so the bedroom was dainty. Somehow, before he had even met her, Chris had known how she longed to escape to a surrounding of feminine beauty when she doffed the white coat that signified Dr. Hall and became simply Samantha again. Delicate flowered curtains of sprigged muslin danced in the gentle breeze, and the same lavender and green flowers reappeared on the lightweight coverlet folded so neatly at the foot of the luxurious double bed. The dresser and bed were painted white, as were the walls, and small throw rugs on the hardwood floor picked up the motif of lavender and green. The effect was a charming relief from both the rich if practical heaviness of the den and the bright tropical colors dominating the decor of the first-floor living area.

There, in a large single room off the tiny kitchen, a riot of color brought the spacious sofa and soft easy chairs, the draperies and trim, to vibrant life. A small wood dining table was set up with four carved armchairs at the end nearest the kitchen, and even the mats laid on the table repeated the tropical motif. Although the colors were bright and the floral print large, the size of the room was more than sufficient to handle the lively design, and the effect was at once individual and charming. Again Samantha sensed Chris's taste as well as his wealth in what she saw. His hand seemed to touch all her life, she thought as she surveyed her new world with pleasure. It was a frightening thought but also an exhilarating one.

As she walked out the door a few minutes later,

Samantha stopped to write a message on the board posted conveniently at the entrance to the clinic saying where she had gone. She laughed at herself, knowing she didn't have to start work until the morning, but felt better for leaving the message. "Just in case of an emergency," she murmured as she climbed into the station wagon.

In a few minutes she had reached the little cove at the end of the road. Dropping her loose smock and towel on the untouched sand, she raced toward the water to swim and frolic like a playful seal. At last, worn out and content, she rolled onto her back to float in the bath-warm sea.

From where she lay she could see the peak of the Mountain of the Sun, the deceptively gentle rounded dome of the volcano. She had been glad to learn that scientists considered it extinct, for the sight of the hardened black rock of an ancient lava flow reaching its dangerous fingers down to the very edge of the sea was an awesome one. As she rocked with quiet rhythm in the cradling swells of the sea, she mulled over what Mrs. Tarai had told her the night before.

No wonder Chris had seemed so understanding about her childhood, she thought. He had lost his mother even earlier than she, and like herself he had been something of an orphan while his father still lived. They had both turned to education as a solution. But there the similarities ended, she realized as she paddled lazily back to shore. He had gone to school and to travel almost to spite his father; she had studied in order to please hers and make him accept her in place of the son he had wanted.

What she'd said to Chris about growing apart from her childhood friends after high school was only part of the truth. It had really happened earlier, during those years when she'd skipped one grade after another, always leaving her friends behind and ending up in classes with children one or two or three years her senior. When she'd graduated from high school she'd been only sixteen and already separated from those early friends. Then came college, where she'd been very happy and made new friends. But she'd completed college in three years, and then had chosen a medical school with an accelerated program. She'd hoped that by attending medical school year-round she could beat the clock's ticking so loudly, numbering the minutes her father had left. But the clock had won the race, and her father died in her final year of medical school.

Suddenly the rush had had no purpose. Her plan to work with her father, making his life easier, and eventually to take over his practice had evaporated when he died. She had earned his respect at last; that she knew. But she was not sure she had ever earned his love.

As she toweled herself dry, Samantha remembered those painful months when she'd realized her lifelong plans held no meaning, and she had to find some other purpose. She'd never considered giving up medicine; her search was simply for the best way to use her medical training.

At last she'd found it when a missionary spoke to
her class about the need for physicians on many of
the outlying islands of the Pacific. Her sense of
adventure was piqued by the idea, as was her lingering need to find a mission, a new purpose for her life.
So she trained especially for such a job, studying a
broad spectrum of medical practice and adding postgraduate work in tropical diseases. Then came the
applications, assembling a dossier, asking for references, traveling for interviews. She had more than
one offer, although several places rejected her on the
grounds that at twenty-six she was simply too young
to accept the responsibility of practicing medicine in
such isolated and difficult conditions. Among the offers, however, was one from Good Providence, and
after much consultation and many hours of agonized
thought, she had signed a one-year trial contract to
serve on this remote Micronesian island.

She stretched out lazily on her towel after moving
it carefully into the shade. Now she was here, though
it all still seemed more than a little unreal. She felt
very young and rather awed by the responsibility she
had undertaken. But she believed the job to be important and felt she could make more of a personal
contribution here than she could working in a hospital or even in a small town in the United States. The
people of Good Providence needed her and the life
on the island intrigued her.

She gazed up at the purple dome high above her. In
her mind she traced a path down from the mountain's peak to its gentle slopes, rich with sugarcane

and pasturelands, polka-dotted with the houses of herdsmen and farmers and those workers who chose to live in the hills. Prominent among those small buildings even in her mind there was one magnificent home, the Girard family mansion.

She tried to picture the Big House as it would appear during the day, its whiteness shimmering in the brilliance of the tropical sun. The flowers whose rich perfumes had pervaded the night air and still lingered in her memory would be lovely to look at in the light of day. The spacious courtyards inside the house and the gardens that surrounded it would glow with the velvet colors of orchids, bougainvillea, passionflowers and myriad others whose names she did not yet know.

From the house her mind wandered to what intrigued her even more—its owner. Restlessly she rolled over onto her stomach, pillowing her head in her folded arms, her senses filled with the memory of the preceding evening. In the warmth of the afternoon sun, her body glowing from its encounter with the refreshing tanginess of the sea, it was all too easy to slip back into the remembered glory of that final embrace.

She didn't know what to make of it or whether she dared to believe Chris could already feel the same attraction and the same warm interest in her that she did in him. It was all happening so fast. She'd had her share of male companions in college and afterward, but never had she found herself so deeply aroused by a man or so enmeshed in thoughts of him.

It seemed to her she was still surrounded by the faint light scent of his after-shave as she lay alone on the beach.

Suddenly a shadow fell across her. Startled, she rolled over abruptly only to feel her heart leap unreasonably within her breast.

"Chris," she breathed in surprise.

He looked down at her, his slender height emphasized as he stood above her. "You seem so comfortable, I'm almost sorry to disturb you," he said quietly.

Hastily she sat up, acutely aware of the revealing nature of her bikini. As she looked at him, her face suffused with the warmth of an attractive blush, she noticed that he, too, was dressed for swimming. His powerful thighs and his broad chest glowed with a deep tan showing through the dark hair that grew thick and wiry on his skin. His suit was tight and brief, displaying rather more of his male strength than she wished to see. And yet her eyes were drawn irresistibly to him and she couldn't look away from the virile picture he made.

But when she glanced at his face, she regretted her lack of self-control, for his expression told her without doubt that he knew of her inspection. To her relief, he offered no comment; but his eyes dropped from hers meaningfully, and he returned the compliment by looking appraisingly at her own form. She fought the urge to pull her towel around her, suffering his gaze in silence even though his lingering eyes raked her skin as though he had stroked the length of her body with one of his lean and powerful hands.

When he spoke, however, his voice was as neutral as his subject. "Have you swum?"

She nodded, incapable of speech.

"Well, would you like another dip?"

This time she shook her head. Shrugging, he dropped his towel next to hers and walked toward the water. Knowing his back was safely to her, Samantha followed him with her eyes. In their embrace she had sensed the strength of the rippling muscles in his legs and back, but his grace surprised her. He walked like a man who knew his own body well and enjoyed it in all its capacities.

At the water's edge he turned abruptly, grinning broadly when he saw her eyes fixed on him once again. Angry at herself for being caught staring a second time and annoyed at him for taking such obvious pleasure in her interest and her embarrassment, Samantha stretched out on her stomach, determined to ignore him and just enjoy the warmth of the afternoon sun. But her mind was filled with thoughts of Chris and every nerve in her body was alert for his return.

When he flung himself down beside her a few minutes later, her nostrils twitched pleasurably at the enchanting scent of sea and sun he retained on his body. He moved close to her, and she could feel the heat rising from the sun-touched skin of his thigh now pressing lightly against her own. The contact sent a thrill through her and she wanted to stay like this forever.

"You're in the sun, you know," his voice came lazily into her consciousness.

"Mmm," she murmured, knowing she should move but incapable of breaking the single point of warm gentle contact that their legs made.

"Here, I'll put some tanning oil on you. Then you'll be all right."

Without waiting for her consent, Chris leaned casually across her to get the lotion from her bag. The touch of his leg lying fleetingly on her own was electrifying in its impact, and she held her breath as he rummaged with casual possessiveness in her purse. Only when he had removed the burning pressure of his leg from her thigh could she breathe again, and then with unconscious irony she clenched her fists in the intensity of her effort to mimic his relaxed attitude.

He was so close she could sense when he sat up in order to open the bottle of tanning oil. She spoke compulsively as she waited nervously for him to smooth the oil on her body.

"How did you find me?" she asked in a voice she hoped sounded lazily relaxed.

There was a note of contented laughter in his voice as he answered, "Your compulsiveness gave you away."

When the rise of her shoulders indicated her perplexity, he explained, "The note on the clinic message board? You said you'd be here 'in case of emergency.'" He chuckled softly as he placed the bottle on the sand beside his towel. "I figured this was an emergency," he said. Then he leaned very close to her to whisper the final words, "I needed the doctor."

Whatever Samantha might have said in response vanished from mind as she felt his hot breath against her ear. Then he lowered his hand slowly to her back, preparing to smooth the lotion on her waiting sun-warmed skin.

His hand moved in slow gentle circles across her taut skin. At first his motions were broad and sweeping, covering her shoulders in swaths of delicious sensation as he massaged oil into the tense muscles of her upper arms. Then his movements became smaller, as if he could concentrate on only one tender patch of skin at a time.

Gradually his hand moved downward from her shoulders, and his fingers caught in the strap of her bikini. With an impatient exclamation he sat up and swiftly, with practiced fingers, untied the thin strap.

As Samantha lifted her head to protest, he motioned her to be still. "It's in the way," he announced.

Although a bit edgy, she accepted his explanation, and soon the soothing strokes of his hands making endless tantalizing circles on her supple back began to do their work. Her breathing slowed, and she could feel the muscles of her shoulders and upper arms relax.

His fingertips massaged her spine from the nape of her neck to her waist, delicately but insistently. However, just as she started to feel safe, relaxed and comfortable under his touch, he slipped his hand lower.

"Your legs will burn," he explained, his voice a soothing murmur as his hands stroked oil onto her skin from the base of her high-cut suit down over her thighs and into the sensitive skin behind her knee. Continuing his delicate descent, he smoothed the oil into her calf and over her heel, his fingers pausing to knead her foot with the gentleness of the warm sun itself.

Breaking the hypnotic rhythm only long enough to pour some oil onto his hand, he stretched his arm across her body to reach her farther leg. The casual pressure of his arm across her back and thigh awakened a nerve running deep inside her, and a shiver of sensuous pleasure traced its way down her spine as he repeated the slowly descending massage on her other leg, swirling his hand in steady circles from her hip to her thigh, behind her knee and down to her toes.

When he finished, she felt extraordinarily relaxed, almost somnolent in her comfort. But at the same time every inch of her skin tingled with the intimate knowledge of his gentle sensuous touch.

She rolled over lazily, to thank him and to take pleasure in looking at him again. But when she raised her eyes slowly to his face, the expression she read on it alarmed her. There was a hard gleam in his dark eyes, and his mouth formed a narrow line across his face.

Before she could speak he bent toward her, his face so close she could feel his breath harsh and uneven against her cheek. She gazed at him in troubled fascination, incapable of moving or thinking clearly. Slowly he slipped his strong arms behind her back, lifting her slight body toward him. Awkwardly she grasped at the bra of her bikini, but it had fallen away from her breasts, and she could only attempt to cover her nakedness with one hand as she pushed against his shoulder with her other.

"What are you doing?" she gasped in dismay.

But he didn't answer, silencing her protest by lowering his mouth upon hers. His kiss was hard and possessive, and she struggled to resist the passionate demands of his firm lips and probing tongue.

Yet even as she fought, she was tantalizingly aware of the new sensation of his bare chest pressed against her own. The wiry hair covering his strong muscles teased the sensitive skin of her soft rounded breasts, so that her nipples rose and hardened involuntarily. In every nerve and cell her body was betraying her, offering him a very different message from the one she wished to convey by the delicate hand beating like a captive bird against his shoulder.

The urgency of his mouth upon hers affected her with desire she had never before known. Compulsively she leaned into his embrace, her resisting hand opening involuntarily to stroke his sun-warmed shoulder. He sighed as he felt the difference in her reaction, releasing her mouth at last, only to bury his face in her hair. His hot breath fanned the back of her neck and he murmured inarticulate words. She turned her head to rub her soft cheek against his, stubbled every so slightly with a day's growth of beard, and again he claimed her mouth with his insistent lips.

His kiss was deep and searching, gently persuasive now, and this time her response was all he could have wished for. Surprised by her own unexpected sensuality, she pulled him down to her with reckless abandon, seeking his ever nearer embrace. She felt she would drown in the sweet sensations as his tongue once more began its probing exploration of her mouth.

His hand slid smoothly around from her back, stroking gently along her side until it reached her breast. She inhaled with a sharp gasp of pleasure as his palm cupped her tender breast and his fingers teased her nipple until the ache he roused there descended throughout her body.

"I want you, Samantha," he murmured, his breath warm against her ear.

Although his voice was resonant and throaty, the sudden intrusion of speech broke the spell their desire had woven about her, and Samantha rolled away from him abruptly.

"No," she whispered. "This isn't right!"

He sat up, his dark eyes wide, his hands trembling with the longing she now sought to deny. "What do you mean?" he asked finally, his voice broken with the effort to speak.

She couldn't reply but rolled farther away from him, fumbling awkwardly for her clothes. Not even pausing to fasten the difficult ties of her bikini, she slipped her smock over her head, unaware of what a seductive picture she made as she did so.

At last she spoke, forcing her breath into a regular pattern with the same sheer willpower that had freed her from his embrace. "I'm not ready for this," she said evenly.

He looked at her appraisingly. "You say that now; but your lips, your arms. . .the very warmth of your skin said something very different to me a minute ago."

He spoke caressingly, but she shook her head vehemently. Reaching out with one hand, he stroked her cheek gently. "You can't deny it, Samantha. You wanted this as much as I did."

He was right, and she knew, as well, that it would do her no good to deny the unexpectedly sensuous nature of her response. "I got carried away," she said with appealing honesty. "But. . . ." She spread her hands wide in a gesture of confusion and conciliation.

"But you thought better of it?" His voice shifted subtly, a harsh and strained note entering it now.

She nodded lamely.

"You're a doctor. Surely you know that passion— desire—is a perfectly normal feeling." His voice dropped, coaxing yet strong. "There's something between us, Samantha. You feel it, too. Why deny ourselves this pleasure?"

She looked away, unsure how to answer. She could not speak of her hidden dreams; she wanted passion, yes, but she wanted love and romance, too, not just a momentary fulfillment of physical desire, a brief spasm of pleasure on a sunlit afternoon. Though she laughed at herself sometimes, she still cherished a vision of being carried across the threshold of some vaguely imagined home by a man whose strong arms encircled her as if he would never release her while his lips whispered words of love.

At last she spoke in a low soft tone, struggling to stay calm though the words were torn from her with agony. "Yes, passion is normal. But that doesn't mean I'm. . . ready to. . . ." Her voice trailed off.

"To leap into bed with me?" he finished the thought with seeming helpfulness.

She dug her toes into the sand, burying and uncovering them with the fine white grains. "Something like that," she admitted reluctantly.

"My God, Samantha." His voice was tense, his glance swift and pained. "We're not children. You can't play with me like that."

"I didn't mean to," she said softly, unable to meet the agonized expression in his glowing eyes.

"Maybe. Maybe not."

The cynicism she heard in his voice was unbearable to her. Scrambling to her feet, she confronted him directly, embarrassed as she was.

"You've got to believe me, Chris. I . . . nothing like this has ever happened to me before. I didn't know what I was doing."

He looked at her skeptically. "Do you really expect me to believe that?" he asked, his voice dripping acid.

She shuddered with pain, staring him hard in the face for a moment. Then she could look into those cold hooded eyes no longer, and she turned away.

"You can believe what you want," she said bitterly.

Without another word or a glance in his direction, she bent to pick up her towel and handbag. She longed for him and she knew he wanted her, too. But a man of his obvious skill in knowing what would give pleasure to a woman would not see anything wrong in a casual liaison. An afternoon of lovemaking on the beach, a weekend together at some hotel, and he could walk away.

For her it was different. Whatever he might think, she had never been with a man. There had been opportunities and she had been tempted, but never like this.

She knew how close they had come, how nearly she had betrayed her own dream. Had he not spoken when he did, she would have been lost in a sensuous haze of desire and pleasure from which she could only have emerged later in misery. But he had spoken, and his words were not of love or even affection; they simply expressed his desire for a physical union. Well, maybe that was enough for him, but it would not do for her.

Chris's harsh voice interrupted her uncomfortable reverie. "Here, don't forget this," he said, tossing the bottle of suntan oil at her. "You might need it the next time you go sunbathing."

There could be no mistaking his meaning. He thought she was making a play of innocence, and he was both frustrated and angry. If that was what he believed, she could understand his bitter reaction, and she longed to convince him of the truth. But she believed his way was different from hers, and she knew from even the quickest glance at his tensely held body that this was not the time to attempt to reason with him.

Sighing, she slipped the bottle into her bag and walked slowly toward her car, leaving him standing on the beach. His hands formed tense fists on his powerful hips as his burning stare grazed her back.

She was not sure quite how she felt about Christopher Girard. She found him intriguing and undeniably attractive, yet she sensed in him hidden reserves of feeling that she couldn't begin to fathom but which she knew could spell danger to anyone he regarded as an enemy. Uncertain what she wanted their relationship to be, she knew without a doubt that she could not bear life on Good Providence if he were her enemy.

CHAPTER FIVE

ONLY THE OPENING OF THE CLINIC early the next morning prevented Samantha from wallowing in the mixture of remorse, frustration and anger that had followed her encounter with her striking employer. But if the misery of the night faded in the brightness of the tropical dawn and in the excitement of walking downstairs to her clinic, it didn't disappear. She was already too deeply involved for that.

Her first sight of the neatly arranged clinic, its door open to receive fresh air and new patients, revived her after a poor night's sleep. Even Felicity's appearance offered encouragement. The young woman arrived on time, dressed comfortably but decently in a lightweight skirt and blouse, the same kind of outfit Samantha had chosen for herself. Samantha grinned inwardly as Felicity walked through the door. It was apparent that she had not altogether relished the decision not to wear uniforms, a decision Samantha had reached long before coming to Good Providence and later had communicated to her assistant. While Samantha was attired in a lime green blouse and print cotton skirt, Felicity had come as close as she could to a nursing uniform—a white shirt tucked into a white skirt, white sandals on her feet.

But she was neatly dressed, properly covered and on time, and Samantha sighed with relief at all three indications that her assistant might actually be willing to assist her this day. Felicity turned out to be more than willing, Samantha soon learned. When the first patient walked in the door, the young woman quickly displayed her usefulness to Samantha, a usefulness that went beyond whatever talents for nursing she might later reveal.

Felicity knew everyone in the small island community. With pride in herself and in her new job, she introduced each patient to Dr. Hall, stressing Samantha's title and role in order, perhaps, to feel the glory reflected upon herself. While the patient settled into the comfortable chair across from Samantha's desk, Felicity asked after various family members, spoke politely of current news and often, however unwittingly, gave Samantha a clue to the patient's reason for being there.

"Are your headaches any better now that your son is home to help in the gardens?" she asked one wizened old man. The light in the islander's eyes as he spoke of his son's return and the doggedness of his voice as he revealed his son's imminent departure told Samantha more about a probable source of his intermittent recurring headaches than she could have learned from the most thorough neurological examination she could perform.

"How's your stomach been, Mrs. Johnston?" Felicity asked one obese patient. "Have you been able to eat at all?'' Again the words and the patient's reaction offered Samantha a clue that Mrs. Johnston might be something of a hypochondriac, or that at the least she reveled in whatever illness she truly suffered from.

Of course Samantha knew better than to rush to judgments based on such intuitive reactions. But she also knew that what she was learning through Felicity's casual chatter with the patients could prove very useful, and she quickly discarded her first notion of stopping the preliminary talk, instead using it as a way to introduce herself casually to the patient, to encourage the patient to see her as an interested human being, not as some remote, omnipotent creature called ''the doctor.''

The method seemed to work, for the islanders arrived excited to meet their new doctor, proud that the island now had its own doctor, curious about the petite woman who filled that prestigious and responsible role—and more than a little nervous. But during Felicity's respectful introduction and casual chatter they watched Samantha, just as she watched them. And when she entered into the conversation, asking how long the headaches had lasted or when Mrs. Johnston last had eaten, Samantha rapidly took over from Felicity, asserting her role as she revealed her knowledge, compassionately questioning the woman or man who sat before her on the edge of a chair that seemed to become ever more comfortable.

Not all the patients that first morning were like the old man and the obese woman, individuals with long-standing complaints who sought the doctor out of a need for self-justification or psychological support as much as for physical help. A few came with scraped knees, a bee sting, a sore throat—the ordinary minor aches and pains treated at home for years in the past and undoubtedly, once the novelty of the new doctor wore off, to be treated at home in years to come. But this day, the first day the clinic was open, everyone with any excuse to walk through the door made the pilgrimage to the doctor's office.

The trickle began slowly, a tiny tributary off the mainstream of island life. But by eleven o'clock the trickle had become a stream, and by two it had swollen to a river. When Felicity went to close the door to the clinic at three, there were still patients waiting to get in. Although unhappy about refusing to see anyone who needed her, Samantha knew she had to set down some ground rules. True, the flood of visitors would ease off, but she had to survive during these early days, as well, and she dared not exhaust herself to the point that she couldn't function in a real emergency. She and Felicity had been interviewing patients, preparing charts, examining children and men and women since eight in the morning, and they had hours of office work to do after the last patient went home.

Reluctantly, therefore, Samantha ordered Felicity to close the clinic at three, the posted hour. She reminded herself that there was a big sign in front of the building announcing she was available for emergency help twenty-four hours a day, but she still felt more than a slight twinge of guilt as she watched the islanders walk away from the clinic.

Guilt, yes, but relief, as well, she admitted as she stretched her legs out before her, wriggling her toes appreciatively. If the people outside had no more serious complaints than those who had lined her waiting area during the day, she didn't need to feel much guilt. It was obvious the majority had come only to meet the doctor.

That was acceptable to Samantha, too. She knew the islanders would bring her their serious problems more readily if they trusted her, and she wanted to encourage them to have periodic checkups, to make regular visits and to allow her to practice preventive medicine. But still. . . .

"How many scraped knees did we examine today, Felicity?" she asked with a grin.

"There are a lot more knees left on the island," Felicity warned with a rare answering smile, handing Samantha a glass of iced tea she had just taken from the refrigerator.

Samantha sighed, holding the icy glass against her flushed cheek for a moment. There had been no time for lunch, no time for more than a quick drink of water between patients, and she was very tired. But she was also grateful for the help Felicity had given her, and she was quick to say so.

"You did a good job today," she smiled in gratitude at the graceful woman who now lounged with casual voluptuousness against a filing cabinet.

Felicity didn't respond, but her too often passive face revealed her pleasure in the compliment.

As Samantha sipped her iced tea, enjoying the peaceful break before attacking the files, she found herself admitting that Felicity might turn out to be a real asset to her in her work. Clearly she knew everyone on the island, and more than that, Chris had been right: Felicity had a way with people, especially with children. When she exerted herself, she could make the nervous ones comfortable and encourage the silent ones to talk. But how long would she continue to exert herself?

Samantha's forehead wrinkled in a slight frown. Today Felicity had had a good time. She had looked forward to this; she could revel in being the one who knew the patients *and* the doctor and could bask in the light of her brief importance. But Samantha wondered what the future would hold when the line of patients did not disappear, when the hundredth scraped knee or sore throat had to be tended. Would Felicity still care? And if she was no longer interested, would she do even an adequate job?

Samantha had her doubts, and they were not alleviated by recognizing a touch of disappointment even in herself. Had she really spent years studying tropical diseases and exotic ailments in order to treat scraped knees and the common cold? When she reached that point in her ruminations, she shrugged herself out of her chair with a quick laugh. Surely she couldn't wish for an epidemic of dengue fever or hope that malaria would strike some of the kind islanders who streamed to her door seeking help! No,

she did not; yet as she bent her head over the files
Felicity handed to her one after another, she admitted she really didn't want to spend all her days
cataloging sore throats, either.

Maybe she had more in common with her young
assistant than she liked to realize, Samantha thought
when she rose from her desk several hours later. Both
of them had a talent for taking care of sick people,
both could draw patients out, both could comfort a
child who feared the injection the doctor must give.
And both of them were young, restless, seeking adventure.

There was even more to it than that, Samantha admitted as she sat in her study after dinner. The house
was quiet, the dinner dishes put away, the lights in
the clinic turned off for the night. Felicity had left
before dinner with a promise to return early in the
morning, since Samantha expected another busy day.
But the perfume the young woman wore lingered in
the little house, rising above the smells of antiseptic
and furniture polish that mingled throughout the
rooms. Samantha rose restlessly from her desk. Her
thoughts had turned to Chris often during the day,
but never as forcefully as now, while the tropical sun
blazed for one last moment before it disappeared,
doused as a fire is doused by a final pail of water.

Just as Felicity's perfume lingered in the house, so
did a sense of Christopher Girard pervade the rooms.
The furniture was his or chosen by him. The house
was his. The arrangement of the rooms was his. Even
the food she had eaten for dinner had been selected

by him, or by someone acting for him, before she'd arrived on the island.

Samantha knew that even without those tangible reminders of her enigmatic employer, her thoughts would be filled with Christopher Girard. She might have been able to break off his lovemaking on the beach the day before, but she could not so easily prevent the assault he made even in memory on her mind and heart and body.

Samantha roamed around her little home restlessly. It might be that Felicity and Chris were lovers; it might be that they had been so in the past. But whether she and Felicity shared a current attraction for the tall lean man, it was clear that she shared with Felicity a sensuality she had not known she could experience, even in imagination.

IN THE NEXT FEW WEEKS Samantha's life assumed a routine pattern. The hectic pace of the first hours began to ease as soon as the islanders had met their new doctor, but there was more than enough work to occupy her days and many of her evenings, as well.

Regular clinic hours were devoted to appointments for physical examinations, routine inoculations, prenatal care for women who had always delivered their babies at home. Although the islanders had been receiving needed medical care on Halekai, many had neglected having routine physicals or paying attention to preventive medicine; it just took too much effort to fly to another island for care. So Samantha confronted a backlog of long-standing ailments and

inadequately treated complaints, and she also was
determined to encourage regular checkups for children and adults alike. Under her guidance Felicity
began a file for each member of each family on the
island, charting medical health and problems, treat-
ment and outcome.

In addition, a few hours each day were set aside for
unscheduled visits. Then patients could simply drop
in to see the doctor about an upset stomach or an
unexplained pain or to ask a question. Determined as
she was to encourage the islanders to see her when
they were not trapped in a medical emergency,
Samantha still found it difficult to give them as much
time as she felt each deserved. Inevitably, it seemed,
there was a stream of patients waiting to see her at
the end of each day.

But gradually she worked through the backlog,
and at the end of the third week she began to feel she
had established a pace that was fair and reasonable—
and that she could survive. In all of this Felicity was
surprisingly helpful. Although she balked when her
evening fun disappeared or a free Saturday suddenly
became a day to catch up on patients' charts, for the
most part she was quick to see what Samantha needed and to provide her help. Her manner was sometimes grudging, sometimes supercilious; but she came
to work on time and she stayed late when she was
asked—at least she usually did.

If at times Felicity resented the heavy load of
work, Samantha could understand that. More than
once she realized days had passed since she had last

found time to swim or had eaten dinner without charts spread before her. But Samantha's life was not totally filled with work.

The Widow Tarai came by several times a week, often carrying a pot of chowder that Samantha could heat for her dinner or a loaf or two of freshly baked bread. But even when she arrived empty-handed, Samantha welcomed her with joy. Only with the widow could Samantha relax entirely, knowing she did not have to maintain the distance she did with her patients, and knowing that the motherly woman sought nothing more from her than common courtesy.

Father Ilima often stopped by about dinner time, joining Samantha in a cold drink and for a short visit. At first Samantha thought his timing coincidental, but after a while she realized the good man came when he did on purpose, forcing her to take a break from her work. Sometimes she resented his visit as an interruption, but he never stayed long and she soon came to sense that he was right; even if she returned to her desk immediately after Father Ilima left, the change of pace relaxed her after a hectic day.

Ed Bates, a less frequent visitor, was also a welcome one. He knew a great deal about the islanders, not only the current ones but also those who had founded Good Providence or had lived there in years past. He even provided Samantha with information about the health of the children he taught in the schools, warning her of family conditions that could influence the children's physical or emotional states.

And Ed was good company—relaxed and amusing, but capable of sober reflection and intelligent conversation.

Of all her special acquaintances on the island, only one failed to become a casual visitor, and that was the one person she most longed—and feared—to see. Samantha knew that Christopher Girard was aware of her work. She heard, secondhand, that he approved of one or another of her arrangements; she received an occasional note from him with a box of supplies; his gardener regularly appeared at her door with baskets of fruit and bundles of vegetables from the orchards and gardens of the Big House. But Chris himself stayed away.

Samantha didn't need his presence to be reminded of him. If she had been likely to forget, she wasn't allowed to. For one thing, her patients constantly spoke of Mr. Girard and his help in some matter of importance to them. Then, too, she had the stories of island life Ed Bates told her and Father Ilima's less obvious hints. She found before her constant evidence of the pervasive role Christopher Girard played on Good Providence, and all that she learned added to her growing respect for what he tried to do—and did—on the island.

She learned rapidly that everything Chris had told her about her prospective patients the afternoon they had met was accurate, and much of it proved helpful. Like Felicity, Chris knew the islanders; but he knew much more, and his insights were far more sensitive. He knew which of the islanders suffered from the

kinds of illnesses that would bring them frequently
to the clinic, seeking Samantha's regular ministra-
tions. As a result, the very first time Samantha heard
a distinctive wheeze coming from the waiting area,
she knew from Chris's description that old Mr.
Nakuoro, a victim of emphysema, had arrived. Chris
also knew which parents would bring their children
routinely for checkups and inoculations, and which
ones she would have to seek out. About this, Ed
Bates also provided a wealth of information and offered some strategies for dealing with the most
recalcitrant parents and fearful children.

Chris had even been able to predict who would be
among the few malingerers to seek Samantha's
cooperation in getting around the strict island laws.
The law forbidding anyone who did not work to stay
on the island, combined with the practice of pro-
viding care and support for those unable to work,
tempted a few individuals to try to abuse the system.
Samantha carefully completed a history and physical
examination for everyone who claimed a disability,
but she found it helpful to recall Chris's warnings,
and without exception she found his judgments had
been correct.

It was hard to reconcile the disparate images she
had of her employer, the boss of her island home. On
the one hand there was the sensitive, intelligent, caring, active Mr. Girard who ran Good Providence
with the delicacy of his compassion and the near
autonomy of his power. On the other there was the
witty and urbane host of the dinner party, a man

liked and respected by at least two individuals Samantha had learned to like and respect—Ed Bates and Father Ilima. And then there was the arrogant, self-assured seducer of a hot afternoon at the beach. Samantha found herself as fascinated as she was frightened, and she knew deep in her heart that she longed to learn more about this tantalizing man.

There was one source of knowledge Samantha would happily have done without. That was Felicity, always careful to refer properly to "Mr. Girard" when her mother was nearby, but quick to talk about "Chris" to Samantha. Sometimes Felicity's comments grew reasonably out of a conversation she was having with Samantha, but often she seemed simply to delight in a casual mention of some special place she and Chris had been, a party they had attended, a night spent together on Halekai.

Although Samantha could not be sure, at times Felicity's comments struck her as intentionally barbed. And although she warned herself not to seek comfort in false explanations, it seemed to her that Felicity tended to exaggerate, even to shade the truth when she talked about the things she and Chris had done. Samantha wondered, for example, if Chris had taken Felicity to a particular party or if they had both just attended it independently, a coincidental meeting. Similarly, she wondered what exactly it meant that they had spent the night together on Halekai; had they each stayed on the island for independent reasons, in separate rooms or locations?

In spite of her doubts, however, Samantha knew

that Felicity thought her relationship with Chris was special. And she had to admit to herself that the relationship appeared special enough to be bothersome.

Worst of all, because it touched on Samantha's professional responsibilities as well as her feelings, were Felicity's casual reminders that "Chris" had got her the job in the clinic. Good as she was with patients, careful as she could be about the files, Felicity was still quick to reveal a difficult and lazy streak. Yet when Samantha tried to point out flaws to her or suggest ways to improve her work, Felicity came back with more than one veiled threat.

"Chris didn't say I had to do that," was her answer the first time Samantha asked her to return in the evening to catch up on paperwork.

"No?" Samantha responded with feigned surprise. "But he did expect you to finish your work, didn't he?"

"I guess," came the sullen response. "But I've got a date tonight," Felicity continued after a brief pause.

Knowing Chris was once again away from Good Providence undoubtedly helped Samantha keep herself in control, and she answered quietly, "Then why don't you plan to stay late tomorrow, Felicity? I don't care which night you work, as long as the files are up to date by Friday afternoon."

This suggestion proved the right touch, for it allowed Felicity to cooperate without losing face. But Samantha could sense the threat behind Felicity's words and could smell the tension in the air. Chris, not Samantha, was her boss, Felicity's words implied, and Chris wasn't about to fire her.

Samantha saw only one justification for Felicity's behavior; that is, one justification not based on a relationship she didn't want to contemplate. It had not taken Samantha long to see that Felicity evoked two very different reactions among the native people of her island home. Some disliked her, considering her manner cold and her clothing and behavior simply outrageous. But many offered her a kind of deference born of her beauty, and these people seemed to accept the justice of her skimpy bikinis and her haughtiest smiles. If Felicity had been accorded such deference from childhood, it was not hard to understand the source of her arrogance. It was the arrogance of custom, the tough conceit of a very self-centered and very young woman. If this was the case, then Chris and Widow Tarai were right: Felicity needed Samantha's help. Samantha knew, as well, that she could make very good use of Felicity's help, especially if she could motivate her young assistant to overcome her laxity. But it was hard for Samantha to concentrate on such worthy goals, reached with difficulty in the quiet solitude of her bedroom at night, when she was confronted by the girl herself, lounging arrogantly and altogether beautifully against a file cabinet, as if there were no work worthy of her attention.

Late one afternoon, nearly a month after opening her clinic, Samantha returned from visiting a patient who lived high in the hills. She had stopped at the beach on her way back, grateful for the chance to take a quick swim. Now, as dusk approached, she looked forward to a leisurely dinner and a quiet evening spent reading from a parcel of medical journals that had arrived, weeks late, from the States.

Even as she opened the door to her house, however, Samantha sensed that something was wrong. She stood in the doorway, gazing around her until she realized what looked strange. The chair that normally stood beside her desk was moved to a new position, and the papers on the desk, usually left in neat heaps at the end of the day, were scattered over the top, as though she—or someone else—had been searching for something. More angry than frightened, Samantha stepped inside the house, glancing farther into the clinic office.

It was not only her desk that showed signs of having been disturbed. File drawers were partially open, and on top of one cabinet lay some charts she knew she had seen Felicity put away earlier that day. Other furniture was out of place, sometimes just a foot or two, but enough to be noticeable.

Samantha made a cursory inspection of the other rooms and found nothing amiss elsewhere in the house. Returning to her office, she stood in the center of the room, beating her clenched fists angrily against her hips. Whoever had done this had been fairly careful. There was no startling mess, no obvious sloppiness. Only someone who knew the room well would see that the furniture was out of place, and even the charts *could* have been left on top of the cabinet. But they hadn't been, and Samantha knew it.

With growing anger she stalked out of the house, careful to pull the door shut behind her and to check the lock. It was intact. Whoever had done this damage either had a key or had found the clinic door open, then closed it carefully when the dirty work was done.

Samantha's anger did not ease as she strode the few short steps to Widow Tarai's. She knocked on the door with quick hard fists, hoping to find Felicity alone. She did not want the girl's mother to hear what she was about to say.

"Dr. Hall!" Felicity looked surprised to see her. "Did you come to see my mother? She's not home."

"Good," Samantha spat forth between clenched teeth. "It's you I want to see."

"Is something wrong?" Felicity's gaze was innocent, her brow furrowed in apparent confusion and concern.

"I think you know what's wrong," Samantha responded. "Maybe I'd better come in. You're not going to want the neighbors to hear this."

Felicity held the door open, silently inviting Samantha into the living room. But Samantha stood doggedly in the hall.

"Were you at the clinic tonight?" she began quietly.

"No, I left an hour or so after you did, as soon as I'd finished Mr. Maguro's chart," the girl answered quickly.

Samantha stood in silence, aware how little she knew for sure. She knew only that this was not the first incident to occur in her absence. Drugs had disappeared, sometimes reappearing in unlikely places, sometimes never reappearing at all. Once a windowpane had been smashed, apparently by a rock or a fist, although nothing had been taken that time. In each instance, though Samantha had been away, Felicity could have been near. This was the first time, however, that Samantha had decided to confront her. At last she began again.

"Did you lock up when you left?" she asked, her tone making her words more of an accusation than a question.

"Yes, I did," came the quick belligerent response.

"Are you sure?" Samantha prodded.

Felicity glowered. "I must have. Why?"

Samantha looked at her hard as she answered, seeking in the girl's face the answers she could not get from her words. "Because someone was there this afternoon. Someone who shouldn't have been there."

Felicity's gasp seemed genuine enough, Samantha had to admit. "How could you tell?" she asked breathlessly.

"The chairs were moved about, the file cabinets were open, my desk was a mess," Samantha cataloged in an even voice.

"Why, that's awful!" Felicity cried.

Samantha stared at her, struggling to interpret the look in those large expressive eyes. The young woman seemed genuinely distressed, but Samantha was not sure.

"Yes, it is awful," she pushed on. "You know those files are confidential. It isn't fair to the patients to have just anyone look at them. That's why I'm always asking you to lock up when you leave the place, even for a few minutes."

"But I did, really I did," Felicity cried, her eyes wide with an emotion Samantha could not read.

Samantha shook her head. "I just don't know," she muttered, more to herself than to the young woman standing nearly as tense as she.

"Don't you believe me?" Felicity asked angrily. "What did I do to make you think I'd sack the place, or want anyone else to?"

Samantha turned away. She wasn't sure what to believe. She had no real evidence against Felicity, nothing except the girl's tendency to be lax and her occasional spitefulness. Yet that spite always seemed directed against Samantha, never against the patients. With them she was quick and she was honest.

Admitting this to herself was easier than admitting it to Felicity, but Samantha mumbled something about being too distraught to think straight.

"So you thought just enough to blame me," Felicity grumbled bitterly.

"You were the last person in the clinic, Felicity—" Samantha began.

"And you don't like me anyway," came the quick interruption.

"It's not that," Samantha started to object, helpless before the girl's passion and her own lack of information.

"Well, what am I supposed to think?" Felicity spat back.

Samantha stood very still, her clenched hands betraying how upset she was. "You must admit you've been known to leave the door unlocked, Felicity," she said quietly. "And I think I have some reason to worry about your performance in this job."

"Enough to complain about me to Chris?" Felicity hissed at her.

The bitter argument was halted by the heavy sound of Widow Tarai's footsteps on the walk outside the door. Samantha managed a quick final comment before Felicity's mother approached.

"I haven't complained about you—yet," she whispered. "And I hope you never force me to."

The argument ended abruptly, but Samantha could only wish the problems could also be cut off as quickly. None of the incidents was especially serious or even disconcerting in itself. But the buildup of one after another was demoralizing and very disturbing.

Drugs continued to disappear or to be "misplaced." A medical text vanished from the bookshelf only to appear in the schoolhouse library. The phone rang in the middle of the night, only to go dead when Samantha, thoroughly awakened by the thought of an emergency, picked it up.

Samantha wondered briefly whether the incidents were the work of a man whose disability claim she had squashed and whose fury at her decision was ap-

parent. But he seemed someone who would use up his
anger in one large act, not at all the type who would
pick away with a series of petty acts of vandalism and
annoyance.

Less than a week after her confrontation with
Felicity, Samantha was getting ready for bed when
she saw a tall male figure approaching the house.
Against her will and her good judgment, she could
feel her heart leap with anticipation. Maybe this time
it would be Chris. She paused, one hand on the top
button of her blouse, and watched the man walk
near. As he stepped into the light from an open doorway, Samantha realized that her hope was vain:
whoever the solitary walker was, it was not Chris
Girard.

Disappointed that it wasn't Chris and hoping the
stranger wouldn't knock on the clinic door at this
time of night, Samantha started to turn away. Suddenly she was arrested by something peculiar in the
man's behavior. From behind the curtain she peered
into the street in time to see him look around as if to
make sure no one was watching. Then, apparently
satisfied, he darted off the public road and disappeared behind her house.

Because the backyard was not visible from her bedroom, Samantha raced to the den, anxious to see
what the man was up to. By the time she reached the
window, cautious not to reveal herself, the prowler
had slipped out of sight.

She stood by the window for some time, too nervous to climb into bed. It did not seem that the man

was doing anything seriously wrong, but he was sneaking around her house in the dark. Moreover, he was a stranger—a rare sight on the small island—and Samantha was all too conscious of the recent acts of vandalism that had plagued her.

Quickly she made up her mind and reached for the phone beside her bed. The steady voice of Charlie Tuatara, the chief of police, reassured her; yet there was little he could do.

"We'll keep an eye out for strangers, Dr. Hall," he repeated when she'd finished her tale, "and we'll keep a watch on your place. But are you sure it *was* a stranger?"

"At least not anyone I recognized," Samantha insisted.

"And I'm sure you know all the islanders by now," he agreed.

"I think so. That is. . . ." Samantha hesitated.

"Yes?" Mr. Tuatara's alertness indicated his thorough professionalism.

"Oh, nothing," she ended lamely. And however the policeman prodded her, she resisted mentioning her vague intuition that she could identify the prowler.

There was only one man she had heard about but hadn't met, a man about whom she had felt the vaguest unease growing out of the faint hints she had received from Mrs. Tarai and Ed Bates and Father Ilima. That man was Pete Thompson, the former manager of the sugarcane plantation. She had learned enough to know he was disaffected and to sense that he just might be behind the series of troubling acts of vandalism. Yet could she speak of such vague suspicions? She could not accuse a man she didn't know and couldn't identify; and so, in spite of Mr. Tuatara's questions, she said not a word.

At last the policeman gave up. "You let me know if you see the man again," he said in frustration.

"I will," Samantha promised as she hung up the phone, having gained only a small degree of comfort from the conversation.

When at last she lay in bed in her darkened room, Samantha realized that she still felt very much alone. Sleep came slowly, and with it came little true peace.

SAMANTHA'S PAINFUL SENSE OF LONELINESS was eased but far from cured by a phone call early the next morning. The insistent ringing of her bedside telephone interrupted the brief period of sound sleep she had finally achieved at the end of a long uncomfortable night. Struggling to the surface of consciousness, she answered the phone with a clarity that belied the fog in which her mind still floated.

"This is Dr. Hall," she spoke clearly into the instrument.

"Samantha, did I wake you?"

The voice that resonated along the wires brought into her room the vibrant presence of Christopher Girard. Samantha sat up in bed, nervously twitching the light covers up to her neck.

"No, I . . . I mean, yes, but it's all right," she stammered.

Chris apologized quickly but with the perfunctoriness of one with special rights. "I'm sorry, but I had to reach you today, and I'm flying to Guam in less than an hour."

Samantha made some appropriate response, asked about his trip, answered his polite question about her work and waited to hear the real reason for this sudden call. At last it came.

"We've been invited to a party on Halekai, a week from Saturday, and I wanted to let you know as soon as possible," Chris explained after the few minutes of preliminary chatter had passed.

"We?" she asked, speaking to hide her confusion.

"I've been asked to bring the new doctor—that is you, isn't it?" Chris's attempt to tease her seemed forced.

Samantha stalled, unsure what to say. She wanted to see Chris, but she wasn't certain how wise it would be to accept a formal date with him or to travel to Halekai with him.

"Samantha? Are you there?" Chris's impatience was obvious.

"Yes, I'm just...I don't know, Chris. I'm not sure I can make it."

"Are you busy?" he asked irritably.

"It's not that," she admitted quickly. "I don't think I should leave the island."

Chris hesitated for a fraction of a minute before cutting through her excuse. "You've got to take an occasional day off, Samantha. The islanders will survive without you for one night."

Samantha knew Chris was right, and she knew, as well, how transparent her excuses must be. Still she hesitated. Chris did not wait long before interrupting her swirling thoughts.

"Look, Samantha, you don't have a great deal of choice," he said impatiently. Before she could react he continued, "The party is being given by the governor's representative on Halekai. We can't offend him, so it's pretty much a command performance."

"I see," Samantha answered. It seemed Chris was no happier about this than she, and, unreasonably, that thought caused her heart to sink in her breast.

They made their arrangements quickly, their voices stiff and their manner equally awkward. Then the connection was broken, and Samantha sat alone in her room again.

If Chris had seemed unwilling to escort her, he nonetheless appeared at her door promptly on the night of the party. His formal white dinner jacket set off his tan, and Samantha could feel her chest constricting as she watched him walk across the room to greet her.

He seemed as tense as she felt, but his eyes lighted with pleasure as he openly surveyed her appearance. Samantha had dressed with special care, hoping to put herself in the proper mood for a party. A dress of bold colors clung to her torso, swirling out in diaphanous layers at her knees. The brilliant colors offered a challenge to her red hair, but the gleaming curls met the dare and her eyes seemed as green as the water in the lagoon.

Samantha met Chris's eyes after his frank inspection, catching in them a twinkle that set her pulse to racing. When he spoke his words traveled straight to her lonely heart.

"Shall we start fresh?" he asked with a smile.

Too moved to speak, Samantha nodded shyly, then took the arm he offered to walk with him to his car. On the brief ride to the airstrip they spoke only a little, about neutral, island matters, and Samantha found herself relaxing more every minute.

In the intimacy of Chris's plane, however, she began to grow tense again. Chris helped her secure her seat belt carefully before he took off into the evening sky, pointing the light sleek plane toward Halekai. At once silence descended between them; only the noise of the engines could be heard.

Chris did not seem to object to the silence. Except for a few quick remarks about the flight path and what Samantha might expect the plane to do, he concentrated his attention on flying, almost ignoring his passenger. At another time Samantha might have felt left out, but this night she was glad to have the chance to gather her thoughts. Was it possible for them to start fresh, as Chris suggested? She hoped so, but she wondered exactly what he meant.

The night seemed to fly by as quickly as their light plane had passed the coral atolls on the way to Halekai. Samantha met a great many people she had heard about from Ed Bates or Father Ilima, and she basked in the warmth of their welcomes. The governor's representative turned out to be an officious man, more conscious of protocol than of the true problems the islanders faced. Samantha could well understand why Chris said he would be offended if she failed to appear at his command.

"His wife really runs the show," Chris whispered to her as they seated themselves for the formal dinner.

"You mean...all this?" she asked, her arm sweeping a wide circle to encompass the elegant seating, the floral arrangements, the carefully appointed rooms.

"This...and more," he nodded. "She tells him what's happening on the island, and she drafts his memos for him. They say the governor calls her when he has a problem he can't handle!"

Samantha laughed at the notion of how powerless was the pompous man who now strutted to the head of the table. Still, it was sad that he received all the glory, his quiet wife none. She said as much to Chris, and soon the two were engaged in a conversation that ranged from the growing political power of women around the world to the relative value of personal satisfaction and public recognition. Not until they were interrupted to listen to the formal toasts did their conversation wane.

Even then, the interruption was brief. Although they both spoke politely to their neighbors, in truth Samantha cared only about what Chris said, and he paid attention only to her. She barely tasted the wine and food placed before her, conscious of the satisfying glow that a superb dinner, graciously served, arouses. The flowers on the table and around the room seemed to bring the tropical night into the house, and once dinner was over, the party moved outside to enjoy the night itself.

Soft lights bathed the lawn, illuminating the formal gardens with the silver of moonglow. The scent of tropical flowers filled the air, and a string quartet chose soft slow music as a backdrop.

"Dance with me?" Chris's voice was as soft and persuasive as the cello now playing a poignant melody.

"I'd love to," Samantha murmured, drifting comfortably into his strong arms.

Those arms drew her close and held her there, through one dance after another, through an evening that melted into darkest night. From time to time they talked lazily, desultorily, their comments as much a part of the night as the scent of flowers and the tingle of champagne. But often they said nothing, and then Samantha reveled in the easy movements of the dance, in the nearness of Chris's slim strong body.

As the night wore on, she felt increasingly close to Chris. He seemed comfortable, and his near strength was comforting, as well. Once another man interrupted to ask Samantha to dance with him. She started to pull away from Chris, reluctant but polite. He shook his head, drawing her closer to him and sweeping them effortlessly out of the other man's reach.

"I'm not letting you go so easily," he murmured

into her hair. "I've waited too long for this."

Samantha's heart leaped within her. He felt it, too! Quickly she cautioned herself not to read too much into his simple words. After all, for him it might be only a physical attraction, the desire to hold a beautiful woman close to him. But for her, it was more.

As they swung around the corner of a palm tree at the garden's edge, she realized suddenly how very much more it was for her. Maybe he cared for her, maybe not. But she cared for the lean tall man who now embraced her in the dance, cared for him more than she ever had for any other man on earth. Whatever Chris felt, whatever it might mean to him, she was beginning to fall in love.

CHAPTER SIX

SAMANTHA'S EYES WERE CLOSED and her body drugged by the rapture of the dance. All at once she felt Chris stiffen and, as if unconsciously, widen the space between them. Opening her eyes, she saw a policeman standing nearby, his hand gripping Chris's elbow to gain his attention.

"Sir, I've had a report you ought to know about, from the chief out at the airport," he began, his tone deferential but firm.

"Yes?" Chris's response was businesslike, Samantha noted. She still felt dazed, caught in a dreamworld she didn't want to leave.

"The weather's deteriorating rapidly, sir," the policeman continued.

"Go on," Chris urged. Even Samantha's head cleared suddenly—too suddenly.

The man consulted a small notebook he held in his hand before continuing. "There's a storm coming in from the south, and it's coming fast. Ceilings are dropping rapidly—"

"What are they now?" Chris interrupted.

"About five thousand," came the crisp answer. "Turbulence light to moderate and growing worse."

Samantha turned to look at Chris. "Can we get back to Good Providence?" she asked fearfully.

"If we leave now," he replied firmly.

Their host had made arrangements for them to spend the night on the island so that they wouldn't be flying across the ocean after dark and after an evening of revelry. When Chris had first told her of this plan, Samantha had been startled, but she soon learned that most visitors from the out islands tried to avoid flying at night. There were none of the sophisticated navigation devices on the remote islands that made it possible to fly through clouds and dark elsewhere in the world, and the coral atolls whose patterns made daytime navigation easy were invisible in the cloak of night.

"Is it safe?" she whispered, remembering all she'd been told.

Chris shrugged. "As long as the ceiling stays high enough that we can fly below the clouds, it'll be okay. Bumpy, yes; but safe."

"Couldn't we just wait out the storm here?" Samantha asked nervously.

Chris shook his head. "It could be a passing storm, but what if we were stuck here for days? Would you want that?" Before she could answer, he slipped his hand under her arm and drew her into the shadows. Teasingly he added, "*I* might enjoy it, but...."

Samantha smiled, her arm tingling where his hand lingered in a caress, her heart lightened by his attempt to take her mind off the storm. Certainly he was right, though. If this proved to be a bad storm or if it was the beginning of the rainy season, she wanted to be on Good Providence, not trapped miles away, unable to return.

Struggling to match Chris's light tone, she whispered, "We'll just have to save that for another time. Let's go!"

"Good girl," he returned encouragingly.

It took only a few minutes to make their excuses to their host and hostess and to drive to the airport. A mechanic had already checked their plane and filled its tanks to the top with fuel. Still, Chris walked around the plane slowly, inspecting it carefully before climbing aboard. There he paused, turning to Samantha with a curious expression in his eyes. For a moment he just gazed at her, then he apparently made up his mind.

Reaching behind the seats, he pulled out two life jackets. "Better wear this," he said, handing one to her.

"Chris, is it that bad?" she squeezed out, her throat tight with fear.

"Just a precaution," he assured her. "Sort of like taking an umbrella on a trip to make sure it won't rain."

Samantha struggled to answer his smile with one of her own, but it was a losing battle. In silence she secured the straps of the life jacket as he demonstrated, then tightened her seat belt securely.

The plane took off into a starless sky. Above her Samantha could see nothing, only the wash of a darkened world. Below her, once the lights of Halekai flickered out in the distance, there was only an answering darkness, the deep and unhelpful ocean.

As the plane gained altitude, its steady motion was disturbed by an ever increasing turbulence. Samantha clung to the edge of her seat, seeking something stable in a rocking world.

"Are you all right?" Chris took his eyes off the plane's instruments long enough to glance over at her.

"I guess so," she replied uneasily.

"This is nothing," he called across the small space between them. "Just a little bouncing as we get closer to the bottoms of the clouds. Nothing dangerous."

"Just unpleasant?" she said with an attempt at a smile.

"I'll grant you that," Chris muttered, his hands gripping the yoke as the plane rose on a wave of air, only to be dropped with a sickening thud a moment later.

Samantha couldn't help herself. "Oh, Chris!" she cried out.

Incredibly, he removed one hand from the yoke long enough to pat hers comfortingly. "It's all right, Samantha, honestly. Pretend you're riding on a rough road, in a car with rotted-out springs."

"One of our mountain roads?" she offered gamely.

"That's right," he nodded, his hands back on the yoke and his eyes staring out the window into the gloom. "It's just a rough ride in a bad car, up the side of the Mountain of the Sun."

"Yes, but there's at least a road under me there," Samantha muttered.

Chris laughed. "That's the spirit. I knew you'd be okay!"

Samantha smiled wanly, determined to live up to those words of encouragement. "Why do you keep looking out the window?" she asked. "You can't see anything, can you?"

"I've *got* to see something," Chris explained. "I'm flying by what's called 'dead reckoning.'"

"Bad words," Samantha declared with a weak grin.

Chris tossed his head back in a refreshing laugh. "Sorry. Well, what it means is that I follow a certain compass heading—fly in a certain direction—for a specified amount of time. Then I look around, to make sure I'm where I want to be. If so, I set a new direction, determine a new amount of time, and we're off again."

"If not?" Samantha probed.

"That's why I keep looking out the window," Chris said firmly, "so we'll get where I want us to be!"

"Can I help?" she asked.

"Sure," he responded gaily. "Look off to the right, about two o'clock, for a flashing white light."

"What would that be?" Samantha asked, peering out the window into the unending blackness.

"The light on a buoy off Kanoa Cay," he explained.

"I've never heard of Kanoa Cay," she admitted, still staring into the darkness and wondering how Chris could hope to see something so small in an ocean so vast.

"No one except pilots and a few fishermen know it by name," he explained. "It's one of a series of landmarks we use for navigating. . .and there it is, right where it should be!"

Samantha stared out the window in the direction Chris pointed, but another full minute passed before she made out the tiny winking light several thousand feet below them.

"That?" she asked incredulously.

"That," he nodded. "Now the next one is off my side of the plane, so it'll be harder for you to find."

"Harder?" she echoed with a laugh. "It's a good thing you're not depending on me to navigate."

"It just takes practice," Chris assured her.

For a few moments they were silent, and in the silence Samantha's fears began to grow again. The clouds seemed to be drawing nearer, the buffeting seemed worse, air whistled past her in the light plane. As if sensing her rising panic, Chris began to talk again.

"Not quite like flying in the States, is it?" he offered lightly.

"Is that where you learned to fly?" Samantha asked, half out of interest and half to find distraction from her fears.

Chris nodded, and then, apparently sensitive to her needs, he began to talk more openly than ever before about his years in America, his travels, and even the situation on Good Providence just before he began to run it. If he spoke to distract Samantha, what he said also fascinated her, for it revealed a great deal about the man who guided their light plane through the gathering storm.

He told her about being sent to Halekai for his early education and about living in a series of boarding schools in America, sometimes staying in one long enough to make friends and feel at home, but sometimes being transferred by his father after only a year or even a term.

"Why was that?" Samantha queried.

Chris shrugged. "I suppose he wanted me to get as broad an experience as possible."

Samantha offered no comment, but she found herself wondering if Chris's father had realized how cruel his actions were to a young child, a child made virtually homeless. After a moment of silence she changed the subject, and for a while they compared their experiences in college and in graduate school. Samantha noticed that Chris didn't explain why he'd extended his years of travel and schooling, but she remembered very well what Mrs. Tarai had said: that Chris and his father did not get along, and that Mr. Girard had very nearly paid Chris to stay away from Good Providence.

Chris spoke only of his desire to learn as much as he could about agriculture and business, even about flying. It was up to Samantha to recognize the reason behind his efforts: he had wanted to be ready to help the people of Good Providence when the time came. Still, his voice grew light with pleasure as he talked about his training and his plans for the island.

"And when you came back?" Samantha prompted him as he fell silent.

"I took over," Chris said simply. "The plantations were run down, the crop yield was too low, the equipment was outdated, and even the new stuff was rusty from neglect."

"Pete Thompson's work?" she suggested.

"His *lack* of work," Chris muttered, "and his manner, too. He treated the farmhands badly, and he did almost nothing to supervise the workers, let alone encourage them."

Samantha asked sympathetically, "So you fired him?"

He nodded. "I tried to get him to resign—even offered to find him a new job. But...." His voice trailed off.

"You had no choice," Samantha interjected swiftly.

"I didn't," Chris acknowledged. "It was either fire Pete or battle him every step of the way to make changes. I couldn't fight him and deal with all the other problems at the same time. There was just too much to do."

"The school and the houses and the roads," Samantha listed. When Chris looked at her quickly, eyebrows raised in question, she laughed for the first time since boarding the rocking little plane. "Oh, yes," she admitted cheerfully, "I've been hearing a lot about those days!"

"Father Ilima talks too much," Chris said with a smile.

"So do Ed and Mrs. Tarai," she added.

For a while they continued to talk casually about some of the changes Chris had made on the island. For all his willingness to talk, however, Samantha realized that Chris held certain things in reserve. He minimized his own role in the improvements he had made, and only her conversation with Ed, Mrs. Tarai and Father Ilima made it clear to her just how extensive that role had been. Somehow Chris made it seem as though it was all a coincidence: he returned home and roads began to be graded, houses painted and plumbing repaired, schoolbooks purchased, the sugarcane production raised, the attitudes of workers altered. Samantha knew better, but she respected him for his reticence.

On another matter, however, she was puzzled by Chris's reticence. He made vague mention of other "responsibilities" his father had left for him, but when she tried to question him he changed the subject. Later she tried again, and this time Chris had admitted that some problems remained with Pete Thompson.

Samantha hesitated. A cold band tightened around her chest as she remembered the night the prowler had skulked through her yard, a prowler she was ever more certain had to be Pete Thompson. Tempted as she was to tell Chris about that night, she hesitated. After all, she wasn't sure it had been Pete. So she hinted at her fears awkwardly, but she could do no more than hint.

"I may have seen him around the...the island," she stammered. "Is that what you mean? That he still hangs around?"

"Partly," Chris offered unhelpfully.

"Is there more to it, then? Is he...dangerous?" Samantha spoke more nervously than she realized.

Chris shook his head. "I don't think so," he said calmly, undercutting the confidence of his words by his tone. "Still, he's pretty angry right now."

"Angry?"

"At me," Chris explained. "He resents me." After a brief pause he continued thoughtfully, "I guess he could be vindictive."

Samantha sat quietly for a moment, then continued to probe, curious about the origin of Pete Thompson's attitude. "Is he the extra 'responsibility' your father left you?" she asked.

Looking steadily out the window, Chris seemed not to hear her. Samantha wanted to know what he had meant, and her interest was piqued all the more by his sudden silence. She tried again, and again Chris's lack of response rebuffed her.

The little airplane rose and fell ever more violently in the gusts of wind. Samantha tried to force herself to think about what Chris had told her, to concentrate on possible solutions to the riddle he had posed, to look out the window for their next landmark. But nothing seemed to work. The wildness of the weather and the violence of the ride soon stole every other thought from her mind.

With each minute that passed, conditions seemed to be getting worse. She could make out the faint waviness of the cloud line above her, so near were they to the bottoms of the clouds. Below she could occasionally catch the uneven pattern of a rock breaking through the sea or the luminescence at the coastline of some tiny atoll. And each time she looked it seemed that the clouds were coming nearer—and so was the ocean below.

Hesitant to reveal what were probably silly fears, she could at last stand it no longer. "Chris, aren't we getting awfully near the water?" she ventured in a timid voice.

"Yes," he answered steadily, as if it was completely natural.

His voice gave her hope, but still she pushed on. "Is it. . . safe? Are we going to be all right?"

Even as she spoke she could feel the seat dropping away from her when the airplane descended sharply, as if the road Chris had spoken of earlier had suddenly collapsed.

"Chris!" she shrieked, her hands grasping for his arm.

"It's all right," he shouted, his shoulders tightening as he fought with the careening yoke. "It's just an air pocket. We'll be out of it in a minute."

In just seconds Samantha could feel the upward pressure on her seat while the plane rose as swiftly as it had fallen before. She clung to the seat, her teeth gripping her lower lip in a determined struggle not to cry. But her pulse raced and her eyes were wide with fear.

When she could make herself move at all, she turned her head to glance over at Chris. He continued to fight for control of his craft, his eyes darting across the panel before him, seeking first one instrument and then the next. His hands were white as they strained against the yoke. But for all his concentration he showed not a single sign of nervousness, and Samantha took comfort from the quick wink he gave her when he had no time to speak. She could see why the islanders looked to Chris for solutions to apparently insoluble problems. He was the kind of person you could rely on in a crisis.

Suddenly off to the right Samantha caught a glimmer of light. She turned quickly to Chris to see his reaction.

For a moment he took his hand off the yoke to pat hers. "Yes, that's Good Providence," he said quickly.

Samantha's sigh of relief was cut off abruptly when the plane bumped violently on an updraft. She gasped in terror while Chris, with calm concentration, struggled to line the plane up with the runway. Lights blazed along the edge of the airstrip, and as the plane turned for the final approach, Samantha realized how unusual it was for the runway to be so well illuminated. She turned to ask Chris but saw he had no time for questions.

Not until they had touched down with a squeal of rubber tires on the airstrip did Samantha exhale normally. Then she peered out the window, squinting into the bright lights. First one was extinguished, then another, and then there was only one pair of lights beamed at the plane, the lights of a single car.

Chris nodded his answer to Samantha's unspoken question. "Automobiles. Probably every one on the island. They knew we'd welcome a sight of home!"

Although he spoke lightly, Samantha felt a great flood of relief and pressure. The islanders had known it would be difficult to see a tiny airstrip on a tiny island in the midst of a vast dark ocean, so they'd done what they could to ensure a safe return for Chris and Samantha.

On steady ground again, Samantha felt the tension flowing out from her. But when she and Chris had thanked the islanders and watched them depart, she realized that even as she had relaxed, he became more and more tense. His shoulders were taut and he strode with obvious anger around the plane, checking to make sure it was tied down securely, in case the storm grew worse. Samantha followed him mutely, confused by his sudden anger and afraid to speak, though she sensed his anger was not directed at her.

The drive to her house passed in silence. It was not until Chris had walked with her into her house that he spoke again.

"That wasn't a very pleasant ride, was it?" he said as they stood in the doorway.

"Not very," she agreed.

For a moment there was silence between them, a silence Samantha finally broke with an awkward invitation to Chris to come in for a drink. He shook his head.

"It's late. You're tired. I'm tired." Each phrase was a labored statement.

Samantha shrugged. "I'm more excited than exhausted," she told him truthfully.

Chris beat one fist into the palm of his other hand. Once again his shoulders grew tight and tense, but this time his words explained his actions to a watchful Samantha.

"I'm sorry this had to happen," he exclaimed. "I felt so rotten for you in the plane!"

"It's okay, Chris." Understanding his anger was directed at himself for putting her through the terrifying ride, she hastened to reassure him. "I guess I'm a bit of a coward."

"No, you're not," he responded energetically. "That was a frightening ride, and a dangerous one. You were about as brave as anyone I've ever flown with."

"I didn't feel very brave," she admitted, glowing from his words of praise. It seemed as though Chris really cared how she felt, really worried not only about having risked her life—however small the risk had been—but even about having upset her. That recognition spread a warm glow through her chilled body and went far toward wiping out the horror of the traumatic flight.

"Samantha," Chris began, then paused. His eyes holding hers in a gaze she dared not break, he moved toward her until only a single short step separated them. Without saying a word he slipped his hand around hers, walking silently with her through the clinic to the living room. He didn't have to lead her; they walked side by side until they reached the puffy sofa that dominated the room. Then he sat down, drawing her beside him, still without a word.

As Chris slipped his strong arm around her shoulders, Samantha felt a wave of release flood through her. It was as if, having trusted Chris with her life on the plane, she no longer had to fear him. She felt as secure in the warm circle of his arms as she had while dancing with him in the tropical night on Halekai just hours—and light-years—ago. She snuggled against him, burrowing into him like a young animal, seeking warmth and comfort.

Chris seemed content just to hold her quietly, stroking her hair with his sure strong hand. As his hand brushed across her head from front to back in a soothing pattern, his palm felt hard against her forehead, his fingers delicate in her short curls. She sighed with pleasure, nestling close to his chest.

"Better than the plane?" Chris asked, his voice a tender caress.

"Much better," she responded with a soft smile. "As nice as dancing in the garden."

"Close your eyes and maybe you'll see the moonlight again," he whispered.

Samantha closed her eyes, seeing imprinted on her lids the soft glow of moonlight on the garden. Her nostrils were filled not with the scent of tropical flowers but with the heady warmth of the man who held her now.

"Can you see it?" he asked softly, his breath teasing her ear with soft waves.

"Mmm." Samantha managed no more than a gentle murmur of assent, too peaceful and happy to bother with unnecessary speech.

Chris's lips, close to her ear, began to move against the sensitive skin beneath the line of her hair and along her neck. His breath grazed her like the wings of a butterfly, and his lips made a moist warm pattern on her neck.

Sighing with unconscious seductiveness, Samantha half turned in his arms to meet him in the embrace. Her mind no longer had the power to reason; her heart felt warm and safe; her body yearned to meet his in ultimate closeness.

Chris inhaled sharply as she moved against him. "Samantha," he whispered, his call half a warning, half a plea.

She couldn't bring herself to speak, couldn't say what she wanted. But her body said it for her, her arms entwined around his neck and her spine arching toward him.

Chris leaned toward her, his head dark above her. Slowly he lowered his lips to hers, claiming them with a passion marked by a possessiveness she had never felt before. His mouth captured hers, his lips and tongue exploring hers no more eagerly than hers responded to him.

Samantha ran her hand through Chris's hair, still damp from the rain that had begun as they left the airstrip. She inhaled the warm moist perfume of his skin and the different scent of his rain-touched hair. Part of his cheek was rough with the stubble of new beard. She brushed her lips along the line of his beard, so that the light stubble tingled against her sensitive lips. She traced the very tip of her tongue along the same line, tasting the slightly salty tang of his skin as she registered the various sensations, now rough, now smooth. At last she lay back in his arms, her green eyes wide to meet his dark ones.

For a long moment he stared into her eyes, and in his smoldering pupils was a question Samantha understood with her heart if not with her mind. She answered only by closing her eyes, half-consciously inviting him to continue, but uncertain how to make her invitation more direct.

Chris needed little encouragement to lean toward her again, his lips lightly grazing her eyelids and nose, her cheeks and her chin, before homing in once more on her willing mouth. He brushed her lips tantalizingly with his own, then pressed more deeply against her mouth, encouraging it to open to his desire. His arms tightened convulsively about her as he felt her respond, and his body stiffened against hers in an ever closer embrace.

Suddenly Chris broke that embrace, pushing Samantha away from him with a small exclamation.

She gazed up at him like an injured animal, surprised by his abrupt movement.

"Enough!" he muttered in a strangled cry.

"What is it, Chris? What's wrong?" she cried in confusion.

He looked at her tenderly, his eyes moist and dark with desire. "It's enough for now," he said, pulling her upward not to be closer to him but to sit beside him, leaving a small painful space between them. Only when Samantha sat quietly by his side and their breathing had eased to normal did he speak again.

"Don't get me wrong, Samantha," he said quietly. "I want you. My God, how I want you!"

Samantha shivered at the force of his words, but she could say nothing to him.

"It's just that you're exhausted, and it's nearly morning, too," he explained. Placing his hand under her chin, he tipped her head up so that she had to return his prolonged gaze.

"I don't want to make love to you when you're half-asleep," he continued, his words sending a thrill down her spine. "I want to make love to you when you're awake, when you know what you're doing and what I'm doing," he concluded with tender force as he rose from the sofa.

Pulling her to her feet, he leaned down to kiss her lightly, affectionately, on the lips. Samantha yearned for him but made no move. Chris stood silently for a moment, then pointed out the window with a grin.

"I was about to say good-night to you, but it looks as though good-morning would be more apt," he announced lightly. Drawing her against his chest for a final embrace, he whispered close to her ear, "Sleep well, my brave little one."

Then, before she could even return the wish, he was gone. The pale rays of light slipping through the window announced that, like the rain, the strange, tense, wonderful night had passed.

CHAPTER SEVEN

SAMANTHA AWOKE A FEW HOURS LATER to greet a brilliant day. The storm had apparently abated during the night, leaving no trace but a scent of fresh moisture on the air.

Stretching lazily, she reminded herself it was Sunday. There were no regular clinic hours today, and since she had expected to be on Halekai until midmorning, she had no obligations. Barring an emergency, the day was hers to enjoy.

She rose slowly from the bed, luxuriating in her rare free time. There was no need to rush, no reason to toss on her clothes and swallow a hasty glass of orange juice while sorting through notes about a patient's condition. But as she washed the last traces of her brief night's sleep from her eyes, Samantha admitted that her sense of infinite well-being did not really come from having a free day.

A warm flush rose to her face in spite of the cool water she splashed on her cheeks. She knew very well why she felt so good on this sunny morning. She was in love!

When she thought of the night before, Samantha's heart filled to the brim with emotions she could barely recognize. But she knew what they added up to, and that was love.

Somewhere between Halekai and Good Providence; sometime between the moment when Chris first looked at her last night and when he parted from her with a kiss; somehow, among the dancers and the talkers and the tired members of the elegant little string orchestra, she had found love.

Every moment of the evening on Halekai came back to her in poignant detail. She could smell the flowers and hear the violins as clearly as she had last night. She could taste the herbs in the salad more distinctly than she had when the dish rested before her on the linen cloth. She could remember what the governor's representative said and what his wife said, and what the man who wanted to dance with her had worn. And she could remember Chris.

She remembered everything about Chris. She could see the appreciative glitter in his eyes when he walked into her house and she could visualize the twinkle those eyes had held when he told the other man she would not dance with him. The sensation of his strong arms holding her as they danced and the light pressure of his long body swaying against hers as the music played were so real she ached to embrace him again. She remembered the scent of his hair and the crispness of his dress shirt, the feel of his cheek touched by the faintest possible stubble of beard.

In the warm safety of her room, each memory was a pleasant one. Even her memories of the flight home took on a new interpretation. No longer did fear interpose itself between her and Chris as he sat so steadily before the yoke, as he guided the little plane safely through the storm and winked to encourage her and give her hope. Yes, he was a man to count on; he was a man to love.

Twirling about on her toes, Samantha hardly tried to suppress the wordless song that rose to her lips. No one could hear her; she was alone and she could do as she pleased. She could shout her love to the desk and the bed and the lamp, and they wouldn't tell a soul!

As she whirled to a stop before her unmade bed, Samantha was suddenly halted by a disturbing thought. She couldn't tell a soul. She didn't want to tell anyone. In fact, she was afraid to mention her love, for she was unsure whether that love was truly shared.

Sinking onto the bed, she rolled over to lie on her back, staring sightlessly at the white ceiling. In the silence she saw the events of the night before in a new way. Chris had never spoken of love to her. What he had said was that he wanted her, he desired her. And she didn't doubt the truth of that. But was there nothing more to his feelings than passion? She shared his passion—she had learned that about herself—but she felt so much more, it was frightening.

Another thought occurred to her as she rolled onto her stomach. Their relationship, whatever it was, had certainly changed last night. The beauty of the dance, the closeness she had felt as they spoke together, the fear aroused in her by the airplane ride—all had combined to have an effect on her. Her emotions were less in check than usual; her defenses were down. She needed to be held, protected, sheltered, and Chris had been there.

She shook her head. That was rationalizing. It had taken so little to destroy her defenses against him that it must have been every bit as obvious to Chris as it was to her that she had welcomed his advances. She had sought his embrace, and not just because she'd been frightened.

Samantha rose wearily from the bed. But as she pulled the sheets tight and fluffed up the light cover, her mood began to change once again. Maybe he didn't love her—yet. Maybe she cared more than he did. Still, he wasn't faking in his embrace or in his kisses, as tender as they were passionate. He felt something for her, and she for him. Suddenly it was very, very good to be alive.

When the phone rang an hour later, Samantha grabbed it off its cradle with confidence, sure it was Chris. She was not disappointed.

"Samantha? I waited till I thought you'd be up." Chris's strong voice was energetic with life.

"I've been up since eight," Samantha admitted. "I couldn't sleep."

Chris chuckled deep in his throat. "I had the same problem."

Samantha couldn't bring herself to answer, so she sat in tense silence awaiting his next words.

"I wanted to see you today, but something's come up," Chris said easily. "Tomorrow? Maybe we could go for a swim before dinner?"

Chris's words made Samantha's heart first soar, then plummet, then soar again. He had wanted to see her, so he did care! But then, that vague excuse, "something's come up." Still, he was asking her to see him the next day.

She answered more quickly than she could have expressed the thoughts that flew like birds through her mind. "That'd be nice. I should be done here about five."

"Fine. I'll pick you up."

As if being connected by only a phone wire was too painful, they soon broke the connection. But long after she had hung up, Samantha stared at the phone, hearing Chris's voice echo through her head.

She spent the rest of the day quietly, getting some work done, writing a few letters, straightening up the house. Late in the afternoon she went to the beach, too lazy to swim but glad to lie in the heat of the declining sun. Tomorrow at this time she would be with Chris, here, on this beach, perhaps. Tomorrow they would plunge together into the chill of the sea, then escape together to the heat of the sand, where they could lie side by side, serene and at one. Samantha shivered with anticipation. It seemed tomorrow would never come.

NOT ONLY DID IT COME, but it was an extremely busy day. Although Chris was never far from Samantha's thoughts, she had no time to dream about her date. In fact, she almost missed it.

Felicity, who could be so fine an assistant, was in

one of her bad moods. From the moment she walked
in the door, her behavior was sullen and difficult.
She barely performed her work and she took an extra
long lunch break on a day when she might well have
skipped lunch in order to help Samantha.

When the girl finally sauntered back to work, well
after two o'clock, Samantha was thoroughly exasperated. She had received a phone call to drive into
the hills to deliver a baby, and she had been stalling,
waiting for Felicity's return.

"I've tried to cancel the afternoon appointments,"
she told the sullen girl while she tossed instruments
into her medical bag. "But I couldn't reach everyone, and Mrs. Nakuoro is coming in to pick up some
medication, so you'll have to stay here. You can use
the time to sort through these charts," she added,
motioning toward the pile on her desk.

"Couldn't I put a note on the door?" Felicity
asked, obviously reluctant to stay in Samantha's
absence.

"And what about the medicine for Mrs. Nakuoro?" Samantha pointed out. "And Billy Rubins
needs his bandage changed. You can do that,
too."

Felicity hedged. "Shouldn't you do it?"

Samantha halted her rush to stand in angry silence,
her hands on her hips. With an extreme effort she
managed to speak softly. "Normally I'd like to see
how his leg is, but that will have to wait till tomorrow. Meanwhile the bandage must be changed, and
you are perfectly capable of doing that. You can also

make an appointment for him to see me tomorrow, anytime after one.''

When Felicity said nothing in response, Samantha could feel her short supply of patience evaporating. "Felicity? I have to go. It's Kiri Lawrence, and it's her first baby. Okay?''

At last Felicity nodded, obviously balking at being forced to work, but apparently loath to say anything more. Frustrated as she was, Samantha had no time to spare; so, tossing her medical bag into the little station wagon, she drove rapidly up to her patient's mountainside home.

The hours passed swiftly as Samantha provided what comfort and help she could to the frightened young woman giving birth far from her home on a neighboring island. Kiri Lawrence had come to Good Providence when she'd married, and happy as she was, she missed her family and her true island community, most of all at this time. But when Samantha handed her the perfect infant, diapered by one neighbor woman and wrapped in a blanket loaned by another neighbor family, Kiri Lawrence smiled. All at once she was a mother—and she had found a new home.

A smile echoing the young mother's played about Samantha's lips as she guided her car back down the mountain and toward the clinic. So often medicine dealt only with the hopeless and the deadly, but today she had seen new life come into the world, and she had helped. That baby was as healthy as it was because she, the new doctor on the island, had taught the mother how to prepare for it: what to eat, how to exercise, when to rest. She had been with the frightened mother, a friend among the other friends who came to help. It was a good feeling.

Realizing she would have to rush if she was to change her clothes before Chris arrived, Samantha slammed the car door and raced to the clinic. It wasn't quite five o'clock, so she was not surprised to see the door open. Felicity was supposed to stay until five before locking up.

But Samantha's headlong race to the door halted at her first sight of the open room. The clinic was in a shambles, furniture broken, papers strewn about, a window smashed. And Felicity was nowhere in sight.

As Samantha looked around her in shock and horror, she heard the sound of a car in the street. She could not take her despairing eyes off the vision before her, but she was aware of footsteps approaching along the walk. It was Chris.

Relief flooded through Samantha when she recognized Chris's steps. Her warm memories of their night together returned in spite of the anguish she now felt, and she welcomed his sympathy as much as she needed his help. She turned to him gratefully, longing to be held and comforted by him in her confusion.

"What is it? What's happened?" Chris demanded as he looked past her into the clinic.

Samantha shrugged helplessly. "The same thing that's happened before, I guess," she said at last.

Chris looked at her sharply. "How could it have happened again? Wasn't the place locked up?"

"Apparently not," Samantha responded unhappily.

"Well, wasn't anyone here? Where were you?"

Chris's rapid-fire questions struck Samantha like bullets when it occurred to her that he was blaming her for what had happened. It was as if he thought her negligent and believed that negligence had caused the ransacking of the clinic. Numb with pain, she stammered, "I had to see a patient! I was delivering Kiri Lawrence's baby!"

Although he seemed to accept that she had left the clinic only to perform her duties elsewhere, Chris still offered no words of apology. In his frustration he continued to hammer at her, "And where was Felicity? Surely you didn't leave her in charge here?"

Driven to fury even while understanding the cause of his anger, Samantha snapped back at him, "I had to leave her in charge. I couldn't just close the clinic, and she is my assistant."

"Yes, but you should have known better," he insisted. "You shouldn't have left her alone like that."

Hurt that Chris could continue to blame her and filled with jealousy over his double standard—she had to be perfect, but Felicity could get away with far, far less—Samantha bit her lip to keep from shouting. When she felt she had regained some measure of self-control, she responded quietly, bitterness obvious in her face as well as her words.

"What else am I supposed to do, Chris? She's all I've got. And *you* assigned her to me."

Chris was silent for a moment, but his next words held no plea for forgiveness. "I thought you'd be able to see her strengths—and her weaknesses. You can't leave her alone and expect her to work."

"Am I her boss or her baby-sitter?" Samantha longed to cry out. But catching herself before she spoke her thoughts, she asked resentfully, "Surely you expected she'd do her work, didn't you? Why else did you make her my assistant?"

"She's got real nursing talent," Chris said quietly. "You've admitted that yourself."

True as this was, Samantha refused to dignify his comment with so much as a nod of agreement.

Chris shook his head, hesitating a moment before continuing. "She needed a job; you needed an assistant. It seemed to make sense."

When Samantha remained silent, he tried again. But his answer was vague and his expression veiled. "Look, Samantha," he began, "I had to do something for her. I had . . . a responsibility for her."

Samantha's heart contracted, and fury mingled with pain in her eyes. "So you saddled me with her? You met your 'responsibility' by giving me someone totally irresponsible as an assistant?" She paused, then spoke again, her voice a cry of pain. In it was all her latent jealousy and all her fear. "Why, Chris? Why did you do it?"

Chris looked at her as though he was about to speak, then turned his head away. His shoulders sagged as he said, "I had my reasons, Samantha, but I'm not free to tell you. I *can't* tell you."

The anguish of a physician whose patients had been betrayed mingled with the greater anguish tearing through Samantha—the agony of learning that her worst fears about the man she loved were true. It seemed to her that Chris had all but admitted he loved or had loved Felicity. Had she been his mistress? Was she still? Samantha couldn't see past her jealousy to look at Chris. She could see only her own pain, not the troubled expression on his mobile face.

In her misery, her voice was taut and her words sarcastic. "Oh, I understand all right," she snapped. "I think I know perfectly well about those noble motives of yours, and I don't find them very noble at all!"

"What...?" Chris looked at her sharply, his eyes wide with a confusion she refused to acknowledge.

"You don't have to play innocent anymore, Christopher Girard," she shot back at him, her voice cracked from the strain of not crying. "I know what it means when an attractive man feels a special 'responsibility' toward a woman like Felicity. You don't have to play games with me."

Chris stared at her, his eyes darkening like the sky over Halekai as the storm approached. "I don't believe you know what you're saying," he whispered at last.

"Oh, I know all right," she spat out.

"Do you think. . .?" He hesitated, apparently incapable of speaking.

"Do I think you and Felicity are lovers? Is that the word you can't seem to recall?" Samantha looked directly into his dark eyes. "Yes, I do. Or, at least, I think—I *know*—you've been lovers. Maybe it's over now." She paused, still anxious to give him the chance to say something to prove her wrong, some words of affection and comfort to show her it was all a foolish nightmare, and soon she could awaken to the warm reality of his tender embrace.

"So you think Felicity's my mistress, or has been," he said slowly. He seemed to be keeping something in, waiting, as she waited, for understanding.

Samantha nodded, holding her breath in hopes of his denial.

"And you think I got her the job out of some sense of duty? That I thought I owed her something?" he continued, his voice steady but his eyes flashing with an emotion Samantha could not decipher.

"You keep talking about responsibility," she reminded him.

"Yes," he said, "and I believe in doing my duty. But you're accusing me. . .of foisting an incompetent on you in order to salve my conscience, is that it?"

Samantha shrugged, but inside the doubts began to rise. When he put it so bluntly it seemed impossible. Chris cared about the islanders, and he always seemed to act for their sake. And yet she had the evidence before her, and he hadn't denied her accusations.

She didn't know what to think. People she trusted and respected, like Ed Bates and Father Ilima, seemed to think Chris was an entirely good man. Widow Tarai had nothing but praise for him, especially for his efforts to help Felicity. Still, it was possible she had been ignorant of the affair; maybe it was even probable. Yet Ed and the priest seemed to know everything that happened on the island. Other men might excuse someone like Chris for having an affair with a young woman in his charge, but Ed would not, and certainly Father Ilima would not. But on the other hand, there were all of Felicity's comments, some of them crude and obvious, and there was the fact of Chris's placing her in this job.

Granted that Felicity showed some talent for nursing, but that was not enough. She was flighty, difficult and so obviously irresponsible that Chris could blame Samantha for leaving the clinic open under her care. If Chris had no responsibility to the islanders, it would be more reasonable that he try to help out a young woman like Felicity. But he did have that other responsibility, and it was one that seemed to weigh heavily upon him. He would not do something to harm the island's residents unless he was driven to it out of desperation. And what could cause such desperate need, unless it was indeed true that Felicity was his lover? Why else should he owe her so much that he would give her a job she didn't deserve, a job that jeopardized the success of the clinic and even the well-being of the islanders?

It was hard for Samantha to believe that Chris

would risk doing harm to the islanders for any reason. Yet Felicity was an attractive woman, a very attractive woman. She had an unusual degree of sensuality, which she was happy to flaunt before anyone and everyone. That Chris responded to such a woman could not be doubted. He was a passionate man, as Samantha's own experience showed all too clearly.

When she reached this point in her ruminations, Samantha felt all but convinced once again. There was no solution except the one she hated to believe in, the one she had accused Chris of and which he had not denied. Out of some irrational forlorn hope she tried one more time.

"Do you have another explanation?" she asked. Her voice turned the words into an accusation, but she ached to make it a genuine question, a question he could answer simply, directly, satisfactorily.

Chris looked at her from under his heavy eyelids, his eyes dark with smoldering emotion. For a moment the space between them was filled with a silence so intense it seemed almost tangible. At last he spoke.

"No explanation you'd accept right now," he said evenly.

His voice resonated with a bitterness Samantha found as confusing as it was distressing. It made no sense. If he was guilty, he had no right to be bitter, unless perhaps he was angry that she had found out and that thus he had lost his chance to have her as a lover, as well as Felicity. The thought made her shiver with painful jealousy and angry pride.

But perhaps he wasn't guilty—the thought crossed her willing mind once more. If that was the case, he would have every right to be bitter toward her for saying what she had. A spark of hope lighted in her heart, and she fanned it with every power she had. She was almost ready to believe she had been wrong. One word from him, one real attempt at explanation, and she would have tossed aside her jealousy and her doubts. But he didn't give her that word.

At last she spoke again, her voice an anguished whisper. "So you don't deny it," she exhaled slowly.

Chris shrugged. "What's the point in denying it?" he asked.

Samantha looked up in time to catch the flicker of pain crossing his brow. Yet even as she stared at him, his face grew still, and she wondered if she had interpreted his expression correctly.

"You could if it wasn't true," she suggested, praying he still would offer a solution.

"Would you believe me?" Chris asked.

Again his tone was enigmatic. Although Samantha thought there was just the touch of a wish in that tone, she couldn't be sure. Perhaps it expressed only belligerence, a self-satisfaction so great that it mocked her good opinion of him. She was too confused to respond to his question, and after a short pause Chris continued to speak in the same ambiguous tone.

"That's what I thought," he said.

His voice sounded tired, and his shoulders drooped. But even as Samantha looked at him, strug-

gling to decide which feelings were the true ones,
which false, he snapped his shoulders back and
pulled himself up to his full height. Glaring down at
her, he looked deep into her troubled eyes. A flash of
light seemed to travel across from his dark eyes to
hers, which were wide open to accept what he offered.

"I'm disappointed in you, Samantha," he said
coldly.

Taken aback, Samantha could only gasp and echo
his words. "*You're* disappointed in *me*?" she cried
out.

He nodded soberly. "I thought you had better
judgment. I thought you knew something about
people—about me," he said tiredly. "I thought,
after Saturday night, that you understood me." He
paused, then added in a tight voice, "I guess I was
wrong."

Before she could respond to his strange words, he
had stalked out the door.

"Chris, I..." Samantha stammered, struggling to
find the words that would keep him there.

"Yes?" He paused in the doorway to turn toward
her.

His expression froze her courage. She couldn't say
what she wanted to say. Instead she managed only a
lame question. "What am I supposed to do...about
all of this?" she asked, motioning vaguely around
the ransacked clinic.

Chris shrugged. His tone was even, his words prag-
matic as he listed suggestions that were more nearly

orders. It seemed from his matter-of-fact manner that he would do his duty, though he had no interest in the problem. "Start taking inventory," he began the litany. "See what's missing. Let me know what you need. I'll get it cleaned up tomorrow and replace the supplies as soon as I can."

When Samantha stammered a word of thanks, he looked at her from under his heavy lids. "Did you think I'd shirk my responsibility?" he asked sarcastically.

She shook her head sadly, her eyes glued to the floor. By the time she lifted her head to look at him again, he had disappeared.

CHAPTER EIGHT

SAMANTHA SURVEYED THE RUINS of the clinic glumly once Chris had gone. All around her lay evidence of the work of the people who had ransacked the place, the people she could only consider criminals. Why they should have wanted to be so destructive was something she couldn't hope to understand, but destructive they had been.

Tears burned hot and painful in Samantha's eyes. It seemed as though every time she began to feel at home on Good Providence, every time she felt the islanders had welcomed her, something happened to prove she was wrong. Today she had helped Kiri Lawrence to deliver her baby and, even more, to become a part of her community. When the baby was born, Kiri had smiled shyly at the neighbors who stayed with her and then had smiled gratefully at Dr. Hall. Samantha had felt a little bit like Kiri, first frightened and disoriented, then suddenly accepted by the people of the island. But now this!

And Chris's reaction—so unexpected, so cruel— had been the final blow. It was bad enough to see the evidence of the islanders' dislike of her and her clinic strewn on the floor in front of her. But to have

Chris belittling her, blaming her—that was too much!

To be fair, she admitted as she kicked an open file out of the way, she could not say the islanders disliked her. Most seemed not just to accept her but to welcome her, as well, and those few people she had told about the rash of incidents at the clinic insisted it was the work of one person, or at the most a small group. They could not—or maybe they would not—tell her who might be creating so many problems; but they all said to Samantha, over and over again, that the islanders wanted and needed her and liked her, as well.

And to be fair to Chris, Samantha had to admit that he hadn't really blamed her, not after his first shocked reaction. Still, she remembered with a stab of pain, he had all but acknowledged the fact that hurt her most of all: the fact that Felicity and he had been lovers.

Shaking her head angrily, Samantha stood in the center of the room. "This isn't helping any," she muttered under her breath. "I'd better get to work."

Knowing that Chris would send over a crew to straighten up, Samantha didn't bother to move anything except her patients' files. She would not leave those scattered on the floor or the desk where anyone could see them. But the rest of the mess she left untouched. She knew that however angry Chris was, he would not neglect his duty.

"At least he won't want to upset Felicity," Samantha whispered angrily as she searched for paper to begin an inventory. "He'll help the islanders all right; he'll do what he said he would for me in the clinic...just as long as I watch over Felicity for him."

Shaking with anger, Samantha had to fight to calm down enough to start the inventory. She walked cautiously around the room, peering into overturned boxes and behind cabinets to see what had been misplaced and what had been broken or stolen. Her list grew slowly: a bottle of medicine missing from one shelf, another smashed on the floor, a chair with a cracked leg that could probably be repaired, a sensitive instrument that was damaged beyond repair.

The work barely seemed to progress as the long minutes went by, and then the first hour and a second. Samantha could feel exhaustion seeping into her body. There was nothing physically demanding about the work—the hard labor would be performed by Chris's men and women the next day. Yet although her efforts were not tiring, Samantha felt drained. The emotional strain caused by both the destruction in the clinic and the argument with Chris was almost more than she could bear.

As the hours passed, Samantha felt the muscles at the back of her neck growing tense and tight. Her back ached and her shoulders ached, and hunger gnawed at her stomach, for she refused to give herself time off to get anything to eat. Far from being a lazy evening of swimming followed by a pleasant dinner with Chris, this had turned into a terrible night of painful work and even more painful thoughts.

At last the inventory was completed. Hot and miserable, Samantha sat at her desk, trying to figure out how to work in the clinic during the next few days until Chris was able to replace the broken or missing items. Fortunately, only a few important things were damaged; there was more mess than actual destruction.

Grateful for that at least, Samantha worked steadily at her desk, nibbling at a dry sandwich while she copied the lists to give to Chris. Suddenly she was disturbed, as if some noise had attracted her attention. She glanced up, then bit her lip at the sight of a stranger standing in the doorway. She could not be sure, but she thought it was the prowler, the man she believed to be the worrisome Pete Thompson.

She looked at him quickly, and a shiver of fear crept along her spine. Although Samantha told herself not to be ridiculous, she felt there was something mysterious about the way the man had just appeared. There had to be a perfectly simple explanation, she chided herself. She had been concentrating on her work and he had walked up quietly; that was all. But she couldn't rid herself of the feeling that this man was indeed the prowler and that he represented some very real danger to herself or her work.

"What do you want?" she stammered at last, trying to remind herself that he might just be a patient. "May I help you?"

For a moment he didn't reply, and Samantha sensed something defiant about the way he stood there lounging against the door, staring at her.

When he spoke at last, his words should have dispelled Samantha's fears, for they were ordinary words spoken in an ordinary tone. "Looks like you've had some trouble," he commented casually, motioning around the room.

Samantha's eyes followed the wave of his arm. She was startled by the pale color of his skin; though his arm seemed strong, almost wiry, it looked unhealthy. She glanced at his face, catching a glimpse of his pasty skin before his eyes bored into her from across the room. Nervously she forced herself to respond to his comment.

"Yes," she said quietly, "things are a bit messy. But I can still see patients, if that's what's worrying you."

She paused, hoping he would identify himself and then offer some acceptable reason for sauntering in after the clinic's regular hours, so late at night. If he was there for medical help, she would know how to react and what to do.

"Oh, I'm not worried," he said sarcastically.

"Well, then," she asked a trifle impatiently, "what can I do for you?"

The man said nothing. His posture suggested he was waiting for her to speak again, and while he waited he was content to study her with an insolent expression on his strangely white face. Samantha could feel the color rising to her cheeks under his steady patronizing stare. Her mind worked quickly. The doctor in her noted his pale color and wondered whether he had been sick or simply out of the sun for a while. But all the rationality of the doctor could not prevent the fear shaking the woman she also was. He was too strange, and he frightened her too much.

To hide her fear, she slowly rose from the desk. When she could see him more nearly eye to eye, she paused, standing behind the desk and leaning against it lightly for what security it seemed to offer. Only when she believed herself in control again did Samantha speak.

"Can I do something for you? If not, would you mind leaving?" she asked politely. "I have a great deal of work to do."

At last the man spoke to her once more. "You can do something for me," he began softly.

As he spoke he took a single slow step toward her, and Samantha could feel herself cringing behind the desk. She forced herself to stand in place as though unmoved by his tone or his approach. By a sheer effort of will she made herself appear in control.

"Yes? What's your name?" she asked politely, reaching for some papers on her desk in her most professional manner.

The man stopped walking, and Samantha took comfort in that. Still, his body had assumed a new position, and it seemed almost as though he swaggered while he stood in the same place.

"My name is Pete Thompson," he announced evenly.

A thin tremor of fear worked its way along Samantha's nerves, yet there was also relief. At last the

"Only those that dry quickly. Nothing's worse than having to tote along a bunch of soggy garments that weigh a ton," Susan told her.

"What about our heavier garments?"

"They never get washed," came Susan's laughing reply. "Our next full rest day it would be a good idea to air all of them."

Rock joined Beryl when she returned to the tent area. "I think it's time we had a little talk," he ordered, his eyes on her damp hair waving softly down her back.

"What's there to talk about? I thought you settled everything back at the ravine."

"Come with me," he insisted. He took her arm and strode purposefully toward a grove of trees.

"Don't manhandle me!" Beryl flared as he pushed her to a seat on the ground and towered over her.

"Manhandle?" He grinned mockingly. "If that's all you know about it, the men in your past must not have been much."

Beryl itched to slap the mocking smile off his face. "And I suppose you think you're the answer to every woman's prayer?"

His arms shot out and he grabbed her by the shoulders, pulling her hard against his chest. For a moment her luminous green eyes met his glittering black gaze before his mouth closed over hers in a plundering kiss. His lips, hard with anger, forced hers apart, his tongue probing the sensitive inner recesses of her mouth.

At first she struggled, refusing the response he was trying to force from her. She fought to remain passive under his kiss, but the erotic demands of his told her about Pete Thompson during their plane ride to Halekai, that night that seemed to have taken place so many years ago. Pete was "jealous"—was that it? Or had "vindictive" been Chris's word? Whichever, Chris had seemed to think Pete was a source of trouble. Maybe he wasn't really dangerous—more of an annoyance, had been her impression from what Chris had said—but he might well be responsible for everything that had been happening in the clinic from the day of her arrival until the present.

Thinking of the present whipped Samantha out of the world of memory and into the world of reality. In that world, speculation about Pete Thompson faded before his presence in the room, not twenty feet from where she sat.

Samantha forced herself to speak calmly, as though she had entertained none of the thoughts rushing through her head. But as she maintained an outward studious calm, she had the uncanny feeling that Pete Thompson knew exactly what she had been thinking and that he could sense exactly how nervous those thoughts had left her.

"Am I right that you don't have a medical problem? Nothing I can help you with?" she asked with apparent placidity.

"That's right," he said, smirking at her from his position across the room.

"Well, then," she began, rising from her desk again as if to dismiss him, "there seems no point in your staying, Mr. Thompson."

"Well, now, maybe *I* can help *you*," he suggested, his voice ripe with impudence.

"Oh, I don't think so," she said, willfully misunderstanding him. "I've got this nicely under control," she concluded, wishing it were as true about her confrontation as it was about the supply lists she flourished at him.

Pete took another step toward her. "Aren't you a little bit curious, doctor?" he asked, his emphasis making a mockery of the formal title he accorded her.

She looked at him silently, unsure how much she needed to humor him. But he no longer seemed to require any encouragement. Taking another step toward her, cutting the distance between them with his giant stride, he continued to speak; and his tone turned his polite words into a challenge.

"Wouldn't you like to know what's been going on here?" he asked.

Samantha steadied herself against the edge of her desk. "Look, Mr. Thompson," she said evenly, though her palms were wet from fear, "it's late and I'm too tired to enjoy this game. Why don't you just leave?"

Pete shook his head soberly. "When I'm ready I'll leave," he said, the tension in his face heightening the threat in his words.

It seemed to Samantha that the more distance she tried to put between them through her words and stance, the more he narrowed the gap between them and the more of a bully he became. With gleaming eyes he watched her fumbling for the speech that would force him to leave. Her mind clouded over with exhaustion and fear, and the right words seemed further away than ever.

As if sensing her increasing insecurity, the rapidly rising fear that threatened to engulf her, Pete Thompson closed the small distance between them with a few long strides. His eyes glittered, and it was obvious to Samantha that he reveled in his new power, taking pleasure from the fear she tried to hide.

Samantha stood motionless like a trapped animal as Pete walked toward her. His eyes were narrowed to intense slits of light in his washed-out face, and his hair was rumpled as if his restless fingers had traveled through it a dozen times. She could see his hands tremble, though whether they shook with excitement or nervousness she couldn't determine. One part of her mind noticed all this and more: his thin mouth, the rigid set of his shoulders, his pale skin. But another part raced through all he had said and done, seeking an answer, a way out.

When he stood less than a foot from the desk, Pete stopped his relentless approach. His eyes riveted hers, forcing her to stare back into their depths. He leaned against the desk, bringing his weight to bear on it as if it were some insurmountable object he was trying to push aside. She stared into his eyes, his gaze hypnotic in its intensity, terrifying in its cruel indifference.

Suddenly Samantha broke the mesmeric hold of

his eyes upon her to search restlessly around the
room as if seeking another person, an answer, an
escape. There was none. She was alone.

As abruptly as she had broken the stare, so quickly
did Pete move, coming around the desk to stand
beside her. His eyes gleamed with power, his hands
twitched and his lowered eyebrows cut a rift into the
pale skin of his forehead.

Samantha knew she had to move. She didn't want
to risk actually tangling with him, for, even aroused
as she was by anger, she doubted her strength.

She slipped past him quickly, making for the front
door. Even if no one was outside this late at night,
she knew she could run into any house on the street
for shelter. But Pete Thompson knew that, too.

Quick as a lynx he turned, cutting off her route of
escape. "Not so fast, doctor." His voice was a wicked snarl.

"Don't you touch me," she breathed at him as he
moved closer to her.

He shook his head as if in disbelief. Without
another word he reached his hand out toward her.
But Samantha was too fast for him, shaking off his
hand and stepping back out of reach. He closed in
again, this time gripping her upper arm with fingers
surprisingly strong and no longer trembling. Now, it
seemed, he was in control and he knew it.

She could feel his breath hot against her face as he
leaned toward her. Bending her arm back, he was
forcing her into an embrace that made her sick with
fear and loathing. Samantha fought him, thrashing

about in her mind for an escape. She knew she had to act swiftly if she was to act at all.

As he bent his head toward her face, she whipped around, pulling herself loose from his grip and racing for the door. But her headlong thrust was abruptly halted as she caught sight of Chris walking toward the clinic entrance.

Fear vanishing in a dizzying flood of relief, Samantha felt the tears start to course down her cheeks. Her breath came hard as she cried out his name, a single word of pain and hope all in one. Her cry echoed through the clinic and out into the night, but she was past caring. All that mattered was that she was safe. Chris was there and she was safe once more.

Chris stalked into the clinic, taking in the vision before him with a strange savage look in his dark eyes. For a moment the only sound was Pete Thompson's labored breathing echoed by Samantha's panting gasps.

"What's going on here?" Chris spat out angrily.

Samantha hesitated, unsure how much of her suspicion to reveal in front of Pete. She still had no proof, only questions. But she hesitated too long, and Pete broke the momentary silence with an implication so grotesque she might have laughed had she not been so overwrought.

"What's it look like?" he asked, his voice insolent and rough.

Samantha whirled around to stare at him. He was leaning against a cabinet, his shirt loosened above his belt, his eyes hard. He leaned back as though he were perfectly relaxed, but the tension of his shoulders gave him away, at least to her intense stare.

Chris turned slowly to look at Samantha. She met his eyes, ready to cry out her accusation against her attacker, her belief in his complicity in all the destructive incidents at the clinic. But she couldn't read the expression in Chris's eyes. Rather than being open and concerned, it was enigmatic.

Samantha felt the icy fingers of fear stealing around her heart once again. It seemed she could scarcely breathe. Surely Chris couldn't believe what Pete Thompson was insinuating.

She spoke quickly. "Mr. Thompson came in after hours, Chris. He wouldn't say why he came, but...." She paused, unsure whether to speak first of her suspicions or of his attack.

But Chris gave her no time to decide. His voice was deep, and his tone seemed almost sarcastic as he interrupted, "I think it's pretty obvious why he came."

Samantha's breath came so sharp and hard it hurt. She was all too aware of how she appeared: her face was flushed, her shirt wrinkled, and a red mark burned on her arm where Pete's iron hand had held her. She didn't need a mirror to know she looked like someone who had been in an embrace, as indeed she had. But it had been an *unwilling* one! Surely Chris could sense that from the anger in her eyes!

Forcing herself to breathe calmly and ignoring Pete Thompson's complacent leer, she began again in a low tone, "Chris, Mr. Thompson walked in here while I was working, made a number of nasty and insinuating comments and then...." She paused, gathering strength for what she must conclude. "Then he attacked me!"

Chris glanced over at Pete, who smiled at him with a slight shrug, then returned his deep gaze to Samantha.

"Is that what happened, Samantha?" he asked quietly.

"Yes," she responded evenly, her voice masking the pain that gnawed at her heart.

At last it seemed Chris was willing to act. The hesitation he had shown at first, the apparent unwillingness to act directly against Pete Thompson, disappeared. Turning to the pale man Chris spoke in measured tones.

"I'm not sure what you're doing here, Pete," he said, "and maybe it's best if I don't know. Why don't you just leave now, before something else happens?"

Although the words were quiet and the statement more a suggestion than an order, Chris's stiff back and his expression made clear the nature of his command, and Pete lost no time in obeying.

Samantha watched uneasily as Pete walked to the door without a word. Only after he had disappeared did she turn again to Chris, still unsure why Pete had come or what exactly was going on between the two men. Yet as she began to speak, to ask Chris the questions that burned inside her, she saw his dark eyes become hooded once more, and the words failed her.

Walking quietly across the room toward her desk, she called over her shoulder to Chris, "I'll get that list of supplies for you." She fought to steady her voice and speak of neutral things, as if their earlier fight and the more recent strange events had not occurred.

"Thanks," Chris responded evenly. "That's why I'm here."

By the time she turned around again with the list in her hands, Samantha felt as though she had regained control. Perhaps she could talk with Chris now, she thought hopefully. But his eyes were still veiled, and she waited for him to speak first.

Chris remained silent for a long and painful moment. When he spoke, his words offered no encouragement to Samantha, for his tone was flat and his topic business.

"I came back to pick up the list..." he began, then paused significantly.

In spite of her better judgment, Samantha could feel her heart begin to pound with hope. But his next words removed that ray so faint, so deeply desired.

"...and to tell you I'm going away for a few days," he finished the sentence. "That's why I came by tonight. I didn't want you to think I'd forgotten my promise to get whatever supplies you needed, and I knew I'd be leaving first thing in the morning."

Again he paused, and Samantha held her breath, wondering why he was leaving so suddenly, where he was going and, most of all, how she could break through the barriers they had built between them.

Chris gave her no time to solve that last problem before his voice interrupted her thoughts. He was explaining his sudden departure, and his words cut through her like a knife.

"Felicity's missing."

In spite of her anger and her pain, Samantha was curious. "Missing?" she echoed.

Chris nodded. "She disappeared, apparently sometime after you left to go to Kiri Lawrence's. She never showed up for dinner, and her mother's worried."

Samantha nodded unhappily. She felt sorry for Widow Tarai, but her pride and her anger were piqued by Chris's concern.

"So?" she prompted him at last.

"So I'm going to try to find her," he responded simply, as if it was totally natural for him to interrupt his busy schedule and leave all his responsibilities behind in order to chase after an incompetent, frivolous, difficult woman. *His* woman, Samantha reminded herself bitterly.

"I'll start out on Halekai," he continued his explanation as Samantha seethed with anger. "While I'm there I can give your list to one of my agents, and he'll arrange for the supplies to be sent to you."

Samantha handed him the list without a word. Chris's eyebrows lifted ironically, and he smiled wryly at her.

"Is something wrong?" he asked, his tense voice belying his easy words.

Samantha glanced up at him in despair. She refused to wallow in jealousy before him when he knew perfectly well what was bothering her.

At last he broke the silence. "There isn't anything much to say, is there?" he suggested in a voice tight with tension.

"Chris," she began, awkward but determined not to let him leave without hearing his side of the story. Still, the irony in his eyes doused the fire in her heart and removed her ability to say another word.

"You're jealous, is that it?" he stated quietly. When she couldn't answer, he reached his hand toward her face, lifting her head with an insistent finger under her chin.

"Is that it?" he asked again. Still she couldn't answer.

Chris dropped his hand, and Samantha felt as if his finger had raked an indelible line across her chin, though he had barely touched her.

"Samantha..." he began, then hesitated. Gathering himself together, he seemed to force himself to speak. "Can't you see how wrong you are? It's not what you think."

"No?" she asked incredulously. "You saddle me with Felicity for some vague reason, you leave Good Providence to search for her...." She paused, then continued in a pleading voice, "What am I supposed to think?"

Chris shook his head sadly. "I'm sorry, Samantha, and for more than you know," he said quietly. "You're quick enough to accuse me, and not just of having an affair with Felicity. You seem to think I could ignore the needs of the islanders; you seem to think I just don't care. But you should know better.'' His voice quavered with feeling as he insisted again, "You *must* know better!''

Samantha's eyes sought his dark ones, glimmering from behind their fringed lids. "Why?'' she asked in pain. "What am I supposed to believe?''

He returned her gaze openly, and Samantha's heart quailed before the brilliance of his eyes. She longed to tell him so many things, to ask him still more. She wanted to ask him what his relationship with Felicity really was, for her heart tripped with anxious hope at the mere thought that she might have been wrong in her interpretation. She wanted to tell him of her suspicion that Pete was the prowler, to ask him if Pete could be behind the incidents at the clinic, to warn him of Pete's vague hints of responsibility and to share with him her intuitions about the man. She longed to tell him how she really felt—about Pete, about Good Providence, about him. But she was too frightened, too insecure, and she couldn't bring herself to speak of all that filled her heart with pain, with anger and with hope.

Chris looked at her closely for a long moment, then at last he turned away. She could not see the expression in his eyes or read the slump in his shoulders. She could only sense the tumult of emotions rising from deep inside him.

"I'll see that you get the supplies, Samantha,'' Chris muttered as he stood in the doorway. "And you should know that Charlie Tuatara is looking into the vandalism. He'll keep an eye on you—on the clinic—while I'm away.''

Samantha nodded. Every ounce of her energy was needed to keep from crying out in anguish; she had no breath to speak.

She watched Chris's back until he had disappeared from sight. Then she sank to the floor, the hot tears spilling out of her eyes to burn a path down her cheeks. She clenched her fists in frustration. She could see no way to convince him that he was wrong, no way to tell him of her love.

For the second time in a single day, Chris had been there when she needed him; he had come to her rescue. But for the second time in the same day he had also failed to explain his relationship with Felicity. If she had misunderstood him, he had made little effort to ease that misunderstanding, and it seemed there was not a thing she could do.

CHAPTER NINE

SAMANTHA STRUGGLED to keep the clinic open and to take care of her patients without either adequate supplies or an assistant. Her struggle was not made easier by her need to fight for calm. She was curious about Felicity, anxious about Chris and torn by emotions that threatened to spill over like a waterfall at the height of the rainy season.

Hampered because she lacked this or that drug, one or another piece of equipment, and frustrated because she had to cancel routine appointments for lack of time, Samantha collapsed into bed each night in a state nearing exhaustion. But she knew as she felt the covers soothingly embrace her aching body that it was probably good she was so tired. At least she could sleep, however uneasily.

Her dreams were filled with vague fears of Pete Thompson, though she heard he had left the island and Charlie Tuatara, the chief of police, dropped by each day. She was haunted by a painful jealousy about Felicity and still more by a desperate need to talk to Chris, to hear from him, to seek an explanation. She kept going because she had to, because her patients depended on her; but she was like a robot

who knew only how to work. And the longing she felt
for Chris was so intense it could not be dulled by the
exhaustion that otherwise numbed her, body and
soul. That agony alone she could feel, and it burned
into her like a brand.

Two days passed in a haze of painful speculation,
false hopes, sharp despair and work. Always there
was work. Illness and accidents did not stop happening just because she felt unfit to deal with them. So
she continued to work and to wait for a word from
Chris, a word about Chris. The word did not come
by mail or phone, directly or indirectly; only the patients kept coming.

On the afternoon of the third day, the pilot of
the Inter-Island DC-3 arrived at the clinic bearing
welcome boxes of supplies and some unwelcome
news.

"These were sent over from Halekai, Dr. Hall,"
he announced with a grin as he lugged the first box of
drugs over to her desk.

"Wonderful!" Samantha nodded in response. At
least one of her worries could be laid to rest, she
realized as she quickly checked through the boxes
that the pilot continued to carry in.

"That's everything," the young man said a few
minutes later as he placed a padded container on top
of the pile. "Is it what you needed?"

"Yes," Samantha answered quickly. "Thanks so
much." She paused, anxious to know what the pilot
had heard from Chris. Chris must have given him the
list of supplies, but the young man had offered no ex-

planation. At last Samantha asked tentatively, "Did Mr. Girard tell you to bring me all this?"

The pilot nodded calmly. "Toby, his agent, did it. I guess it was ordered Tuesday, but some of it had to be brought in from Guam." He looked curiously at the padded box. "That was what I was waiting for," he said.

Recognizing his curiosity and grateful for his help, Samantha opened the box to show him the gleaming instrument inside. "It's a tonometer," she explained. "You use it to test for glaucoma."

"How does it work?" he asked curiously.

"It measures the tension inside the eye—that's called the intraocular pressure," she explained. "You use it right against the eyeball, sort of like this," she added, bouncing the sensitive instrument off her finger to approximate its actual use.

The pilot watched admiringly while she carefully packed up the equipment again. "I guess it's important, huh?"

Samantha nodded. "With one of these I can check for glaucoma and possibly save someone from going blind. I'd call that pretty important!"

The pilot nodded with a sense of pride. They exchanged a few more pleasantries about their work, and Samantha struggled to remain casual and optimistic. But she soon realized he had nothing to say about Chris. Either Chris had not seen the pilot or had given him no message. Grateful as she was to have a resupplied clinic, Samantha could not halt the wave of disappointment that swept over her when the young pilot prepared to leave. Her heart sank as she realized he was her best contact with Chris, and he had proved to be no contact at all.

At the door, the pilot turned back to face her once more. Pointing to the boxes he had stacked neatly by her desk, he said jauntily, "It's a good thing that stuff arrived when it did."

"Why?" Samantha asked, made curious by the mystery of his pause.

"Remember that storm threatening when you were on Halekai?" he asked casually.

She nodded, wincing at the other memories his words evoked.

"Well, that was just the beginning," he announced portentously. "The rains are really starting now. They're working their way east and north. We should be getting them in a few days."

Samantha shivered, sensing the significance of what he said. "Does that mean you and...other pilots...won't be flying into Good Providence any-more?" she asked anxiously.

He shook his head. "Oh, I'll come when I can," he said with the jaunty grin of the would-be hero. Without realizing how deeply his words affected her, he went on lightheartedly, "And Mr. Girard's a good pilot, too. He'll be in and out pretty regularly. But there'll be times..." he concluded in vague warning.

"Times?" she prompted with a question.

He nodded. "The rains can knock out just about anything," he explained. "Roads, phones, crops—or planes. We do our best, but...." He trailed off, cer-

tain she would understand the implication of his unspoken words.

She did, all too well. Quickly she thanked him
again for his help and his warning, then closed the
door behind him, anxious to be alone to think and to
wonder.

Samantha had heard tales of the rainy season before, of days and weeks when the skies poured forth
water unceasingly, when the power went out and
roads washed away, and the earth sloughed off the
hills like dead skin, taking grass and flowers and
crops on a headlong rush to the sea. She knew that
the succulent fruit and lush vegetation that blessed
this tropical island resulted from the long months of
heavy rain. She knew that the waterfalls and rivers as
well as the cisterns that supplied water year round
were getting low and that the rains were a necessary
part of the natural balance of life on the island. She
knew that the islanders welcomed the rains for their
crops and their water supply. But she also knew that
what the pilot implied was correct: without enough
rain, the island could die; with too much, it could
die, as well. Inexperienced and filled with doubt,
Samantha faced the oncoming rainy season with awe
at the power of nature and the delicate balance of
natural and human life, but she faced it also with
fear.

Her fear was increased by Chris's continued silence. He had not called or sent a message. For
another day, as water began to drip from the laden
clouds, Samantha waited, hoping she would hear if

not from Chris, then at least about Chris. But when Father Ilima left after his regular visit without once mentioning Chris, Samantha could stand it no longer. Somebody must have heard something from him, and she had to know.

She walked quickly through the increasingly heavy rain to Widow Tarai's. Knocking lightly on the door, she was grateful to be admitted promptly. Mrs. Tarai took one look at her dripping hair and seated her in the kitchen, thrusting a coarse clean towel into her hand.

"No raincoat or hat?" she chided Samantha.

Samantha shook her head weakly. "Everyone says you have to learn to live with the rains," she pleaded her innocence.

"Live with them, yes." The old woman glared with mock anger at the young physician. "Drown in them, no!"

Samantha smiled. Tense as she was, she was comforted by the woman's fussing like a mother hen welcoming another chick under her wings. But thinking of herself as one chick reminded her of Mrs. Tarai's other chick, the missing Felicity.

Returning the damp towel with a word of thanks, Samantha gratefully accepted the fresh coffee her hostess handed her. Over cups of the steaming rich brew the two women talked casually for a few minutes. Finally Samantha gathered her courage to ask what the widow had learned of her daughter.

"Nothing." Mrs. Tarai shook her head sadly. The energy she always seemed to exude suddenly dissipated, and the old woman seemed to shrink before Samantha's sympathetic eyes.

"Hasn't Chris—Mr. Girard—told you anything?" Samantha asked, aroused as much by her concern for Mrs. Tarai as by her anxiety about Chris.

"I'm sure he's doing everything he can," came the widow's quick assurance. "He's probably just too busy to call."

It was clear to Samantha that in Mrs. Tarai's eyes Chris could do no wrong. She did not want to injure her friend's faith, but she grew angry at this new evidence of Chris's thoughtlessness. He must know how desperate Widow Tarai would be, yet he couldn't even take the time to call.

But when Mrs. Tarai spoke about how grateful she was to Chris, how good he was to take time from his work to look for Felicity, how concerned and caring he was, Samantha was forced to recognize how different his actions appeared to her friend and to herself. To Mrs. Tarai his efforts were heroic, though also typical, and his silence seemed reasonable. Maybe Chris had nothing to report; when he did, she would hear from him.

As the widow spoke, Samantha realized how it might appear to her. To her it would seem that Chris cared about Felicity, as he did about all the islanders. He cared enough to leave his home and his work for Felicity's sake. And it could even seem kind not to call Felicity's mother with every bit of news, every rumor. Perhaps it was better for him to wait until he had something definite to say before he contacted her.

Against her will, Samantha had to acknowledge that Mrs. Tarai might be right. Chris was doing a great deal for her and for her daughter. If his motivations were questionable, if he had been Felicity's lover, at least he accepted his responsibility. Yet, somehow, knowing that he was not so bad as she had decided he was did nothing to lighten the burden Samantha carried.

When she started toward the door an hour later, Mrs. Tarai handed her an umbrella.

"You can drop it off tomorrow, but you use it tonight," she said with a firm nod. "You'll have to get yourself a slicker or a good umbrella," she added firmly.

Samantha blushed like a child. "I will," she promised, opening the umbrella as she prepared to walk home through the steady rain.

"One other thing," Mrs. Tarai warned, keeping Samantha at the door. "You be careful driving. The roads in the hills get mighty slippery this time of year."

Samantha nodded quickly, her steady voice belying her quaking heart. "Yes, I've heard. I've got chains in the car."

"Good. Be sure you know how to use them, and watch out for floods, too."

"I will," Samantha reiterated her promise to the mother hen whose wings seemed to offer such tempting shélter. "I know the streams can flood quickly."

"*Very* quickly," warned Widow Tarai, "and the roads can just about wash out in an hour."

Samantha fussed with the latch on the umbrella, and as if sensing she had frightened the young woman, Mrs. Tarai spoke again, this time in a softer voice.

"You're new here, that's all. You'll catch on quickly. And the rains can be beautiful, too," she said gently.

Smiling gratefully at those kind words, Samantha ventured forth into the rain she would have to learn how to live with if she was to stay on Good Providence.

Samantha's education progressed quickly. In the next several days the rains never once let up. The temperatures remained mild and in some ways the rain was pleasant. Samantha soon learned why it was that many of the islanders disregarded the rain, behaving as if the sun were shining. Many eschewed the umbrellas and slickers Widow Tarai considered essential, letting the warm water soak their hair and sluice over their lightly clad bodies. Samantha learned the pleasure of swimming in the rain, of smelling the scent of tropical blossoms made even headier by the moisture that clung to their petals, of feeling the soft water caress her skin. But she also learned of the power of the rain.

By the end of the week, even the paved roads in the village were covered with mud. Patients coming down from the hills spoke of swollen streams and gardens flooded by the never ceasing water. Other patients simply canceled their appointments, choosing not to face the long trek down from the hills, a trek that was always unpleasant during the rainy season and could even be dangerous.

Early one afternoon, several days after she had last seen Felicity's mother, Samantha sat quietly at her desk. The clinic phone was out of order for the second time in the week, and her last scheduled patient had failed to show up for an appointment. She was trying to sort through papers, trying *not* to sort through the hopeless cycle of thoughts about Chris. Suddenly Mrs. Tarai tapped on her door.

Surprised to see her standing without even a raincoat on, Samantha hastened to invite the widow in. But Mrs. Tarai shook her head, rejecting Samantha's invitation as well as her offer of a towel or a hot drink.

"I just got a phone call for you," she panted in her anxiety to speak quickly.

"Catch your breath! It's all right," Samantha urged her. She assumed that since the clinic phone was out of order, the patient who had missed his appointment had called Widow Tarai to apologize. She asked if that was the case, but Mrs. Tarai shook her head swiftly.

"No, it's an emergency," she gasped, still short of breath but determined to speak.

Samantha stiffened, her mind filled with business, her hands quick to pack equipment even as the widow relayed the message.

"I couldn't get the name, the connection was so bad," Mrs. Tarai said apologetically, "but it's up in the hills. Someone's been injured: he fell, or a tree fell on him; I'm not sure. But it sounded pretty bad.''

"Where?" Samantha asked tersely.

"Up the mountain," the widow answered quickly, referring to the island's massive extinct volcano.

Samantha thrust a pen at her. "Here, write down the directions for me," she commanded as she continued to gather her equipment together.

In a few minutes Samantha had added tourniquets and splints to the medical bag that always stood ready in a corner of the room. Scrawling a hasty note on the message board outside the clinic, she ushered Mrs. Tarai out the door ahead of her. Pausing only long enough to check the lock on the door and to grab the paper on which the widow had written directions, she raced to her car. There was no time to bother putting on chains, but she made sure they were in the back seat when she tossed in her equipment. Then, with a quick nod and a glance at Mrs. Tarai still standing in the rain, water dripping down her nose and off her dress, Samantha put the car into gear and headed toward the rounded shape of the Mountain of the Sun.

The first minutes of the trip were reassuring. The rains had eased somewhat, and the condition of the paved road through the village had at least not deteriorated. Mud washing down from the hills crossed the road in long patches, and everywhere there lay slick spots to be negotiated. But Samantha could feel her shoulders loosen as she relaxed, realizing this was no worse than she had seen before. She was beginning to get the feel of driving on the mud-slicked roads, so they no longer frightened her unduly.

Yet as she headed up the mountain, leaving the paved road behind, she admitted she had relaxed too soon. The higher she drove into the hills, the worse the road seemed to become.

If the mud slides grew narrower while she climbed steadily upward, this was more than counterbalanced by patches where there was no road, or at least none she could readily discern. Peering through the windshield, now washed with rain, now cleared for a moment by the reassuring swish of the wipers, Samantha swept the forest with her eyes, seeking the thin light line that was the road. Sometimes it was there, no longer light but still clear enough to follow; but all too often there was nothing to be seen except matted underbrush, twigs and streamlets of water careering down the slope of the mountain.

The higher she drove, the worse the conditions became. The road grew winding; it twisted and curved narrowly, oozing like a snake among trees heavy with rain, leading dangerously close to the steep edge of the mountainside. She bit her lip in her effort to follow the tortuous path ever upward. Frightening as it was to trace its winding route through the standing trees and fallen trees, over the streams and through the streams, she knew it was the only route to the distant cabin where a man waited for her help. If she lost this trail that seemed almost to try to shake her free, she would be truly lost, and so would the injured man.

Eyes narrowed in search of the road, Samantha

guided her car inches to the left, inches to the right, always moving it cautiously but steadily forward. A stump reared abruptly in the very middle of the road, and she eased her car to the left of it. A mad rivulet careered across the trail, and she pushed forward steadily through it, scarcely daring to breathe until she reached the other side and learned her decision had been correct: the water was not too deep to ford; her car had not flooded.

More than once it seemed she couldn't continue. The road, always narrow, had been cut to barely half its normal width by the fallen debris of the rains. What once had been dirt had now congealed into mud that threatened to clog the car's wheels, then force them to spin and send her flying off the road in a sickening skid that could only end when the car crashed hundreds of feet below on the valley floor.

Still Samantha pushed on, driven by her sense of duty and her determination to prove something to herself. She could do it; she could survive the hardships here and do the job she had been hired to do. All those people who had refused to hire her because she was too young, all those men who had rejected her application because she was a woman—she would show them all. And somewhere, deep in her anxious mind, another thought resided. She would show Chris he had been right to hire her. She would show him how brave she could be and how strong. Maybe he would still feel he had been wrong about her ability to judge people, but she would not let him be wrong about his decision to hire her. His judgment had been correct, and she was determined to prove that to him and to herself.

As she bit her lip in determination, Samantha suddenly realized there was no road ahead of her. The path had been washed away! She tapped the brakes quickly, carefully, knowing she could not slam them on or she would skid—into the forest or over the edge of the cliff so close beside her. Terrified, she eased the car to a stop, then clambered out to look around.

The road seemed to disappear. Ahead of her was only a rushing stream where she had remembered a dirt road to be. Either the water had washed the road away or the road lay under the stream, but in either case, she could not drive a quarter mile farther.

Samantha walked carefully to the side of the road. Clinging to the dark mushy bark of a water-soaked tree, she gazed cautiously about. To her right there were more trees, the low heavy trees of a tropical rain forest gradually giving way to the higher trees of the mountainside. But to her left all she could see was the gray veil of the rain. Here was the very side of the Mountain of the Sun, the sheer edge of the cliff along which ran the little-used road to the summit. In the rain even the sheer drop of the cliff was invisible, a hidden enemy waiting for her first mistake.

There was no choice: she had to continue on foot. Returning to the car, Samantha stopped only long enough to don a rain hat and tighten the slicker around her. Then, medical bag in one hand and a bundle of tourniquets and splints in the other, she continued on up the mountainside.

She forced herself to concentrate on her climb, picking her way carefully along the inner edge of what had been the road. She knew she had less than a mile to go, probably less than half a mile. Under other circumstances, even on the mountain that would be only a half hour's walk. But this was no pleasure hike on a sunny day.

She followed the edge of the stream, certain she would thus be tracing the normal course of the road, and in just seven or eight minutes she had cleared the worst of the washout. Once again the mud path beckoned her onward, and she sighed with relief.

Tightening her grip on her supplies, Samantha trudged along the path. The rain trickled down her hat and inside the neck of her slicker. She shivered in spite of the sultry weather, and she found herself thinking longingly of the hot bath she could indulge in when she returned to town.

All at once it struck her: she might not be able to return to town that night! With the road washed out and her car waiting half a mile from the cabin, she might have to stay with the injured man. It would depend on his condition.

"No sense in worrying about that now," she said out loud, her voice jaunty in an attempt to restore her good spirits. "If he's not hurt too badly, maybe he can make it to the car with my help. If not—well, I'll think about that later."

Those encouraging words brought her within sight of the path leading from the road to the cabin. It looked just as Mrs. Tarai had described it. A small path led off to her right, a path slightly overgrown with weeds but still clear and easy to follow. She turned up it, walking briskly now that she was within reach of her goal.

The cabin appeared like a mirage behind the gray veil of the rain. Samantha scampered up to it and climbed the three shallow steps to the door, evaluating as she went how difficult it might be to help her patient down those steps.

Later, she reminded herself with a toss of her damp curls. *First, let's get in and see how he is.*

The door gave easily to her hand. Unlocked doors no longer surprised her. She knew that some of the islanders left their cabins open and stocked with food for hikers or hunters who might need them in an emergency. Even more, Samantha was grateful the door was open, for it suggested her patient was able to walk around. But then he had managed to call her or get a message through to her, she reminded herself as she shook off her wet clothes at the entrance. That meant he had been conscious, at least a few hours ago.

"Hello," Samantha called as she pushed open the door. There was no answer. Quickly she slipped out of her slicker and hat, letting them fall unceremoniously to the floor.

"Hello?" she called again, walking uneasily into the room. Even though she knew she would be welcomed by the injured man, she still felt uncomfortable walking into someone else's home without his knowledge.

"He must have passed out," Samantha muttered to herself as she felt on the wall for a light switch. Finding one, as she expected, near the door, she flipped it up; but the room remained as dark as a cave.

"Just what I need," she breathed in exasperation. "The power's out."

She flicked on the torch she carried with her, sweeping its strong beam around the dark room. A table, a few chairs, an old sofa appeared briefly in the light, one after the other, then disappeared in the shadows as the beam passed them by. But there was no one in the room.

A second pass of the light around the room revealed a door to the right and one to the left. Following the steady beam, Samantha swiftly crossed the room to the right. There was the kitchen, compact and fairly neat, although a coating of dust lay on all the furnishings.

"Wrong side," she whispered, speaking to feel less alone. She walked quickly back across the all-purpose room she had entered first. "Not much of a housekeeper," she added as she felt her leg break a cobweb she had brushed against.

The other side of the cottage must house the bedroom, she decided. Here she expected to find the injured man, resting or perhaps unconscious from the effort it had taken him to send a message to her and then to crawl back to bed. She called out again as she entered the room, to warn him of her approach and not to frighten him if he was conscious.

"It's Dr. Hall," she cried cheerily as she approached the doorway to the bedroom.

But there was no answer to her call. And, Samantha discovered when she played her flashlight around the room, there was no one in the bed.

"What's going on?" she muttered to herself as she flashed her light quickly here and there, illuminating one by one the corners of the room in which she stood. The only other furnishings were a low chest and a straight-backed chair, both devoid of any signs of human life. There was one door still closed, and Samantha moved hastily to open it. Her nervous act revealed a closet as empty as the bed had been.

She moved quickly around the cabin once again, examining the kitchen and the living room more carefully this time. She looked behind the sofa, but there was no one lying there. She checked for another door, one that might lead to a storeroom or pantry where the injured man could have fallen, but there were no other doors. Impossible as it seemed, the cabin was empty.

Could he have tried to go outside, she wondered. Stuffing her arms into her slicker and tying her hat loosely on her head, she pushed her way out into the rain. Struggling against the wind, she worked her way around the house, thrusting aside bushes and tripping over roots and bushes that had not been cleared in a very long time.

It doesn't seem as though anyone lives here, she mused when she reached the low steps again. She climbed them heavily, anxious and perplexed, then stood quietly once she was at the doorway.

Puzzled by the lack of any signs of care outside the house, Samantha walked through the three compact rooms one more time, moving very slowly. She had been too anxious to find the injured man before and so had paid little attention to the condition of the cabin. But now she looked more closely at her surroundings, noticing for the first time that the dust in the kitchen was matched by dust in the living room and dust in the bedroom. Hanging from the corners were long tendrils of cobwebs, and more cobwebs were draped across the dusty shades on the lamps.

Yet as she studied the rooms more closely still, she realized they were more than dusty. It was not just that whoever lived in the cabin was a poor housekeeper; it seemed that no one lived here at all.

Samantha strode across the living room to the kitchen, opening cabinets to find shelves without dishes and yanking at drawers to find them empty of silverware. There were no pots, no pans, no canned goods, no preserves. The only sign of habitation she found was a single rusty spoon pushed far back in a drawer.

Quickly she crossed to the bedroom, noting as she walked through the living room the complete absence of magazines, coats, a book, a guitar—anything to indicate someone had been there recently. In the bedroom she discovered more of the same—more of nothing. The closet was empty, the bed unmade, the pillow flopped on the bare ticking of the mattress.

She bent down to touch the mattress, feeling its rough cover and playing her light over it. There were no drops of blood, no indentation where someone had rested his sore body. It was all too obvious that no one with an injury had lain on that bed in the past few hours. No one had been in this room or in the cabin for a long, long time.

Suddenly Samantha was attacked by a terrible notion. Could she have come to the wrong place? She thrust her hand into her pocket in search of the paper with Mrs. Tarai's directions. Unfolding the small sheet with hands that trembled, she stretched it on the bed and shone her light at it. No, she had followed the directions exactly. She was not in error.

Perhaps Mrs. Tarai had made a mistake, though. That was possible, but if so, there was nothing she could do up here. Not surprisingly, there was no phone in the cabin. Few of the mountain cabins had phones, and certainly not one that was rarely inhabited. If Mrs. Tarai *had* got the directions wrong, the only way Samantha would find out was to return to the village. That was the only thing she could do.

A long sigh was the only evidence of Samantha's frustration—and her exhaustion. But even those seconds seemed wasteful, and in a very few minutes she had donned her waterproof gear again and started back to her car.

As she made her way through the underbrush toward what was left of the dirt road, Samantha tried to fathom what could have gone wrong. The widow had said the phone connection was so bad she couldn't understand the caller's name. It was certainly possible she had misunderstood the directions, too. Yet if she had had any doubts she would have mentioned them to Samantha. She had not seemed at all unsure of the location of the cabin. It made no sense.

Samantha clung to the trees on the inside edge of the path as it led past the edge of the cliff. The road was, if possible, even worse than before, and her footing was less secure. She clenched her teeth in a paroxysm of fear while she fought to control that fear. Forcing herself to breathe deeply and steadily, she talked to herself encouragingly, concentrating on first her right foot and then her left. She used every trick she knew to prevent her fear from blinding her, from letting her slip.

Not until she had strapped herself securely into the dubious shelter of her car did she allow the thought that had begun in the deserted cabin to reach the surface of her mind. Then, as she sat quietly, trying to calm herself before beginning the downhill drive, she put into words the question that had haunted her frightening walk from the cabin to the car.

"Did someone send me up here deliberately? Was it all a wild-goose chase?" she asked herself in a whisper of ice. "But why?" she cried out loud. "Who would do that? Why would anyone want to?"

She forced herself not to consider the possible answers to the questions she had to ask. Time enough to look for answers when she was back in the village, when she knew for sure it had been a wild-goose chase. Right now she had something more important to do. She had to survive the storm and get back down the mountain.

Cautiously she put in the clutch and released the hand brake. Holding her breath with anticipation, she turned the key. The car coughed once, as if sputtering from the water that had poured on it all day, then the engine caught.

"So far so good," Samantha murmured to herself as she eased the car forward on the beginning of the downhill trek.

The first mile or so went more smoothly than she had dared hope. The car crawled forward, barely seeming to cover any ground. But when she looked at the changing terrain she knew she was making good progress. The trees grew denser as she moved down the mountainside. Soon she had left the fir trees behind, slipping again into the tropical rain forest where lush ferns and low bushes competed for growing space on the jungle floor. Each change in vegetation heralded her progress, and she pronounced the names of the trees and bushes she recognized when first they came into view.

It took all her courage to concentrate on the forward movement of the car, ignoring the wash of rain on the roof, the mud slicks where once there had been road, the cascading waterfalls so beautiful at a distance but now so terrifyingly close. Still she pressed on, each moment and each foot she passed giving her more courage to face what might appear around the next hairpin turn.

As she descended, it seemed as though the rain drummed ever more militantly, and Samantha knew she was not exaggerating the increasing depth of each stream she eased her car across. Before one swollen stream she had to stop to get her bearings. The road, such as it was, forked, and both paths looked equally likely—and equally dangerous. Consulting her notes, she decided the right-hand fork was correct, so she prepared to ford the rushing stream.

She eased her foot off the clutch and added pressure to the gas pedal, waiting for the car to move forward once again. But it didn't budge. The wheels spun and the car whirred in place, and the sounds she heard sickened her with fear. Quickly she eased up on the gas pedal, determined not to dig the car into the mud. Shifting the car into reverse, she tried again, lifting her foot off the clutch with infinite care and starting the smallest possible flow of gas with the lightest possible tap of her other foot on the pedal. Still the wheels spun, and the car moved only an inch backward before settling more deeply into the mud.

Again Samantha tried, and yet again, easing the car first into low, then reverse, then low again, to rock it forward and back. She tapped the gas pedal so gingerly it seemed no gas could flow, turning the steering wheel first left, then right in an effort to free the car. No matter what she did, however, the car budged no more than an inch or two. The only direction in which she seemed to make progress was the one she didn't want: downward, ever deeper into the mud.

"Damn it!" she cried at last, biting her lower lip in frustration. "I guess I'll have to walk."

Castigating herself for being foolish enough to stop the car in the mud before the stream, Samantha tied her hat tightly in place, buckled up her slicker and prepared to set out. Although she told herself she'd had no choice but to stop, since she was unsure of the route, she was too frustrated, too wet and too scared to forgive herself for her error.

She started to open the door, then paused. It was fine to say she should walk, but where should she walk to? The cabin was clearly the closest shelter, and it would do for a few hours or even a day. But there was no food, maybe not even running water, and there was no way she could contact the village. Besides, she couldn't predict how long the storm would last. It might rain for days, weeks, without pause, and she might be trapped on the mountain the whole time. No, however tempting it seemed, the cabin would not do.

She had no choice. It was farther and it would be a horribly difficult walk, but she had to go down the mountain, not up. She had to go to the village.

Her calm decision seemed perfectly reasonable until Samantha opened the door of the car and stepped out into the rain and the wind. She knew the weather had been worsening all the time she was out, but in the shelter of the car she hadn't realized the full magnitude of the storm.

Water swirled around her from her head to her feet. The wind made froths of foam on the rushing stream before her and whirled gushes of water into her eyes. Frantically Samantha held on to the door of the car, seeking in its hard surface a link to something stable, something protective in a world of nature gone berserk. But she had to leave, and she knew she had to leave quickly. The longer she delayed, the higher the streams she would have to ford, the deeper the swirling waters, the madder the wind. It was time to go.

Taking a deep breath to steady herself, she released her grip on the door of the car. However useless it was, stuck in the mud before the raging stream, it was the last familiar thing she knew. With great reluctance she forced herself to take first one agonizing step away from its sanctuary, and then another.

The wind blew at her, threatening to upset her precarious balance. She had left her medical bag in the car, knowing she would need her hands as well as her feet to make the descent. Now she grasped at first one branch and then another, stepping from bush to bush as she neared the water.

Gazing at the rushing stream before her, Samantha knew a moment of paralyzing fear. Never had she seen water churn like that down a mountain. Never had she been faced with the need to cross such a maddened stream. Yet she had to; there was no choice.

As she looked about for a foothold in the raging waters, a branch to cling to, a stump to lean on, she suddenly heard another sound over the rumble of the stream and the gushing of the water-laden wind. It was the sound of an engine—an automobile engine.

Samantha inhaled sharply, torn between joy at the thought of a companion, a rescuer perhaps, and the equally insistent notion that the car might bring more trouble. She looked about quickly, wondering whether to try to hide. But she had no time to act, for the car was coming closer every moment, its engine sputtering in the rain but sounding louder even as she tried to think about what to do.

As she stood before the silt-laden stream, frozen with fear and with hope, the car burst into view from behind the gray wall of rain. It was the Land Rover Chris used in the hills, and he was at the wheel!

Samantha sighed with relief, then waved frantically at Chris as though unsure he could see her. He halted his car just short of the raging water, slammed the door to keep out the rain and swiftly crossed the stream.

"Chris! I'm so glad to see you," Samantha shouted with joy.

"Later," he commanded, interrupting her words of thanks and relief. "We've got to get out of here."

"My things," she cried, pointing back at the car. Now that she was sure she would be safe, it seemed wrong to leave her newly stocked medical bag behind.

Chris looked at her with his hands on his hips, exasperation obvious in his eyes. "Must you—" he began, and then his eyes cleared and his face relaxed in a momentary grin. Laughingly he announced, "You want 'em, lady—you got 'em!"

Leaving Samantha standing at the edge of the

stream wondering how it was that he could stride through the water with such apparent ease, he took two or three long steps to her abandoned car. Turning to look at her with a curious expression on his face, he called back, "You locked it! Who'd you think would steal anything up here?"

Grinning weakly, Samantha dug into her pocket for the keys, then tossed them up at him. She was too relieved to think of the truth: that someone might have enticed her up the mountain in a storm and that such a person would hardly scruple to steal medical supplies.

More quickly than she could have thought of this answer, Chris had unlocked the door and retrieved her bag. In two steps he had reached her side again and stood before her with a smile. "Is that it?" he asked with exaggerated politeness. "Can we leave now?"

Nodding sheepishly, Samantha took the bag from his hands. "Thanks," she whispered.

"You hold the bag and I'll hold you," Chris instructed when they had covered the short distance to the stream.

"I think I can make it across alone," Samantha offered with a bravery she didn't quite believe.

Chris shook his head. "I've risked my life for that bag, and I don't want it to float off downstream. You'd probably make me swim after it, anyway!"

Laughing in spite of her fears, Samantha grasped the bag firmly under one arm while Chris wrapped both his strong arms around her, lifting her casually into the air. As he stepped into the swirling water, she could feel his feet search for firm places among the slippery rocks. Scared as she was, she admired the ease with which he strode across, the ease with which he carried her. And frightening as was their passage across the swollen stream, she could feel herself relaxing into the strength of his embrace.

Once across, Chris put her gently back on the ground. For a moment he looked down at her, as though he was almost reluctant to release her. But shaking himself abruptly, he motioned her toward the car.

"Let's go," he urged as she paused to shake off her drenched slicker. "The storm isn't getting any lighter."

Samantha hastened into the car, tightening her seat belt with shaking hands as Chris wiped off the moisture from the inside of the window.

"Ready?" he asked.

She nodded, all at once too weak to say a word. It was enough to sit next to Chris in the safety of his car, to leave the decisions and the problems to him.

She expected Chris to start the car immediately, but his impatience seemed to vanish; now he apparently felt no rush. He sat quietly looking at her. The open gaze of his laughing eyes gave way to a strangely veiled expression, and Samantha could feel her heart tighten as she waited for him to speak.

"What is it?" she asked at last, too uneasy to sit still.

"Why were you up there in the storm?" Chris answered her question with one of his own.

"I got an emergency call," she explained quickly.

Chris said nothing. After gazing at her for another long silent moment, he slowly withdrew his eyes from hers to stare ahead through the foggy window to the storm. Samantha couldn't fathom his expression, but he offered no words of explanation. Instead, in a silence so frustrating she could taste it, he slipped the car into gear and started to maneuver it cautiously down the muddy road.

"Chris?" she began tentatively.

His only response was to shake his head as if discouraging conversation.

"But—" she started again, only to be interrupted.

"Not now," he insisted. "I've got to pay attention to the road."

As they continued down the treacherous path, Samantha realized he was right. The conditions were far too dangerous for him to be distracted by any discussion. But she was terribly confused.

The warmth of his greeting, like his relief at finding her, had been unmistakable. It seemed he had come looking for her, since he offered no other reason for being on the mountain and since he had headed his car back toward the village as soon as she was inside it. Yet there was something wrong. He had helped her out, maybe saved her life, but he didn't trust her enough to explain what was troubling him.

He knew something about that cabin or about her trip up the mountain, and he would tell her nothing.

Was it about Felicity? Did that cabin hold special memories for him? Had it once been occupied in a way he could not—or would not—confess, and now he wanted to forget that?

All her joy at the moment of their greeting, all the pleasure she had taken from the affection in his eyes and the warm strength of his arms, threatened to disappear as swiftly as the mud below them was swirling down the mountain. She ached to be off the mountain so they could talk: somehow she would persuade him to tell her the truth. Even the worst truth about Felicity would be better than not knowing, unless the truth was that Chris still loved the sultry beauty.

Samantha shuddered, a shiver born of fear rather than cold. Although Chris glanced at her for a fraction of a second, he said not a word. As they made their way carefully down the mountain, Samantha knew she longed for the moment they could talk, but she dreaded it, too.

CHAPTER TEN

THE MINUTES PASSED SLOWLY as the car slipped and slid down the mountainside. Chris said almost nothing, concentrating on the road with absolute intentness. Aware of the ever worsening conditions, Samantha understood his silence and respected it.

Water washed down on them from above and swirled below the wheels of the Land Rover. Low branches scraped against the side of the car and bushes felled by the storm threatened to block their route to safety. Everywhere lay debris; mud clogged the gullies, and flowers curled up in protest against the violence of the assault. Not a bird could be seen or heard, although the wind would have wiped out the delicate song of any who tried to brave the storm.

More than once Samantha thought they wouldn't make it. At the least, she was sure, they would have to abandon the Land Rover and walk the rest of the way. Oddly, that thought did not frighten her. With Chris near, she felt safe.

But finally the car twisted around the last bend in the high mountain road to emerge onto the main route, the one leading to the village. Even slicked by mud, the wide road seemed a sign of civilization.

Samantha sighed. The hot bath she had dreamed about hours ago would soon become a reality. She looked forward to sinking into the soothing steamy bathwater as much as she looked forward to getting out of her soaked clothes.

All at once she realized Chris was not heading toward the village. "Where are we going?" she asked, perplexed by his route.

"To my place," he responded shortly as he maneuvered around an empty wagon stuck in the mud at the side of the road and abandoned until the rains eased.

"But I've got to get back to the clinic," she protested. "I'll be needed there if the storm continues like this."

Chris shook his head. "You won't do anybody any good if you catch a cold."

"But—" she began, only to be overruled by his swift interruption.

"My house is much closer," he explained evenly. "It'd take us at least another half hour to get to yours."

Still she looked at him, frowning in concern.

"Don't worry," he said, a hint of a smile in his voice. "I promise to take you home just as soon as you've dried off."

Flushing, Samantha could find nothing more to say. What Chris suggested was perfectly reasonable, but she felt uncomfortable nonetheless.

The silence between them remained unbroken until Chris had pulled the Land Rover up in front of the Big House and motioned Samantha to run ahead of him. Swiftly she opened the door and preceded him up the broad stairs to the house, as imposing behind its curtain of rain as it was on a starlit tropical night.

"Up the stairs to your left," he called as she hesitated in the foyer.

When she continued to stand as if too weak to move, he took a long step toward her. "Shall I carry you?" he suggested, a mocking light in his dark eyes.

"Oh, no," she murmured in confusion. "It's just...." She paused, then continued awkwardly, "Where am I going? What am I supposed to do?"

"There's a guest room at the top of the stairs, the first door to your left. You can use it to dry off, take a bath, whatever," he explained.

Samantha was too exhausted to think clearly. All the pressures of the day—the challenging ride up the mountain alone, the emergency or fake emergency for which she had been summoned, the difficult journey back down the hillside with Chris—had caught up with her, and she didn't know what to think or to say. Was she to bathe in his house, apparently empty except for him? What was she to do with her wet clothes, and what could she wear after her bath?

When Samantha continued to hesitate at the foot of the stairs, Chris grinned up at her wickedly. "You do know how to take a bath, don't you?" he asked.

She blinked in surprise at his teasing question. In her continued silence he interjected a few more telling words.

"Because if you don't, I'd be happy to help you," he suggested with a wide smile.

Before he could take a step toward her, Samantha had fled up the stairs, hearing his shout of laughter as she slammed the door of the guest room behind her.

Twenty minutes later she rose from the steaming bath reluctantly. Knowing she should return to the clinic as soon as possible, she had stripped off her clothes, hung them efficiently with a forlorn wish they might dry, filled the tub with hot water and quickly scrubbed herself until her skin glowed. At that point she could no longer maintain her resolve to be brisk and practical, and she had allowed herself to sink deep into the soothing heat of the water, feeling its warmth ripple on her skin.

Luxuriating still more, she had lazily examined her surroundings from the depths of the glistening tub. A thick pile carpet of richest brown covered the floor, and rose and white tiles climbed the walls in an intricate and irregular design. The shower curtain made a splash of rosy flowers against a white background, and towels of deep brown, rose and the purest white hung from gleaming steel racks. Just as Samantha's eyes appreciated the echoing tones of the dominant colors in all their richness, so her nostrils twitched pleasurably at the floral fragrance of the soap bubbles that tingled and broke all about her.

At last she forced herself to awaken to reality. It was time to return to the world of storms and hard work, of mysterious feelings and events she couldn't understand.

Climbing from the tub, she felt the last bubbles of

soap burst on her tingling skin. They seemed a protective coating that disintegrated minute by minute, forcing her to return to a harsh world. She knew she must go back to that world, but she ached to live out the dreams that filled her heart with longing and charged her body with unknown desires.

A glance at her blouse draped on a chair to dry showed her it was as wet as it had been when she'd placed it there. The sheen of water still made it glisten in the artificial light.

As she snuggled her right foot into the welcoming pile of the carpet, Samantha heard a knock on the door.

"Yes?" she called uneasily.

"It's me, Samantha," came Chris's strong voice.

Samantha wrapped herself in one of the thick towels, the largest she could find, and walked quickly to the door. "What do you want?" she called.

"Open up," he commanded lightly.

Samantha hesitated, acutely conscious that the towel knotted tightly around her offered only precarious covering.

"Come on, Samantha," he called impatiently. "I just want to give you something."

Reluctantly she slid the door open a crack, looking out to see Chris dripping wet, as wet as she, and dressed in no more than what she wore. His hair gleamed with the sleekness of a seal's back, and his eyes twinkled maddeningly as he acknowledged her disarray.

"I like your costume," he said with a grin. "But I

think this might be more practical," he added, holding out a large cotton garment.

"What is it?" she asked in confusion, reaching out with one hand while she clutched the knot of the towel with the other.

"A shirt," he said with a smile. "I can't offer you much else in the way of clothing, but this might just be long enough to do."

"Thank you," she returned uneasily as she stepped back into the room, preparing to close the door.

He blocked the door with his hand. "That *is* quite a costume you've got on," he said, his eyes raking her up and down.

"Chris," she warned nervously.

He laughed. "I know. You've got to get back to the clinic. You might be needed there." Having admitted that, however, he paused, looking closely into her wide eyes. "You might be, it's true. But if it wasn't for that. . . ."

Samantha could feel the warmth rising to her cheeks as he hesitated significantly. Her heart yearned for him and her body longed for the warmth of his close embrace, warmer and more soothing than the heat of the bath and infinitely more exciting.

His dark eyes shone as he looked at her, and his body swayed toward hers an almost imperceptible fraction before he spoke again with words that threatened to unnerve her.

"You're needed here, too," he said quietly. Then he stepped away from the door, leaving a wet path of footprints to show where he had walked.

Shaken by his words and his tender look, aching for him in every inch of her body, Samantha reluctantly closed the door and returned to the bathroom. The shirt Chris had given her was large, with long tails. It would cover her adequately for the drive to the clinic, especially since she could put her slicker on top of it.

Grateful for his thoughtfulness, Samantha slipped her arms into the long sleeves, pausing only to roll them up enough to be out of her way. As she buttoned the shirt from top to bottom, she knew it belonged to Chris. Soft from wear, it was apparently one of his favorites. Her skin thrilled to the touch of the cloth that once had offered his skin the same protective covering.

"Ready?" he asked a few minutes later as she emerged from the room.

Like her, Chris had toweled himself dry quickly, and his hair still glistened with water. Unlike Samantha, however, he was fully dressed in clean khaki pants and an open-collared shirt. Samantha became painfully aware of how brief a "dress" Chris's shirt had made and of how little she wore underneath.

As if he sensed her discomfort, Chris held her slicker for her without comment. As soon as she had buckled it securely, Samantha nodded briskly.

"I'm ready," she declared, moving toward the door in proof.

"Then let's go," he announced cheerfully, slipping his hand under her elbow as though he were about to escort her to a party rather than through a driving rainstorm.

"Can't your gardener take me back?" Samantha asked, suddenly realizing Chris intended to brave the storm again. "Or could I borrow a car?"

Chris shook his head. "Theo's helping out at home, and there's no car to borrow."

"I'm sorry, Chris," she exclaimed, realizing how much of his time she was taking. There were undoubtedly other problems on the island, but he had chased up the mountain after her, waited while she bathed, offered her clothes and now was going to drive her home.

He smiled as he paused before the massive door. "My pleasure," he answered with a bow of mock formality.

"But really, Chris," she protested. "You've got so much to do, and—"

"You're important, too, and I'm glad to help," he interrupted jauntily.

She flushed with happiness at his words. She could feel his breath light on her face when he leaned toward her once again. But even as she braced herself in willing anticipation of his touch, he straightened up abruptly.

"We'd better get you back," he muttered, his voice low and uneven. Pausing with one hand on the door-knob, he added, "You tempt me, Samantha Hall. You really do."

Samantha shivered at the force of his words, at his voice that radiated tenderness and passion, affection and power.

As he swung the door open to the world once more, Chris shifted the subject. He joked with her as they walked outside, announcing, "It's still raining," as though he had made a momentous discovery. He talked as if he was not racked with the same feelings that stunned her, but the quaver in his voice gave him away.

Although the ride to the village was accomplished in near silence, Samantha felt perfectly comfortable. From time to time she glanced at Chris, not to seek in his face confirmation of what she had heard in his voice but simply to take pleasure in looking at him. She could feel the light pressure of his arm against hers as he leaned forward to shift gears. She could sense the heat rising from his body in spite of the dampness and the rain. More than once, when she glanced at his face, she caught his eyes, his dark sparkling eyes searching for her own. In spite of the hazardous road conditions, it seemed Chris could no more ignore her than she could ignore him.

In what seemed like minutes they had reached Samantha's house. Chris didn't hesitate at the car but walked in beside her.

"We could both stand something to eat," he announced once they were out of the rain.

"There's some soup in the refrigerator," Samantha suggested. "And I've got cheese and fruit, too."

"Fine," he nodded. "It'll heat the soup while you change."

Samantha hesitated, thinking it was her home and therefore her responsibility to cook. But Chris interjected lightly, "Don't you think you should get dressed? Someone might come by, after all, and you are, hmm—" he hesitated, grinning "—shall we say you're 'interestingly attired'?"

For the second time that afternoon Samantha fled up the stairs to Chris's joyous laugh. But this time, embarrassed as she was, she shared his joy.

When she returned to the kitchen a few minutes later, however, she could sense that Chris's mood had changed. The light had dimmed in his eyes, and his greeting was no more than a perfunctory suggestion that they eat at once.

Samantha tried to make conversation during the quick meal, but Chris barely responded to her questions about the damage the rains were creating on the island. Only when she had cleared the table did he really start to talk. Then, to her dismay, his voice turned cold; once again, as so often before, he seemed determined to keep something from her.

He began with what seemed an innocuous enough question, but his tone undercut the potential concern in his words. "Why did you go up the mountain alone? Didn't you know it would be dangerous?"

Samantha replied calmly, although her heart beat painfully fast in its effort to keep pace with his shifting moods. "I had a patient to see," she explained quietly. She tried to justify his apparent accusation of carelessness by telling herself he might resent her taking chances, perhaps because she had unwittingly forced him to come to her aid. Although that could explain his annoyance, his reaction still was unfair.

Even as Samantha tried to fathom his motivations,

Chris spoke again. "A patient?" he asked in an odd tone. "Who was it?"

"I don't know," Samantha responded innocently.

Chris seemed incredulous. "You went to see a patient whose name you didn't know?"

Samantha nodded, bridling at his tone but struggling to speak evenly. "Mrs. Tarai took the message for me," she began, interrupting herself to explain. "The clinic phone was out because of the storm."

"Yes?" Chris prompted impatiently.

"Well, the connection wasn't very good, I guess, because she only learned that someone—some man— was injured and needed my help," Samantha concluded quietly.

"Some man?" Chris asked. "You don't know who it was?"

"No," she responded, and her voice revealed anger at last as she continued, "I still don't know who it was."

Chris hesitated, looking at her curiously. "You mean you never saw the man?"

She shook her head, frustration obvious in the furrows above her eyes. "No, I don't know if I went to the wrong place or what, but there wasn't any injured man at the cabin."

For a moment there was silence, each of them mulling over independent but apparently painful thoughts. When Chris spoke again, it seemed he was finally willing to reveal something he had hidden, and his tone was no longer brusque. But his words were shocking.

"You mean Pete Thompson wasn't up there?"

Samantha looked at him with the startled eyes of a fawn. "Pete Thompson?" she asked in perplexity.

"That's what I said," Chris responded grimly.

"No," Samantha asserted quickly. "I didn't see Pete there. I didn't see anyone!"

"You're sure? No signs of anyone?" Chris's gaze was probing and deep, his eyes flashing dark fire.

As annoyed as she was puzzled, Samantha replied testily, "Of course I'm sure. Do you think I'd go on a wild-goose chase like that for fun? I don't even know if there's someone else lying in a cabin up in the hills waiting for me now!"

When Chris didn't answer but only turned his face away from her, biting his lip in thought, Samantha lost her patience.

"What is it? What's wrong?" she asked.

Chris rose swiftly and walked to her side. Pausing with his hands on his hips, he stared down at her for a long moment. Then the tense light in his eyes gave way to a softer look, a look of warm concern. Samantha could feel the icy band about her chest melting in the warmth of that gaze, and she began to breathe normally again.

"I know this is hard for you," Chris said softly, stroking her damp hair with a gentle hand. "I just don't want to make it worse."

"The worst is not to know, Chris," Samantha breathed.

The lean man nodded firmly, but for a long moment he said nothing, just holding her in gentle connection by the tender touch of his hand.

Samantha sat in absolute stillness as he ran his hand over her hair again and again. She could feel the anger and the pain being stroked out of her, and with them, too, went the last of the terror from her trip into the hills. Minutes passed as they stayed like that, she sitting, he hovering over her, gentling her as if she were a skittish colt.

Finally Chris stepped back with a sigh, gazing at Samantha for a long moment before he resumed his seat across the table. His fingers played with the coffee mug before him in a silence neither could break. At last he began to speak, his arms resting on the table and his eyes following her earnestly as he told his story.

"I came by here about one. I knew your phone was out of order, so I thought you might need something," he began.

A warm glow began to spread through Samantha's body as she listened to Chris's quiet voice. "Thanks," she interjected softly.

The words seemed wholly inadequate for all the care Chris had provided that day, but he sloughed it off with a shrug. Quickly he resumed his story, as though she had not interrupted at all.

"I saw your message on the board outside," he continued, nodding vaguely in the direction of the message board Samantha always used when she left the clinic unattended.

Chris grimaced, and Samantha looked at him curiously. "I should say I saw what was left of your message," he explained. "Most of it had washed away."

Samantha bit her lip, but Chris went on without giving her a chance to speak. She made a quick mental note to come up with something better than a chalkboard for messages in the rainy season, then let the thought slip in the tension of the moment.

"I could make out enough to realize you'd gone into the hills and...." For the first time since he'd reseated himself to tell his tale, Chris hesitated, and his eyes dropped away from Samantha's. When he continued she had the distinct impression that he'd decided not to tell her the whole truth.

"I figured Mrs. Tarai would have brought you the message, so I went over there. I thought she might know where you were."

"I tried to leave directions on the board," Samantha defended herself.

"Yes," Chris admitted. "But they puzzled me."

"Puzzled you?" she echoed.

Chris seemed not to hear the question in her tone but went on quickly with his story. "Mrs. Tarai gave me the directions she'd given you, and I decided I'd better follow you."

Although some vague feeling warned her not to ask, Samantha had to know. "Why?" she queried gently.

Again Chris hesitated, and again his answer was less than satisfying. "I thought you might need some help if the injured man was hurt badly," he said.

Samantha sat quietly. There was something false about Chris's story, but she couldn't put her finger on it. He could have asked Charlie Tuatara to send someone after her; the policeman had deputies trained for such events. But it was more than that. At last she asked evenly but with an intent to probe, "Is that all?"

Chris shrugged off the question. "I've had some first-aid training, you know."

"I know," Samantha acknowledged. "But. . . ." She paused, unsure what to say, only sure that Chris had not told her everything he had thought. His anger and tension earlier in the conversation lingered in her mind. What he had said didn't justify either anger or such tension. Something was missing.

Remembering one of his earlier remarks, Samantha tried again. "Why did you say my directions puzzled you?"

"Oh, I just couldn't make them out," Chris responded casually.

Suddenly Samantha rose from her seat, walking swiftly toward the door.

"Where are you going?" Chris asked, pushing his chair back with a decisive movement.

"I want to see the message board," she replied evenly. "I want to see how much of the directions had washed away."

Chris motioned her back to her seat with a sigh. "All right," he exclaimed. "They weren't that bad."

"Well, then?" she probed, determined to get to the bottom of this, convinced that there she would find the solution to Chris's strange inconsistent moods.

Chris looked at her with hooded eyes. "The cabin you described is uninhabited," he said at last.

Samantha nodded brusquely. "I know," she responded quietly. Again she was knifed by the thought that the cabin might once have been shared by Chris and Felicity. But Chris's voice overpowered even that painful image.

"You knew that? Then why did you go?" he insisted.

"I know it now," she explained. "I didn't know it then." Quickly she told him of her fruitless trip up the mountain, her careful search in and around the cabin, her fears that she'd been sent on a false errand.

"I don't understand it, Chris," she concluded a few minutes later. "Could Mrs. Tarai have got the message wrong?"

"I don't think so," he answered solemnly, grimly.

The pause that followed his words grated on Samantha. Finally she asked the question that concerned her most.

"Do you think there's someone up the hills, in some other cabin? Someone who needs me?" Her voice quavered as she spoke.

Chris shook his head. "No, I think you went to the right place. We'd have heard by now if someone was missing or injured. Somebody would let us know," he reassured her.

Samantha frowned. "I don't understand, Chris.

You think Mrs. Tarai took the message down properly, and you think I went to the right place." She paused in thought, then cried out, "But there wasn't anyone there!" She turned to look at him, pleading with her wide eyes. "What's it all about?"

For a moment Chris said nothing. It seemed his gaze met her own reluctantly, as though he wanted still to hide the truth from her. But at last he spoke again.

"The cabin used to be Pete Thompson's," he announced quietly. "He used it for fishing, hunting, that kind of thing. He didn't live in it regularly, but it was usually pretty well stocked."

Samantha bit her lip in confusion. "Pete Thompson," she echoed. "But why would I . . . ?"

Her sentence trailed off, and in the silence that followed she was suddenly assailed by a thought too painful to put into words immediately. She remembered the night Pete had come to the clinic, and she remembered all too well Chris's strange reaction at seeing her with the other man. She let the suspicion grow, and as it did it seemed her sense of understanding grew, too. Finally she could wait no longer. Gazing at her fingers as they played nervously on the table, she spoke in a low voice.

"Is that why you asked me if I knew whose cabin it was?" She paused, but she had to go on. "Is that why you wondered about my going up the mountain alone?" Still staring at her entwined fingers, she refused to meet his gaze.

Exhaling sharply, Chris reached across the table to

grasp her restless fingers with his own. He held her hands silently for a moment, until she had to look up at him. Locking her eyes with his steady gaze, he said softly, "I was worried about you. Can't you understand that?"

Samantha sighed deeply. "Yes," she admitted. "But you seemed so angry, I thought, well...." Again her voice trailed off. She couldn't put into words the thought that had assailed her, the thought that Chris had believed she would go up the mountain to meet Pete Thompson, that she had an appointment—even an assignation—with him.

Chris understood without her speaking. Shaking his head soberly, he looked at her for a long moment before answering. But his words offered total reassurance. "I never believed Pete that night," he said quietly. "I just wanted him to think I might have."

Relieved as she was, Samantha couldn't ignore the fact that Chris still hadn't explained everything, including why he might want Pete to believe such a lie. But he seemed to be genuinely concerned for her, and that thought melted the tiny remnants of the storm's chill in her heart. Maybe he had followed her up the mountain because he would help any islander he thought was in danger, but somehow she doubted that. Samantha's heart told her what her head tried to ignore: that Chris had followed her because he cared about her, cared enough to leave his work and risk his life for her.

The thought was warming, and knowing the answer to just one question relieved some of the tension

Samantha had lived in all through the long day. But even though one puzzle seemed to be solved, another remained. Why had she been called to the cabin? Although she was loath to endanger the precious mood that had come with Chris's last words, she felt she needed answers to the questions that lingered. Reluctantly she spoke up again.

"Do you think Pete's been hurt? But then, where was he? And if he wasn't hurt, why do you suppose he had me called to the cabin?"

Chris shrugged. "I'm not sure. I don't think he was injured or he'd still have been there. And you said there were no signs anyone had been there recently." He looked at her sharply, turning the statement into a question by his glance.

"That's right," she affirmed quickly, safe on factual ground again. "The place looked deserted—no, unused. As though no one had been there in ages."

"Then I don't understand it," Chris admitted. "Unless. . . ." It was his turn to hesitate uncertainly.

Samantha finished the sentence for him, confident now that he had never doubted the truth about her encounter with Pete in the clinic. "Unless he wanted to get me alone up there?" she asked, shivering at the thought of the danger she might have been in.

Chris nodded. "But I don't believe that," he said quickly.

"Are you trying to make me feel good?" Samantha asked lightly.

"No," Chris answered solemnly, "I'm telling you what I believe. Pete can be difficult, even malicious.

But he's not a bad man; he's not violent. I don't think he's really dangerous.''

"Then why would he have sent the message about the injury?'' she persisted.

"I'm not sure.'' Chris spoke in a meditative voice. "But if he's the one who's been creating trouble in the clinic, then this fits the pattern. He's just making mischief, trying to harass you.''

"He's succeeding, not trying,'' Samantha said glumly.

His quick smile was sympathetic. "Yes, and he's harassing me, too.''

Samantha looked up at him.

"He keeps me busy,'' Chris explained. "I have to chase down supplies for you, chase up mountains for you. . . .''

Samantha's eyes dropped, but before she could speak in apology, Chris laughed out loud. "I don't mind,'' he insisted. "But there are better things I could do with my time, better things we could do together.''

Samantha tried to change the subject. "Have there been other incidents around the island?'' she asked. "Incidents he might have caused?''

"Some,'' Chris admitted, but he would say nothing more about them. After a moment he added a quiet warning. "Remember, we don't really know if it was Pete who enticed you up the mountain. We don't know if he's responsible for any of this.''

"We don't *know*,'' Samantha agreed, "but it's a pretty good guess.''

"It is," Chris acknowledged solemnly.

"So what do we do?" she asked into the void of their silence.

"*You* don't do anything," was his sharp reply.

Surprised, Samantha looked at Chris across the table.

"You do your work and take care of yourself," he insisted. "I'll handle Pete Thompson."

Samantha's eyebrows rose quickly at his patronizing words. "I can help," she asserted with pride.

Chris smiled quizzically. "Yes, by leaving it to me." When she continued to glower at him, he added with a sigh, "Look, Samantha, you've got a lot to do here—"

"So do you," she inserted hastily.

Chris nodded, admitting the truth of what she said. But as he continued to speak, his tone made clear that he wanted her to keep out of this as much as she could. "I know Pete Thompson. He's my problem—mine and Charlie's. You leave him to us."

Samantha recognized in Chris the same proud independence she felt in herself, and silently she admitted he had the greater right, even the greater ability, to deal with Pete.

"Good, that's settled," Chris finished briefly. "But tonight Pete's not here," he added with pleasure. Rising in a leisurely manner from the table, he stretched luxuriously and continued speaking in languorous tones. "There were no messages on your board, there weren't any patients waiting outside, and there's nothing else I must do." Smiling at her across the table, he stretched out his hands toward her and concluded, "We've got some time for ourselves tonight."

Samantha reached across the short distance between them to take his hands in her own. "It's pretty late," she murmured.

"It is, and I won't stay long," he responded softly, drawing her toward him around the sharp edge of the table. "I just want to forget for a few minutes that there are people out there who need us, and one person who wants to create problems. I want to forget there's a storm raging outside."

He slipped his arms gently around her, stroking her back as he pulled her closer to him, so close that she had to snuggle her head against his chest. All the while his voice continued, a low and tender murmur reaching through her ears and mind into her heart.

"I just want to hold you for a moment," he said softly. "I want this to be the whole world...just us, just this room."

Samantha sighed with pleasure as she felt his heartbeat throb through her. Shyly she stretched her arms around his back, embracing him and drawing him close. Her cheek pressed into his chest, a button leaving its mark on her delicate skin, the lines of his ribs strong and hard under the thin layer of protective flesh.

They said not a word. None was necessary. It was enough just to feel so close to another person, so close and warm and secure. All the doubts that had assailed Samantha in the past vanished in the tenderness of Chris's embrace. Passion was not far away, but for a moment it, too, was stilled, and they knew a peace as perfect as it was rare, as wonderful as it was fleeting. Perhaps it couldn't last, but for the moment it was enough.

It was Samantha who broke the silent embrace. Exhaustion had taken its toll on her that day, and she exhaled with a sound that was half sigh, half yawn.

"Tired?" Chris held her away from him to look at her sympathetically.

"A little," she acknowledged reluctantly, loath to release him from their tender embrace.

"Let's sit down," he suggested gently. Without another word he led her into the living room and eased her into a seat close beside him.

Samantha rested against the arm that wrapped her shoulders securely. With a sigh more of pleasure than sleepiness, she eased her head back against Chris's shoulder.

"Comfortable?" he whispered, his breath soft against her ear.

She nodded. "I could stay like this forever," she admitted.

"Only till my arm falls asleep," Chris warned with an affectionate smile.

For a few minutes they spoke easily, desultorily. It didn't matter what they said. They spoke of everything and of nothing, hearing only the sound of each other's voice, not the words or the ideas expressed. Chris's voice was low and resonant in Samantha's ears. It was a soothing voice, a rich voice that vibrated to the depths of her consciousness. She let the words wash past her, hearing only the rich resonance of the beloved voice.

Suddenly she realized Chris had said something about Felicity. "What did you say?" she asked abruptly.

Chris smiled quietly. "Weren't you paying attention?" he teased her.

Samantha shook her head. "I guess not," she said, struggling to keep the tension out of her voice. "You said...?" she prompted.

Smiling patiently, Chris repeated his comment. "I said there's still no word about Felicity. I've had people asking all over Halekai and up north through the islands."

Samantha stiffened at this proof of his cruelty. He had been talking about Felicity, as though she could care what happened to the girl. It didn't seem to occur to Chris that she might object to his caring what happened to Felicity, his continuing concern for his former mistress.

How dared he speak of that woman, his lover, while he was embracing Samantha! What kind of man would hold one woman in his arms and talk about another! Angrily Samantha drew away from Chris, her body suddenly stiff and cold.

"What is it, Samantha?" Chris asked, concern obvious in his voice.

She couldn't speak. Silently she shook her head, drawing still farther away from him on the sofa.

"What's the matter?" he asked again.

Samantha glared at him. How could he pretend he didn't understand? He cared for her, it seemed: he had demonstrated that in the storm. But he could still think it was perfectly all right to care for Felicity at the same time. If he chased up a mountain for her, he chased all over the islands for another woman.

"You know what's wrong," she hissed in proud anger.

He stared at her, incomprehension clouding his eyes. Suddenly he seemed to understand. Rising abruptly from his seat, he glowered down at her, his dark eyes smoldering.

"Is it that old thing again, Samantha?" he asked impatiently. "I thought you'd outgrown that."

"Outgrown it?" she echoed, rising to her feet in fury.

"All right," he hastened to soothe her. "Bad word choice." He paused for only a few seconds before continuing in a strong clear voice, "But I thought we'd got past all that. . . all that petty jealousy."

"You call it petty?" she seethed at him.

"You don't?" he retaliated in growing anger. Gazing down at her, he seemed about to grab her with his strong hands once more. Instead he sighed, hesitating before speaking once more. "No," he said in a resigned tone, "I guess you don't."

"Should I?" she asked sarcastically.

He looked at her with an expression she couldn't understand. "You'll only believe what you want to, Samantha. I can't change that."

Samantha stood quietly, her hands clenched into

fists by her side. She could think of no way to express her doubts and her confusion, her hopes and her fears all at once, so she said nothing. Into the silence came Chris's final words.

"I can't change what you think, Samantha. And sometimes, when you're like this, I don't even want to try."

Those few words, full of anger, frustration and pain, echoed long after Chris had stalked across the room and closed the door firmly behind him. Samantha braced herself for the bang when he crossed the threshold, but he didn't give himself the pleasure or the release of slamming the door. It was as if he, like her, was too drained even for that act of defiance, that final passionate statement.

CHAPTER ELEVEN

THE RAIN CONTINUED. Hour after hour it poured from the skies as though it would never stop. The wind dropped, its ceaseless howling replaced by the steady drumbeat of the rain. Days passed, wet morning followed by wetter afternoon and then by the blackest night, and still the rain continued.

Samantha saw nothing of Chris during the next few days. She worked in the clinic catching up on charts, since many patients canceled their routine appointments. Stacks of old medical journals she had stored for a quiet day confronted her, but all they could do was make her feel vaguely guilty. She had neither the energy nor the discipline to study.

The days passed slowly, the nights were bleak. Many an hour when she could have been doing paperwork or reading, Samantha gazed sightlessly out the window into the gray wash of the unending rain. More than one night she lay awake long after climbing into her bed, wearily listening to the rain beat taps on the roof. And still she heard nothing from Chris. It seemed to Samantha as if she was in suspension, merely waiting without volition or purpose.

One afternoon as she sat lackadaisically at her window with a journal resting on her lap, the lights in the clinic suddenly sputtered, then flickered out. The gray haze outside offered little illumination, certainly not enough light to read by. So, nervous and grateful for an excuse to leave the clinic, Samantha decided to go to Mrs. Tarai's. Scrawling a quick note on her message board, now protected from the rain with a wooden cover, she sloshed along the street to the widow's.

Even in the dark and without their usual cups of steaming coffee, Samantha found comfort in sitting quietly with Mrs. Tarai. The plump woman took her in like a waif, and her casual certainty that the power would soon be back was a tonic to Samantha's overwrought nerves.

"The generator's out; that's all, my dear," said Mrs. Tarai, patting Samantha's hand comfortingly.

"The generator that supplies the whole island?" she asked in fear.

The widow nodded. "It probably was damaged by the storm," she explained.

"But the rain could go on for days," Samantha anxiously pointed out.

"It's all right, dear," came the soothing reply. "There's a backup generator. We should have power again in just a little while."

Samantha tried to imitate the plump woman's casual air of unconcern, but she found it difficult. Her nerves, already taut because of the fight with Chris, seemed pulled as tight as the strings of a violin, pulled to a tension at which they must soon break. No lights, no electric power, and still the rains came down.

The power had not returned an hour later when Samantha buckled her slicker around her to walk back to the clinic. She held on to the widow's final reassuring words as the two women said goodbye before opening the door to the gray wet world.

"Any minute now, you'll see," Mrs. Tarai reiterated as she shook Samantha's hand in parting.

Samantha nodded in thanks in a last effort to appear comforted, then headed back through the rain to the clinic, lighting her way with a lantern borrowed from Mrs. Tarai, so dark had it grown even in the late afternoon.

Back home, Samantha tried to read by flashlight, fighting to remind herself that this was only an ordinary power failure, that there was a supplementary generator, that everyone on the island was surrounded by the same daytime dusk that surrounded her, that workers were undoubtedly trying to solve the problem even as she thought about it. But still her uneasiness grew; still her nerves pulled ever more taut. Minutes passed, then hours, and still the island was in darkness. Whatever the emergency generator was supposed to do, it did not seem to be doing it.

As night fell, the darkness intensified. Samantha had only her flashlight and a few candles for illumination, so after a cold early dinner she decided she might as well try to catch up on sleep.

Even her bed seemed hot and damp. The humidity

in the room had risen steadily with the long days of rain, and the sheets felt uncomfortably heavy. She tossed restlessly from one side to the other for more than an hour before she finally dozed off. But the sleep, however slow in coming, was doubly welcome. She needed the rest, and she needed the escape sleep brought.

Samantha had been asleep for several hours when she was aroused by a loud knocking at the clinic door. "What...?" she muttered in confusion as she jerked awake. She had no time to sit in bed and wonder, for the pounding was as loud and continuous as it was frantic.

"I'm coming!" she shouted, reaching for her robe. As she raced down the stairs she knew her cry had been useless; she couldn't have been heard over the rain, let alone the knocking. But the sound was so frantic she'd felt compelled to respond as quickly as she could.

Still pulling the tie on her robe with her left hand, she yanked open the door with her right, swinging it wide to the rainy night. Three men stood there, supporting the inert body of a fourth. Even as she reached forward to look at the man they carried, she heard Chris's voice. She raised her head to meet his eyes for an instant, and in that instant she caught a glance of understanding. Then she was all business again, as was Chris.

"It's Pete Thompson," Chris shouted over the splash of the rain. "He's been hurt, and he's been out in this for some time."

Without another word Samantha led the men into the examining room. Two of Chris's workers joined him in bearing the limp form to the table.

"Up here," she directed efficiently, shining her flashlight to show them how to place Pete on the table. "What happened?" she asked tersely as she began her first hasty examination of the injured man.

"Here, Tom. Mark, light over there." Chris paused only to position his two helpers with lanterns before answering Samantha's question. Then, as he added the beam of his flashlight to the steady dull glow of the lanterns they had lighted, he explained quickly, "A couple of us went up to the emergency generator with Charlie Tuatara to find out why it wasn't working." He was still panting from all the effort and the rush. "That's where we found Pete. Charlie's up there now, directing repairs."

Samantha looked up sharply for a moment. Chris nodded, his lips pursed. "Yes," he answered her unspoken question. "He may have knocked out the main generator—he probably did. Anyway, he was sure working on the backup."

Samantha bent quickly to her task again, forcing herself to think of Pete not as a troublemaker but simply as a human being who needed her help, a patient. All her professional training came to her aid, but it was still difficult not to be angry.

Chris's breathing returned to normal. "We can't be sure exactly what he was up to, but he'd climbed the fence around the emergency generator and was inside the protected area."

"I don't see signs of electrical burns," Samantha noted.

Chris shook his head. "I didn't think so. We found him unconscious, out cold on the ground. He might have fallen, knocking some equipment off with him, or maybe he was just prowling around and something fell. But when we found him he was pinned under a steel rod."

Samantha winced. "That explains his leg," she said, gingerly pulling aside the trousers she had cut with a single swift motion.

"Broken?" Chris leaned over to look.

"Compound fracture," she responded. "And he's lost a lot of blood, though all the bleeding seems to have stopped—for now at least." She took a single step back from the table, placing her hands on her hips and looking down at the battered body stretched helplessly before her. "I don't suppose there's any way we can get him to Halekai?" she asked Chris wistfully, knowing in advance what his answer had to be.

"Not in this rain," came the quiet response.

"Well, then, there's no choice, is there?" Samantha's question was purely rhetorical. She knew she had no choice, and neither did Pete Thompson. She would have to do the best she could, and her best was all the medical care the injured man could hope for, perhaps for many days.

Although her question required no answer, Samantha was grateful for Chris's confidence in her. "There's no choice," he echoed simply, and his tone suggested that Pete was in good hands, that there was no need for another choice.

She began to gather her equipment together, thinking quickly of what she would need. As she prepared a table with all the drugs and instruments she was likely to use, she talked steadily, using the sound of her apparently calm voice to take her mind off her fears.

She directed Chris's assistants, Tom and Mark, to place their lanterns where they would offer the greatest amount of light for her work, then she showed them how to shine their flashlights directly at the operating field. Tom and Mark would provide the only lights she would have throughout the surgery, and Chris would be her only assistant.

"Your first-aid training is about to be tested," Samantha quipped to Chris as she began to scrub for the operation. She pointed to the soap and scrub brush as he stood waiting. "You'd better scrub, too. I'm not sure what you'll end up doing," she admitted as Chris hesitated before the sink.

"Anything I can," he responded quickly.

"I know that," she answered softly. "I'm glad you're here."

"Not half as glad as I am that you're here," he whispered to her while reaching across to hand her a towel.

With Chris's words ringing in her ears, Samantha approached the table on which Pete Thompson lay still unconscious.

"I hate to give him morphine when he's already

out," she commented, "but once I get started he'll come around fast enough."

She paused, then looked up at the three men waiting silently for her directions. Chris was right: he would help in any way he could, and she knew Tom and Mark would, as well. But they could only assist her. It was up to her to make all the decisions, to take all the actions; and a man's life depended on her.

Drawing in one final deep breath, she began to speak. "After I start the IVs and cover up that leg with a sterile bandage, I'm going to check for abdominal bleeding; then I'll get to work on the head wound—cleaning it, sewing it up. If there's no abdominal bleeding, that's the only one that might bleed again, and he can't afford any additional blood loss. Next I'll check his leg, reduce the fracture, get it in a cast. Then I can clean up any other lacerations, and we can move him a little to check for other injuries." She paused, looking at each of them in turn. "Okay? Any questions?" Again she paused, giving them a chance. When no one spoke she asked one last time, "Are you ready to start?"

The three men nodded solemnly, and Chris gave her a quick thumbs-up sign. "Just tell us what to do, doc," he said with a jaunty smile.

"I'll tell you what I'm doing, or going to do, as we go along." She spoke calmly to reassure her assistants and herself. "First I'm going to start two IVs. I'll have to push fluids into him." Biting her lip in frustration, she added, "It'll have to be saline and water, with Dextran for a plasma expander, since I can't type and cross blood. And an antibiotic to prevent infection. I'll start two million units of penicillin. No morphine for now.''

All the time she spoke, Samantha's hands were busy. Turning to Chris she added, ''I'll use a local for the head wound, but I'll have the narcotics all set up to go. As soon as he begins to move, and I mean the least twitch, you'll have to inject the morphine into the IV. Here's the syringe.'' She glanced quickly at Chris, who nodded to show he understood what she wanted.

''I wish I had something better for an anesthetic,'' she muttered as she slapped the back of Pete's hand to raise a vein. Slipping the needle into the nearly flaccid vein, she acknowledged what the facts were. ''I don't have anything else, so this had better work!'' She checked the flow of the intravenous before taping the needle securely into place, then repeated the procedure on his other hand.

''Okay, that's done.'' Turning to Chris she cautioned him, ''Watch the blood pressure carefully. I want to hear about every change. Okay?''

''Right,'' he replied smartly. ''That I can do.''

Samantha nodded. A sympathetic thought floated through her mind that this must be nearly as frustrating for Chris as it was for her. Both of them knew how limited her equipment was, how hampered she was in her work. He had to feel very nearly helpless as he watched and waited for her commands. And she—she could only think of the well-stocked hospital in Halekai, the proper drugs and the fancy machines, the trained nurses and anesthesiologists and surgeons who could do what she was trying to do in half the time and with twice the grace. But there was no choice. And, she reminded herself as she draped a sterile bandage over Pete's crushed leg, there was no time even for sympathetic thoughts.

Once the leg was protected by its sterile drape, she examined Pete carefully for abdominal bleeding. Finding no evidence of an internal injury, she then turned her attention to the wound on his forehead. It had obviously bled profusely when he'd been injured, but the bleeding had stopped some time before. She injected a little Novocain around the wound, then waited briefly for it to take effect. Finally she was ready to set to work.

As she vigorously scrubbed the wound and lined up the edges of skin to suture them closed, she spoke to the three men, first telling them what she was doing and then voicing one of her concerns.

"Do you have any idea how long he'd been lying there? It would make a difference to how I'd treat his leg if I knew," she explained as she deftly tied off the first stitch.

Chris shook his head. "Five hours? Six? I'm not sure," he answered.

"It can't have been more than three or four hours, Mr. Girard," Mark broke in for the first time. "Charlie had my boy check around there earlier, and he didn't see anyone."

"Are you sure?" Samantha asked eagerly. "It really matters."

"I'm sure, Dr. Hall," Mark nodded, secure in his knowledge and proud to be able to help. "You couldn't have missed Pete if you were anywhere near the generator, and my boy was patrolling up there. He's pretty careful, too."

"That's true," Chris agreed. "If he says Pete wasn't lying there, he wasn't." Chris paused for a moment of thought. "I suppose Pete could have been hiding nearby, but he wasn't at the generator and he hadn't been injured. And that's all you care about, right?"

"Right," Samantha echoed, grateful that at least one problem was solved for her. "Now I can go ahead and take care of that leg properly. Thanks, Mark." Above her white mask, her eyes smiled briefly at the man who held the flashlight with such steady patience.

"Okay. That finishes one part," she announced a few minutes later as she set aside the first group of instruments. "Now to the leg."

She moved quickly to the other end of the narrow table, motioning to line the lights up properly again. For a few moments she worked quietly to complete her preliminary examination of the broken leg, checking the pulse in the ankle and top of the foot to see if the circulation was adequate, then testing for nerve and muscle damage as best she could. Finally she straightened up from the table, stretching to ease her cramped muscles.

"That all seems fine," she announced. "Let's get to it."

Working together, Samantha and Chris shaved the leg and washed it thoroughly with a strong soap, being careful not to injure the wound further. Since Pete's blood pressure had remained stable, she was able to give him some more morphine.

"This is going to be the bad part, so let's keep him quiet," she warned as she changed her gloves, gathered her instruments and prepared to work on the wound.

Tom directed the beam of his light at the center of the open wound, and Mark moved around behind Samantha to shine his light over her shoulder. Chris watched the blood pressure, handed Samantha instruments as she called for them and sometimes anticipated her needs. But in spite of their steady assistance and calm support, Samantha felt very much alone.

Carefully she began to snip away at the tissue around the opening. "What I'm doing is debriding the wound," she explained. "Getting rid of anything that's hopelessly damaged."

She grew silent as she excised the last of the damaged skin. Putting aside the instruments she'd been using, she motioned to Chris to help her drape the leg again with a clean sterile covering. Then she picked up her scalpel. She had to enlarge the incision in the skin in order to expose the broken bone.

Cautiously she probed inside the wound, examining the ends of the bone carefully. She removed the small fragments she found, lining up the larger ones to help the bone in its process of mending.

As she searched for any remaining fragments of tissue or bone, she explained, "The greatest risk is infection. That's the real problem, not the fracture itself."

She probed cautiously around the site of the fracture, talking sporadically. "I've got to clean out the wound, get out all the debris. Then, if I just line the bones up properly, the leg will pretty much heal itself."

While she spoke her hands were constantly busy, searching, moving, lifting, working. At last she had finished cleaning out the wound.

"Okay, Tom. Give your light to Mark for a moment; I want you to pull on that leg when I tell you to."

"Pull on the leg?" Tom asked in astonishment.

She nodded. "That way I can line up the broken bones."

Quickly demonstrating what she wanted done, Samantha asked Chris to double-check Pete's condition, then while Tom pulled on the leg she aligned the broken bones as they slid apart. Finishing up her work with the torn muscles, as well, she washed the wound one last time before preparing to close it. Cautiously she drew the skin together, closing the wound by lining up the edges of skin, being careful not to pull them too tightly.

"That's it," she breathed at last when she had put the last neat stitch in place. "Let's get the plaster ready."

Stretching with relief at her first break in nearly an

hour of painstaking work, Samantha directed the three men in preparing the materials to make the cast. The fracture was bad enough and the swelling marked enough to require several thicknesses of sheet wadding under the plaster cast, and she placed those with care. Then she began to wind the wet sticky material that would harden into a cast around the injured leg, struggling to prevent its slightest movement.

"Don't you cover the toes, too?" Mark asked, made bold by their successes so far.

Samantha shook her head, continued to wind the fabric with its sticky plaster coating around the leg. "We keep the toes out so we can check the circulation as the leg heels," she explained.

Tom interrupted, "You mean if the toes get purple?"

"Yes, or if they're cold," she nodded. "We can test for muscle and nerve injuries later, too. Once Pete's awake I can ask him to wriggle his toes or I can see if he senses a pinprick on his foot. That way I can keep track of how he's doing, find out if the bandage is too tight, all sorts of things."

Mark subsided, obviously impressed more by this one small detail he could comprehend than by all the use of drugs and instruments he couldn't fathom.

A few minutes' more work completed setting the leg, and Samantha was ready to turn to the minor lacerations Pete Thompson had suffered. She washed with care once more while Tom and Mark cleaned up the operating area and at her direction Chris reviewed the instruments. Every minute or so he walked back to the examination room to take Pete's blood pressure and check his pulse, calling the results in to Samantha.

Returning to her patient, Samantha reviewed his vital signs for herself before beginning to search for further injuries. As she examined him thoroughly from head to foot and from one side to the other, she called out her results to Chris.

"Lacerations on the right shoulder and arm. They'll need suturing. One on the neck—just cleaning will do. Nothing on his chest or left side."

Looking quickly at Chris's assistants, she continued, "Let's turn him over now. Watch that leg," she cautioned as they prepared to lift him. "Good. Now just hold him like that for a moment."

The two men struggled to keep Pete steady while she studied his back. "Okay," she motioned to them. "Nothing there but bruises. Those'll heal without our help."

Mark and Tom helped her lower Pete on his back on the table when she'd finally completed her minute examination. "Another half hour should do it," she said in encouragement as she prepared to clean and sew the remaining wounds.

"We're all right." Chris spoke for the three men. "You must be exhausted, though."

She shook her head. "Not now. It'll hit later."

Then for a few minutes the room was quiet except for the sounds Samantha made in her work. She worked quickly, deftly, washing the wounds with water and then painting them with antiseptic, putting in a few stitches in one cut on Pete's shoulder and a few more in one on his arm. Finally the last wound was painted, the last suture tied.

"I just have to give him a tetanus booster and we'll be done," she announced as she straightened up from the table.

"Now what?" Chris asked shortly thereafter, when she had completed the final necessary injection.

"Now we get him in bed, keep him immobilized and give him antibiotics," she announced as she stripped off her sodden gloves.

"Do you want to keep him here?"

Samantha grimaced. "Not really. But I'll have to. He can't be moved for a few days, even if the weather were to clear."

"When could he be moved?" Chris asked.

"Well, ideally not for a week or more," Samantha began thoughtfully. "That's a pretty bad fracture." She hesitated, then added, "Still, he ought to have X rays, and an orthopedic surgeon ought to check my work." Shaking her head, she concluded, "I guess as soon as the weather lifts I'd be for trying to move him. I'd be happier if he were in a hospital now, but...." Her voice trailed off as she shrugged, indicating her helplessness.

"Okay, we'll move him as soon as the weather clears," Chris decided. "I don't think that'll be too much longer, either," he said comfortingly.

Wearily Samantha showed Mark and Tom where she kept a spare cot. She found sheets for them and then worked on arranging a way to elevate Pete's leg once he was in the cot.

When the bed was made, the three men carried Pete to it carefully, helping Samantha to arrange the pillows under his leg. Once he was settled into the bed, they all stood back, looking with some awe at the man who had caused them such trouble, the man whose life they had worked together to save.

"You did a superb job, Samantha," Chris said admiringly to her while she fussed at the edge of Pete's bed.

"I couldn't have done it without you," she said truthfully. She included them all in her glance, but her eyes lingered longest on Chris's lined face.

"Will he sleep for a while?" Chris asked, turning away quickly to deflect the praise from himself.

Samantha nodded. "He should be out for hours, even without any more morphine."

"Good." Chris spoke decisively. "Then it's time for you to get some sleep, too."

Samantha shrugged. "Someone will have to watch him," she began, but Chris interrupted.

"Someone will," he said quickly. Asserting his authority for the first time since he'd knocked on her door hours before, Chris spoke hastily to his two men.

"Mark, you wait here. Keep an eye on Pete and call out at once if you notice any change."

Before Mark could even agree to his task, Chris had turned to Tom. "You go to Widow Tarai's and bring her back here."

"Chris," Samantha cried out, "you can't wake her! It's the middle of the night!"

"Is it?" he asked ironically. "Take a look out the window."

Even through the rain, Samantha could see the dim gray of a wet dawn. She had worked almost through the night, and a new day was ready to begin.

"Go on, Tom," Chris urged, and Tom, stopping only long enough to pull on a slicker, headed out the door.

"Okay, Samantha." Once Tom had stepped out the door and Mark was seated beside Pete Thompson's cot, quietly repeating the minute instructions Samantha had recited to him, Chris turned his attention to the exhausted woman. "It's time for you to go to sleep," he announced firmly.

Samantha's protest was feeble. "What about Pete?"

"You told me he'd sleep for hours," Chris asserted smoothly. "Mark's with him now, and Mrs. Tarai will take over when she arrives."

"But he's my responsibility," Samantha protested.

"That's right." Chris nodded his agreement. "You're his doctor, and he's going to need you to be his doctor. He doesn't also need you to watch over him when he's asleep!"

Samantha nodded tiredly. Suddenly what Chris said made a great deal of sense. She had done her part, and Mark or Mrs. Tarai could take over now. They were both conscientious, and they would be cautious, too. They wouldn't hesitate to call if they needed her. Pete Thompson would be all right under their watchful eyes, and she could get some of the rest she needed so desperately. Without that rest she couldn't help Pete when he did need her, and she couldn't help anyone else who might come to the clinic seeking her aid.

Knowing that Pete was safe, Samantha relaxed. Chris could set up a nursing schedule; Chris could work things out with the widow and Mark and anyone else he chose to ask for help. All at once Chris had taken over, and it seemed perfectly natural. Her part was done, her responsibility taken care of for now, and it seemed right that Chris take charge once more.

Sensing the change in her mood, Chris slipped his arm tenderly about her shoulders. "Are you ready to go upstairs now?" he whispered in her ear.

Nodding sleepily, Samantha leaned back against his strong shoulder, feeling his arms embrace her and hold her up.

"Relax, Samantha. It's all right," he whispered soothingly as he led her to the foot of the stairs.

As Samantha gazed at the flight of stairs, they seemed to multiply before her eyes. Instead of extending up a single story, they suddenly extended many stories, farther than she could see, certainly farther than she could walk. She sighed wearily, girding herself for the climb, but Chris didn't hesitate.

Scooping her up in his arms, he carried her easily

up the flight of stairs. Samantha snuggled against his chest, feeling comfortable and at home.

He carried her into her bedroom and set her gently on the bed. Without a word he began to untie the robe she still wore, the robe she had worn under her sterile gown during the surgery. She was too sleepy to protest, and she felt too contented to be disturbed by his touch. All night long he had worked beside her, helping her and guiding her by turn. And now he was supremely gentle and affectionate.

When he slipped the robe off her shoulders and eased her into the bed, he leaned over to kiss her lightly on the forehead. Pulling the covers up to her chin, he spoke a few soft words of farewell.

"Sleep well, my love," he whispered in a voice she could barely hear, in a tone that also seemed to speak of love.

Samantha barely remembered his good-night kiss, barely noticed when he walked out the door. But as she fell into the dreamless sleep of the exhausted, those words echoed in her mind. She wondered whether he had actually spoken or whether she had only dreamed such tender words of parting.

CHAPTER TWELVE

DREAM OR REALITY, the words Chris had whispered echoed through Samantha's mind when she awoke several hours later. She had slept past the middle of the morning and rose refreshed, feeling newly born into a good world. She moved slowly, luxuriating in the moment of freedom before her return to work. As a result, she had not even finished dressing when Mrs. Tarai tapped on her door.

"Come in," she called cheerfully after the woman had identified herself.

"I heard you moving around and I thought you might like this," Mrs. Tarai said with a smile, handing her a cup of tea.

"Oh, lovely," Samantha thanked her. Seating herself on the edge of the bed, she sipped the steaming liquid with pleasure. Even in the heat of the tropics, the constant rain made everything damp, and a hot drink on a clammy morning was welcome.

"The power's back on, then?" she asked.,

Mrs. Tarai nodded briskly. "It came on several hours ago, not long after Mr. Girard left here. Charlie must've got it going again."

Thinking of the generator and how it had been broken made Samantha wince. But, unsure how much Chris had told Mrs. Tarai about Pete's injury, she decided not to mention the suspicious circumstances in which he'd been found.

"Has Pete been sleeping all this time?" she asked the widow as she slipped into her skirt.

"Yes, he has," Mrs. Tarai said importantly. "I would have called you if there'd been any change. That's what Mr. Girard told me."

"I'm sure you would have," Samantha responded. "That's why I could sleep—I knew Pete would be safe under your eye."

"Are you done now?" Mrs. Tarai smiled self-consciously at Samantha's words of praise and prepared to take the empty cup downstairs.

"Yes, thanks," Samantha responded politely, before adding, "And you ought to go home for a while. I can take care of Pete again."

But Mrs. Tarai shook her head. "Mr. Girard said I should try to help out at the clinic today. He said there'd be lots of people coming in after a night like last night."

Samantha shrugged. Pete would be quiet for the next few days, between exhaustion, pain and the drugs she would give him, and very few patients bothered coming to see her in the rains. She couldn't really imagine needing an assistant. On the other hand, she wouldn't object to whatever help—or company—the widow could provide. Last night's encounter with Chris had left her keyed up; it would be good not to be alone during the long day before she could expect to see him again.

By evening she was even more glad that Mrs. Tarai had offered to stay. The combination of the ceaseless rain and the black night following the power failure had finally produced patients for her in abundance. In addition, sick as Pete was, once he regained consciousness fully he took a lot more of her time than she'd anticipated he would.

Pete needed to be watched closely, for the blood loss he had suffered had been fairly severe, and he remained weak. Giving him routine antibiotics was easy, but giving him medication for pain was not. Samantha wanted him to be comfortable; regardless of how he'd behaved, he was a human being—and he was her patient—so she cared about what happened to him. But he was too weak to tolerate the doses of narcotics he needed to control his pain. When she raised the dose of drugs, his blood pressure dropped, and he lapsed into a sleep approaching semiconsciousness. But when she reduced the drugs, he moaned constantly, unable to get the rest he needed if he was to heal properly. At least every half hour she had to check on him and adjust his medications. He couldn't be left alone.

Pete was not the only patient demanding Samantha's attention. Young men came in with contusions suffered when they had tried to clear the roads of fallen debris; a woman had burned herself lighting a lantern; children were scraped and bruised from playing outside in the storms and inside in the dark.

One elderly man had fractured his arm when he fell
down a flight of stairs. It was a simple fracture, and
Samantha had no trouble setting it. In its simplicity it
contrasted sharply with her efforts of the preceding
night, but it brought back the trauma and the beauty
of her work. All her fears of what she didn't know
and what she couldn't do had surfaced last night, and
still she had done what she had to, and she had done
it well.

All day long people came to the clinic. They came
with minor injuries and small problems for the most
part, but all were injuries and problems only Samantha could cure.

Mrs. Tarai did her best, but her best was very
limited. She had no training in either first aid or nursing. She didn't even seem to have any aptitude for
assisting Samantha. She forgot the names of instruments right after Samantha identified them; she
helpfully placed a bandage on one child's arm only to
have Samantha realize later it was not a sterile bandage and the wound was open. She tried, but she
created almost as much work as she did help.

One talent she had was for talking to the patients.
She could comfort a crying child and calm a worried
parent; she knew everyone on the island and could
entertain them when Samantha fell further and further behind in her work. Soon Samantha learned it
was best to send Mrs. Tarai out to the waiting room
and to do all the rest of the work herself.

In an odd way, the more Samantha watched Mrs.
Tarai fumble at her work, the more she realized how

helpful Felicity had been. Felicity's work was erratic; she did what she felt like and all too often that meant she didn't do what Samantha told her to. Still, with patients Felicity always behaved well. It was not only that she had training in first aide or that she knew the names of most instruments and illnesses. She had an instinct for doing the right thing, a real talent.

As the day wore inexorably on toward evening, Samantha realized more than once that she missed Felicity. Her lips curled wryly at the irony of her recognition, but she knew it was true.

Shortly after seven she closed the door of the clinic on the last patient. "I guess that does it," she said wearily to Mrs. Tarai.

"I made you some dinner," the good woman responded softly. Before Samantha could thank her, she interjected, "I'm sorry I'm so little help, Dr. Hall. I just don't know what I'm doing."

Samantha placed her arms around the woman's soft form and gave her a quick affectionate hug. "You helped keep me sane today. That's a big help all in itself."

The widow shook her head. "I know I'm not much use, not like Felicity."

Grimacing inwardly, Samantha forced herself to smile outwardly. "Felicity has a rare gift, Mrs. Tarai. But you were here all day when I needed you."

"You'll have to get some sleep, after what you did last night," the elderly woman announced.

Samantha shook her head. "I'll be fine. I'll just

make up a bed near Pete's cot, so I can hear him if he needs me.''

"Let me do it,'' Mrs. Tarai pleaded.

But Samantha would not be moved. "You just get a good night's sleep and come back tomorrow to keep things quiet, in case it's another day like today,'' she insisted. Then, over the widow's objections, she thanked her again and ushered her out of the room.

Sighing deeply, Samantha seated herself before her rapidly cooling supper. She'd had no time for lunch, and her lost night's sleep was overriding her good morning nap. Hungry as she was, she could barely eat. She was too tired, and too concerned about Chris.

During the day she had heard nothing from him. Her phone was still out of order, but she had expected to receive a message at the least. Stretching sleepily as she rose to wash her dishes, Samantha shook her head. No, to be honest she had expected to see him, not just to receive a message. After what they had shared last night, even before his parting words—the words of a dream that echoed in her ears and in her heart—she couldn't believe he would let a day go by without coming to visit her.

But the evening wore on, the gray sky growing black as night approached, and still she hadn't heard from him. About nine, after giving Pete another injection, she threw some blankets onto the sofa in the living room. If her rest was going to be interrupted by his helpless groans and periodic demands, she knew she must try to go to sleep as early as possible.

She had just placed her pillow at one end of the couch when there came a knock at the clinic door. "Chris?" she called anxiously as she hastened to open the door.

But it was Mark, not Chris. Swallowing her disappointment, Samantha motioned Mark into the clinic.

"I hope you're not hurt, Mark?" she asked quickly.

"No, I'm fine, Dr. Hall," he responded awkwardly. "Mr. Girard sent me."

"Chris sent you? But why?" she asked.

"He wants me to stay and watch Pete Thompson tonight," Mark explained casually. "Mr. Girard heard you'd been real busy, and he thought you could use a hand."

"Well, it has been busy," Samantha began slowly, but quickly she made up her mind. "No, Mark. You've been working all day, too."

"No, I haven't, Miss...I mean, doctor," Mark's words tumbled from him. "Mr. Girard made Tom and me go home right after we left here. I'm supposed to stay here tonight, then Tom'll be around tomorrow to see what he can do for you."

Samantha thought rapidly. It was obvious that Mark expected to stay. It was his job, and she must let him do it for that reason alone. But it was even more than that. In his eyes shone a light she had not seen before last night. It was obvious that he took pride in this new responsibility. He'd proved himself the night before; Chris knew it and Mark knew it, too, and he was proud on both accounts.

"That'll be great, Mark," Samantha said quietly as soon as she reached this point in her thinking. "You can use the bed I'd set up on the sofa," she added, motioning toward the living room. Quickly she rehearsed her instructions, telling him to call if Pete seemed restless, if he moaned during the night, if his condition changed in any way. As she prepared to go upstairs to her room she reminded him once more, "You just call me if you need anything. Okay?"

"Yes, ma'am. That's fine," Mark responded happily, importance radiating from his eyes. "You get some rest now."

"All right, Mark." Samantha thanked him seriously, fighting the smile that threatened to rise to her lips and undercut the pleasure he was taking in his new task.

As she curled up in her bed a few minutes later, the smile still hovered about her lips. Maybe Chris had been too busy to come to see her, but he hadn't been too busy to remember her. Tender thoughts of his kindness and his attention stayed with her as she drifted off to a sound night's sleep.

SHE CLUNG TO THOSE TENDER THOUGHTS in the next several days. In between the bumps and bruises, the wounds and sprains, she reminded herself that Chris had shown both kindness and attention when she needed it. Every night Mark came to watch over

Pete. Every day Tom came to help in the clinic, to fetch supplies for her, to clean up debris outside her house. Every day the widow came, too, offering her calming presence to the patients, her good food to Samantha and her ready ear to anyone who wanted it. But Chris never once came, though she soon learned why.

Her patients chatted freely while Samantha cleaned their wounds, bandaged their arms and strapped their ankles. Thus she heard stories of Chris's ceaseless work on the island. One day he was in the hills with Charlie Tuatara, checking the roads and placing crews to work on them. Another day he was at the water cisterns, setting up spare tanks to catch the overflow, so unnecessary now but so welcome when the rains would pass. And many days he spent in the lowlands, supervising the work on the plantations and farms, trying to help the islanders to salvage what they could of this year's crops.

Samantha knew he was busy. His work was essential, his responsibilities tremendous. But hers were, too, and she still found time to think about Chris, to long for him and miss his reassuring presence, unsatisfied just to receive his messages from Mark and Tom. In time the phones were reconnected, and then Samantha's heart began to grow lighter. She felt sure it would not be long until she heard directly from Chris.

On the fifth day Samantha cut open Pete's cast partway. It was time to inspect his leg. Pete was fully awake now, regaining his strength rapidly. He re-

mained immobile, so Samantha felt no fear. But she
was grateful when Tom offered to help. She didn't
need any assistance in handling the bandages or inspecting the injury, but she still felt very uncomfortable around Pete. Even drugged as he was, he
managed to exude an inherent nastiness that made
her want to cringe before him. With Tom's steadying
presence she found she could manage the necessary
examination and rebandaging quite nicely, and afterward she quickly gave Pete his daily massive dose of
penicillin, his smaller dose of streptomycin, a second
antibiotic and his pain medication. Through it all
Pete watched her scornfully, offering no cry of pain
and not a single word of thanks.

Besides her hope, what helped Samantha the most
during this long period was the gradual daily im-
provement in the weather. As Chris had predicted,
the storms had begun to ease almost immediately
after the night Pete was injured. In spite of her tension and her continuing state of near exhaustion,
Samantha could feel her heart growing more buoyant
as the gloom began to lift.

Each day the sky grew a little lighter, the rain a little less persistent. At dusk and dawn there was a trace
of color on the horizon that had been lost for more
days than Samantha could remember. In the afternoon the rain slowed to a drizzle, and then at last it
stopped.

Clouds hung low in the sky, but not too low to prevent a glimpse of the sun, not too low to keep an
airplane on the ground. And so, one morning when

Mark was preparing to turn over his duties to Tom, the pilot of the Inter-Island Airline arrived at the clinic.

"I hope I'm not too early," he greeted Samantha with the air of nonchalance she had learned masked a careful pilot and kind man.

She looked at him, perplexed. "Too early for what?"

"To pick up that patient," he explained lightly.

Samantha stared at him. "Pete? I didn't know he was supposed to leave today."

Even as she spoke, Tom came racing to the door. "I'm sorry," he shouted as he came into view. "I was supposed to get here early today to tell you, but I got held up. The road's out again," he added in disgust as he stood panting at the door.

"Not again," Mark groaned. Turning to Samantha, he shrugged helplessly. "I guess it's a good thing Mr. Thompson'll be off your hands today. I'll be going up to help Mr. Girard, and I bet Tom will, too."

Samantha's heart leaped at the sound of Chris's name. Nervously she asked, "Is that where he is today? Working on the road?"

Tom nodded. "He's been working somewhere all the time. Mr. Girard just never lets up!" He shook his head in wonder at the energy of his employer. As if reminded by that thought of his own responsibilities, Tom spoke swiftly to Mark. "You're right—as soon as we help get Pete Thompson to the plane, we're supposed to join the road crew."

Turning to Samantha, he added politely, "Mr.

Girard thought you wouldn't be needing us anymore. Is that all right?''

"Of course," Samantha affirmed. "You've both been a tremendous help, but with Pete gone and the rains clearing, it should be a lot quieter here. I'll be fine now, and—'' she stumbled over the name but finally managed to conclude her thought ''—Mr. Girard needs you.''

By the time she had prepared Pete for his flight to Halekai and given his medical charts to the pilot, who would hand them to the nurse meeting their plane, the waiting room was beginning to fill. Seeing this, Tom asked anxiously, "Are you sure you won't need us? Mr. Girard would understand—''

Thanking Tom again, Samantha cut him off rapidly. "No, you go along now. Both of you," she added with a laugh when she saw Mark hesitating as if to speak.

Samantha knew they had to go. Without Pete around her work would be much easier, and the road had to be repaired. Still, she felt sad to watch them leave. Not only had they been helpful and unfailingly cheery, but they had been an immediate link to Chris. Each time Tom or Mark spoke of work being done on the island, he spoke of Chris. Each time one of them appeared, it was a reminder to Samantha that Chris was still thinking about her. In her haze of work and worry, that was a comforting thought.

As the next few days passed, the crush of Samantha's work began to ease. The clearing weather meant fewer accidents; less difficult tasks for the island workers created less call on her talents. Samantha kept busy nonetheless, but she also began to catch up on her rest. She was grateful for that, because the more time she had, the more she could afford to realize her exhaustion. With each passing day she let herself think more seriously about Chris. The fear nagged at her that she might have misunderstood him, that he might truly still love Felicity. Maybe he even felt that if Samantha objected to his having two women, he didn't need her at all!

But in spite of the fear, in spite of all her attempts to tell herself not to build up her hopes, her heart raced with joy. Knowing how she felt, she could well imagine Chris was simply waiting to be free of the pressures upon him, free to attend completely to her, before he called.

She could almost believe that. Knowing how she felt each night when she collapsed into bed, Samantha could sympathize with the exhaustion Chris must be facing. She had a lot of responsibility, it was true. But he had all that and more: he was out working with the islanders, digging roads, moving water tanks, clearing debris. And he even had responsibility for her. If it hadn't been for his efforts, Tom and Mark would not have come to help her. The pilot would not have known to pick up Pete Thompson if it hadn't been for Chris's thinking of her needs, watching the weather and taking on yet another responsibility.

Accepting all that made it easier for Samantha to wait to hear from Chris. Still, with each passing day she fought her nerves and her excitement, growing even more anxious to hear Chris's knock on the door, more alert when the phone rang or the mailman walked by at noon.

The sun was shining in all its glory the day the mailman delivered a note from Chris. Recognizing his distinctive tan stationery, Samantha could almost believe the weather was an omen. She shrugged off her superstition with a laugh, then hastened inside to read the note in private, tearing open the envelope with fingers that twitched nervously.

It was an invitation to dine at the Big House two nights later. The note was typed and its language seemed formal, almost a formula. But at the bottom Chris had added a private note in his strong clear handwriting: "It's been too long."

Samantha's heart echoed those simple moving words. It *had* been too long. Moreover, two additional days, forty-eight hours and then some, must yet elapse before she would see Chris. It was definitely too long!

The clock marked the passage of the hours with no more haste or leisure than usual. But to Samantha each hour was composed of hundreds of minutes, each minute of hundreds of seconds. Nonetheless, the hours did pass, and at last it was time to dress for dinner with Chris.

In spite of the formality of the invitation, Samantha harbored a lingering hope that she would be the only guest. She longed to see Chris alone, to talk with him and learn from him whether he shared her memories of their night with the injured man. Yet she hadn't been able to ignore the heavy chugging of the Inter-Island DC-3 arriving and leaving twice in the late afternoon, or the higher, lighter sound of a private plane, perhaps a jet, circling over the landing field. In spite of her desires, she suspected it was indeed a large party to which Chris had invited her.

She chose her costume with anxious care. Her dress had to be suitable for a private party or a large one, a few casual friends or many unfamiliar people. And it had to be something special, something that would delicately evoke a special mood without revealing every emotion that churned within her. At last she selected a dress of starkest white, its plainness relieved only by the white embroidery on its bodice and by the straps that crisscrossed her back. The simplicity of the dress underscored her flaming hair and made her light tan glow; subtly, without flamboyance, it also played up her gently rounded figure.

Samantha did not have to park her car outside Chris's house before she realized this was no private party, nor was it a small get-together of island friends. Lights blazed throughout the Big House, and music drifted out across the damp lawn. In her excitement Samantha let out the clutch on her car before she had shifted into neutral, so it was with a grinding crunch and a final few bounces that she pulled up before the Big House.

"Announcing yourself, Samantha?" Chris's voice floated out to her, his tone light with humor and irony.

Too embarrassed even to pause to check her hair or lipstick, Samantha managed an apparently casual wave to Chris as she prepared to step out of the car. Puddles of water stood between her and the steps, and she glanced at her polished white sandals ruefully.

"Get out the other side," Chris suggested. "It's drier there."

Samantha leaned across her small car to open the door on the passenger's side. Chris was right: the ground sloped down from right to left, making the earth on that side of the car considerably drier. Grimacing, she wriggled across to the right-hand door, silently cursing the hard, separate bucket seats and the obtrusive gear shift as she moved. At last she had maneuvered herself out of the car and across the short distance to the front steps of the Big House.

"You made it," Chris said, reaching toward her with both of his hands.

He might have been simply welcoming her to the party, knowing how busy she had been at the clinic. Or he might even have been referring humorously to her awkward maneuverings in the car and her gingerly trail around the mud puddles leading to his front door. But the way he held her hands and the warm light in his deep eyes suggested that he meant something far more important. Samantha's heart filled as it responded to the look in his eyes. He was glad to see her, there could be no doubt about it.

Their private moment was precious to her, but it was poignantly fleeting. No sooner had Chris spoken his few words of greeting than another car drove up.

"It's a large group tonight," he said softly as they watched Theo, his gardener, park next to Samantha's automobile. It seemed there was more than a touch of sadness in his voice as he recited what could have been no more than a fact.

Samantha remained silently by his side while he welcomed the new arrivals, the last Theo had driven up from the airport. She greeted them with a trembling smile, achingly aware of how good it felt to stand next to Chris. As soon as the guests had climbed the stairs, he drew her to the side of the wide steps, where the hyacinth blossoms wafted their fragrant scent from the lawn.

"This is probably our only chance to talk," he explained hastily. "It'll be hectic tonight."

"What's the party for?" Samantha asked, tremulously aware of how near he stood.

He shrugged. "It's in honor of a friend of mine. You'll meet him later."

Samantha stared at her shoes, half noticing a spot of mud soiling their glossy whiteness. She could think of nothing to say, no small talk to fill the uneasy silence. But the silence didn't seem to bother Chris. He gazed at her quietly, as if content just to pass his eyes over her again and again, drinking in the sight of her to quench some endless thirst.

When he spoke at last, his voice was husky. "You're very beautiful, Samantha," he murmured close to her ear.

Samantha felt her body sway toward his, but in her

insecurity and her confusion she held herself rigidly back. It was one thing for him to say she was beautiful, even to single her out when she arrived. But the fact remained that days had passed since she had last seen Chris, and that their last two encounters had been confusingly, shockingly different.

Maybe it was enough for him just to invite her to a party and assume they could pick up where they had left off. But they had left off in each other's arms, with words of love after a night of trauma. And she could not so easily forget the time before, the time that had also begun with gestures of love yet ended with words of jealousy and anger. She was ill at ease, needing to know what Chris felt. She needed to hear from him the truth about Felicity, no more half-truths and no more evasions. Most of all she needed to hear him say words of love once more, this time when she was awake and could be sure they were not a fantasy occurring in a lovely dream; when she was secure and no longer jealous.

She waited, but Chris offered no such words and no explanation. He seemed content just to stand near her; she was too unsure to be at such peace.

Half-aware of her intention, she heard her voice break into the silence. "Who's your friend?" she asked, saying out loud the first neutral thought that came into consciousness.

Chris started abruptly. For a moment he stared at her as if he had no notion of what she was talking about, then he roused himself to speak.

"His name is Jacques LeTort," he said flatly.

"Jacques LeTort? The actor?" Samantha's expression echoed the surprise in her voice.

"Yes, he lives on Atanoa, about a hundred miles from here," Chris answered. His face seemed veiled, his tone ambiguous.

"And he's a friend of yours?" Samantha asked again.

Chris nodded. "He's very nice. You'll like him," he commented, slipping his hand under her arm to turn her back toward the well-lit doorway.

As Chris escorted her up the stairs and into the reception area, Samantha felt vaguely dissatisfied. She knew she had interrupted a moment of special importance to Chris, and maybe to herself; as well, and she could tell from the rigidity of Chris's upright back that he was tense, perhaps displeased with her. Yet she had felt helpless, unnerved by the power of his gaze, by the emotions that threatened to overwhelm her.

When she stood alone with Chris it had been as if she were floating above a beautiful coral garden far out in the ocean. To see the garden and become at one with the fish swimming in it, she would have to lie still, to be absolutely peaceful, even passive. But she feared drowning and thought that only by kicking with all her might could she stay above the surface. When she kicked, she destroyed the beautiful scene and lost her chance to be a part of it; had she not kicked, she might have drowned.

Yet even as Chris introduced her to first one and then another of the guests who had flown in earlier that day, Samantha knew she was rationalizing. Perhaps she would have drowned, but it was also possible she would have swum beautifully, in absolute security, with Chris by her side.

A change in Chris's voice broke through her musing as all of his earlier introductions and even her responses had not. "Samantha, this is Jacques LeTort," he announced with an odd inflection.

Overwhelmed as she was to be meeting the world-famous actor, Samantha couldn't help stealing a sideways glance at Chris as he completed the introduction. But his expression was veiled, so that she couldn't be sure if it was ironic humor or something else that made his dark eyes glitter. She murmured an appropriate response to the white-haired man, who offered her a hearty handclasp. As she stumbled for the beginning of a conversation, Chris startled her further by preparing to walk away.

"I'll leave you two alone to get acquainted," he said evenly. An odd smile dented his face as he caught the appeal in Samantha's green eyes. "I'm sure you'll find lots to talk about," he announced.

Biting her lip in annoyance Samantha looked at Chris hopefully once more, but he merely grinned knowingly. With a casual wave of his hand, he walked across the wide room to speak with another guest. With growing discomfort Samantha watched him leave. He had managed to stay for a few minutes with each of the dozen people he had introduced her to, but this time he had left almost immediately. It was as if he wanted to make her uncomfortable by abandoning her with the famous actor; and, she admitted ruefully, if that was his goal he had succeeded.

She turned back to face her companion, a flush mounting to her cheeks. Confronted with the famous smile flashing at her, a smile she had often seen magnified many times its normal size on movie screens, she felt like the country mouse abandoned in the big city. She couldn't think of a single thing to say that might possibly interest Jacques LeTort. Looking at him, she was awed by his graceful stance, his shock of wavy white hair, his immense personal charm. He seemed to exude the wisdom of an elder from the firm body of a man far younger than his fifty or so years.

All Samantha could think of was the Jacques LeTort of films and newspaper articles. The titles of his films, including two for which he had won awards, raced through her mind as if they were being run by on a screen. The names of the characters he had played and the names of his leading ladies galloped by next; then came a series of disparate images of him from his films: Jacques LeTort on horseback, in military garb, on the steps of the White House, at the controls of an airplane, leading a team of explorers down the Amazon. These pictures were superseded by a series even more distressing: Jacques LeTort holding a beautiful brunette, kissing a voluptuous redhead, bidding a stoic farewell to a delicate blonde.

What could she say to such a man? He wouldn't want to hear her gushing about his marvelous talent like some witless schoolgirl. Yet how could she begin?

"Chris said you live near here?" she half stated, half asked, a stammering beginning.

To her surprise, Jacques LeTort responded more than pleasantly to her overture. Either she had lucked upon a topic that interested him or he was unfailingly polite, but he drew her slightly to one side, away from the path of casual chatter and white-coated servants offering glasses of champagne. The deep voice she knew so well from the films grew soft and warm as he talked of his island home to her, only to her.

"Atanoa's about one hundred miles from here, virtually due north," he began. "It's small, even smaller than Good Providence, and I'm the only European there."

As he spoke, Samantha remembered what she had read about his home. He had purchased a tiny island and turned it into a retreat, a place he could use to escape the pressures of fame. Remembering this, she began to warm toward him and to feel her fears vanish.

"Do you live there all alone?" she asked when he paused.

Jacques shook his head. "I have a housekeeper and a gardener, and there's a small colony of Micronesians on the island," he explained. "In fact, when I bought the island I had to agree to leave them strictly alone."

Samantha's expression revealed her curiosity, and

Jacques obliged with further explanation. "You see, they live as they have for centuries—probably for a thousand years or more. The government wanted to give them the chance to continue to live as they had." He hesitated, then continued with a slight frown, "Yet they were anxious to sell to me. I suppose it makes sense. The government needed money, and since I was willing to accept their conditions, it worked out for all of us."

"Do you ever see the others?" Samantha asked, eyes wide with excitement at this glimpse into so unusual a life.

"Oh, yes," Jacques laughed. "Not often, but I've been invited there several times." He paused, then changed the subject slightly, but not in a way that would make Samantha feel she had asked a rude question. In fact, as he leaned toward her she realized he was very nearly confiding in her. In an odd way it didn't surprise her, for she found herself wonderfully comfortable with Jacques. Already she had replaced her impression of him as a famous actor with a new impression, that of a man who was totally sincere and perhaps a little lonely.

"You see, I bought the island to be alone, yet I don't want to cut myself off entirely. I think I'm a little like the Micronesians who live on Atanoa. They want to live as they always have, but they want to know about the other world, too. Maybe then they can go back to their lives, knowing just how little they are missing!"

"So you visit them or you fly out here to sample

our lives, but then you're glad to go home. Is that it?'' Samantha asked sympathetically.

"That's it exactly." Jacques nodded until his silver hair shimmered. "Chris was right," he added with a smile. "I do like you!"

Feeling the color rise to her cheeks, Samantha made it her turn to change the subject. For the next few minutes they spoke casually about the party, the beauty of the room illuminated by flickering candles, the brilliant jumble of colorful clothes worn by the guests. Jacques asked Samantha about her work on the island, how difficult she found practicing medicine alone and how she liked her new life. With each passing moment she felt more and more comfortable, forgetting Jacques's impressive background and enjoying his pleasing manner.

When a servant came around to announce that dinner was ready, Jacques slipped his hand under Samantha's arm. "You're my partner, you know," he explained as she glanced up at him curiously.

Surprised as she was, Samantha was also pleased. If she couldn't be with Chris, then she would gladly share the dinner hour with this lively, intelligent and urbane man. She laughed at herself as he ushered her to her seat.

"What's so funny?" Jacques leaned over to whisper as they spread their snowy linen napkins.

But Samantha refused to answer, too embarrassed to tell him she had been remembering how terrifying she'd found him at first.

The arrival of a servant with a salad of asparagus

tips and sliced tomatoes prevented her from saying anything more, and for a few minutes Jacques, too, was absorbed in the delicious meal. As the dinner progressed, they chatted pleasantly together, sometimes speaking to a near neighbor or joining in the general conversation. But the group around the table was too big to sustain a single discussion, so most of the time Samantha found her attention focused on Jacques.

The food was lovely, the service unobtrusive, the wine golden and slightly sweet. The only light was provided by the flickering yellow and orange candles, and the odor of tropical flowers in the same fiery colors scented the air. Increasingly Samantha felt herself falling under the spell of the evening, and increasingly she grew mellow and open to everything around her.

More than once she glanced to the head of the table where Chris sat. On either side of him was placed the wife of a government official, and he didn't seem to find their simpering questions absorbing. More than one of Samantha's glances was intercepted by his flashing eyes, and she felt rising in her a warm glow that owed nothing to the golden wine or the excitement of sitting next to Jacques LeTort.

In a sudden lull in the conversation, she heard one of the women question Chris about a recent trip he had made to Halekai. "Did you find the flight very rough?" she asked.

Chris nodded. "It was right after the storm, really the first fairly decent day."

"Was it safe?" the woman persisted, shivering with delicious anticipation of his response.

Chris shrugged. "I had to go. There was someone I had to meet there."

As he spoke, he glanced across the table to Samantha, as if to see whether she had heard. Samantha could feel her face burning with anguish and with anger. He had been to see Felicity; it had to be that. When he was too busy to come to her or even to call her, when the weather was so bad he as much as admitted it might not have been safe to fly, he had still gone after Felicity!

Furious with him for his duplicity, furious with herself for indulging in false hopes, Samantha stiffened her shoulders and lifted her wineglass to her trembling lips. In a single swallow she drained the contents of the glass, then motioned to the waiter to refill it.

Jacques's voice recalled her to her social obligations, and she made a quick response to his quiet question. Then, drawing her lips into a thin line, she made up her mind. If Chris could treat her so casually, she could do the same to him. Jacques seemed friendly enough, and he was sophisticated enough to respond to her lead. She knew it was childish of her, but a little flirtation with Jacques just might put Chris in his place.

Another quaff of the golden wine gave Samantha the courage she needed to begin. Leaning close to Jacques, she whispered softly into his ear. To someone looking from across the table, someone like

Chris, it would seem their conversation had taken a sudden turn. Their behavior must seem more intimate. In fact, she had asked Jacques to pass the pepper—that was the only thing she could think of, but at least it was a start.

Over the rest of dinner, Samantha indulged in a friendly flirtation with Jacques. He seemed perfectly willing to follow her lead. In fact, he seemed to enjoy what she was doing and responded in kind to her throaty laughs, her intimate asides, her private smiles. She harbored no worries that he might misunderstand her, for he seemed to sense she was playing some kind of a game, and like her he kept his distance.

It was Chris she wanted to mislead, not Jacques LeTort. Yet whenever she looked at his end of the table from under her thick lashes, Chris either ignored her or merely grinned at her, his lips curling slightly in a knowing fashion.

When dinner was over, he approached Samantha for the first time since he had introduced her to Jacques. "Having a good time?" he asked, steering her away from the others for a moment..

"Super," she breathed enthusiastically. Putting every ounce of effort into her response, she looked up at him in what she hoped was a mysterious manner and confided, "You were right. Jacques is fantastic!"

To her shock, Chris just lifted up his head and howled. "I'll tell him that," he promised.

Perplexed, Samantha struggled to maintain the

facade. "Oh, you don't have to," she said. "I will."

Chris shook his head at her as though she were a fractious little girl. "It won't work, Samantha," he warned, a smile still wrinkling his face. "I won't believe you."

She looked at him in silence, too stunned to do more than try to appear at once innocent of his meaning and stunningly sophisticated. "Jacques would never try to take my woman from me," he said with a knowing smile.

Before Samantha could respond, Jacques had re-appeared, and she had to stand quietly while the two men talked. What did Chris think he meant by calling her "my woman"? Samantha knew she should be furious with him for taking her so for granted, especially after he had neglected her in the past few days. But she couldn't convince herself to be angry at his unwarranted possessiveness, his proud certainty. As she listened to his resonant voice respond to some comment Jacques made; as she looked about at the room he had caused to be filled with people from all over the islands, with sweet flowers and gleaming candles; as she stole a glance at his strong and shapely body, she began to bask in a renewed glow of sweetest emotion. He exuded such a glow, and he awakened it in her. She couldn't resist his appeal.

"Samantha's agreed to come to Atanoa," she heard Jacques say to Chris, trying to include her in the conversation once again.

"I'd like to...someday," she admitted, suddenly

contrite as she recalled her behavior earlier that evening.

But Jacques seemed to take no note of her discomfort or to remember her flirting words and manner.
Smiling at her pleasantly, he said, "I don't give out
vague invitations, and I don't accept vague answers.
How would next weekend do?"

Samantha looked from one man to the other, unsure what to say. Before she could answer, Chris interrupted.

"That's no good for me, Jacques. How about the
following one?"

Samantha's eyes opened even wider. "Are
you...? I mean..." she stammered.

Chris rested his hand on her shoulder in a light
possessive gesture. "Are you asking if I'm invited,
too?" he quipped teasingly.

She shrugged, aware of the warm light clasp of his
hand and unwilling to put into words the questions
that coursed through her mind.

"Well, I am," Chris answered his own question
with a grin. Leaning close to her, he whispered so
that even Jacques couldn't overhear, "I told you it
wouldn't work!"

Blushing furiously, Samantha stood in abashed
silence. When she had accepted Jacques's casual invitation during dinner, she hadn't realized he meant
her to come to Atanoa so soon—and certainly she
hadn't realized he meant her to come with Chris. She
hesitated, feeling she ought to back out, fearing what
might be expected of her on such a trip and wonder-

ing exactly what Chris thought their relationship was to be. Yet she was tempted, and not only by the thought of spending more time with Jacques or seeing his private island.

"So, the weekend after next?" Jacques echoed Chris's suggestion, looking at her encouragingly.

"I don't know," she stammered. "I'm not sure...."

"You promised," Jacques reminded her with a smile.

Samantha raised her eyes to meet Chris's teasing ones. In his eyes hovered a smile and a challenge that she could read, but there was also something else, something not so easily defined. Was it hope? Her heart throbbed with painful joy as she reached this interpretation. Suddenly she knew she must go to Atanoa, and she must go with Chris.

"All right." She looked at Jacques when she agreed shyly, but her words and her hope were addressed to Chris. "In two weeks."

CHAPTER THIRTEEN

"THERE IT IS!" Chris called out exultantly as he banked the light plane sharply to the right. "Do you see it?"

"It's so small!" Samantha stared out the window at the tiny atoll that was Atanoa.

"Jacques's house is at the west end," he explained, easing up on the throttle so that the plane seemed to float over the water.

"And the village? The Micronesians?" Samantha asked eagerly, straining to identify the few signs of habitation on the island.

Chris shook his head. "Their houses are deep in the forest," he said. "You might see some canoes off the north coast, but otherwise you could barely tell the island was inhabited."

"But where are the people?" Samantha asked, puzzled.

"They'll be in their houses while we land," Chris answered. He paused to lower the flaps on the plane. His voice disappeared in the sudden rush of air, and he postponed the rest of his explanation until they had landed safely on the gravel runway and taxied over to stop beside Jacques's light twin-engine.

Samantha trailed behind Chris as he walked around the plane. While he tied it down and checked the ropes, he returned to her question. "Even though Jacques has been here for a half a dozen years, he gets so few visitors that the islanders still tend to hide when they hear an airplane. Later on, though, they'll come out to the beach. But I'm not sure if we'll be able to go to the village. And if they don't feel like letting us see them, we won't see a single person!"

"You mean at the village?" she asked as she reached her suitcase down from the plane's small hold.

"I mean anywhere," he answered evenly. "In the village, on the beach, out at sea. They've managed to live here alone, keeping to themselves, for a long, long time. You could walk all around the island and barely know anyone lived here except Jacques, unless you knew exactly where to look!"

"That's amazing," Samantha mused while she followed Chris along the edge of the runway, apparently toward a solitary unattended Jeep that sat there as if awaiting them. She felt odd, almost reborn, arriving on this lovely but alien island. All through their hour's flight she had felt as though she were being transported to some fantasy world.

In the swift airplane they had flown past one tiny atoll after another, over a hundred-mile chain of incredible green and brown outcroppings in a world of endless ocean. The sun glittered on the water, sparkling its palest turquoise and deepest purple with flecks of gold. It was a wondrous world, and she had felt a part of that wonder.

Chris's greeting early that morning had been a gentle kiss, so gentle she could barely feel the brush of his lips against hers, yet so tender that the light imprint remained on her mouth and in her heart. During their trip he had not been too busy with the work of flying to talk to her about all sorts of things, from the route they followed to the identity of each of the named islands they passed. Tacitly she had avoided asking him any questions about his search for Felicity. She was willing to accept the present as it was, to accept it and enter into it fully. For now it was enough.

Samantha's musings ended abruptly when Chris lifted her suitcase into the Jeep. "What are you doing?"

"Getting ready to drive to Jacques's," Chris answered with a smile.

"Shouldn't we wait for Jacques or someone to pick us up?" she asked. "You can't just drive off in someone else's car like that."

Chris laughed. "Around here you can," he explained as he ushered her into the vehicle. "Jacques usually leaves a car out here with the keys in it."

"But isn't that awfully tempting?" she suggested hesitantly.

"Only to someone who wanted to steal a car," Chris responded, easing the clutch out. "Who's going to steal a car around here?" he continued a minute later as he guided the car toward the gravel runway that doubled as a road.

Samantha shook her head, unsure what to say.

"The villagers aren't interested in cars," Chris commented. "I don't think anyone realized—not even Jacques when he first moved out here—how committed those people are to living in the old way. They like it like that, and they don't want to change."

"How about somebody flying in?" Samantha suggested after she had digested this information.

"The island is private; the runway doesn't even show on navigation charts," he responded. "The only people who come here are Jacques's guests."

Chris paused while he twisted the wheel of the car to avoid a tree stump in the hard-packed dirt of the road, then concluded, "If anyone landed here in an emergency, Jacques would be happy to help out, and that would include the loan of the Jeep. But otherwise...." He let his voice trail off, as if there was no need to say anything more.

Samantha was still puzzling over this strange, almost idyllic life when Chris stopped the car before Jacques's low-slung house. At her first sight of the building, she snapped out of her pondering. Chris's house was impressive, quite marvelous in its history and its reflection of his family. But Jacques's house was something from another world.

No, she revised that opinion a moment later when she had studied the exterior more closely. It was something from this world. It fitted the tropics and this private hidden life perfectly.

The house had just one story, but it sprawled

across a fairly large base, curving around trees and gardens and small ponds. Most houses are landscaped; first the house is built and then flowers and bushes are planted to suit the house. But Jacques's creation reversed the process. It was as if the land had been "house-scaped," Samantha thought whimsically as she surveyed the scene before her. It seemed as though the house had been integrated into the natural world, as though it had been planted to suit its surroundings. The effect was fantastic but very, very right.

"Welcome to Atanoa." Jacques's handclasp was as warm as his voice. "Did you have a good flight?"

For a few minutes they stood by the Jeep exchanging the usual pleasantries, then Jacques raised his hand to halt the small talk.

"Here I am wasting time. We can talk later. Now, though, I've got a treat for you," he concluded. Standing with his hands on his hips, he paused as if to tease them.

"Were you able to get permission for us to go to the village?" Chris asked.

"I was indeed," their host responded exuberantly. "But tonight is a feast night," he added, "and they'll be busy all afternoon preparing for that. So if we're going we've got to go at once." He turned politely to Samantha. "Are you sure you're not too tired?" he asked solicitously.

"Tired? I was just hoping we could go," she admitted.

"Good," he responded swiftly, patting her warmly

on her arm. "Let me just pick up the baskets," he added vaguely before disappearing into the house.

"What did he mean?" Samantha asked Chris when they were alone.

"I'm not sure," Chris admitted. "We'll have to ask Jacques when he returns." Motioning to the villa they stood before, he added, "It's a fantastic house, isn't it?"

Samantha nodded, too excited about their pending visit even to pay much attention to the unique house. Chris reached over to squeeze her hand, and she looked up at him quickly. A golden light gleamed in his dark eyes.

"Glad you came with me?" he asked softly.

Samantha's answer, a murmured yes, was lost to Jacques's return. But the memory of Chris's expression lingered with her during the ride to the village, even through Jacques's fascinating story of the villagers' lives and his minimal interactions with them.

Quickly he traced what was known of the history of the island, pointing out that most of the information came from legends. "Scholars all over the Pacific are still trying to piece together the story of all the migrations from one island to the next and to work out all the interrelationships among different groups," he commented as he concluded his brief history lesson.

"Do they know what Atanoa means?" Chris asked.

"It comes from legend, too," Jacques explained. "According to the Marquesans, Atanoa was the first woman. Their Eve, I suppose."

"Who named the island?" Samantha queried next.

Jacques shook his head. "No one's really sure about that. The people here have always called it Atanoa, and that's interesting, too, since the Marquesas are in Polynesia. But it's got that name in their stories and dances, and they tell of a migration here from another island, one where the sun stopped shining."

"The sun stopped shining?"

Jacques nodded. "It might have been a period of storms or even an eclipse, but it was probably a volcanic eruption. The ash could have darkened the sky, so the sun would seem to disappear."

"Then they moved on because they were frightened?" The suggestion came from Samantha.

"More likely because the crops were destroyed and the land was dead," Jacques explained. "There's usually a practical reason for the most fantastic events, I've learned. Their dances and legends tell it all."

Samantha's voice revealed almost as much envy as interest. "Have you actually seen any of the dances?"

Jacques smiled. "A few, but it's taken a long time, and there are still many things they do not show me." He paused, then began the story of his introduction to the Micronesian culture. "When I first came to Atanoa, I stayed away from the village entirely," he explained, adding quickly, "I still go there only when I'm invited."

"How did you meet the villagers, then?" Samantha asked

"I was out on the beach a lot, of course, and one day two of the men—two of the elders, I learned later—came up to me. They'd obviously known about me even before I arrived, and apparently they'd been watching every change on the island, from the workers who built the house to those who leveled the field for an airstrip, and then they'd been watching me." Jacques paused, grinning before he continued, "I guess they approved of what they saw, because they invited me to the village."

"And since then?" Samantha prompted.

"Since then, about once a month I'm invited up for a visit, and very occasionally, like today, I've asked permission to bring a guest or. two. I've been there for dinner and I've seen some of their dances. But they've never invited me to a feast or a religious celebration, and I doubt they ever will."

"What's in the basket?" Chris asked Jacques when he had finished his story.

"An offering," his friend explained. "I always bring something, every time I go." He smiled ruefully. "It's not all that easy to come up with an appropriate gift, either."

"Why?" It was Samantha's turn to ask the question.

"I don't want to bring something that's not from their world, and I don't have very many things they would value."

Samantha sat quietly. It had never occurred to her to consider how worthless most of the things she cared about would be to people living in primitive fashion on a remote island. The tools Jacques could offer to make the villagers' work easier would also destroy their life. The delicacies of food, fancy materials, furniture—all were either useless to the islanders or inimical to their way of living.

"What did you bring this time?" she asked, awed by the thoughts Jacques's words had aroused.

"Pineapples and mangoes and several loaves of a sweet bread," he answered. Smiling at Samantha he added, "And they'll probably give us pineapples and mangoes and some sweet bread to take back with us."

"Really?" Her voice revealed incredulity.

"Really. We exchange gifts to show we mean each other no harm. We are friends, or at least not enemies."

Samantha was still pondering this last notion when Jacques pulled his car into a small clearing in the underbrush. "We walk from here," he explained as he climbed out of the car.

Each of them carried a basket of food, for Jacques pointed out that each must be accepted into the village, even if only for a short time. "There's no danger," he said quickly as he handed Samantha her laden basket. "This is just a formality. But without it we'd be considered rude."

"Like tracking mud into someone's house?" Chris suggested lightly.

"More like slapping your host in the face," he replied in a friendly but warning tone.

In spite of the warning, or perhaps because of the

symbolic baskets, they were all greeted warmly at the edge of the village. Just as the first houses came into view, they were met by a young man dressed only in a short skirt composed of large leaves woven in a sturdy and attractive pattern. He and Jacques exchanged a few words in a language neither Chris nor Samantha recognized, then he led them into the village.

The small village was nestled into the shelter of the rain forest. The overhanging branches of jumbled bushes and trees arched out from the jungle floor to cover the village huts with their cool protection. The sun filtered through the trees, making patterns of blackish green and white on the ground and touching the straw walls of the huts with tinges of golden yellow.

The huts were rounded in shape, one story high and roofed with something that looked like thatch. Each hut was raised on stilts to protect its inhabitants from animals and from the sudden floods of the rainy season. But now the ground was dry, the huts mostly empty and dark. From one large hut in the center of the village, voices could be heard, presumably the voices of the adults. Except for their guide, there was not a grown man or woman to be seen.

But everywhere there were children. On the ground, outside the huts, climbing in trees, playing in the splotches of sunlight or sitting quietly in the dark shadows, there were children. Whatever they were doing, they had one thing in common: all were naked to the sun that would beat on them mercilessly when they left the shelter of their jungle homes.

The young man who had escorted them to the edge of the village disappeared with a quick indecipherable word to Jacques.

"We're to wait here," Jacques explained easily. He alone seemed unperturbed by their host's strange disappearance. In a moment his security was proved correct, for from one of the central huts an older man issued forth, his arms folded across his immense chest.

Warning Samantha and Chris to stay where they were, Jacques walked toward him, bowing his head slightly. The older man returned the bow, then reached out to shake Jacques's hand. It was clear that this was one of the village elders, and that he and Jacques had exchanged greetings first in the local manner and then in the European way. The two men spoke briefly together before Jacques motioned to Samantha and Chris to walk close.

Quickly Jacques performed the introductions, announcing that Ma'anoa was the village chief and that he welcomed his new visitors to his home. Samantha and Chris made appropriate responses translated by Jacques into the local language, and then Ma'anoa surprised them by speaking in English.

"You are welcome," he said, his words clear although strongly accented.

"Ma'anoa does us honor by speaking English," Jacques announced, cueing Samantha and Chris to respond with words of thanks. In a few minutes the ceremonies of greeting were over, and Ma'anoa retired to his hut, motioning the young man who had met them to take over.

With Jacques's sponsorship and Ma'anoa's approval, Samantha and Chris were made welcome everywhere in the village. They toured through the communal building where women were preparing food for the feast that night. They walked to the door of more than one hut, peering in at the woven mats that provided the main furnishings. They spoke to the children, with Jacques serving as interpreter, and joined in a ball game some teenage boys were happy to demonstrate. But one hut remained closed, and that they were not allowed to explore. There the adult men of the community were preparing the ornate costumes and materials for body painting they would need for the evening's celebration.

All too soon it was time to leave. Jacques led Chris and Samantha in offering thanks to the villagers for their hospitality and for their gifts. As he had predicted, the three returned to the car laden with produce and baked goods almost identical to those with which they had arrived. The fruit grew wild on the island, the bread was a native delicacy, and both symbolized the friendship between the village hosts and their guests.

Throughout their ride back to the villa, Samantha and Chris plied Jacques with questions about what they had seen. During their visit to the village they had known better than to ask questions, only to listen to what the guide said. Now they threw their questions at Jacques, asking about the tools the women used, the ceremonial foods they were preparing, the toys the children had. Jacques answered as best he could; his contact with the villagers combined with his extensive reading provided him with many explanations. But he could tell them little about what went on in the closed hut.

"I know from what I've read and seen that each dance tells a story," he summarized as he parked the car. "The body decoration differs for each dance, too. In some dances the men are hunters and carry spears; in some they tell of their trips to another island, and they mimic the long ride in large canoes. But what ceremonies they'll do tonight and why they are so restricted, I just don't know."

"Do the women ever dance?" Samantha asked as they paused outside the villa.

"Yes," Jacques hastened to explain. "The women do dances for the harvest, and many of the stories about history and legends are told by the women. They sing and chant, too, but apparently tonight it is only the men who are dancing."

Jacques guided Samantha through the doorway into the large open foyer of his house. As she looked around the interior for the first time, she was struck by the vast difference between the world they had just left and the world Jacques had created for himself. Everywhere around her were signs of wealth and comfort. The furniture was light colored but sturdy, the draperies a silvery beige, the walls plain stucco but decorated with intricate carvings on a good light-toned wood.

Yet as Jacques ushered them into an open court-
yard where lunch was to be served, Samantha realized there were almost as many similarities between
the two worlds as there were differences. Although
Jacques had made use of modern materials and
equipment in designing and furnishing his house, it
all blended into the natural world. Not only the shape
of the house, but even the colors inside it reflected
the vegetation outside. Deep greens and browns provided touches of color to relieve the beigy gray of the
house without making it too bold or bright. The
wood tones were light and prominent; wood, stucco
and the softest fabrics were the dominant materials
to be seen.

And there was another similarity, a more profound
one, Samantha reminded herself as the afternoon
wore on. Like the villagers, Jacques had chosen this
home as a retreat. His was a private world, an isolated world, far from the excitement he could have
known as a movie star. For all the tropical luxury of
his magnificent house, it was a home, not a show-
place. And like the villagers he allowed very few
visitors to see him in his home.

As she dressed for dinner, Samantha sighed with
pleasure. In still another resemblance to the Micronesians living in seclusion on Atanoa, Jacques treated
his guests very well. All during the afternoon he had
suggested activities, but always offered choices and
never pressured them. If they wanted to swim when
he did, that was fine. If they would rather sail or explore a tidal pool or walk out across the coral crust in

the shallow part of the lagoon, that was fine, too. And if one or both of them had preferred to lounge inside the house or even to sleep away the afternoon, Jacques would have encouraged that, as well.

As it happened, everything he suggested sounded superb to both Samantha and Chris, and they had indulged themselves in a series of pleasures, first swimming, then sailing, then diving off the boat to snorkel in a deep blue pool, then returning to shore to wander barefoot along the beach. Samantha found herself relaxing more and more as each minute passed. Jacques was good company, not obtrusive but witty and charming. It was as delightful to be with him again as she'd anticipated.

But being with Chris was even more wonderful than she had dared to hope. With no work and no responsibilities, no pressures and no arguments, they could simply enjoy each other's company. Jacques seemed to respect their closeness without feeling—or making them feel—isolated. So they could walk happily together, swim gleefully and talk companionably, drawing closer to each other with every shared experience and every passing moment.

By the time dinner was served, Samantha's heart was aching with the fullness of her love for Chris. Her doubts had vanished, carried away by the water that had caressed their bodies in the afternoon, the icy fears had melted in the heat of the golden sun. She was content.

As the plates were removed Samantha gazed at Chris across the table, not for the first time during the delicious meal. In spite of Jacques's intelligent conversation, even in spite of his presence, she was drawn constantly to look at Chris.

His black hair was blown untidily by the breeze that billowed the curtains in the wide-open window. He reached for his coffee cup, and his eyes caught hers. In their dark depths she saw the flame burning brightly. She knew his look of hungry desire was met by her own. She could feel the flush creeping up her cheeks, but she felt no shame, no hesitation. Desire flashed between them, so sudden and so intense she felt it must be obvious even to Jacques.

She averted her eyes in confusion, unable any longer to bear the heat in Chris's gaze. But in her mind she still could see the look on his face, a look of desire and of love. Whatever had happened between Chris and Felicity was in the past, she told herself. Now it was her he loved; it had to be so.

It was not quite ten when Chris suggested turning in for the night. "It's been a long day and I'm tired," he announced with an exaggerated yawn.

"It's too early for me, but if you young ones want to call it a day, I can understand," Jacques said with a quiet smile. "I'll read for a while, I imagine."

Samantha had to fight against the color that threatened to flood her face. She sensed in Jacques an understanding she could wish were not there, an assumption she wasn't yet ready to make. Her thanks to Jacques for the day and her good-night wishes were subdued, and she barely nodded at Chris when he motioned her toward her room, just down the hall from his own.

He offered no words of farewell but simply stood by her door until she had opened it, then walked silently away. Samantha watched him as he covered the few yards from her door to his own, but she could speak no more than he.

A few minutes later she had bathed and slipped into her nightgown. Nervous and too overwrought to seek sleep, unsure what Chris intended, she pulled her light robe over her embroidered gown and walked to the window. Turning her back on the lush greens of the carpet, bedspread and plump armchair, she gazed out to the sea.

There were no lights to interfere with her view of the ocean and the stars. On the water a silvery streak marked the moon's reflection, and silver glistened from the crests of the waves that broke against the shore. In the pure black of the sky, the stars winked on and off, adding their shimmery pinpoints of light to a world dazzling in stark black and silver. The crests of the waves and the light from the moon seemed to shimmer in the darkness, and Samantha felt her heart slowly ease from its tense beating until she was at one with the dark and silvery sheen outside the window.

She stood there in silence, willing herself not to think of Chris, not to confront the choice she would soon have to make. She had stood at the window for some minutes when she heard a knock at her door.

There was no sudden leap in her blood, no frightening shock. As she walked to answer the door, she knew she had not been standing at the window to look at the moon reflected in the sea. She had been waiting for this moment...for Chris.

When she opened the door and saw Chris standing there, his hair damp and the scent of soap and water rising from his skin, she knew her choice had been made. If she had hoped to reason with herself, to maintain a calm distance, the sight of him fresh from the bath, dressed in a robe as thin as her own and considerably shorter, destroyed those hopes. But when she gazed at his dark eyes, smoldering with a fire she could feel arising within her, as well, she knew it didn't matter if her calm power of reason was lost. She was in love, she believed she was loved in return, and she knew she wanted what Chris wanted.

Chris spoke not a word, nor did she break the silence that surrounded them. She stepped back from the door, letting him walk past her into the room without so much as a gesture of invitation. He knew the invitation was given, and he knew why.

She smiled tremulously at him, not frightened but still nervous, unsure of herself or what to do. But Chris needed no guidance. He reached toward her with one hand, palm turned up in unspoken appeal. His arm moved so slowly she could scarcely breathe as she watched the inexorable approach of his expressive hand. Her breath stopped for a moment when he first touched her, his fingers light on her cheek. Then the air escaped in a sudden expulsion from her lungs, a release of all the pent-up tension building in her over the past hours and through the recent months.

She longed to bury herself in Chris's arms. She was ready to embrace him and hold him as close as she could; but he held her off with a look, still tracing one finger slowly upon the tender skin of her cheek. She ached with the need to embrace him, but he would not hurry. It seemed he had to explore every inch of her face with his fingertips. His fingers, so hardened by work, were light and caressing on her face. He explored her cheek, her chin, the sensitive skin beneath her ears and behind her neck. He traced a light line around her lips, down her nose and across each finely arched eyebrow. It seemed he couldn't know her too well, and he would not be rushed in his knowing.

He leaned toward her at last, but when she moved, yielding herself to him, he held her back, still denying her the pleasure of his embrace. Standing just inches from her, his loose robe caressing her limbs in the soft ocean breeze, he bent his head toward hers. Her mouth ached to feel his against it; but he did not offer his lips to her.

Instead he used them to follow the path his fingers had blazed onto her skin. With soft kisses he traced the route of his fingers from her cheek to her ear and back to her eyebrows, down to her eyes, then to her nose. Samantha inhaled sharply as his breath caressed her mouth, but his lips skimmed over her willing ones to move to her chin and then down to her neck.

"Chris," she breathed, pleading with him in the single word.

He leaned back from her for a moment, his eyes locked to hers with a question hers answered all too willingly. Her body trembled as he hesitated, trembled with a depth of desire she hadn't known she could feel. Her nerves were on fire and her whole body was alight with sensations she hadn't known were possible.

She could hear him breathing unevenly, rapidly, as he hesitated. Then, with a sudden inhalation, he hesitated no longer. Lowering his mouth to hers, he claimed her lips with a passion he had never before revealed. His once gentle kisses were hard and demanding, his mouth tense against her own. But she met the hunger of his lips with an equal hunger, and she could feel the effect her reaction was having on him.

Chris's lips explored her own, demandingly, with ever increasing passion, Samantha raised her arms to reach beyond his neck. Her hands moved slowly down his back, feeling his muscles rippling beneath the thin protection of his robe. In spite of the cooling breeze, heat rose from his skin in waves as she touched him, her hands as soft and exploratory on his back as his fingers had been on her face. Yet the intensity of their kiss was almost too much for her. Her hands moved convulsively, tightening still further behind him as she unconsciously sought an ever closer embrace.

Their kiss did not end. It seemed it could never end. They knew each other too intimately, and they knew each other not at all. The more he demanded of her with his restless hands and probing lips, the more she longed to yield herself to him, to melt into him in absolute surrender. And the more she demanded of him with her clenched hands and soft lips, the more he leaned into her, yielding himself to her aroused desire.

Samantha couldn't think or breathe or sense herself apart from him. She couldn't know where her lips ended and his began. She felt outside herself, beyond herself, transported to some alien and fantastic world; yet she was more aware of every inch of her body and every emotion that coursed through her restless heart than she had ever been before.

Chris's breathing was hoarse and ragged in her ear. His hands moved restlessly on her body, kneading the muscles of her back, then soothing the skin through the light fabric of her gown. Then they moved slowly, questingly, from her tingling back.

In spite of the rapid heartbeat she could feel against her cheek, in spite of his uneven and rapid breathing, Chris moved his hands with careful control. They were light and tender on her body, gentle on her waist and sides. Still holding her close with one hand, still exploring her mouth inexorably with his, he reached up to the single tie that clasped her robe at her neck. Without a wasted motion he undid the knot, then slid his hands inside the robe to her naked shoulder.

Her skin welcomed his touch, though his hand left a burning path wherever it moved. His fingers were as light on her thin collarbone as they had been on her eyelids, and when he slipped his hand under her gown to caress her still more intimately, his fingers left an ache of new knowledge each place they touched.

At last he broke off their seemingly endless kiss, but it was only to free his mouth so that it might follow his restless fingers. Easing her shoulders out from her robe, he let it fall to the ground. Slowly he bent his head to her neck, brushing her flaming skin with his tender lips. His mouth moved delicately over her neck and shoulders and down to the line of her low-cut gown.

Samantha gasped with pleasure as his lips sought skin never touched by the sun. With his first gesture of impatience, Chris pushed himself away from her just long enough to grasp her gown at the waist. Then with a swift single gesture he lifted the gown above her head. She felt its touch like gossamer as it rose over her body and beyond her head, and then she stood before him unclothed, her body freed to the kiss of the night breeze and the unblinking gaze of his smoldering eyes.

For the first time since he'd entered the room, Chris spoke. But his words, filled with love and wonder, were unnecessary. All Samantha heard was the sound of his voice, resonant and deep and broken in the depth of his emotion.

As he gazed at her, Samantha could feel a flush rising in warm color along her skin. But she welcomed his eyes for all that, shy but glad to stand there before him.

It was long before Chris moved. When he did it was to reach out for her small hands with his large commanding ones. In a silence that spoke more than words, he enclosed her delicate fingers in his, drawing her hands to his lips and kissing each finger one by one. Then he led her hands to the sash of his own robe and with a silent gesture encouraged her to untie it. Shyly she slipped the knot on the sash and, with Chris's help, loosened the robe about his body.

At last they stood together in the delicate light of the moon, as naked as the sea that washed outside the window, as private in the world they had created as were the isolated villagers living in a timeless paradise. Theirs, too, was a paradise, and time stood still for them as they waited in the shimmering light.

Chris's eyes were dark with passion, but his actions throughout their hour together had been restrained, affectionate and controlled. So, too, he stood now, the glint of the moon silvering his body with a lovely sheen, silvering Samantha's skin to match. They did not speak or rush to embrace, though Samantha could see Chris trembled as she did, and not because of the cooling breeze that wafted in through the open window.

As Samantha waited, her breath coming unevenly, Chris seemed to be waiting, as well. But at last he acted, reaching toward her with both his arms and scooping her up into the air. He cradled her in his arms for a moment, bending down to kiss her gently, almost reluctantly, then raising his head while he held her close to his sturdy chest.

Samantha could feel his heart pounding against her ear, and she heard her own beat in rapid unison with his. She knew if she was to stop Chris it must be now, before he carried her to the wide soft bed that filled the other side of the room. But she made no move to stop him; she did not want to.

Yet when Chris took his first step, it was not toward the opposite side of the room where the soft bed waited for them. Instead he moved easily to the window, carrying her as if she were no weight at all.

"It's beautiful out there," he said, his voice uneven in spite of his ordinary words.

It hurt Samantha to rouse herself to speech, but he seemed to expect it. With difficulty she forced herself into consciousness and murmured her agreement.

"It's a fairy-tale world, isn't it?" he continued softly. His breathing remained harsh, but it was less ragged than a moment before.

Samantha couldn't answer. She nestled closer to him, and she heard the sharp intake of breath as he reacted to her gentle movements. But he did not echo her gesture. Instead he put her slowly down, keeping one arm tight around her shoulders and helping her to stand until she was steady on her feet. In distress and confusion, Samantha looked up at him. She couldn't understand what had happened or what was to happen next.

Chris paused for several minutes, as if he was waiting for his heart to beat more normally and his breathing to become less a frantic gasp for air. At last he spoke again, his voice as softly caressing as his hands and mouth had been just moments before.

"This whole island is like a fairy tale," he began gently. "The Micronesians living out their dreams, Jacques living out his."

He paused, and Samantha, feeling his eyes upon her, nodded wordlessly.

"It's a world where dreams should come true," he went on musingly, gazing into the distance.

In her confusion Samantha could think of nothing to say. Her eyes followed his, looking into a distance she could not see.

Suddenly he turned to her with an easy grin. The tension had gone out of his body; his breath was light and his back curved softly. "I bet when you were a little girl you dreamed about having a big wedding," he said, smiling tenderly at her.

Samantha shrugged, shocked by his sudden change of mood and subject.

"Well? Didn't you?" he pursued.

"I suppose so," she admitted, reluctant to speak, and even reluctant to remember the dreams she had relinquished so long ago, dreams he somehow had sensed.

"Flower girls and a ring bearer, and stirring music and a high wedding cake, too," he continued, looking at her closely.

When Samantha failed to respond, he probed further. "I'm right, aren't I? All of that and a honeymoon, as well, and a very special wedding night?" His voice had grown soft and tender.

Shyly Samantha nodded. He was right: for all her years of rigid training, her cool professionalism and her self-control, she had treasured those traditional dreams. And Chris had seen them, had recognized the soft, old-fashioned Samantha behind the modern, determined career woman.

"Then that's what you'll have," he said, looking down at her gently.

Samantha grew very still. Uneasily she pondered his words, at last driven to speak. "I don't understand," she said quietly.

"You should have your wedding party and your wedding night," he responded.

Samantha grew cold. It seemed he no longer wanted to make love to her, and that was what she wanted. Her dreams of flower girls and honeymoons seemed very remote. Chris was here, and it was Chris she loved, not some mythical man in a top hat waiting for her at the end of a red-carpeted aisle.

She snuggled closer to him, suggesting in her wordless innocent way that she wanted his embraces. But he held her off with an arm tight around her shoulders. Driven to words, she stumbled, speaking of her desire in the most veiled language she could find.

"That's all in the past now," she murmured, reaching up to caress his lips with her hand, pleading with her body for his touch.

"It's in the future, too," he responded.

Samantha bit her lip in frustration. How could she say what she wanted? How could she put it into words? Even as she struggled to find the language she needed, Chris turned her slowly toward him. Holding her gently, so near she could feel the heat rising from his body but just distant enough that they didn't touch, he looked deeply into her wide eyes, examining her dilated pupils to their depths.

"Don't you understand, Samantha?" he asked, amusement and affection, passion and frustration mingling in his tone.

She returned his gaze uncertainly, then shook her head. She did not have the strength to speak.

"I love you," he said simply. "I'm asking you to marry me."

"Marry you?" she breathed in confusion.

"Yes." He laughed out loud. "Is it so hard to understand? I thought it was a very simple question."

Samantha looked at him with eyes that registered a mixture of emotions as profound as his own.

Chris sighed with exaggerated exasperation. "Anyway, the answer is simple. You have only two choices, Samantha: you can say either yes or no."

Smiling up at him freely at last, Samantha sighed with deepest pleasure, happiness filling her heart. "Then the answer's yes, Chris. Oh, yes!"

Chris reached for her without another word, folding her close to his chest and caressing her back. Again Samantha felt the hard desire rising in him as it was in her, and again she pressed closer to him, silently offering him her body as she already had her heart and her life.

But Chris held her away gently. "No, Samantha,"

he said, gazing longingly into her eyes. "God knows I want what you're offering. I want you so badly it's going to take everything I've got to walk out of this room. But that's what I'm going to do."

"Why, Chris?" she cried in passion and loss.

"Because I know your dream, and because this is an enchanted island where dreams come true," he said, kissing her lightly on the tip of her nose.

"But, Chris—" she pleaded.

He interrupted, "No. In time, Samantha. We'll have years together, and I want to give you everything I can, everything you've ever dreamed of. And that means I'm going to leave you tonight."

Samantha's arms dropped by her side. In spite of the desire churning through her body, she understood what Chris was doing. The sacrifice was as great for him as for her. He had made that clear in his words, his actions, his beating heart. Silently she handed him his robe; tenderly he draped hers around her shoulders.

As Samantha gazed up at Chris when they stood by the open door of her room a few minutes later, the love in her eyes was answered fully by the love in his own. She could only believe that he was right. Atanoa was an enchanted isle, and every one of her dreams would come true.

CHAPTER FOURTEEN

IT WAS THE SUN STREAMING IN through the open window and dancing lightly on her eyelids that awakened Samantha the next morning. She stretched like a contented cat, moving each limb and sensing each muscle with the pleasure of being alive. Lazily she opened her eyes, smiling at the sight of the golden gleam the sun had made on the bedroom walls. It was a lovely day, a day to spend in the sun, a day to be with Chris. It would be a perfect day.

Laughing aloud with joy, Samantha slipped eagerly from the bed. Dressing quickly in a bathing suit and tossing her light shift on top, she grabbed a towel and a pair of sneakers, then headed for the door.

Early as it was, she decided to wake Chris and convince him to go for a swim before breakfast. After all, they had only one full day at Atanoa. *And we're engaged,* she reminded herself with a smile. *I can wake him up if I want to.*

Chuckling at the happy absurdity of that thought, Samantha paused momentarily in the hall outside Chris's bedroom, nerving herself for the first sight of the man she loved—the man who soon would be her husband. She rapped gently on the door, then

waited in excited anticipation for his welcoming
words.

"Come on in." The words were simple, but the
voice was Chris's, and that was enough to make
Samantha's skin glow. She opened the door quickly
and stepped into his room.

Chris sat on the edge of the bed dressed only in his
red bathing suit. One foot was clad in a scuffed white
sneaker; the other rested across his knee, the laces of
a dirty twin sneaker dangling like the strings of some
balloon a child held unconsciously. Chris looked
young and healthy and vigorously alive.

If Samantha had any doubt of her welcome it was
dispelled by the glance he gave her. Dropping the untied sneaker to the floor, he opened his arms in warm
greeting.

"Come here, woman," he teased in his deep voice.

Suddenly shy, Samantha paused with one hand on
the doorknob and whispered her suggestion. "I
thought we could go for a walk before breakfast."

Chris smiled. "I'd planned to wake you as soon as
I was dressed," he admitted. "It's a perfect day for a
walk. But first. . . ." His open arms invited her near,
completing his thought with a gesture at once sweetly
tender and compelling.

Samantha walked to him and balanced herself
lightly on his lap. Feeling his chest contract as his
breath caught suddenly, she was no longer shy. This
was the man she loved, and he loved her. Happily she
nestled into his lap, treasuring the strength of his
arms encircling her. With a contented sigh she wrig-

gled closer to bury her face into the soft flesh of his neck. The warmth was shared, and it was a long moment before she could rouse herself to speak.

"Did you sleep well?" she asked at last, more to hear the sound of his voice than to know whether he had dreamed of her—or dreamed at all.

"Not badly," Chris whispered, tightening his arms around her as he spoke. "But I'd have slept a lot better if I'd been with you."

Samantha had no response but to burrow more deeply into his neck. If hugging him was no way to hide from him, she didn't care: she had no desire to hide any thought, any single feeling, from Christopher Girard.

There was no need to speak. The touch of their bodies against each other, the scent of their skin, the gentle unevenness of their breathing said it all.

At last, however, Chris moved slowly, almost reluctantly. "I suppose we ought to go," he suggested.

"I guess so," Samantha agreed. "At least if we're to take a walk before Jacques expects to meet us for breakfast."

"Then hop up, Samantha." Chris feigned annoyance. "You've put both my legs to sleep!"

They were still laughing five minutes later as they walked down the stairs, hand in hand. When Jacques greeted them from below, Samantha started to pull her hand free, but Chris held it tight. Knowing what Jacques was undoubtedly thinking, and knowing that he was only partly correct, Samantha could feel a blush climbing to her cheeks. But before her face could be tinted even more rosy by embarrassment, Chris interrupted, and the words he spoke made her glow instead with happiness.

"Congratulate me, Jacques," he announced proudly. "Samantha and I are going to be married!"

"You *are* to be congratulated!" Jacques hastened to meet them on the stairs. Extending a hand to Chris and another to Samantha, he squeezed their hands warmly. "You're a lucky man, Chris," he added with a flash of the smile that charmed millions when it was projected on a movie screen. Turning to Samantha, he leaned close to kiss her on the forehead. "I wish you the very best, my dear," he said with a sincerity she couldn't doubt.

"Thank you," she whispered. "I think I'm pretty lucky, too!"

Jacques nodded vigorously. "If I didn't believe you already knew it, I'd tell you just how lucky." His statement was firm. "Chris is a good man. I hope you'll be very happy...both of you," he concluded with another squeeze of the hands he held.

"Enough!" Chris laughed an embarrassed protest. "It's time we went for a walk. If I'd known you'd fuss like an old mother hen, I'd never have told you!"

Jacques shook his head. "I'd have known anyway," he insisted as he shooed them out the door for their walk, clucking like the fussy mother hen Chris had called him.

Early as it was, the sun shone brilliantly upon them. Samantha blinked at the stark whiteness of sunlit beach after the cool interior of Jacques's house. With Chris holding her hand her pleasure at the bright day before her was increased. She knew such glorious peace could not last forever; the real world of work and routine lay just over the glittering green ocean. Yet for however long this special time lasted, she wanted to appreciate it, and she felt sure that with Chris beside her she would have more than her share of glory and of peace in her life.

As if sensing the depth of her wandering thoughts, Chris remained silent. But it seemed he could also read her mind, for just as she reached the end of her train of ideas, he squeezed her hand, the hand he held so comfortably in his own.

They wandered along the empty beach, often in silence, sometimes pointing to a tree or a shell, a bit of seaweed brown from exposure to the air, a rock polished so smooth by the waves that had tossed it on the shore that it seemed to masquerade as the egg of some mystical seabird. When they spoke it was of various things: important, trivial—the judgment others might make bore no relevance. If Chris said it, it mattered to Samantha; if Samantha spoke, Chris cared. A story about the clinic, something Jacques had mentioned at dinner, the sound of the waves lapping unevenly against an outcropping of coral, the dew glistening on the flowers that grew in the grass where the beach melted into the forest—all were a part of the world they shared, and so each had its significance.

Samantha buried her toes in the damp sand as they

STORMY PARADISE

trailed along the beach together. Her nostrils expanded delicately to the delicious scent of the orchids that grew wild all around. The heat of the sun was pleasant on her bare shoulders, and the air was as fresh as her love.

"Samantha." Chris's voice seemed different, and Samantha turned to look at him when he called her name.

"What is it, Chris?" she asked, oddly aware of a change in his mood.

"There's something I'd like to talk to you about," he began hesitantly. "We've got the time now, and it's difficult to find time to talk on Good Providence."

Although she told herself not to be silly, Samantha felt apprehension shiver along her spine in spite of the tropical sun. With difficulty she managed to keep her voice even as she quietly prompted Chris to continue. "Yes?"

"I know it's something you've thought about," he began slowly, "and I guess I've always put you off when the topic came up before. But I really shouldn't, not any longer."

It seemed to Samantha that her throat was closing up. Her breath came hard and her back grew tense. She knew what Chris was going to tell her, and she wasn't sure she wanted to hear his story. Without a doubt it had to be the story of Felicity, and that was more than she could bear. To have that woman interrupt her happiness again seemed as unfair as anything Samantha could imagine. Yet she did not speak; she could not speak, not in the few seconds it took for all her thoughts to assail her mind and for all her pain to burrow into her heart.

As quickly as she reached a conclusion, even more quickly had Chris continued his speech. "Samantha, do you know what I'm saying? I want to tell you about Felicity." He tugged on her hand as if to be sure he had her total attention.

"No, Chris!" The words thrust themselves from Samantha only half-willed. "I don't want to hear about it. Not now!"

Chris's easy steps halted. Pulling her around to face him, he asked, "Why not? I don't understand."

He didn't say what both knew to be true: that many another time Samantha would have been all too glad to hear the story, that she'd been curious and annoyed and aroused in the past at the thought of learning the truth about the girl whose behavior and even appearance made her such a source of jealousy. Now Chris just looked at her, and it was enough to send these thoughts fleeing out of her agitated mind.

Samantha flushed under his steady gaze and his unspoken criticism. She could not say all she thought. She was afraid to hear the truth, afraid to hear that Chris *had* loved Felicity, even if it was a thing of the past. Another part of her was torn, however, for she really wanted to hear the whole story. And she honored Chris for wanting to tell her the truth. Still, she couldn't bear to listen now, not on this first morning of perfect happiness.

With a reluctance born of fearing the truth and the end to such happiness, Samantha tried to make her feelings clear to Chris—at least as clear as they were to her. She looked him steadily in the eye as she began to speak.

"It's not that I don't want to listen to you," she said slowly. "It's just that I don't want you to tell me now...this morning." She hesitated, then looked up at him pleadingly. "Can you understand that?"

There was a quizzical look in Chris's eyes as he returned her steady gaze. The furrow in his brow made it seem as though he would object, but at last he shrugged his agreement.

"All right, Samantha. If that's the way you want it," he said.

"It is," she announced with a firmness she didn't altogether feel. She knew she had given up something by refusing to listen to his story, and she knew she might regret that. But for the moment, at *this* moment, she could not let Felicity come between her and her love.

Their leisurely steps soon took them back toward the house. Although they continued to hold hands and to talk companionably, Samantha felt subdued, even a little sad. Something was missing, and she knew she was at least partly to blame for the loss of their idyllic pleasure. But her slight tinge of regret was suddenly shattered by Jacques's appearance on the path before them.

"Chris," he called out as soon as they could hear him, "I've got a message for you! It's urgent."

Grasping Samantha's hand more firmly, Chris broke into a trot. With her shorter legs, Samantha found it hard to keep pace, but she was as concerned as he.

"What is it?" Chris halted abruptly in front of Jacques.

"Charlie Tuatara called from Good Providence." Jacques bit off each word crisply. "Felicity's been found!"

Samantha could feel her heart freeze as Jacques spoke. What would Chris say? What would he do? Surely he could no longer care about the other woman, searching for her and chasing her from island to island. But when Chris spoke it seemed her assumption was wrong.

"Did the message say where she was?" Chris asked quickly, already turning his steps toward the house.

Jacques nodded. "She's up north, though Charlie didn't think she'd stay there long. He told me you'd better hurry if you want to catch her this time."

"I will," Chris said, his voice grim and determined. "I'll leave at once."

"Yes," Jacques agreed hastily. "I'll help you get ready."

Through her despair, Samantha could hear the two men making plans. Suddenly it was as if she were no longer with them. She heard Chris say something about a fuel stop for his plane and something else about a second plane, but the words made little impression on her icy heart. All she knew was that Chris was once again leaving her to seek Felicity.

"Samantha? Didn't you hear me?" Chris's voice interrupted her reverie.

"What?" she muttered in a tight voice.

"I asked if you would help me pack," he said, squeezing her hand as they neared the house.

Struggling to contain her fury and her pain, Samantha tried to pull her hand away from his, but he held on too tightly. With difficulty she murmured an answer she longed to spit out. "No. I'm going for a walk," was all she could manage.

If Jacques was surprised at her tone, he was far too polite to show it. Chris, however, was not so reluctant to reveal his feelings.

"Samantha, what's the matter now?" he asked in obvious annoyance.

"Nothing," she whispered, fighting tears with anger. "I'm going for a walk."

"Samantha!" Chris's voice echoed his confusion after her as she raced off down the same path on which they had so happily begun their walk an hour before.

"I'll be back before you leave," Samantha called. With those words she fled to the beach, desperate to be alone yet still hoping, against all good sense, that Chris would follow her.

But he didn't follow her, and it was a sad young woman who retraced her steps to the house half an hour later. She had reached no conclusion during her walk, but she knew she had to talk to Chris before he left to see Felicity. What she would say she didn't know, but she couldn't let him leave without some words—if necessary, some confrontation. They couldn't part like this.

From the moment she saw Chris, Samantha knew that he, too, had resolved to speak. He motioned her toward the waiting Jeep.

"I've already said goodbye to Jacques," he announced. "Hop in."

Samantha stared at him in confusion. "Are you taking me with you?" she asked. She had never dreamed of that possibility. What a difference it would make! She held her breath in excitement, but Chris's curt reply destroyed her hope.

"Only to the airstrip."

Hiding her renewed misery, Samantha obediently climbed into the seat beside him. For the first few minutes of the ride, both were silent. Then abruptly Chris began to speak.

"You wouldn't listen before, when I could have talked slowly and told you the whole story," he said. "Now you must."

In spite of her good resolve, Samantha couldn't subdue her angry tongue. "More excuses, Chris?" she snapped out at him.

He shook his head in fury, out of patience at last. For the first time ever, Samantha experienced the full force of his anger thrust directly at her. "You've never given me a chance, Samantha," he cried. "Even now, even after last night, you're so filled with pride that you won't trust me." He paused, then delivered a final blow. "One of these days that stubborn pride of yours is really going to hurt you!"

For the rest of the brief trip Chris maneuvered the car along the narrow road without a word. Anger was obvious in his rigid back and taut face. Too scared and too chastened to speak, Samantha sat beside him in agonized silence.

Only when they had reached the strip and Chris leaned over to pull out his suitcase from the back seat did he speak again, and then his words were brief, his tone surprisingly quiet.

"Just for a minute, suppose everything you believed were true." He paused, then continued steadily, "Felicity's in trouble. Shouldn't I help her? Wouldn't you want me to help her?"

Chris stared hard at Samantha, waiting for her to speak. In her turmoil she couldn't find the words to undo the damage her pride had caused. And before she could gather her thoughts, he had turned away.

"Chris..." she called after him a few seconds later. But he had already reached the plane. Waving frantically to catch his attention, Samantha leaped from the car as he taxied into place.

She could not be sure, but as she drove back to the house she told herself over and over again that Chris had seen her. Just before takeoff he had waved, and it had to be at her, since there was no one else. He had to know that she was sorry for her stubbornness, sorry she hadn't given him the chance to explain. She was still jealous, and maybe she always would be, but Chris's words echoed in her ears long after she parked the Jeep in front of Jacques's remarkable house and entered it, oblivious to her surroundings.

"Wouldn't you want me to help her?" Of course he should help Felicity: it was the humane thing to do, the only decent thing.

And even more, his other words, those tantalizing words that made her wish she had been patient enough and brave enough to let him speak: "Suppose everything you believed were true." *Suppose*—that was the word that lingered in her mind, all the rest of that long day and through many days to follow.

Back at the house, Jacques greeted her as if there had been nothing strange in her behavior—or in Chris's leaving. "Chris arranged a private flight out for you," he said quietly.

Samantha nodded. She had forgotten that Chris's departure left her stranded unless Jacques would fly her back to Good Providence. But Jacques didn't need to; Chris had thought of everything.

"What time?" she asked.

"Any time you want," her host responded. "The pilot will be here in about half an hour, but Chris told him you should stay as late as you want, even until tomorrow morning."

It seemed to Samantha that Jacques knew how upset she had been and, though he sympathized with her, he thought Chris was in the right. Now he was reminding her, however, indirectly, that Chris had shown his concern for her and had made generous arrangements to look after her.

Samantha roused herself to respond politely. "I think I'll leave right after breakfast," she said numbly.

"There's no need to rush away," Jacques urged. "You could still swim and sail."

Samantha shook her head. Jacques's offer was kind, and it might have been a callous rejection of his hospitality, but she couldn't bear to stay on this enchanted isle—not without Chris. Now Atanoa seemed an island of ogres and nightmares, and she had to leave.

"Thanks, Jacques, but I'll head for home," she said firmly, adding a few words of politeness before following him to the dining room.

Her scanty breakfast over, Samantha thanked her host and returned to her room to pack. She stripped off her bathing suit, pulling on a random pair of slacks and a casual shirt, then stuffing the rest of her clothes into the suitcase. With every item she tossed in, her pain intensified.

Torn between lingering fears and growing faith, between anger at herself and an increasing sense of understanding, Samantha said a subdued farewell to Jacques and began a plane ride she barely remembered when she reached Good Providence. The flight had traversed the same series of volcanic islands and coral atolls she had found so lovely the day before, but this time she hadn't noticed them. Only one thought kept running through her mind: what should she do?

By the time she entered her small house she had all but decided she would leave Good Providence when her contract expired. This constant conflict was tearing her up. She loved Chris desperately—the ecstasy of their love was wonderful; but the agony of her doubt and fear was nearly as great.

Yet her contract had months to run, and she would not break it. She could send her notice in to Chris that very day, giving him plenty of time to find a replacement. But she would not leave until her replacement arrived.

Samantha's heart sank as she thought of leaving Good Providence. She had become attached to the people and to the island, and she loved her work. She did something worthwhile on the island, and she knew it would be hard to find another job as purposeful and exciting as this. Yet she couldn't stay forever in a state of emotional limbo. She couldn't live in the alternating heaven and hell she and Chris seemed to create.

Nor could she write the letter of resignation, she found later that day as she sat before her desk. She had selected a piece of paper, filled her good pen with ink, cleared her desk of its usual pile of books and charts. But she could not write the first line. "Dear Chris?" Of course, but somehow not for a letter of resignation. Yet she could hardly write, "Dear Mr. Girard." This was the man who had asked her to marry him the night before!

I'll do it tomorrow, she promised as she pushed herself away from the desk after a fruitless half hour. Although she repeated the word "tomorrow" like an incantation, she knew she was lying. She could not leave Good Providence—or Chris.

Maybe Felicity had been Chris's mistress. Even so,

Samantha knew that Chris loved ~~her~~ now. ~~She had~~ only to recall the day and night on Atanoa to still her doubts. She thought about Jacques's reaction to Chris's leaving. The great actor clearly thought his friend was right to go to Felicity, and Samantha knew this was not the reaction of a sophisticated man-of-the-world discussing a former lover in front of a current one; it was the reaction of a decent man. And, increasingly, it was a reaction Samantha could share.

These thoughts churned through her receptive mind when she climbed into her bed late that night. She had waited up past her usual bedtime, hoping she would hear from Chris. She longed for the chance to talk to him, to listen to the story he wanted to tell. But there had been no word, and at last she had to go to sleep. Tomorrow would be Monday, a working day and a day when she might expect to hear about Chris, if not from him.

But in the morning all she learned was that he had not returned to Good Providence. Wherever Chris had gone from Atanoa, it was not back to the island. There was a rumor that he had been seen on Halekai, another that he had flown to Guam, or even to the States. There were rumors, yet no one seemed to know for sure.

Samantha thrust herself into her work. She saw few people except her patients, but Mrs. Tarai came by at least once each day. Although Samantha enjoyed her company, it seemed that the plump woman was behaving rather strangely.

It was not like her to walk to the clinic every day, especially if Samantha had visited her the same day. Yet now in the evening the widow would often show up again, "to sit and chat for a spell," she would explain. That, too, was unusual. Like Samantha, Mrs. Tarai had much work to do, and it was only rarely that she could be convinced to sit still and talk.

Her manner also seemed unusual, almost constrained. She talked about the still-missing Felicity as she always did, and she informed Samantha of the current island gossip, including the news that Pete Thompson was out of the hospital and was rumored to have been spotted on the island. But always she seemed to pull herself up short; she seemed to be holding something back.

More than once Samantha thought about asking point-blank what was going on, but she couldn't bring herself to do that. One time she did ask if anything was wrong, but the widow denied that anything bothered her. Samantha knew Mrs. Tarai was as honest a person as any she had known, yet she couldn't ignore her suspicion that the elderly woman was hiding something.

Several days passed, disquieting in their very sameness. Samantha was mildly disturbed to know Pete had been released from the hospital; but knowing there was nothing she could do about him, she had to rely on Charlie Tuatara to watch for him. It was one more reason for her to miss Chris, however, and one more reason to feel anxious about him.

Late one afternoon Samantha sat quietly at her

desk. She knew she should take advantage of her rare free time to go for a swim, but she couldn't make herself walk up the stairs, find a bathing suit, change and then proceed to the beach. It all seemed like too much effort, so she continued to sit limply at her laden desk.

"Hello, Dr. Hall." The words were simple, the voice familiar and disturbing.

Samantha looked up sharply to see Pete Thompson swing himself into the room, using his crutches with the ease of practice. Her professional eye took in his sickly appearance: his skin looked damp and pasty, and his eyes glittered as if he was running a fever. But he moved with surprising speed to stand near her desk.

"I happened to be on Good Providence, so I thought you might be able to take a look at my leg," he announced. His eyes watched hers narrowly and his voice, though flat, held some veiled threat.

Samantha shrugged. She was determined to treat him with professional distance and aplomb and to get rid of him as quickly as she could. "Is your leg bothering you?" she asked, motioning him to sit on the examining table.

"Some," he admitted, wincing involuntarily as she manipulated the toes that stuck out from the foot of the cast.

"The color is good, your foot feels warm enough, and you apparently can move your toes all right," she announced a moment later. Straightening up, she asked, "When's your next appointment with the surgeon?"

"About a week."

She turned her attention to his head wound. The line of stitches was neat and smooth, she observed with professional pride, and the wound seemed to be healing well.

"You're doing all right," she said as she concluded her examination. "I think that leg is just bothering you because you're using it too much. You should stay off it as much as possible, walk only when you have to."

Pete nodded in apparent agreement, but he seemed in no rush to get off the examining table. Samantha turned her back on him to wash her hands, hoping he would understand her silent message that he should leave. As if he did, Pete rose awkwardly from the table, maneuvering his crutches under his arms like an expert. But once he was on his feet again, he paused, looking at Samantha with a taunt in his eyes.

"I've seen your man recently," he said, insinuation obvious in his voice.

Samantha said nothing, but her heart contracted painfully. She couldn't speak, not even to rebuke Pete for calling Chris her "man." Maybe he had some news about Chris, and even news passed along by this vermin would still be more than she'd had in days.

"He was on Halekai," Pete concluded in a lazy drawl.

"Oh?" Samantha prompted him reluctantly. She hated asking anything of Pete Thompson, even hinting for a bit of information, but she couldn't resist.

"Yeah, on Halekai," Pete drew out his story, teasing her cruelly. "And he wasn't alone."

A knife sliced into Samantha's heart. She couldn't bring herself to ask, but she also couldn't walk away.

"He was with Felicity," Pete continued once it was apparent she wouldn't question him. He started toward the door, his gait an uneven swing. At the entrance he paused, turning to look Samantha directly in the eye before adding his final blow. "They looked pretty friendly."

With those words he was gone. Samantha sank into her chair, her good sense fighting with her immediate reaction of burning jealousy. Of course Chris was with Felicity; he was trying to help her. But Pete had implied so much more.

Samantha knew she shouldn't trust Pete, although there seemed no reason for him to make up such a story. What she knew about Pete Thompson made every word he spoke suspect. With difficulty she forced herself to put his tale out of her mind. His was a warped existence; there was no way she could understand what motivated him.

Thinking of how disturbed Pete was, Samantha could feel the cold band of fear wrapping itself around her chest once more. Beyond the lingering jealousy she felt, there was no reason his taunting should have upset her so; but it did. She didn't trust Pete, and not only about telling the truth.

In less than ten minutes Samantha had made up her mind. She would sleep in her old room at the widow's for a while, returning to the clinic in the daytime to work. Maybe it was silly, but knowing Pete was around and listening to his taunts had frightened her. She would be glad for Mrs. Tarai's company and she could sleep better for the security of not being alone.

As THE NEXT FEW DAYS PASSED with no unusual events and no sign of Pete Thompson, Samantha began to feel she had made too much of his casual visit. She even started to accept with her heart what her head had already told her: that whatever might be the whole truth about Chris and Felicity, Pete's story was not to be trusted. Still she lingered on at the widow's, taking comfort in the good woman's company. Although she worked each day at the clinic, she was strangely loath to remain there at night.

Mrs. Tarai had encouraged her to stay as long as she wanted. "That extra room just sits there empty," she said each time Samantha suggested she should leave.

One time she had even added what Samantha knew to be a heartfelt confession. "I get lonely sometimes now that Felicity's away," the old woman had said. "I knew she'd leave someday, but not like this. It's the not knowing that's so hard to take...."

Samantha had offered what words of comfort she could. However she felt about Felicity, she could understand the fear and the pain in a mother's heart.

Sometimes when Samantha walked into the widow's house at the end of the working day, it seemed as though the greeting she received was even

greater than could be explained by the woman's loneliness. New furrows wrinkled Mrs. Tarai's forehead,
and her eyes glinted with what seemed like relief
when she first saw Samantha as dusk approached.
Samantha puzzled over this, wondered if she was
reading too much into an expression of kind concern,
and tried to put this additional mystery out of her
head. There were too many others there, too many
unsolved problems.

One night, as the two women sat reading in silent
companionship, the phone rang. Mrs. Tarai answered it but quickly handed it to Samantha.

"Dr. Hall? Come to the clinic, please. It's an
emergency!" The voice at the other end of the phone
was breathless.

"Who is this? What's wrong?" Samantha cried as
she motioned to Mrs. Tarai to hand her the already
packed medical bag.

"Come quickly!" were the fading words before
the connection was broken.

"What is it?" Mrs. Tarai asked anxiously.

Samantha shook her head. "I'm not sure, but they
said it was an emergency, so I'd better go."

"Where?" The question was sharp and urgent.

"At the clinic," Samantha called back over her
shoulder as she trotted out the door.

The switchboard operator on the island knew
where she could be reached and transferred her calls
automatically to Mrs. Tarai's each night. Thus
Samantha could not know whether her patient had
been to the clinic or was just going to meet her there,

but she knew she must move quickly. It was urgent.

Arriving to find the clinic dark and empty, she opened the door and flicked on the light. Now she would have to wait, unable even to prepare for whatever medical emergency she might be faced with.

Her wait was brief. Before she had slipped into her white lab coat, a shadow filled the doorway. It was Pete Thompson. He walked in slowly and closed the door with a single deliberate action. Samantha couldn't be sure, but she thought he locked it, as well.

She glanced at him to see if he had been hurt once again. But he appeared as he had the last time she'd seen him, pale and somewhat weakened, yet otherwise whole.

She shivered in spite of herself. It seemed obvious that Pete had no reason to call her to the clinic, no legitimate need for her help. His very presence made her uncomfortable.

"What are you doing here?" she asked when she was sure her breathing was controlled. Though she tried to speak casually, she was all too aware of an unsteadiness in her voice.

"I thought you might be lonely," came the drawling response.

Samantha did not dignify his words with an answer, but that did not bother Pete. Leaning lightly on his crutches, he continued to speak in a lazy tone, as if he had all the time in the world.

"I know your man's still away, still off with his girl friend, so I thought you might just welcome my company."

"Not really," Samantha said, striving for a flippant tone.

"Are you sure?" Pete asked, edging nearer with his uneven gait.

"Quite sure, thank you," she responded icily.

"That's too bad." Pete shook his head with mock despair. "I think I'll just stay anyway."

"Why are you doing this, Pete?" she asked, annoyance and a tinge of fear showing in her tone.

"Why?" He drew himself up with the support of his crutches. His voices grew cold as he spoke, and his body was rigid with tension. "I'll tell you why," he hissed. "I had a good thing going here before Christopher Girard came back. And what does he do? He fires me!"

"He'd have kept you on if you'd cooperated," Samantha observed evenly. "He would have liked you to stay."

"I'll bet," Pete spat out. Black anger shot forth from his eyes. "He was quick enough to get onto me. I couldn't do anything to please him."

"Did you try?" Samantha asked. Fascinated by the quicksilver changes in Pete's mood, she also knew that if she could keep him talking she might be able to calm him down, although it seemed a forlorn hope that she might also encourage him to see reason. So she coaxed him, asking questions about his work on Good Providence before Chris's return, asking him about the old days under Chris's father.

The tense moments dragged on, each an unendurable weight to be borne. As Pete spoke, he admitted everything she had feared. He more than confessed he was responsible for all the trouble on the island; he bragged of his work.

"Your trip to the mountains in the storm? That was me," he smirked at Samantha. "The power failure? Oh, the storm helped me there," he explained with a play at modesty, "but I did most of it."

"All to get back at Chris?" Samantha asked quietly.

"That's right. I wasn't going to let him win, not me. He had dreams for this island, and I'm making damn sure he doesn't get to see a single one of those dreams come true."

There was a bitterness in his voice. Samantha knew he was unhappy, and she could feel sorry for him. After all, Chris's father had let Pete run the island any way he wanted, and so he had been a powerful man. No wonder he had become the way he was. But overriding her sympathy was a revulsion so great she could barely keep from shouting out at him. Instead she turned away in disgust and frustration.

But Pete hadn't finished. "There's one more thing I'm going to do before I'm through," he said, his voice threatening, his eyes cold and direct.

Samantha's blood raced like fire through her veins. Pete's look was too direct, his meaning too obvious to be ignored.

"Why, Pete?" She continued to appeal to his questionable powers of reason.

"Because there's nothing that will hurt Chris more than if I take his woman."

"How can you be like that?" she cried, in despair of helping him.

Pete shrugged. "That's the way I am," he announced with more bravado than understanding.

"Even if it were true that you could hurt Chris that way, I'm not his woman," Samantha tried one more time.

But Pete just laughed. "Don't bother," he spat out, lurching toward her, brandishing one crutch as if he could use it as some kind of a weapon. "I know better than that. You can't lie to me now."

"I'm not lying," she began.

Pete's interruption was swift and final. "You can't stop me, either."

As he lurched another step toward her, Samantha danced sideways, trying to get around him. He was slower than she, awkward because of the heavy cast immobilizing one leg. But while she had been trying to reach him through conversation, he had maneuvered her into a corner, and she felt trapped. She looked around quickly, trying to find something to throw at him, some way to distract him. But there was nothing.

Swiftly she reached a decision. She would have to tackle him, or maybe trip him. Although he was accustomed to walking on crutches, he had to be unsteady, and that would give her a chance. It went against her desire to help him and even more against her code as a doctor; she would have to hurt a patient, a pathetic helpless man. But she had no choice.

She paused, waiting silently for her opportunity. She felt sorry for Pete. He was even more stubborn than she had been about listening to Chris.

As she watched Pete's mobile face reflect his anger, bitterness, bravado and fear, Samantha knew he could not hurt her. Only she could hurt herself, and she hoped it was not too late to undo the damage she had done with Chris. She hoped the next time she saw him she would have the courage and the self-control to listen to him.

Even as she reached this resolution, Pete took one more step, swinging confidently on his crutches. Then, before he could come any closer, Samantha heard voices outside the door.

"In here!" she shouted. "Please, I'm in here!"

The door burst open, its lock shattering with the force of the men behind it. Samantha looked over with a flood of relief. It was Chris, with Charlie Tuatara and her old friends Mark and Tom.

Chris glanced at her quickly. "You're all right?" he asked hastily.

When she nodded that she was, he turned to face Pete. The concern his eyes had expressed for Samantha faded, to be replaced with a hardness she had never before seen. His eyes seemed like lumps of coal, so black and final was their look.

"You've done it now, Pete," he said flatly. "You've said enough to put yourself behind bars for a long, long time."

"You heard?" Samantha had to interrupt to ask.

Chris's voice did not change. Without turning to

look at her he spoke coldly to Pete. "I heard. We all did. You can't get out of it this time."

With a dip of his head he motioned to the other men to approach. Quickly they tied Pete's hands together with a length of hemp. "Take him away," Chris said, spitting out the words as though there were a bitter taste in his mouth.

"How can I walk?" Pete protested sullenly, raising his joined hands to Chris in a gesture half of threat, half of supplication.

"That's your problem," Chris shot back.

"Chris," Samantha spoke in quiet warning.

"Mark and Tom will help you." Chris amended his earlier statement with apparent reluctance. "But I'm not taking any chances this time."

Ten minutes later Pete had been hustled from the room, leaving Chris alone with Samantha. "Are you really all right?" he asked, his eyes soft and moist.

She nodded. "He didn't touch me."

"I know that," Chris said, shaking his head impatiently. "I told you we heard the whole thing. But he was pretty rough anyway."

"I'm all right," she answered softly.

"Frightened?" His voice was tender.

"Relieved," she admitted.

For a moment there was silence between them. Chris looked at her hungrily but did not move to touch her. Samantha stole brief glances at him, then looked away.

"You were very brave," Chris said at last. "You don't know how much you helped us."

"Helped you?" she asked. All at once she realized what must have happened, and the questions began to pour out of her. "Were you hiding there? Outside? How did you know he was here? How long were you there?"

"One at a time," Chris laughed, holding up his hands in mock protest. Silently he drew her down to sit on his lap on the sofa. His hands stroked her hair softly, as if he was trying to comfort her. "Let me start at the beginning," he suggested, looking steadily into her eyes as he added, "the morning I left Atanoa."

That was too much for Samantha. She couldn't bear the gaze of his deep eyes nor the dreadful thought of that morning. Filled with memories of her stormy pride, her fears and her hopes, she slipped off his lap. But he caught her hand and pulled her down beside him on the sofa. Placing his hand under her chin, he lifted her face so that she had to look at him.

"Listen to me, Samantha," he began. "Let me tell you what happened."

She nodded, willing herself not to lapse into jealousy, but to listen with the openness of her attempt at understanding.

Chris spoke quickly, as if anxious to get this done. "You remember the message—that Felicity had been found?"

Samantha forced herself not to wince at the sound of the name she had grown to dread, and Chris continued without interruption, "Well, that was only part of the message."

Surprised, Samantha looked up at him, waiting anxiously for him to continue.

"Charlie had called all right, and he'd found Felicity." He paused for a fraction of a second, then added under his breath, "That story can wait." Without giving Samantha a chance to respond, he hastened on with his tale.

"The other part of the message was that Pete had been found, as well. . . on Good Providence. Jacques didn't know whether to say that in front of you, because he thought it might alarm you."

Samantha moved uneasily, and Chris quickly added, "I disagreed with Jacques. I only wish he could have seen you tonight! Then he'd know just how brave you are!"

Laughing in spite of herself, Samantha settled back to hear more of Chris's story. With a deep breath he continued, "After talking to Charlie again, while you were out walking, I decided not to tell you about Pete." Chris didn't pause when he referred to her angry walk on Atanoa, and she struggled not to interrupt.

"Charlie and I talked for a long time that morning, trying to decide what to do. By then we knew Pete was behind a lot of the problems on the island, but we couldn't prove it. Do you understand?" He paused to look at her before modifying one important statement. "That is, we couldn't prove it. . . until tonight."

"Tonight?" Samantha echoed, an idea beginning to form in her clouded mind.

Chris chose his words with care. "The situation had become pretty desperate, Samantha, and so I'd become desperate, too. When Charlie suggested his plan to me I was reluctant—but I decided we had to try it. There was a chance it might work, and nothing else had."

"What was his plan?" Samantha asked, struggling to breathe through the cold weight that pressed on her chest.

Chris paused. When he continued his voice was soft but steady. "Charlie suggested I make it look as if I'd gone away. He figured that would bring Pete out into the open. Then, if we had him watched all the time, we could finally catch him at something. That way we'd have proof at last."

He paused, waiting for Samantha to speak. When she didn't he continued, "I flew from Atanoa to Halekai, made sure I was seen there, then placed my plane in a locked hangar. The police on Halekai helped me get back here in secret, and I've been on the island ever since, hiding out."

"But why didn't you tell me?" Samantha cried out in misery after she'd admitted the logic of the plan.

Chris looked at her steadily. "Charlie thought, and I agreed, that Pete would probably come to you to find out where I was. If you'd known the truth it would have been harder for you to act natural. This way—"

"This way I had to be worried half-sick, and... and you lied to me!" Samantha interjected angrily.

"I'm sorry, Samantha." Chris spoke pleadingly.

"But we had to do something. We couldn't go on like that forever. The island would have been destroyed." He paused. "And it *did* work," he reminded her softly.

"Yes, but—" she began.

It was Chris's turn to interrupt. "I know it was frightening for you, and I hated lying to you. But I swear you were never in any danger—none."

She looked at him in doubt.

"Really." He gazed at her tenderly. "Do you think I'd have let you be?"

"I don't know what to think," she replied.

"You were never alone," Chris went on, obviously hoping that the facts would help. "Ed or Father Ilima, Mark or Tom watched you all the time. Charlie knew every move you made. Someone was outside the clinic each night, until you went to Mrs. Tarai's." He paused, then added quietly, "I was so glad when you did that."

"Did she know?" Samantha asked in sudden suspicion.

"Yes," Chris admitted. "I needed to tell her because there were times Charlie's men couldn't very well be with you. In the evenings, for example, before it was dark enough to hide outside. So she'd come over."

Samantha thought silently. That explained Mrs. Tarai's frequent visits and her strange nervous behavior. Grudgingly she realized that Chris was right about one thing: had she known the secret she might very well have revealed something of it to Pete.

And if he felt that there was something unusual going on, he would not have been so quickly flushed out.

"You knew she was over here at night?" Samantha asked softly. She couldn't quite bring herself to admit her discovery to Chris, but she could hint that she recognized his constant concern.

He smiled. "I knew where you were and who you were with every moment," he confessed. "You've been watched and tailed and spied on." With a grin he concluded, "You've got very few secrets left!"

Finally Samantha began to relax. A smile played on her lips as she put together the story Chris had told her, but it was replaced by a frown as she remembered the events of the evening.

"Someone was watching the clinic tonight?" she asked.

Chris nodded. "Charlie was here; Mark was with me. When Mrs. Tarai called to tell us about your message, we picked up Tom and hurried over. We arrived just after Pete walked in the door: Charlie was just beginning to get nervous! But we were here in plenty of time—we heard everything."

"Then it's over now," Samantha breathed in nervous relief.

"It's over," he soothed her encouragingly. "He'll be in jail on Halekai first thing tomorrow morning, and that'll be the end."

Samantha sighed. She was exhausted by her ordeal but overwrought by all that had happened, and she was still unsure what to say to Chris. She turned to him, longing to speak to him and to hear the explanation she had put off so long. But before she could even tell him she wanted to listen to him now, she heard a light tap on the door.

"That'll be Mrs. Tarai," Chris said, looking down at Samantha reluctantly. "I asked Mark to have her come over here to be with you."

"But Pete's gone. . . ." In her confusion Samantha stumbled over the words.

"And you're exhausted," Chris observed. "You shouldn't be alone now."

Samantha blinked, her eyes heavy and her body drained of all its energy. As she tried to rise to greet the widow, Chris motioned her to rest. He started to stand up, then leaned close to her, whispering a few tender words in her ear.

"I should be the one to stay with you," he said softly, adding with a chuckle, "But I think the neighbors might talk."

Samantha gazed after him in exhausted bewilderment as he said a casual greeting to Mrs. Tarai, then walked to the door. There he paused to speak again. "Get some rest, Samantha; we'll talk tomorrow. And, Samantha. . . ."

She looked at him as he uttered one final thought. "Thank you. Thank you for everything."

CHAPTER FIFTEEN

IN THE MORNING Samantha awoke befuddled, and not only because she'd slept poorly after her exhausting encounter with Pete. She felt drained. It was with the greatest difficulty that she rose from bed, washed and dressed and prepared for work. As the day passed without a word from Chris, she realized she again felt she was in some kind of limbo, waiting.

She remembered all of Chris's words and actions from the night before; she remembered the love and concern in his eyes and the tenderness in his voice. But she also remembered the day of his departure from Atanoa.

Although he'd explained the days of silence that had followed that morning, she was disturbed, for still she hadn't heard the story of Felicity. Now there were more hours of silence, hours that quickly wore on to be a day, and then a second.

Others told Samantha that Pete had been taken to Halekai; he was in jail awaiting trial. But Chris didn't call to give her the welcome news. Others told her that Chris had gone to Halekai, presumably to make sure Pete stayed in jail. But again it was someone else who gave her that news, not Chris.

On Saturday morning Samantha sat in a silent clinic, acutely aware of the long day that stretched before her. There was no work to fill her time, nothing she had to do, and for the first time in her life there was nothing she wanted to do. Nothing, that is, except see Chris. The last she had heard, he was still on Halekai. She had no reason to believe he would return this particular day, though she felt sure that he would come to see her when he did. She felt driven toward him by some inexorable force, a force that denied her few remaining doubts. Thus, in a silence so oppressive she could feel it surrounding her, she waited.

When Chris appeared in the clinic doorway, Samantha wasn't surprised. But the sight of him standing there, dressed in a trim red bathing suit, made her heart turn over.

"It's a good day for a picnic," he said quietly.

Samantha's mind whirled with his words. *A good day for a picnic? Just that, when there was so much to say?*

"The sun's bright, there's not a cloud in the sky, but there's a bit of a breeze," he continued, as though her silence held an objection to his assertion that it was a good day to be outdoors.

Samantha stared at Chris when he'd finished his weather report. Meeting his gaze, she averted her eyes from his face. He was so lean and strong it made her heart ache to look at him, to notice how his bathing suit emphasized the very maleness of his form.

When she continued to sit in silence, Chris made an exasperated sound. Dropping the shirt he carried onto a chair, he took a step toward her. There was a grin on his face, but there was also a dangerous glint in his eyes.

"If you're not in a bathing suit and ready to go on a picnic in five minutes, I'm going to help you change," he threatened.

He meant it. There was a look in his eyes that said he would enjoy every moment of the process, too. Without a word Samantha fled up the stairs to change. As she did, she realized a smile was hovering about her face for the first time in days. There might be painful moments ahead, but she would be with Chris. As she descended the stairs, she realized with a clarity so sudden it made her heart stand still that she loved Chris's unpredictability, the exciting sense of life in him that let him be master of an island one moment and the next a boy playing hooky from school to go on a picnic.

Samantha's heart was still pounding from her haste and her excitement when Chris ushered her into his waiting car. He tossed her towels next to the wicker picnic basket. She had barely fastened her seat belt when he had the car in gear and was careering along the road past the village.

"Where are we going?" she asked, though the question she longed to ask was, *where have you been?*

"On a picnic."

"But where?" she insisted.

"I thought since we were in bathing suits we'd go to a beach," came the unhelpful response.

That was the way Chris responded to all her questions. His tone was light, his mood teasing. He offered no bit of information about his plans for the day, not where they were going or how long they would be gone, and he answered her questions with jokes, if he answered them at all. When Samantha finally gathered her courage to ask him about the past few days, he adroitly changed the subject.

Throughout their ride he evaded her questions about Pete and about Halekai, about his disappearance and his plans. The only things he would talk about were neutral topics: her work, the weather, the beautiful scenery through which they drove. When he spoke of her work, he needed no encouragement from her; as always, he seemed to know what she had been doing, who was sick on the island and even that the Bascomb twins did not have measles.

When Chris pulled the car off the road onto a secluded pathway, Samantha looked at him in exasperation. "For someone who's never around, you sure seem to keep tabs on everything."

It was Chris's turn to be silent. His only response was a grin as he lifted the picnic chest down from the car.

"Can you carry these?" he asked, loading her arms unceremoniously with a blanket, four towels and a small straw bag.

"And if I couldn't?" she muttered testily.

He shrugged. "Then we'd do without towels."

With that straightforward response he led the way toward an overgrown path.

"Are we going to walk through there?" Samantha looked askance.

Chris nodded. "The car won't fit," he said with a wicked grin.

Grimacing, Samantha adjusted her awkward load and followed him along the weed-covered path. With her eyes on the path and her mind on Chris's strange behavior, she did not notice when the path ended. But when Chris stopped she was forced to stop, too, and she raised her head to see a magical world.

They were in a secluded cove, one she had never before discovered. From the look of the path, very few people had ever found this hideaway, and no one had been here recently.

The beach curved around in a horseshoe, opening out to the sea. Palm trees grew almost to the edge of the water on one side; the other was protected by a rocky cliff. Bird tracks crisscrossed the sand no human foot had marked in a long time. The golden sand sparkled from the glow of the sun; the water glinted with flecks of gold. The only sound disturbing this new Eden was the cry of a bird as it sought shelter in a palm.

"Chris, it's beautiful," she whispered as she gazed about her in awe.

He nodded. "It's as pretty as I remembered," he admitted. "I haven't been here in years."

"I saw the path was overgrown," she observed as she helped him pin the blanket to the sand with the picnic basket at one corner and shoes at the others.

Chris smiled, but his smile was tight. "I found this place one summer, when I was home from school for a while. I used to come here a lot then."

Samantha looked across the short distance to where he stood. "Sort of an escape?" she suggested softly.

"You might say so." Chris paused, as if remembering those lonely days so long ago. "It was mine anyway, a place where I could be alone—and no one could find me. Even then, though I walked down that path nearly every day, it was narrow and I was careful not to bend the branches. You'd have had to know exactly what you were looking for if you were going to find it."

Samantha stood quietly. There was so much she wanted to say, yet she lacked the words that could make up for the lonely pain of such a childhood. It was Chris who broke the silence between them.

"Let's swim," he suggested, tossing his shirt on top of the pile of towels.

Samantha hesitated. In the moment of their silent communion she had felt very close to Chris, close enough to be ready for his story—about Felicity and about the past few days. Yet before she could act on her new courage, Chris interrupted her ruminations.

"Do you walk to the water on your own or do I carry you?" he asked, taking a step toward her as if to act on his threat.

Samantha raced across the beach ahead of him, hearing his shout of laughter as he chased her to the ocean. Still running, she flung herself into the embrace of the waves, falling forward to be immersed in the ever moving sea. Chris followed right behind her, running with high quick steps until the water reached his thighs before he suddenly disappeared below the surface in a long knifing dive.

His lean body broke through the waves in less than a minute and he turned away from the beach. With a powerful stroke he headed out to sea, beckoning Samantha to follow. She hesitated for only a moment and then began to swim steadily after him.

With every stroke she could feel her tension disappearing. The water rushed over her, soothing her and cleansing her of all the pain and doubt of the past days. When she neared Chris she rolled onto her back. Panting from her hard swim, she rested, gasping until her breath returned. As her heart slowed to normal, she could feel her anger draining away. Suddenly she felt free again, free from the burden she had carried far too long.

As if sensing the change in her mood, Chris swam up to her. Rolling onto his back, he, too, floated peacefully, buoyed up by the rich salt water. When they had rested for a few moments he flipped onto his stomach again, then dived suddenly beneath the water. Samantha had barely had time to wonder where he had gone when he appeared on her other side. He smiled, then disappeared again, diving repeatedly and always popping up to grin at her.

It was irresistible. He was like a young porpoise, playing because he had to play, because he was too

alive not to swim and dive and experience all that life
offered. Samantha laughed to see Chris frolicking in
the sea, apparently as carefree as a child. That
thought caught at her. He could not have been so
carefree when he was young, she realized. As a child
he had come here to escape, and, he implied, he had
come here alone.

Pushing her saddening thought aside, Samantha
followed Chris on his next dive, then on another. She
chased him under the surface, then raced away with a
swift stroke when he turned toward her. Like a pair
of porpoises they dived and raced, bumped into each
other and swam side by side. When at last, by mutual
consent, they turned to shore, Samantha was giddy
with laughter and totally relaxed. She felt like a child
again, innocent and free.

Chris tossed her a towel and she rubbed her curly
hair till her scalp tingled. Then, patting her skin dry,
she sank in healthy exhaustion on the blanket.

"Oh, that felt good," she laughed as she stretched
herself luxuriously. "I haven't had such fun in a long
time."

Chris smiled down at her without a word. In his
eyes shone a light so intense she had to turn away.
But when he knelt by the picnic basket and concentrated on pulling out a carafe of wine and two
stemmed glasses, she turned toward him. Without his
eyes gazing at her, she could watch him once again.
Chris uncorked the bottle, then poured wine into
each glass, moving deliberately. Then with a flourish
he offered one of the glasses to Samantha.

"Pretty fancy for a picnic," she said as she accepted the glass with a nod of equal formality.

"It's a kind of celebration," he explained.

"What's the occasion?" she asked curiously.

But Chris shook his head. "That comes later. First, let me tell you about Pete and...some other things, too."

Against her will, Samantha stiffened. The resistance she fought rose in her again, and she could feel her courage drifting away on the receding waves.

As if sensing her tension, Chris went on quickly. He seemed determined to speak and to make her listen. "You probably heard we took Pete to Halekai the morning after we caught him at the clinic. I stayed on there. I had to fill out some papers, and the police made it clear that my testimony could make a difference."

He paused, looking far out to sea with eyes that narrowed in remembered anger. When he spoke his voice carried firmly, although his teeth were clenched. "I wasn't going to take any chances on that scoundrel's getting away again!"

In the silence that followed his assertion, Samantha spoke softly, "So now you know he's in jail?"

Chris nodded, his shoulders still hunched, his voice bitter. "He is, and he will be for a long time. I've also seen to it that when he gets out of jail he'll leave the area."

Samantha looked at him in curiosity.

"He won't be allowed to return to Good Providence," he explained grimly. "Merely setting foot on the island will be enough to send him back to jail, and no one on Halekai is likely to want to hire him."

"What will he do?" Samantha asked, torn between her sense that Chris had no choice and the conflicting belief that Pete should be given another chance.

It seemed that bitter as he was, Chris shared her philosophy, for he shrugged and admitted, "I've already started making some contacts for him on other islands. I'll try to help him find a job, maybe on Guam or in the States." He paused, then said somberly, "I don't think Pete's really all that bad. It's just here that he went wrong."

Samantha nodded gratefully. "I think you're right." A sobering thought crossed her mind. Tentatively she asked, "But will he accept your help? After all, he doesn't like you very much."

For the first time since he'd started talking about Pete, Chris's face wrinkled with a smile. "That's the understatement of the decade! He hates me!" After a moment he went on thoughtfully, "I think you're right, though. I'll have to make sure he doesn't know I'm responsible for any job offers he might get. But that can be arranged."

Samantha agreed quickly, then sighed with relief. It seemed as though Pete Thompson would not be a problem for Good Providence—or for her while she remained there. That last thought sent a shiver down her spine. She still hadn't decided how long she could stay on Good Providence, though she had never been able to write that letter of resignation.

She wouldn't willfully leave, yet she didn't know what to do.

As she sat musing about her uncertain future, she realized Chris had continued to speak. His tone had changed, and his eyes searched hers as he began his next sentence.

"While I was on Halekai, I saw Felicity."

Although Chris's voice was flat, almost expressionless, his words cut through Samantha. It was no more than she expected, but still it hurt to hear that the rumors were true. Struggle as she might against her jealousy, thinking about Felicity—and worse yet, thinking about Chris with Felicity—made her stiffen.

She withdrew her eyes from Chris's face. But Chris would not let her turn away. Slipping his arm around her, he drew her so near she could feel the grains of sand clinging to his damp chest. The heady male scent and those of sun and salt rose from his skin, and she had to fight to keep her head.

"You're going to listen to me this time, Samantha," he said. The smile playing subtle magic on his face could not wholly hide the firmness of his voice.

Samantha said nothing, just waited, barely able to breathe as he went on.

"I'm going to tell you the whole story, and you're going to listen," he repeated. "You're not going to interrupt with that tongue you wield like a scalpel!"

Frowning, Samantha sat quietly in the unyielding circle of his arm. His eyes might be sparkling with humor and his voice firm with certainty, but his arm was strong and warm against her skin. She stiffened her back, resigned to hearing the worst but glad at least that she would be hearing it all.

Chris spoke slowly. It was obviously hard for him to talk, but it was necessary, too. "I had to see Felicity," he began, ignoring the increased rigidity of Samantha's back. "I had to find out if she was involved with Pete."

Samantha leaned back in the circle of Chris's arms to look up at him in shock. "With Pete?" she echoed.

Chris's nod was grim. "Well, you know, she'd disappeared about the same time the trouble started, and . . . for one reason or another, Mrs. Tarai thought she might have been involved in some of Pete's mischief-making." He paused, then spoke into Samantha's silence. "Mrs. Tarai was pretty worried."

Samantha didn't know what to think. At last she murmured, "And had she? I mean, had Felicity . . . ?"

"No." On this point Chris's voice was firm. "I never thought she'd do that. She's restless, but she couldn't have been an accomplice to what Pete was doing."

Samantha nodded slowly. That was her sense of the girl, too. She could imagine how Felicity might have become involved with someone like Pete, maybe even out of anger at Chris when his attentions began to shift; yet doing intentional harm to the island and its people seemed unlike her.

Chris continued, his voice a steady ripple over

Samantha's surging thoughts, "I had a long talk with her once I'd finally tracked her down. It was as I'd expected; she'd just gone to Halekai as so many of them do, because she was restless. She wasn't satisfied with life here, and she thought she could make a new life for herself—maybe at the resorts or even in the big hospital. Oh, yes," he said in answer to Samantha's unspoken question. "She admitted she even looked for work as a nurse's aide, but she didn't find anything."

"She's good," Samantha said with difficult magnanimity.

"I think so," Chris acknowledged. "But she had no references; she couldn't cite any job experience or she'd have given herself away. She was determined to leave here, and she thought the only way she could do it was to run away, to hide."

After a brief hesitation he went on, his voice soft and thoughtful, "I guess I wasn't really surprised when she ran off. I'd expected it for a long time. She'd been restless for years and really wanted to leave Good Providence, but Mrs. Tarai wanted her to stay."

Samantha wondered bitterly if it was only the widow who had pressured Felicity into staying on Good Providence, but Chris interrupted her thoughts.

"Mrs. Tarai had asked me to help when I first came back home. I agreed to do what I could. I thought she'd make a good assistant for you, and I hoped a job she liked might help her to settle down, at least for a while," he added.

"You tried," Samantha managed to say with what she hoped was polite consolation.

Chris shrugged. "I owed it to her," he said simply.

Although she had promised herself she wouldn't react to his confession, Samantha could feel her shoulders pulling back at his words. Her body tried to withdraw from Chris's encircling arm.

Undoubtedly sensing her shrinking movement, Chris pulled her closer to him. He forced her to look at him as he quickly finished his explanation. "I owed her something...because she is my half sister!" he announced all at once.

As Samantha looked at him in shock and confusion, a pattern began to form in her mind. Many things she had not understood began to make sense, even before he said another word. She realized how similar Chris and Felicity were, in nature as well as in appearance. Both were dark and well built, both passionate and alive. Yet the drive and the kindness that adversity had developed in Chris was atrophied or even soured in Felicity. They were alike enough to be sister and brother, but they were very, very different.

Relaxing now, Chris still kept his arm around Samantha as he told her the story.

"My father was Felicity's father," he began. "Her mother was a young village woman who left the island even before Felicity was born." Chris's voice turned bitter. "I gather my father gave her no choice, but she got back at him. She appeared one day at the

Big House when the baby was just a few months old, handed the child to him and then disappeared.''

"So Mrs. Tarai isn't Felicity's mother?" Samantha asked in confusion.

"No. She'd been my nurse, and when Felicity's real mother abandoned her baby, she agreed to raise Felicity as her own child.''

Chris paused, then added, "My father paid her to do it, I'm sure; but I don't think she'd have cared about that. I think she simply had the decency to do what my father wouldn't: give a helpless little girl a home. It didn't matter to her whose child it was. The baby needed a home; that's all.''

"Did you know about Felicity when you were growing up?" Samantha asked, giving up her struggle to imagine what Daniel Girard must have been like. A man who could abandon his pregnant mistress, ignore his son and give away his daughter was beyond her comprehension.

Chris shook his head. "No one did, or at least that's what my father thought. Everything was handled really quietly; my father saw to that," he added under his breath.

"He was anxious enough for the story not to be known that he arranged for Mrs. Tarai to leave the island for a while, smuggling the baby off with her. When she returned, a few years later, it was as a widow with a young child. No one was going to count the exact years, and anyway, she wouldn't have cared. All she cared about was the child, *her* child as far as anyone seemed to know.''

"Then how did you find out?"

Chris grinned. "How'd you expect? From Pete Thompson."

He nodded grimly in response to Samantha's wide-eyed stare. "Pete had been working for my father, and he stuck his nose into anything he thought might help him. Here was a good story, a hold over my father and, he thought, a hold over me, too."

"So Pete told you, figuring that way you'd keep him on?" It was easy for Samantha to make the obvious guess.

"That's right. After all, it worked with my father," Chris admitted seriously. But he concluded with bitter strength, "It sure didn't work with me!"

Samantha spoke her thoughts out loud. "Then you felt you had to do something for Felicity, of course." She paused before asking abruptly, "Did you tell Mrs. Tarai what you knew?"

Chris shook his head. "She'd really come to think of Felicity as her daughter, I think, and anyway, everyone else had. I couldn't let her down. But sometimes I think she knows. Sometimes she looks at me and...." His voice trailed off. "It doesn't matter anymore."

"Now that you know where Felicity is, will you be able to help her?" Samantha asked softly, her voice revealing the care she, too, could feel now that her last nerve end of jealousy had been soothed.

Chris smiled. Releasing her at last from his embrace, he stretched lazily. "I've already arranged for her to go to nursing school in the States," he told her with a smile. "You've said she's got talent, and I think that'll give her a real challenge. When she gets out she can do what she wants and go where she wants."

"Maybe by then she'll be ready to return to Good Providence," Samantha suggested.

"Would you welcome her back?" Chris asked, looking closely at Samantha as he spoke.

Samantha flushed, embarrassed for all she had thought and said to Chris about his relationship with Felicity. But she forced herself to answer his question, and to answer it honestly. "Yes," she responded, "now I could welcome her back." Thoughtfully she added, "Especially if she was a nurse. We could really use a fully trained nurse on Good Providence."

Chris smiled tenderly at Samantha, gazing deeply into her eyes for a moment before turning away to reach for something in the picnic basket. With his back to her he said, "But it'll be years before Felicity's ready to help, even if she does return. You can't wait that long for an assistant."

Straightening up, he handed her half a dozen manila folders, each with a name typed on the outside, each name followed by the significant letters R.N.

"Nurses?" Samantha asked, looking at him perplexed.

"I started searching for an assistant for you as soon as Felicity left," he admitted. "I'd thought about it even before, when I saw how busy you were, but I kept hoping she'd take hold." Motioning to the folders sprawled on Samantha's lap, he added, "I figured you'd have to make the final choice, but I did what I could for you."

"This is great," Samantha declared, quickly glancing through the files. "They all look good," she announced a few minutes later. "It'll be a hard choice."

"You'll have to make it quickly, though," Chris warned.

"Why?" Samantha asked. She would be glad to have help in the clinic again, especially the assistance a trained, responsible nurse could provide. But she had survived without help ever since Felicity had left, and there seemed no reason to rush now.

Chris pulled her into his arms with a sigh. "Because it's not only your patients who are going to be making demands on your time," he said. "You're going to be busy with things besides medicine from now on!"

Samantha had no difficulty understanding Chris's implications, and she snuggled into his arms happily. "I'll get to the folders again tonight," she promised.

But he shook his head. "I'll give you a one-day reprieve. Tomorrow will be time enough. If you make up your mind then, you can have someone here in a few weeks."

"A few weeks?" she exclaimed. "You can't get someone to come out here that quickly."

"Oh, yes, I can. Every one of those applicants is willing to start work immediately." He flashed her a wicked grin. "I made that a condition of employment."

Samantha laughed. "You *are* anxious! Maybe I should look at the folders this afternoon."

Chris leaned over and brushed her lips with his own. "Not this afternoon, and not tonight. You'll be busy."

He drew her close to him, his leg firm against hers as he kissed her again and again without rest, until she could hear the pounding of her heart match the rapid beat of his own so close to her ear. When at last he pulled himself away from her, it was to look at her with yearning in his eyes.

"Still, you'd better get to it first thing tomorrow," he teased. "I'm not a patient man."

Samantha chuckled deep in her throat, then reached up to pull him close to her again. But Chris gently untangled her arms from around his neck.

"There's something else I want to give you," he said softly.

Reaching into the picnic basket again, he pulled from that cornucopia a small dark velvet box. Handing it to Samantha, he murmured, "I told you this was a celebration."

Samantha held the box in one tight hand, prolonging the moment. She was sure she knew what the box contained. It had to be a ring, and the occasion Chris expected to celebrate would be this day of their formal engagement.

Lifting the cover at last, she looked inside the box. But no sparkling gem met the light in her eyes. Instead, folded in a tiny square was a piece of heavy paper.

Before she could open it, Chris clasped her hand in his. "I know you were expecting a ring, Samantha," he said wistfully. "But a formal engagement's the one dream I'm going to deny you."

She looked at him, puzzled by the mixture of regret and warm joy in his voice.

"It'd be lovely to be engaged," he continued, "but we've waited too long." Planting a quick kiss on the tip of her nose, he added, "I told you I'm not a patient man!"

With that reiteration echoing in her ears and a happy confusion reigning in her heart, Samantha slowly unfolded the heavy paper. Spreading it open in her hand, she read the words printed in formal Gothic letters on the rich vellum:

You are invited to celebrate the marriage of
Samantha Hall and Christopher Girard
in the village square
at dusk.

"Tonight?" she breathed when she read the date printed at the bottom.

"Tonight," he repeated.

"But. . ." she sputtered in excitement and surprise.

"Do you mind? Is it too fast for you?" Chris spoke rapidly in his concern.

That quieted Samantha. Her arms circling his

neck, she drew his head down to hers. "No, Chris. It's what I want, too."

"Your dress is ready—it's at Mrs. Tarai's. I'm supposed to get you there by five." Chris spoke brightly now, telling her of the plans he had made and the joy he had taken in preparing to surprise her. "Ed and she will stand up with us, and Father Ilima will perform the ceremony."

"In the village square," Samantha whispered, re-reading the printed invitation.

"In front of all the villagers," Chris pointed out. Drawing her close to him, he asked anxiously, "Will that bother you? They feel that you belong to them, you know."

Samantha shook her head with a warm smile. "It's just as it should be, Chris."

She snuggled close to him, relaxing into his steady embrace, hypnotized by his repeated words of love. She echoed his words and his promises and matched each kiss he gave her with one of her own.

"Don't you want that picnic?" he murmured at last, sighing with pleasure.

"Not especially," she admitted with a quick smile.

"A swim, then?" he suggested, moving slightly away from her on the sun-warmed blanket.

"No, thanks," she answered jauntily, wriggling over to lie next to him once more.

"Samantha, I've told you I'm not a patient man," he mockingly complained as she moved her leg against his.

"And I've made it pretty clear I'm not a patient

woman,'' she responded with a grin. Leaning over him, she brushed her lips against his, first lightly, then with an ever greater pressure as she could feel his desire rising to meet her own.

Chris groaned lightly. "We'll be late for our own wedding," he protested. But his protest was feeble, and it was belied by his hands stroking her bare back.

Samantha only laughed. "It's not even noon. That invitation said 'dusk,'" she observed with a pretense of rationality.

"But your dreams? All those special little girl's dreams?" he whispered a few minutes later when Samantha knew she was trying his patience almost beyond the limit.

Pausing for breath, she spoke. "I've got everything I ever dreamed of. There's nothing more I want."

Chris rolled her over, his arms tight around her, his heart pounding like the sea in her ear. There was nothing more to say.

Hours later, as they stood hand in hand in the village square, Samantha shared a quick secret grin with Chris. He had been right: they were almost late for their own wedding. But it wouldn't have mattered if they had been, for nothing could go wrong this day.

As the sky turned to fire over the ocean, they joined their hands in love and joined their lives with vows spoken before all the islanders. Later the people of Good Providence continued their celebration with dancing in the square and at the beach, but Chris and Samantha retreated to their private world. Standing

on the front steps at the Big House, they watched the
stars wink on over the high rounded dome of the ancient mountain.

"Welcome home, Samantha," Chris said softly as
he guided her up the steps.

"It *is* home," she echoed, walking close beside
him, secure in a love as strong and eternal as the
Mountain of the Sun standing guard over their island
paradise.

Harlequin Presents

ALL-TIME FAVORITE BESTSELLERS
...love stories that grow
more beautiful with time!

Now's your chance to discover the earlier great books in Harlequin Presents, the world's most popular romance-fiction series.

Choose from the following list.

Harlequin ◆ Presents

ALL-TIME FAVORITE BESTSELLERS

Complete and mail this coupon today!

Harlequin Reader Service

In the U.S.A.
1440 South Priest Drive
Tempe, AZ 85281

In Canada
649 Ontario Street
Stratford, Ontario N5A 6W2

Please send me the following Presents **ALL-TIME FAVORITE BESTSELLERS.** I am enclosing my check or money order for $1.75 for each copy ordered, plus 75¢ to cover postage and handling.

☐ #17	☐ #35	☐ #41	☐ #66	☐ #73
☐ #20	☐ #36	☐ #42	☐ #67	☐ #75
☐ #29	☐ #38	☐ #50	☐ #70	☐ #78
☐ #32	☐ #39	☐ #62	☐ #71	

Number of copies checked @ $1.75 each = $ _____
N.Y. and Ariz. residents add appropriate sales tax $ _____
Postage and handling $ ___.75___
                TOTAL $ _____

I enclose _____
(Please send check or money order. We cannot be responsible for cash sent through the mail.)
Prices subject to change without notice.

NAME _____
                           (Please Print)

ADDRESS _____ APT. NO. _____

CITY _____

STATE/PROV. _____

ZIP/POSTAL CODE _____

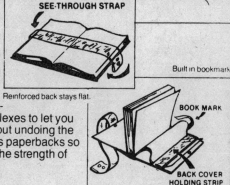

SUPERROMANCE

Longer, exciting, sensuous and dramatic!

Fascinating love stories that will hold
you in their magical spell till the last page
is turned!

Now's your chance to discover the earlier
books in this exciting series. Choose from
the great selection on the following page!